In the
HEAT
of the BITE

LYDIA DARE

sourcebooks
casablanca

Published by Sourcebooks Casablanca, an imprint of Sourcebooks, Inc.
P.O. Box 4410, Naperville, Illinois 60567-4410
(630) 961-3900
FAX: (630) 961-2168
www.sourcebooks.com

Printed and bound in the United States of America
QW 10 9 8 7 6 5 4 3 2 1

To Sabrina Jeffries, Deb Marlowe, Claudia Dain, and all of the other ladies and gentlemen of Heart of Carolina Romance Writers ~ Thank you so much for your support and your belief in us, and for answering all of our questions over the years.

One

Cooper House, London—April 1817

SISTERS WERE A BLASTED NUISANCE. AND IT MADE NO matter whether the sisterhood came by blood or by coven. Rhiannon Sinclair had often wanted to dispense with them all and be afforded a chance to live a normal life. Yet she found herself chasing her younger sister from Edinburgh to London just so she could ensure her safety.

Rhiannon paced the entryway of her aunt's home on Hertford Street, smarting more than a bit at not having been invited to wait inside in a parlor. Instead, the Coopers' butler had looked down his craggy, beaklike nose as she explained who she was and why she'd come. Then he'd left her standing in the entryway while he walked much too slowly down the corridor. If the disdainful servant wasn't careful, she'd hit him with a bolt of lightning and show him the error of his ways. Perhaps he'd move a bit faster if she did. Before she could summon even one thought of a storm, he vanished around a corner.

After what felt like a lifetime, the butler returned and nodded briefly at her. "You may follow me, Miss Sinclair." What had taken the man so long? Had he gone to hide the silver before showing her in? That was as likely as not. There was no wonder what her aunt had said about her.

With a beleaguered sigh, the servant led her to a tidy blue parlor where her aunt and new uncle waited. The pair had been married less than a year, so Rhi didn't know Mr. Cooper well at all. But her Aunt Greer was another matter entirely. In fact, the aunt in question was her mother's younger sister, and unfortunately Rhiannon knew *her* quite well.

"My dear!" Aunt Greer gushed. "It's so nice to see you." As fraudulent as ever. The woman even tried to hide the brogue she'd been born with. And her tone was so sickly sweet that it made Rhiannon want to cast up her accounts. Because, truth be told, her aunt resented her more than a little. She'd resented Rhiannon enough to take her younger sister to London in the dead of night, and she had left Rhi at home with nothing more than an absentminded father and a house full of servants for company. "What brings you to Town, dear?"

As though she didn't know. What brought Rhiannon to Town? How could the woman even say that with a straight face? Rhi took a deep breath as thunder rolled outdoors. "I came ta check on Ginny. Could ye send someone ta fetch my sister? I'd like ta speak with her."

Aunt Greer sucked her teeth lightly, a habit that had always annoyed Rhi to no end. "Unfortunately, she has already retired for the evening." She raised her eyebrows at Rhiannon. "Perhaps another time?"

It was rather late. But Rhi didn't mind waking Ginny, if need be. "Certainly, she's still awake. If I could just see her for a moment." She pointed down the corridor. "Which way ta her chambers?"

"Not now, Rhiannon."

Thunder rumbled outdoors again.

"As I said, Ginessa is already abed. So, let me walk you out, dear," her aunt said as she grabbed Rhiannon's elbow in her gnarly little grasp and shoved her toward the doorway. Of course, Rhiannon could make the woman release her. She could do it in a way her aunt would never forget with a nicely aimed bolt of lightning. But it would probably be best not to burn those bridges in case she had to cross them later.

Her aunt's voice dropped to frantic whisper. "My husband is not aware of your particular affliction, Rhiannon. And I'd prefer to keep it that way. Keep your powers in check when he—or anyone else, for that matter—is present. Your mother never managed it. But you are still young enough to learn."

Rhi tried to keep the scorn from her voice when she replied, "I'm sorry ye were no' born magical, Aunt Greer. There's no' much I can do about that. But, really, ye should have accepted the situation by now."

"I will never, ever accept that my sister was born an anomaly. And you and your little coven of witches will never have my approval. In fact, from this point forward, I plan to limit your access to Ginessa so you don't inhibit your sister's chances of a successful launch into society. Her name will not be associated with scandal. *Do you hear me?*" She hissed the last.

"A successful launch into society?" Rhi's mouth fell open. Truly it was the last thing she expected her aunt to say. Ginny was barely seventeen and a rather naïve seventeen at that.

"Don't look at me like that, Rhiannon Sinclair."

"But Ginny's so young." And London would swallow her whole.

"Well, you're not her guardian, are you? Besides, your father welcomed my invitation."

Papa probably hadn't lifted his head long enough from whatever tome consumed him to even hear a word Aunt Greer had said. He couldn't possibly think *this* was a good idea, not if he'd actually thought about it. Her aunt had never offered a thing where either she or Ginny was concerned. Not until now. Rhi must be missing something, but whatever it was escaped her completely.

"How did you come to be here?" Aunt Greer's frown deepened. "You didn't travel south with that coven in tow, did you? I won't have you hurt Ginessa's chance at finding a *proper* husband."

"Proper husband? What is that supposed ta mean? Are ye plannin' ta marry her off ta some blasted Sassenach?" Rhiannon hissed.

"Better than what she'd find in Scotland."

Rhi sucked in a lungful of air. "Why can she no' marry a man from Scotland? Ginny *is* Scottish, after all."

"Because in Scotland, *Ginessa* cannot escape the taint of your creation, Rhiannon." Her aunt sighed deeply as though dealing with her was the worst sort of trial. "And

I'll expect you and whoever you brought with you to return to Edinburgh as soon as possible. I'm certain your fondest wish is for your sister to find happiness."

Of course, she wanted Ginny to find happiness. But there had been no reason to remove her to London in order to do so. Rhiannon was the older of the two. And *she* had never been launched into society. Her aunt would never do such a thing. Not with all the resentment she held in her heart for the members of the *Còig*, members of the coven of witches she'd so badly wanted to belong to when she was younger. Unfortunately, only the oldest daughter in each family was born magical. Her aunt had never recovered from the slight of being second born.

"The taint of my creation is the least of yer worries," Rhiannon warned.

Her aunt's shoulders went back, and she lifted her nose a little higher in the air.

"Know this, Aunt," Rhiannon said, as she pointed a finger in the woman's face. "I willna allow ye ta run roughshod over her life just ta spite me. Or ta spite the fact that ye were born average."

Rhiannon could almost see the storm cloud forming in the air. Her aunt could as well, if her smirk was any indication. Unfortunately, Rhi's powers were often ruled by her emotions, and while most people could blink back the tears that welled behind their lashes, the telltale patter of raindrops in a room full of people could give her aunt much more insight into Rhiannon's feelings than she wanted her to have.

Rhiannon turned on her heel and fled. The butler looked supremely satisfied as he quickly opened the door. Rhi was surprised not to feel the press of his boot against her backside as she neared the threshold. He yelped lightly as she passed him. Teach the English dog to mess with Rhiannon Sinclair. She'd hit him with the force of power that one might feel after dragging one's feet on the carpet, for which he should be immeasurably thankful as she could have done much worse.

Rhiannon slipped out into the dark night. She was quite used to skulking about under the moonlight. And with her powers, she had little fear that anyone would accost her and do her harm. So, she took a short walk to Hyde Park, where she could take a seat on a bench alone and plan what she would do next.

She hadn't expected her aunt to ask her to stay with her. In fact, Rhiannon had already sent her belongings on to Thorpe House in Berkeley Square, the home of her coven sister, Caitrin, now the Marchioness of Eynsford, and her wolfish husband, Dashiel. Rhi supposed she probably should have mentioned as much to Cait, but her friend would forgive her popping in unannounced since they hadn't seen each other in months.

Cait would welcome Rhi into her home, unlike Aunt Greer.

In all honesty, she hadn't expected Aunt Greer to welcome her with open arms, but couldn't her aunt at least have allowed her to *see* Ginny to be sure she was all right? Rhi sighed. Apparently not. Aunt Greer had treated her as she always had. Not as a revered member of the *Còig*. Not as someone with superior strength and cunning. Not as someone capable of being loved.

She treated her as something vile. Something that should be squashed from the face of the earth.

A lone tear trickled down Rhiannon's cheek as a raindrop landed atop her head. Fantastic. She'd be drenched within moments if she didn't pull herself together. Yet the longer she sat there, the more distraught she felt and the angrier she became.

Rhi jumped to her feet. The wind swirled around her, raising her hair and the trailing end of her traveling dress in its haste to circle her. She glanced about the park. Thank goodness she was alone. She could have the devil's own temper tantrum, and there wasn't a soul to watch. Lightning flashed and thunder boomed overhead. Rhiannon raised her hands in the air and called the wind and the rain, stirring it to the point where she was drenched within seconds.

She felt only slightly better. So, she stomped her feet and the air crackled with her anger. Better. Much better.

∽

Despite the chit lounging across his lap, Matthew Halkett, the Earl of Blodswell, had more than a meal on his mind. He needed to find his new charge and be sure all was well with the newly reborn Scot. Alec MacQuarrie had turned out to be more work than he'd ever expected. When Matthew had first met the gentleman in the lowlands, the Scot had seemed a gregarious sort; and when they'd become reacquainted later in the Highlands, Matthew had no idea the man had since suffered a broken heart. If he had known, that might have altered Matthew's decision to turn

MacQuarrie into one of his kind. Now the damage was done, and Matthew had to deal with the consequences, even if it meant following the younger man from room to room as he learned to use his new baby teeth.

Matthew lifted the wench from his lap, wiped his mouth with the back of his hand, and thanked the woman with a soft smile. She curtsied quickly and said, "It was my honor, sir."

Of course, he'd brought her great pleasure before he'd pulled his incisors from the nape of her neck. That was very much the reason why so many women lingered around *Brysi*, the gentlemen's club for those of his kind. They craved the emotion and satisfaction a vampyre could bring. And almost all of them were in it for the pleasure, if not for the coin. He rarely even had to enchant them to make a meal of them. Or to draw one beneath him. Or to do both at once.

"Have you seen Mr. MacQuarrie about?" he asked as she adjusted her clothing.

"He's abovestairs with Charlotte, I believe. I saw him go up there just before you arrived."

He pressed a coin into her palm. "How many of you has he enjoyed tonight?" he asked casually, dreading the answer.

She giggled. "Quite a few. The man is insatiable." She shivered delicately. Obviously, she'd been with him recently, if her reaction was any indication.

Matthew sighed. "I'd best go and find him." He left the chambers and started for the stairs. If he waited for MacQuarrie to be free of the Cyprians who lined these halls, Matthew would have to wait decades. Thankfully, *Brysi* was a safe place for the newborn to test his mettle. Matthew glanced in doorways and down corridors until he finally heard the guttural sound of the man's voice when he moaned.

"Don't," a woman cried.

Oh, good Lord. MacQuarrie could find trouble unlike any other. Matthew didn't even knock. He thrust the door open and stepped inside. He paused when the paramour cried out again.

"Don't... stop!" she begged.

So that was a cry of pleasure and not of distress. Bloody wonderful. Matthew wanted to snort.

MacQuarrie didn't even bother to look up. He had a blonde straddling his lap, where he lifted and lowered her slowly, her bodice down around her waist, her dress up around her hips. Damn it to hell. Matthew hated walking in on scenes like this.

Yet something about it made him pause. A thin trail of blood dripped down the woman's back from where the infernal Scot had failed to seal his lips across her skin properly before he sank his teeth into her.

"Please," she begged, her voice raspy and strained. She glanced over her shoulder and was fully aware that Matthew was in the room. "Please finish it," she cried. She didn't make a move to cover herself. Or to remove herself from MacQuarrie's swollen member.

"Make the seal and finish the chit," Matthew grumbled. He'd told Alec the same bloody thing over and over. She was waiting for the seal, for the transfer of emotions between them, for MacQuarrie to share his desire with her and take her pleasure in return.

Alec looked up and spoke around the woman's flesh. "I don't want to. I don't want to feel it. This is enough for me." He mumbled against her skin, but Matthew heard every word.

"It's not enough for *her.*"

MacQuarrie shot him a look that told him to go to the devil.

What was a mentor for if not to teach? "Finish it," Matthew commanded.

"Bloody hell," the man said as he leaned forward and sealed his mouth over the bite with fervor. The chit cried out in ecstasy, and Matthew turned his head to avoid seeing MacQuarrie shudder beneath her.

What was he thinking? The blasted Scot was in no condition to leave *Brysi,* at least not at the moment. Matthew sighed again. Damn if he wasn't doing that a lot lately. And he didn't even need to breathe. "I'll be back in a few hours, but I expect you to stay here. And to stay out of trouble," he warned as he turned and left.

Alec MacQuarrie's laughter followed him all the way down the corridor. Keeping that man out of trouble was like trying to return a whore to chastity.

He slipped from the club out into the night and walked and walked until the scenery of Covent Garden disappeared behind him. He needed to clear his head and decide what to do about his charge. It had been much easier when he'd tutored Kettering in this life a few hundred years earlier. Was he getting too old to deal with the foolishness of youth? Or was this generation of man particularly trying?

Before he knew it, he'd walked all the way to Mayfair and yet still had no idea of how to continue. Out of nowhere, a crushing wind nearly knocked him from his feet. He braced himself. What the devil? He'd never seen a storm come on so quickly, and he'd seen more than most.

That was when the rain started in earnest. Only moments before, the stars had been twinkling in the sky. Yet now, thunder crashed and lightning flashed. Hail clattered on the cobbled path where he walked. He covered his head with his arm and ducked beneath a tree.

That was when he saw *her*. Standing directly in the middle of the fray was the loveliest sight he'd ever seen in his life. Her black hair was slicked back with water but it trailed all the way down to her waist. Her gown was pasted to her body, sodden with water. She laughed loudly and sardonically as a bolt of lightning flashed at her feet.

The chit was likely daft. Didn't she know better than to stand out in the rain? Likely, she would be killed by the ferocity of this sudden storm if he didn't intercede. Matthew dashed across the park to where she stood. She clapped her hands in time with crashes of thunder that made even him jump. And looked ridiculously pleased by it all. She didn't even see him as he bolted toward her. Had she escaped from Bedlam?

He yelled over the wind and thunder. "Miss? Are you all right?"

She spun to face him. "Oh!" Her eyes flashed with the same ferocity as the storm. Yet the wind calmed and the thunder stopped crashing when her hands dropped to her sides. Then the beauty brushed the sodden mass of her hair from her forehead. "Who are ye?" she asked.

Her Scottish lilt nearly startled him as much as the tone of her voice. She sounded like she'd recently been crying, but with the rain that continued to fall, he couldn't tell if her cheeks were wet from more than just rain. He found himself with the absurd desire to reach out and brush her cheeks dry with the pads of his thumbs.

"Doona tell me ye're some knight in shinin' armor come ta save a lass from the storm?" She laughed loudly, the tinkling sound of it making him want to smile with her.

"Well, actually…" he started. He *was* a knight of old. Or he once had been. Before his first death, but that was well over 600 years ago. Matthew shook his head. "…I was concerned to see a lady about to be overcome by such a vicious storm. I thought I'd rescue you."

The storm clouds lifted. The rain stopped. She glanced down at her drenched gown, which now hugged her body like a second skin, and crossed her arms in front of her chest. And that was when he realized it. She wasn't *caught* by the storm. She *was* the storm. Saint George's teeth! She was a force to be reckoned with. She was one of *them*.

Two

RHIANNON LOOKED AT THE SODDEN GROUND BENEATH her feet and bit the inside of her cheek to keep from laughing. After all, she was fairly certain the handsome gentleman before her wouldn't appreciate her levity at his expense. Still, it was a chore not to giggle at least a little. No one had ever tried to rescue her from her own storm before. Even those in Edinburgh who didn't know she was the source of such occurrences tended to leave her alone in the midst of ferocious winds and pouring rain, more concerned for their own safety. Yet this gentleman had braved the storm to rescue her?

The Sassenach was clearly out of his mind. Or too noble for his own good. Slowly, she lifted her head to peer at him once more. His dark hair was wet from the rain until he shook his head, scattering raindrops about. His hair then curled up a bit on the ends. His strong jaw with a little cleft in his chin seemed well set and determined. But his dark-as-night eyes made Rhiannon suck in her breath. There was something eerily familiar about those eyes. It was almost as though she'd seen them once before in a dream that had ended poorly.

She took a step backward as a sense of foreboding nearly overwhelmed her. The gentleman was more than he seemed. Much more. He was dangerous. She could feel it in her bones, especially when he frowned at her like he was doing now. "Well, the rain has stopped. So I doona need ta be rescued any longer." Rhi backed up again, only to have her right slipper sink into the muddy, grassy earth with a slurping sound. Perfect! She'd ruined a perfectly good pair of slippers with her temper tantrum.

Before she could lose her balance, the gentleman was at her side in a flash and steadying her with a hand on her elbow. "Careful, Miss."

Rhiannon gulped as she stared up into his obsidian eyes once again. Why did he seem so familiar? "Have we met, sir?"

Finally a smile tugged at those serious lips of his. "I am certain I would remember, Miss…?" His brow rose in question, and he waited for her response.

"Sinclair."

"Well, Miss Sinclair of Edinburgh, I believe someone should see you to safety. Pray tell me you're not out here at night all alone." He began to tug her toward a well-worn path.

Rhiannon winced. She certainly was not about to admit to having sent her maid ahead with her luggage to Thorpe House so no one would witness her encounter with Aunt Greer. Especially not to a man she knew nothing about, not even his name. Wait! "How did ye ken I was from Edinburgh?"

She hadn't told him where she was from.

"I know a great many things, Miss Sinclair," the gentleman replied enigmatically. "Now, where is your chaperone?"

She dug in her heels, refusing to move one more inch. Thunder crashed in the sky above them. "Unhand me." *Havers!* She didn't even know the man's name.

The handsome Englishman turned her to face him. One black brow darted upward. "You can harness your thunder. I'm not so easily intimidated."

Harness her thunder? She couldn't believe her ears. *He knew!* How could he know what she was? No one outside her own coven knew except family members. And this man—whoever he was— was certainly not family. Rhiannon tipped her nose back and leveled him with her haughtiest glare. "I doona ken what ye're talkin' about. Have ye been imbibin', sir?"

He snorted. "I don't have time for this, Miss Sinclair. I truly don't. Point out your chaperone, and I'll leave you in his or her care."

"*Mrs.* Sinclair." Rhiannon lied through her teeth. But it was a good lie. After all, a *Mrs.* wouldn't need a chaperone, would she? If this man would just leave her be, she could dry herself with a warm wind and then make her way to Caitrin's home. She'd had as much of his interference as she intended to take.

In an instant the man dropped her arm. His brow crinkled, and Rhi was almost certain he sniffed the air in her direction. Without a doubt he was the oddest creature she'd ever met. And then it hit her. *A creature!*

She looked again into his coal-black eyes, and her heart stopped beating in her chest.

It had been right there all along. How foolish of her to not to have seen it earlier. "Creature" was most assuredly the right word. She hadn't seen *this* man before, but she'd seen one like him. She'd even been enchanted by his dark gaze and lost her will to the blood-sucker. It was not an experience she ever wanted to repeat. She still had nightmares about the encounter, and she had no intention of spending even one second longer in the company of a vampyre.

Rhiannon grabbed a handful of her skirts and bolted for Hyde Park's gated entrance, her ruined slipper squishing the whole way. She raced as fast as she could across Park Lane, down Curzon Street, and around the little jog of Charles Street until she finally reached Berkeley Square, out of breath but still alive.

⁂

Matthew raked a hand through his damp hair as he watched Miss Sinclair escape into Thorpe House without even a look over her slender shoulder. And he knew she was *Miss* Sinclair. He could smell an innocent from ten feet away, and *Miss* Sinclair was as innocent as they came. And lovely, she was that too, even if she did have a temper that lit up the night sky.

Did she truly think she could outrun him in a foot race? Matthew scoffed as he watched through Eynsford's big bay window as she entered a parlor at the front of the house. He could have run from Hyde Park to Berkeley Square a dozen times in the amount of time it had taken her to run from him.

What a mystery she was. Not *what* she was; he'd known instantly she was a witch. After all, he'd known other weather-controlling witches throughout his life-after-death, *her* ancestors to be exact. The revered *Còig*. The mystical coven of witches who had bestowed upon him the most powerful gift he'd ever possessed. Matthew glanced down at the ring he still wore on his right hand. Without that coven, he would have been reduced to skulking around in the shadows for eternity. But they'd given him the ability to stand in the sun as though he still possessed a beating heart, as though he was a living, breathing man.

He turned his attention back to the Marquess of Eynsford's Mayfair home. Miss Sinclair was undoubtedly safe in the company of her sister witch, the new marchioness. He had no reason to remain outside, catching glimpses of her through the front window. But leaving held little appeal. Why had she lied about her marital state? Why had she run from him as though the hounds of hell chased at her heels?

"Lord Blodswell." A soft Scottish voice caught his attention, and Matthew turned to find Caitrin Eynsford by his side. Apparently, he was more affected by Miss Sinclair than he'd initially believed. He hadn't even heard Lady Eynsford approach.

"My lady." Matthew dipped his head to the beautiful blond in greeting. "We meet again."

"Aye." She stepped closer to him and laid her hand on his arm. The night stars reflected in her cerulean eyes as she peered up at him in earnest. "How is Mr. MacQuarrie?"

Matthew closed his eyes to block out her beseeching look. Why would the clairvoyant witch ask him such a question? She had to know the answer. Was she hoping he would deny it? Ease her guilty conscience?

"Managing." Really, what else could he say? Lady Eynsford had broken MacQuarrie's heart when she'd married her Lycan marquess, putting the wheels of MacQuarrie's fate in motion, but voicing the words wouldn't do anyone any good at this point. What's done was done.

The marchioness swiped a tear from her cheek. "Ye followed Rhiannon." She didn't ask the question, just voiced what she had obviously seen with her second sight. What else had she seen?

Rhiannon. The name echoed in Matthew's mind. Dear God, her name was as lovely as she was. All feminine and airy like a summer breeze. "Just wanted to be certain she made it to your home safely."

"Clearly, she did."

"Yes. I—um—Well, she seemed upset." He sounded like a damn fool. Why did he even bother talking to Lady Eynsford? She knew everything anyway. The witch could see the future. She knew much more than he did. She probably even knew why the lass was upset.

"Family has a way of doin' that ta some of us. I'm certain she'll be fine now that she's come ta stay with Eynsford and me for the season. There's no need for ye ta worry. Ye have Mr. MacQuarrie ta look after as it is. I feel certain ye have yer hands full."

And that quickly they were back to discussing MacQuarrie. Matthew nearly groaned. He knew the marchioness wanted him to do the impossible, to somehow return her former friend to the man she'd once known. He couldn't bring himself to crush the little witch's dreams with the truth of the situation. MacQuarrie would never be the same, no matter how Matthew tutored him. Humans were humans, and vampyres were not.

So he said nothing and made no move to leave his spot. He simply stared across the square at Thorpe House. What the devil was he waiting for? To catch another glimpse of Rhiannon Sinclair? No, that couldn't be it. How many women had caught his eye over the centuries? More than he could count. He just wanted a momentary respite from his life, something to distract him from the road ahead.

"I would invite ye in, but I have a feelin' ye should be makin' yer way back ta that monstrosity of a meetin' place ye call a club." She snorted. "A feeding trough is more like it."

If Matthew still had blood flowing through his veins, she would have made him blush. There were some things ladies shouldn't know. Yet Caitrin Eynsford could see it all, even before it happened. She didn't have a choice in the matter. He shook away his thoughts. He'd rather not wonder at the scenes that did play before her eyes.

Matthew nodded a farewell to the marchioness. "As always, you are correct, my lady. Until we meet again." He started toward Charles Street.

"Tomorrow night," she called to his retreating back.

Matthew stopped in his tracks and looked over his shoulder at the blond witch. "Tomorrow night?"

"Lady Pickering's ball. I'll see ye then."

Matthew couldn't help the laugh that escaped him. "I believe your vision has failed you, Lady Eynsford. I do *not* attend balls." Nor did he plan to attend Lady Pickering's, whoever the devil she was.

But Caitrin Eynsford only smiled and then started across the street to her home. Matthew shook his head as he turned back the way he'd come. Lady Pickering's ball indeed. Perhaps this generation of witches had lost a bit of their power. His future most certainly did not involve black evening wear, dancing in a crowded ballroom, or making pleasantries with men who had more money than sense.

❧

Rhiannon thanked the Eynsford butler profusely for the tea service he had delivered. What a kind soul he was. The man hadn't even lifted an eyebrow when she'd entered the home, dripping water and leaving muddy footprints all over his clean floor. He'd even retrieved towels and the tea without a single scowl. How very un-English of him.

After glancing at her ruined slipper one last time, Rhi cringed. The debacle this evening had been all her fault. She had allowed Aunt Greer to upset her, to get her emotions swirling, and that wouldn't help anyone, least of all Ginny. And if she hadn't started that storm, she wouldn't have met that vampyre or ruined her slipper. Just the thought of him made her pulse race anew. What terrible creatures they were, and her storm had *drawn* him directly to her. Foolish, foolish, foolish!

As Rhiannon was in the middle of berating herself, Caitrin bustled into the room with a flourish. Her friend squealed loudly and very quickly tumbled onto the settee beside Rhi. "I'm so happy ta see ye," the blond gushed as she wrapped her arms around Rhi.

"Ye doona have ta smother me." Rhiannon laughed as she pried Cait's arms from around her neck and sat back to look at her. "Marriage does agree with ye, Cait," she admitted. Truly, she'd never seen her friend looking so content. Or so beautiful, nearly glowing with happiness.

"Oh, I couldna smother ye if I tried. Ye can move the wind ta wherever ye need it, ye ninny." She picked up a lock of Rhiannon's damp hair. "What in the world happened ta ye? Did ye fall in a pond?"

"A little rain is all," Rhi murmured.

"Rain? There's no' a cloud in the sky," the blond witch said. Then her blue eyes narrowed. "Unless ye made some, of course. Please tell me ye dinna do that in Mayfair of all places." She sighed loudly.

"Just a wee storm," Rhiannon mumbled as she held her thumb and forefinger an inch apart.

Cait raised her eyebrows. "A wee storm that soaked ye ta the skin? I sincerely doubt that." She shot a pointed glance at Rhi. "Now tell me why ye were upset."

"It's nothin' ta worry about, Cait. Just let it rest."

"It's no' nothing. But ye *will* tell me eventually." Cait sat forward on the settee, and then her nose scrunched up a bit as she looked at the amount of mud Rhiannon had dragged in with her and which now caked the Eynsfords' Aubusson rug. "*Havers!* What did ye do ta yer slipper?"

Rhiannon felt warmth creep up her neck. It was one thing to feel foolish about her actions and another to have someone else aware of her foolishness. She squirmed a bit in her seat. "A vampyre startled me and I stepped in the wrong place is all."

Cait giggled. "If anyone else heard that statement, they'd think ye were mad."

"Aye, they probably would," Rhi agreed. She hadn't thought about how absurd that sounded before she said it, but then her life had seemed so absurd lately.

"Well, in any event," Cait squeezed Rhiannon's hand, "there's no reason ta be frightened of Blodswell. He's no' exactly harmless, but—"

Rhiannon's mouth dropped open. Cait *knew* the vampyre in question? Was London crawling with the creatures? "Do ye ken many vampyres?" She couldn't believe the nonchalant way Cait shrugged as though it was commonplace to befriend such monsters. But then Cait hadn't been with her in Edinburgh when that awful creature had descended upon their coven, hell-bent on destruction.

"A few. But Blodswell is benevolent. No need ta ruin any good slippers on *his* account."

Rhiannon folded her arms across her chest. "Benevolent or no', I'd just as soon no' see him again, or anythin' like him." Besides, she had Ginny's future to worry about. There was no room for dealing with handsome vampyres, no matter how harmless Caitrin thought them to be.

A little twinkle lit Cait's eyes. "Hmm. How *did* the earl affect ye, I wonder?" Cait asked as though she already knew the answer to that question, which only served to make Rhi's face heat anew.

"Blast it, Cait. Ye're no' supposed ta go peerin' inta my future!" She'd told her and told her not to pry into her life. But did the witch listen? Not a bit, apparently.

"Oh, hush." Her friend shushed her. "I dinna go lookin' for ye on a lark." Her voice lowered. "I only took a small peek when yer coach, maid, and trunks arrived at my doorstep and ye werena with them. I had ta be certain ye were all right."

"Are ye done pryin' now?" Rhiannon knew she sounded waspish. Cait couldn't help it if her gift allowed her into the private lives of others. At times, it was as much a hindrance as it was a help.

"Well, almost," the witch hedged. At Rhiannon's grimace, she continued. "I do ken it wasna Lord Blodswell who provoked the storm. Yer aunt always was a spiteful woman." Cait shivered.

"She wouldna even let me see Ginny," Rhiannon sighed. "She said she plans ta present her this season."

Cait gasped as though she was affronted. "She never presented ye! Never even offered ta bring ye ta Town. That horrid—"

Rhiannon's heart twisted a bit. "Evidently I'm no' marriage material." She waved off Cait's protest. "She's right."

"That's ridiculous."

"I ken the truth of it, Cait. I willna suit anyone. There's no' a man alive who could withstand my powers. Or my temperament." She smirked sheepishly at the last and tucked her ruined slipper farther under her skirts.

"I thought no one could ever fit me, either. Until I met Dash."

"Doona make me ill, please. I havena had dinner yet." Rhiannon laughed as Cait swatted ineffectually at her head.

"So, what do ye plan ta do? Free Ginny from the clutches of yer evil aunt? Or are ye goin' home since she willna allow ye ta see her?"

"Hardly." Rhiannon rubbed her forehead. "I'd like ta stay ta keep an eye on her, if that's all right with ye."

"Ye doona even have ta ask, ye ninny. Ye're always welcome here if ye doona mind wild Lycans traipsin' in from time ta time. Dash has become rather close ta his long-lost brothers, and if one of them isn't here, then another one usually is."

The image was particularly amusing, especially as Cait had never cared for werewolves until she'd married hers. But to be surrounded by the beasts on a regular basis was probably fitting, all things considered. "I'm sure it willna be a problem for me."

"Good. I was hopin' that would be yer answer."

"I doona really have another option. If I'm no' here ta keep an eye on things, Aunt Greer'll marry Ginny off ta some old goat just because he is plump in the pockets or has some connection my aunt covets."

"That would be success in your aunt's estimation." Cait cleared her throat. "Did sweet, old Aunt Greer offer any excuse as ta why she is presentin' Ginny and no' ye?" She avoided Rhiannon's gaze.

"She said she brought Ginny ta London because she canna *escape the taint of my creation* back in Edinburgh. So, now, unless I can prevent it, my little sister will have ta suffer some blasted Sassenach for the rest of her days."

Rhiannon jumped as a voice boomed behind her. "And just what is wrong with the blasted Sassenach?" asked Dashiel Thorpe, the Marquess of Eynsford. The golden-haired Englishman crossed the room, his amber eyes brimming with amusement. He stopped in front of his wife and bent to kiss Cait on the forehead. Then he rose to his full height and nodded at Rhiannon. "Miss Sinclair," he said in greeting. "Let's get back to the blasted Sassenach, shall we?"

Rhi almost laughed. How very single-minded of his lordship to not forget the slight to all Englishmen. "It's nothin', my lord."

He situated himself as close to Cait as he could on the settee. "Don't mistake me for a fool, Miss Sinclair. You Scots, lovely as you are, never use the term as one of endearment, and most certainly not after you've used the word 'blasted' to modify it."

Well, what could she say to that? He was right, of course, and had she known he was within earshot, she wouldn't have used the word. Rhiannon rose to her feet to allow them some room and to distance herself from the pair.

"Doona tease her, Dashiel. Rhiannon has had a difficult day," Cait admonished as Rhi moved to a nearby high-backed chair.

The marquess leaned over and sniffed Cait's hair.

"*What is it* with the sniffing?" Rhiannon cried. That blasted vampyre had sniffed her, too. "Is it something that innocent women are no' apprised of? That men like ta sniff ladies?"

"I feel certain there are quite a few things that go on between married couples of which you have not been apprised," the Lycan chuckled.

Again Rhiannon felt heat creep up her cheeks, though she had set herself up for that one.

"Do you want an answer to your question?" the marquess asked softly.

"Would I have asked if I dinna?" she tossed back at him with more bravado than she actually felt.

"Extraordinary beings…" he began and tapped his puffed-out chest.

Rhi snorted. "Is that what ye're calling yerself, now?" she teased.

The marquess' amber eyes twinkled with mirth. "Extraordinary beings, such as myself—and yes, Miss Sinclair, I am quite extraordinary—often have heightened senses. We can smell things other beings cannot."

"Like perfume?" Rhiannon asked.

"Doona ye dare say it, Dashiel!" Cait cried, shaking her finger at him.

The marquess chuckled again. "Yes. Like perfume. And fear. And other emotions that heighten the body's responses." He narrowed his gaze at her. "Did someone sniff *you*, Miss Sinclair? If so, please tell me so I might have a word with him."

"Lord Blodswell sniffed ye?" Cait gasped. "Ye dinna tell me that part."

"This from the all-seeing member of the coven," Rhiannon grumbled as she sat back with a huff.

"Blodswell, eh?" the Lycan asked with a frown on his face. "He has some nerve."

"Doona get yer hair standin' on end, Dash," Cait

said calmly. "I'm certain his lordship meant no harm. It's no' everyday one encounters a witch in the middle of a storm." She shot her gaze to Rhi. "Ye were in the middle of it, were ye no'? Probably stompin' yer feet and causin' the devil of a ruckus, if I ken ye."

"That was *you*?" Eynsford asked as he sat forward. "I was on the way home, and my driver had to stop and wait for the storm to pass."

"It was me," Rhiannon mumbled, quite embarrassed for herself. It was one thing to throw a temper tantrum. It was quite another to be caught at it.

"Blodswell has no idea what he's in for." Cait laughed. She got a faraway look in her eye and then laughed a little louder. "Absolutely no idea." She was obviously seeing visions of the future. And would torment Rhiannon to no end with them.

"Well, then it's a good thing I never have ta see him again," Rhiannon grumbled.

"Oh, ye'll see him tomorrow night." Cait sat back with a satisfied grin.

"What did I *just tell* ye about gettin' involved in my future?"

"Takin' a peek and gettin' involved are two very different things," Cait said primly. "Ginny will be at Lady Pickering's ball. And so, I assume, will ye also."

"I suppose that means we'll be attending as well?" the Lycan asked.

"Oh, I wouldna miss the events of the ball for anythin' in the world, Dash," Cait said, a mischievous gleam in her eye. "Rhiannon, do ye remember the time ye blew my skirts up in front of all the lads at that picnic?"

Did she ever. Cait had been fifteen years old and being a brat of the worst sort. Rhiannon had taken it upon herself to put her friend in her place. Cait had been mortified. And had never forgiven Rhi.

"Revenge is sweet, Rhiannon dear. So, so sweet." Cait's tinkling laughter sent shivers skittering across Rhi's skin.

What *could* Cait have possibly seen? Letting Ginny attend one ball without her would be all right, wouldn't it? Certainly Aunt Greer couldn't get Ginny attached to some smelly, old Sassenach in one night, could she? "I doona believe I brought anythin' appropriate for a London ball."

"Nonsense." Cait grinned. "I have dressin' rooms full of gowns of every color imaginable. Ye'll look stunnin', and I canna wait ta see the look on yer aunt's face."

There was no getting around this infernal ball. "Every color imaginable?" Rhi echoed on a sigh. And the gowns were certain to be the height of fashion, every last one of them, if she knew Cait.

Eynsford winked at Rhi. "I do love to spoil her."

Rhi suppressed a snort. Every man who had ever met Cait loved to spoil her. How did some women get so fortunate?

"Oh, Dash," Cait tapped her husband on the arm to get his full attention, "ye must ask yer brothers ta join us."

So that whatever disaster awaited Rhi could be witnessed by all and sundry.

The marquess laughed. "I hardly think they would attend a marriage-mart ball at *my* request, lass. You are the one who has them all wrapped around your pretty little finger. They could be a little less wrapped, by the way."

Cait leaned up and kissed his cheek. "What fun would there be in that?"

Three

IN ALL HONESTY, MATTHEW COULDN'T REMEMBER the last time he'd had a headache. The details of events became a little hazy after reaching one's 650th year on earth. If he remembered correctly, however, the last one had happened somewhere around 1190 in the Holy Land, back when he was still human. But serving as a mentor to the newly reborn Alec MacQuarrie had brought about a thumping within his skull that was even louder than Miss Sinclair's storm.

Matthew rubbed his temple, hoping to assuage the bloody pain, as he looked at Charlotte, the last Cyprian he'd seen his charge with. She was now lounging across the bed as though she hadn't a care in the world. "What do you mean he went out?"

The blond tart shrugged, and one strap of her sheer chemise slipped down her shoulder. She made no move to straighten her clothing and only shot him a vague look of annoyance. "He said something about a fireworks display."

New Spring Gardens... er... Vauxhall Gardens.

New Spring Gardens was the original name. What the devil was wrong with him? It had been called Vauxhall much longer than New Spring Gardens, certainly long enough that he should remember the damn name. Headaches apparently made his memory faulty. Matthew glowered at Charlotte, not that MacQuarrie's inept decision to leave the club was her fault. Still, there was no one else to glower at, so Charlotte would have to do.

"How long has he been gone?" Matthew threw the question over his shoulder as he started for the corridor. If he was fortunate, he could reach the reborn Scot before he could create any havoc.

"I'm not really sure, sir. How long were you gone? He left fairly quickly after that."

Damn it all to hell.

Matthew barreled out *Brysi's* ornate doors and quickly hailed a hack. He could have run much quicker than he could ride, but *that* would most likely catch someone's attention, something he tried desperately to avoid, if possible. Although with MacQuarrie loose in the city unchaperoned, Matthew's concerns about detection were nothing more than a futile attempt at normalcy. The Scotsman had a way of drawing attention even when he was behaving himself, which he didn't do all that often.

Once he was on his way, Matthew rested his head against the battered squabs as the rickety conveyance rambled from the Covent Garden district toward Whitehall. With his head pounding, he closed his eyes, which apparently was a mistake. *Her* vision instantly appeared in his mind. Drenched from her own storm, her gown clinging to her every curve. Her ebony hair falling over her shoulders. Her soft hazel eyes, which made her seem as vulnerable as a newborn kitten, blinking at him with innocence. Matthew's eyes flew open. What the devil was wrong with him?

The hack finally stopped at Whitehall. After Matthew handed the fare and an extra coin to the driver, he descended the stairs and boarded a small ferry across the Thames to Vauxhall Gardens. The thump of the orchestra and the raucous clatter of applause reached his ears before he had even disembarked. Bloody wonderful! The place was teeming with people, not that he was surprised. Still, that would make locating MacQuarrie all the more difficult.

He clasped his left hand over the signet ring on his right pinkie and started to close his eyes to focus on the infernal Scot. But he stopped himself, remembering the last time he'd closed his eyes mere minutes earlier. The last thing he needed was to see Rhiannon Sinclair's perfect, heart-shaped face again. He'd never find MacQuarrie if he allowed himself to get distracted.

So he did the next best thing and closed *one* eye, which he was certain made him look utterly ridiculous, and tried to seek out his charge. MacQuarrie was most definitely in the pleasure gardens. Matthew could feel the Scot's restless spirit among the humans who milled about. The question was *where*? He ambled along the path toward the supper boxes. After all, Charlotte had said MacQuarrie mentioned fireworks, hadn't she?

"Blodswell!" came a jovial voice from behind him.

Matthew turned to find the aged Sir Ralph Smyth following him down the path, relying heavily on his cane.

"Sir Ralph, how nice to see you." And it was. Two generations ago, he and Sir Ralph had been great friends. But Sir Ralph had aged, while Matthew had not. The passage of time made it difficult to maintain close friendships.

The old man smiled warmly. "I never do get over the resemblance. Such a shame your grandfather didn't live to see you, my boy."

How Ralph would be surprised to know Matthew *was* his own grandfather. But it was part of the ruse. Spending one generation in London and then one in Derbyshire to keep people from realizing he never aged. "So you often say, sir."

"I am glad to see you." Sir Ralph's gnarly hand squeezed the rounded tip of his cane. "I've been meaning to ask you something, Blodswell."

That sounded fairly enigmatic. Matthew stiffened, preparing for the worst. "Yes, Sir Ralph?"

"Well, with your grandfather gone, and your poor father, who I do regret I never got to meet, having both passed, I feel I should step in on their behalf."

"Step in on their behalf?" What the devil was Ralph going on about?

"You're not getting any younger, you know. If you don't find a wife soon, there'll be no heir. No one to pass your holdings to. Your family line will end."

Despite Matthew's headache, he felt the over-whelming desire to laugh, though he held it in check.

Still, the irony was almost too much to bear with
aplomb. Ralph had fought the parson's noose like
nothing Matthew had ever seen before. The man had
been well past forty by the time he finally married,
and even then he had grumbled the entire time, or
so Matthew had heard as he had already retired to
Derbyshire by that point.

"I'm sure I have plenty of time to find a wife." Not
that he had any plans to do so, but there was no need
to voice his intentions.

The old man sighed. "For years I thought the same.
And all I ended up with were two daughters. Lovely
girls, don't get me wrong, but they can hardly carry
on the family name. You don't realize such things are
important until it's too late."

Matthew studied his old friend. His eyes took in
each wrinkle on Sir Ralph's face and even the slight
shake to his hand. "Nonsense," Matthew said with
more levity than he felt at the moment. "You look
like a young buck. I'm sure you could sire sons well
into your nineties." At least that's what Ralph had
often boasted in his younger days.

The baronet laughed heartily. "You are so very like
your grandfather, young man. I'm certain he would
have been very proud of you."

"Well, thank you, sir," Matthew returned with
sincerity. Then he spotted his quarry behind Sir
Ralph. Alec MacQuarrie stood at the entrance of one
of the darkened walks. Matthew watched as the Scot
wiped his mouth with a handkerchief. Bloody hell.
What had he done now?

Matthew's migraine pounded harder.

"Are you all right, Blodswell?" Sir Ralph stepped closer to him.

"I, uh, just spotted a friend."

Sir Ralph looked over his shoulder in the direction Matthew glared. The movement, or perhaps the rage that rolled off Matthew's person, caught MacQuarrie's attention. He nodded his head in greeting and slowly made his way to the pair, tipping his hat at women as he passed them.

"Ah, Lord Blodswell, what a surprise to see you here." MacQuarrie smiled.

"I'm certain it is," Matthew clipped out, "since I was supposed to meet you somewhere else entirely."

The damned Scot didn't even have the good grace to look halfway apologetic. "Well, how fortuitous to see you here instead." Then he turned his attention to Sir Ralph. "Alec MacQuarrie," he introduced himself.

Sir Ralph smiled. "MacQuarrie? If I'm not mistaken, you are a friend of my son-in-law, Pickering."

MacQuarrie nodded. "Aye, I attended Cambridge with Pickering."

Pickering? Dread filled Matthew's soul as Caitrin Eynsford's prediction echoed in his mind. Damn it to hell, he was *not* going to a ball tomorrow night. He just wouldn't do it.

"Sir Ralph Smyth," the old man said, offering his hand to MacQuarrie. "My daughter is hosting a ball tomorrow evening. You should stop by to save poor Pickering from all of his duties. I feel safe in saying he will thank you profusely."

MacQuarrie glanced briefly in Matthew's direction. He shook his head in warning, which of course, the infernal Scot paid no attention to. "It's been so long since I've attended a ball. Poor Pickering, indeed. Do tell him Cambridge men must stick together. I wouldn't miss it."

"Wonderful!" Sir Ralph gushed. "And do make sure you drag Blodswell with you. I have a duty to his grandfather to fulfill."

A look of confusion crossed MacQuarrie's face, but he nodded. "Of course, sir."

"Very well." Sir Ralph turned to leave. "My wife is here somewhere. I really should get back to her before she calls the watch to find me."

As soon as the man was out of earshot, MacQuarrie cocked his head to one side, regarding Matthew curiously. "What exactly does that man owe your *grandfather*? He's old, but he can't be that old."

Matthew glared at his charge. "What the devil are you doing here? You were supposed to remain at *Brysi*."

The Scot shrugged. "I haven't had a nursemaid since I was a boy, Blodswell. I don't need one now."

All things considered, MacQuarrie was still a boy; but this was hardly the place for that discussion. "What exactly were you doing down that unlit walk?" Matthew raised his brow expectantly.

"I was being the man you created me to be."

It took all of Matthew's strength not to grab MacQuarrie by the jacket and toss him into the Thames. But the sot would probably just float his way into another boatload of trouble.

"I didn't make you so you could accost unsuspecting women at Vauxhall. In case you've forgotten, Alec, I made you because it was that or let you die by the frozen waters of Loch Calavie." He shot MacQuarrie his darkest stare. "And because you asked me to save you."

The Scot snorted. "My memory is a bit foggy on all that." MacQuarrie took a step toward Matthew, a frown marring his face. "Why do you smell like Caitrin Macleod?"

Matthew pinched the bridge of his nose. This was the last conversation he wanted to have. "*Lady Eynsford* touched my arm when I made certain her little weather-disturbing sister witch made it to Thorpe House in one piece."

"Rhiannon's in Town?"

"You know her?" Matthew asked before he could stop himself.

"The better question, Blodswell, is how do *you* know her?"

"I'd hardly say I know her. I *met* the chit when she was throwing a temper tantrum in the middle of Hyde Park." A grin tugged at the corner of his lips, no matter how much he wished it didn't.

"You know, all those years I just assumed she loved the elements," MacQuarrie lamented.

"She *is* the elements," Matthew grunted. And a bloody beautiful one at that. "What do you know of her?"

MacQuarrie's eyes danced with pleasure at Matthew's discomfort. Yet the Scot said firmly, "I know she's too bloody good for the likes of one of us."

Well, he wasn't asking to marry the chit. Still, he didn't like the tone in MacQuarrie's voice. "What is that supposed to mean?" Matthew ground out.

"It means that you had best stay clear of Miss Sinclair while she's in Town."

"Indeed? And is that a warning?" Certainly, the young man didn't want to test his mettle against Matthew. He had to be smarter than that, Cambridge man and all.

"Take it as you will. But I'll not allow you to hurt her. And if you even *think* of partaking of any little piece of her, blood or otherwise, I'll stop at nothing to prevent it. Those women are like family to me. All five of them."

"Even Lady Eynsford?" Matthew couldn't keep from goading him.

The Scot's jaw tightened. "Even Cait," he mumbled.

Matthew laid his hand on Alec's shoulder and squeezed. "The lady you were in the shadows with when I arrived—I feel certain she has men in her life, men who feel just as protective over her as you do those five women. Brothers? A father? So, keep that in mind the next time you decide to enchant your next meal. Choose someone who won't be sullied by it."

"She'll not even remember it tomorrow," MacQuarrie grunted.

"If that's the case, why do you feel as though someone like me is not nearly good enough for Miss Sinclair?"

The Scot's black eyes narrowed. Then he nodded tightly.

"If you're in need of a meal, we can go back to *Brysi*," Matthew suggested.

"I'm fine," Alec said as he adjusted his jacket and stood a little taller. "I've been locked up too long. I'd like to see the fireworks."

A curvy blond walked close by and immediately caught the Scot's attention. Matthew punched his arm none too gently and pointed toward the sky. "Those fireworks, lad. Not the other kind."

MacQuarrie grinned sheepishly and followed Matthew into the dark night. The youngster couldn't be trusted to be on his own. Which meant Matthew not only had to endure the boom and crashing of fireworks despite his headache, he also had to attend a ball. A bloody ball. One where he would be forced to keep a watchful eye on Alec MacQuarrie, or else the Scot would land them all in the middle of an entirely different kind of storm.

⤜⤏

"I canna believe ye talked me inta wearin' this," Rhiannon grumbled as she tugged at the bodice of Cait's borrowed ball gown. There simply wasn't enough of it. Not nearly enough.

Caitrin giggled, and her husband avoided looking across the coach at Rhiannon. His eyes were everywhere else. Out the window. On the ceiling. Staring at his Hessians. If that wasn't a sure sign she was indecently exposed, what was?

"It looks better on ye than it ever has on me," Cait admitted. "Does she no' look lovely, dear?" she asked of her husband.

His noncommittal grunt was his only response.

Cait elbowed him in his side. "Dash!" she scolded. "Tell Rhiannon how wonderful she looks."

The Lycan sighed loudly. Then he finally allowed his gaze to dance across Rhiannon's dress. "If you plan to force me to assess Miss Sinclair's cleavage, then yes, she looks... abundant. I mean abundantly beautiful." He leaned over and kissed Cait's cheek, lingering briefly to nuzzle her cheek.

"I told ye." Rhiannon sighed as she sank back against the squabs. "It's no' decent."

"Stir a little wind, Rhi. Yer embarassment's makin' it hot in here." Cait fanned her face. Then she scolded her husband. "And ye need ta behave yerself, Dash."

"I have a feeling I'll have a whole night of behaving myself as I try to protect Miss Sinclair's honor. The men will be on her like hounds on a bone when they see her, and that's not even including my brothers."

Cait rolled her eyes. "Ye have so little faith in them. I'll have ye ken, all three Hadley men have promised ta be their most gentlemanly this evenin'."

The marquess laughed. "That hardly means anything, Cait, and it means even less when Miss Sinclair looks like *that*."

Cait turned her attention back to Rhiannon. "Just think, ye could meet the man of yer dreams tonight," she gushed. Such a romantic. But then Cait sat back against the seat and smirked as though she was the cat who ate the cream. "Or perhaps ye've already met him."

"Doona go peekin' inta my future, Cait!" Rhiannon cried.

"I wasna lookin' inta yer future. I was makin' an educated guess." Cait harrumphed. She patted her husband's knee. "Ye'll want ta get her some of that special punch as soon as we arrive, Dash. Otherwise, she'll be a bundle of nerves and her powers will go off all over the place."

"And getting her foxed will help with that?" He raised his eyebrows at Cait's ludicrous suggestion.

"Of course," she said primly.

The coach rambled to a stop, and Rhiannon forced herself to take several deep breaths as she was presented to the Pickerings. Though they were only fashionably late, the ball was already in full swing. Couples were already dancing, and women fanned themselves from exertion. Rhi glanced around, looking for Aunt Greer and Ginny.

"Do ye see them?" Cait asked as she tugged at her sleeve.

Rhiannon just shook her head. "No' yet." She saw everything else, however. London was quite different from Edinburgh. She'd heard the term "a crush" before, but she'd never actually seen one. Throngs of twittering girls gathered together, as did young bucks, more dignified gentlemen, and a contingent of older women who seemed more intimidating than the whole of the French army. Rhi gulped. How would she ever find Ginny here?

"Perfect," the marquess grumbled under his breath.

Rhi shifted her gaze to Eynsford. "What's the matter, dear?" Cait asked.

"That ol' dragon just looked this way. There'll be no avoiding her now."

Rhi glanced over the crowd and spotted the woman Eynsford must have meant. She was as regal as she was aged. She wore an unpleasant snarl on her face and a large, purple ostrich feather in her turban that was almost as tall as she was. And the woman in question was glaring in their direction. "Who is she?"

"The Duchess of Hythe," he groaned. "She and her decrepit husband were friends of my father's. All things being equal, I'd just as soon never lay eyes on Her Grace again."

Rhi could see his point. The duchess seemed formidable indeed.

"She was a friend of yer father's?" Cait asked. "Ye should introduce me ta her."

"There are a lot of things I *should* do," Eynsford replied. "And yet, I'll avoid it just the same."

"She canna be that bad," Cait insisted.

"I believe you made a similar prediction about my father, love. I assure you she can be that bad, and she is. Her opinion can make or break someone."

Cait giggled. "Then there's nothin' ta worry about. Everyone adores me."

"*Men* adore you," the marquess informed her. "I've not seen the same devotion from women, unless they're of the witchy variety."

Rhi would rather avoid this conversation if possible. Besides, she couldn't spot Ginny from her current position. "I'll just take a stroll about the room and see if I can find my sister."

"I think not, Miss Sinclair," Eynsford said quietly, a low rumble in his voice. "Not unattended at any rate."

"It's a good thing she'll not be unattended then, isn't it, Eynsford?" a familiar voice said from behind them. Rhiannon looked up into the smiling face of Alec MacQuarrie. He held out a hand to the marquess and laughed as the Lycan scowled at him.

"I can't imagine what you're doing here," Eynsford grunted. Everyone knew there was no love lost between the two as they'd both vied for Cait's hand. But her hand wasn't what was important, because it was quite obvious who had her heart.

"Lady Eynsford," Alec said respectfully, with a small bow. However he never looked Cait in the eye. And there was tension about his mouth that wasn't normally there. Clearly, he was still hurting. Rhiannon placed a hand on Alec's sleeve. It wasn't until he smiled down at her, his black eyes glittering beneath the chandelier light, that she realized he was most assuredly different, and her hand dropped from his arm. "Are you quite all right?" he asked pleasantly, but the lines around his mouth deepened.

"I could ask ye the same thing," she shot back.

"As well as I can be, considering the circum-stances." He took her hand and placed it back on his arm. But what circumstances did he refer to? The fact that he'd somehow become a vampyre? Or that Cait had married another? "Take a stroll around the room with me?"

"Of course," Rhi said immediately. Cait gave her a small nod and her husband shot Alec a look that made him chuckle, which seemed completely inappropriate. Nothing about this situation was humorous in the least. The very thought of Alec changing into one of the undead made Rhi immeasurably sad.

"Chin up, Miss Sinclair," Alec whispered dramati-cally as he led her around the perimeter of the ballroom. "Or else you'll shock the insipid English right out of their finery with the little storm brewing over your head." Rhi looked up and, sure enough, a small storm cloud hovered high above the chandeliers. She forced herself to take a deep breath. The cloud dissipated as quickly as it had arrived.

"How did ye ken?" she asked. No one knew about her powers. Not outside the coven. And yet every vampyre she met seemed to be apprised of the fact.

"When I went after Blaire," he began, but then shook his head slowly. "It's a very long story, Rhiannon. I couldn't even do it justice in this setting."

"Will ye give me the shortened version?" she suggested. "Then we can meet tomorrow so I can hear the whole tale."

He inclined his dark head in agreement. "Cait was concerned about Blaire. Said she was being chased by something with dead eyes. So I went after her. I followed the Lindsays to Briarcraig, the captain's castle."

"I thought ye left because yer heart was broken," Rhiannon said, but instantly regretted her words when his cheery façade melted away.

"That, too," he grunted.

"And ye became one of them?"

He nodded slowly. "I did."

Rhiannon wasn't quite sure what to say to that.

"Tell me ye're all right." She stopped walking and looked directly up at him. His once-brown eyes no longer shined back at her. They were black.

"I'm as right as I can be. This does take some getting used to. But I'm managing." He smiled softly at her. Alec was still the same. He was still the jovial, considerate, compassionate man she'd grown up with.

"Who did this ta ye?" she whispered.

"Speak of the devil," Alec murmured just as Lord Blodswell stepped into her path. He bowed to Rhiannon and smiled. "*Mrs.* Sinclair," he began, a teasing smile on his face. "You look so lovely this evening."

Startled, Rhiannon sucked in a breath. Blast him for being so handsome that he stole her breath, and blast herself for letting him do so; because she knew instantly he'd done it. Blodswell had turned Alec into what he was.

"How could ye?" she gasped and covered her mouth.

Someone shrieked as the punch bowl across the room shattered. Lightning had a way of doing that. The Duchess of Hythe screamed aloud as an icicle Rhi had accidentally allowed to form dropped from the chandelier into her cleavage, where it landed directly between the old woman's breasts.

"Rhiannon," Alec warned, "you need to get hold of yourself." He took her shoulders in his hands and turned her toward him. He said quietly, "He *saved* my life. He didn't kill me."

But Blodswell *had* killed him, no matter what Alec said. He wasn't a human any longer. He was something else, something sinister and dangerous.

"I doona believe ye," she said as she shrugged out of his hold and backed away. Thunder boomed outside as she swallowed a sob. She stared into Lord Blodswell's black-as-night eyes and felt the anger as it rose to a crescendo. A footman, standing sentry at the veranda doors, jumped as a tile beneath his feet broke.

"Rhiannon," Cait called from a few feet away. Both she and Eynsford moved quickly across the floor toward her.

But before her friend could reach her, Rhi turned on Lord Blodswell. "How could ye do such a thing?

What kind of a man are ye?" A drenching rain began to pour outside the open doors leading to the balcony. It came down in sheets and out of nowhere.

"I'd like to explain," Lord Blodswell began, with a most irritating, placating look upon his face.

The slap rang out almost as loudly as the thunder outdoors did. Blodswell took the palm of her hand across his cheek and did nothing more than grit his teeth for a moment with his eyes closed before he finally looked down at her again.

"Do you feel better?" he asked as he tested his jaw with his fingertips.

"Hardly," she hissed as the whole room fell silent.

Four

MATTHEW WASN'T QUITE SURE WHAT TO SAY, AND HE was immeasurably grateful when Lady Eynsford slid her hand into Miss Sinclair's and gently tugged her toward an exit.

"*Havers!*" the marchioness exclaimed. "It appears as though ye've torn a flounce. Follow me, dear." Then the two ladies escaped into the corridor.

Matthew had no idea what he was supposed to do in their wake. All of the Pickerings' guests gaped in awe, while Alec MacQuarrie frowned at him.

"Pleased with yourself?" the annoyed Scot asked so softly that no one else could hear.

Matthew would have glared at MacQuarrie with a stare that had felled lesser men, but everyone's eyes were still on him. What he wouldn't give for the bloody orchestra to start playing again; but the musicians seemed as enthralled as all the guests with his predicament. Somewhere in the distance he heard the ticking of a clock and knew that his time was running extremely short. And so was Miss Sinclair's. A generation from now, no one would remember this little incident. He'd waited out worse, but she didn't have the same luxury.

"Apologies," he said to Eynsford who stood just a few feet away, though everyone overheard him as he knew they would. "It's been so long since I've been in polite society, I completely forgot my manners. Please do pass my sincerest apology to Miss Sinclair. She was most appropriate in her reprimand."

A flash of unabashed humor lit Eynsford's amber eyes. Yet he maintained his polite façade as he nodded and said, "I will be certain to extend your apologies to the lady, Blodswell." Then his voice rose just a tad. "However, you may apologize to the lady yourself when you pay a call at Thorpe House tomorrow."

Blast the damned Lycan for enjoying this.

Matthew nodded tightly.

"Viscount Radbourne. Mr. Grayson Hadley and Mr. Weston Hadley," Pickerings' butler intoned.

En masse, the entire ballroom's occupants shifted their focus from Matthew to the three stunned gentlemen standing in the main threshold. Why the devil couldn't the wolfish trio have arrived moments before?

❦

Cait swiftly led Rhiannon to an antechamber that was doubling as a retiring room where they quietly waited for a pair of giggly girls to take their leave. As soon as they were alone, Cait locked the door behind them, which couldn't have happened a moment too soon. The room was quickly filling with storm clouds as the sobs built within Rhiannon. She sank heavily onto a chintz chair.

"Oh, Rhi," Cait sighed. "I canna believe ye did that. I wish Blaire had been here ta see it. Then she could tell ye it was the most bloody brilliant scene that she'd ever witnessed."

"It wasna bloody brilliant," Rhiannon gasped. "It was horrendous. I'll never be able ta show my face again."

Cait covered her mouth and giggled lightly.

And then Rhiannon allowed a watery smile to cross her lips. She'd just broken a punch bowl, nearly knocked a footman off his feet, and dropped an icicle into a fearsome duchess' cleavage, an area where no one had obviously been in quite some time. Then she'd gone and slapped a revered peer of the realm.

No, she'd slapped the vampyre who'd turned Alec into what he was now, the creature who'd stolen her friend's future. And she'd done it in front of the entire *ton*, in the middle of a crowded ballroom where her powers and her very nature could have been exposed. Rhiannon glanced up to find Cait regarding her curiously. "Are ye all right?"

Rhi blew out an exasperated breath. "Ye kent I was goin' ta do that, and ye dinna give me any sort of warnin'."

Cait shrugged. "Well, that's no' entirely true, Rhi. I *did* mention the picnic, if ye remember. And ever since ye arrived on my doorstep, ye've been remindin' me that I shouldna peek inta yer future."

Rhiannon folded her arms across her chest. "Well, ye picked a fine time ta start listenin' ta me."

"Chin up." Cait smiled. "Ye'll want ta get that knock."

Knock? There was no…

A knock sounded at the locked door. Rhiannon gulped and leveled her friend with her most serious glare. Cait could be more than infuriating at times. "Tell me that isna Lord Blodswell."

The blond witch shook her head. "He may be darin', but I doubt even the benevolent Blodswell would attempt ta enter a ladies' retirin' room."

Benevolent. After what the villain had done to Alec, "benevolent" couldn't be used to describe him. Rhiannon suppressed a snort as she rose to her feet. She crossed the small antechamber to the door Cait had locked. "A moment please."

"Rhi, open up!" Ginny's hushed voice filtered through the door. "Before someone sees me."

Rhiannon wrenched the door open and felt the first bit of relief she'd experienced in more than a fortnight.

"Oh, Ginny!" Rhiannon threw her arms around her younger sister. "I've been so worried about ye."

Ginny pulled back from Rhi's embrace. "Ye're worried about me? After the display in the ballroom, ye should be worried about yerself."

"Ye saw that?" Rhiannon groaned. Blast it all. She'd lost her temper again. "How bad is it?" Her aunt would never let her near Ginny now. She'd released lightning indoors, for heaven's sake! She'd never be able to show her face in London again. They'd chase her back to Scotland if she was lucky, and if she wasn't… Well, not that long ago, witches had been put to death.

Ginny grinned. "It could be much worse, but I believe his lordship is smoothin' everythin' over. He said it was his fault."

His fault? What the in the world was Ginny talking about? "Lord Eynsford is takin' the blame for my storm?"

"Was that torrent outside yer doin'?"

"And the one inside. The punch bowl. The footman." The duchess… She couldn't even bring herself to mention the last.

A peal of laughter escaped Ginny as she brushed past Rhiannon into the retiring room. "I had no idea. No one is concerned about the weather at all."

How could no one be concerned about a storm that erupted *indoors*? Were Londoners all mad? "Then what is Lord Eynsford tryin' ta smooth over?"

Ginny shook her head. "Why do ye keep askin' about Eynsford? It's the dark-haired gentleman ye slapped right in the middle of the ballroom who is takin' the blame." She frowned as she flopped into Rhiannon's vacated seat. "By the way, Aunt Greer was traumatized by that."

Aunt Greer could go hang. Rhiannon slumped against the closed door. "*That's* what they're worried about?"

Ginny gazed at her as though she had her gown on backward and her hair was on fire. "Well, ye canna go around slappin' London gentlemen, Rhi."

"Of course no'," she admitted, "but it's hardly more important than lightnin' blasts inside a home." Not that she should complain. If everyone was concerned about lightning blasts and attributed them to Rhi, they'd march her off to Newgate without a second thought.

"Who is the gentleman? And what in the world did he do?" Ginny's hazel eyes rounded as she waited expectantly.

Cait, thankfully, rose from her spot at that point.

"The gentleman in question is the Earl of Blodswell. As ta what he did, I can imagine Rhiannon would rather no' speak of it, and I'd rather the ballroom no' turn inta Noah's flood, if ye doona mind. Three gentlemen have promised me their attendance, and they've no' yet arrived. I'd hate for it ta all be for nothin'.'"

That caught Ginny's attention. "Who are ye waitin' for, Caitrin?"

The marchioness smiled regally. "Relations of Eynsford. Three very handsome, very eligible relations." His brothers, in fact, not that Cait could admit to the unfortunate circumstance of her husband's birth. *Relations* would have to do.

"Indeed?" Ginny sat forward in her seat with rapt attention. "How handsome?"

"Well—" Cait began, but Rhiannon stopped her with a raise of her hands.

"Ye canna possibly want ta marry one of these Englishmen." Hadn't she just traveled south from Edinburgh to prevent such a thing? Well, she'd traveled south to retrieve Ginny, but now keeping her safe from Englishmen was at the top of Rhi's list.

"I doona ken who I want ta marry," Ginny admitted thoughtfully. "I imagine I have no' met him yet. Now, Caitrin, what were ye sayin' about Eynsford's relations?"

"Ginny!" Rhiannon gasped. "Ye canna be serious."

"Well, why no'?" Her sister blinked at her innocently. "Aunt Greer says I have a face that could land me quite a catch. Do they have sizeable fortunes?" She addressed the last to Cait who looked shocked at Ginny's sudden mercenary question.

Rhiannon could hardly believe her ears either. "Did ye *want* ta come with Aunt Greer?"

Ginny nodded. "Papa said I could, and I want ta attend balls and meet lords and—"

"But *evil* Aunt Greer?" Rhiannon's voice rose an octave.

Ginny's eyes dropped to her lap. "I ken she's no' nice ta ye, Rhi—"

"She's never been particularly nice ta ye, either."

Ginny sighed. "No, but she's offered ta present me. When would I get another chance like that? Can ye see Papa leavin' his library long enough ta bring me ta London and take me shoppin' and ta attend balls and soirees and luncheons? I'm sorry she dinna do the same for ye."

All the air in Rhiannon's lungs escaped. She'd come to London, followed Ginny for no reason at all. Her sister was happy with her circumstances and even with their wicked aunt, it seemed. But that still didn't mean Aunt Greer didn't have some ulterior motive. "I willna see ye married off ta some old goat our aunt picks for ye. I want ta see ye happy."

Ginny's face fell. "Ye doona think she would try such a thing, do ye?"

Rhiannon wouldn't have put it past their aunt, but she decided not to say such things to Ginny. Her sister seemed to be enjoying all this, and Rhi didn't want to shatter Ginny's dreams. "I willna allow it," she vowed. "I'll never be far away, Gin. If there's a fellow ye fancy, let me meet him before ye agree ta anythin'. And doona do everythin' Aunt Greer says. Doona let her make decisions for ye."

Ginny's hazel eyes lit up. "Ye'll be stayin' the whole season?"

Rhiannon smiled back at her. "Cait and Eynsford have invited me ta stay."

Ginny leapt from her seat and wrapped her arms around Rhi's neck. "I promise I willna accept any offers unless ye approve."

❧

Matthew turned on his heel, ready to depart the madness of this ball. Why had he even agreed to attend the deuced affair? But someone clutched his arm, and Matthew looked down into Sir Ralph's old eyes. He smiled tightly to the baronet. "I was just on my way home."

"Are you going to let the chit run you off like that?"

"I…" Matthew didn't even know where to begin after that statement. Rhiannon Sinclair was not running him off. He just had no desire to rub elbows with these people. There was no point to it.

"You were right in what you said earlier. It's been far too long since you spent time in polite society. You obviously don't know how to talk to a lady." Sir Ralph directed him to a far corner. "Which is why your father should have sent you to Eton, but that's neither here nor there anymore. I can't even imagine what you said to the chit. No, don't tell me." He raised his hands in mock protest. "I don't want to know. But it's very obvious you need my tutelage. You must be thoroughly enchanted by the lady to have suggested whatever it was that you suggested."

Matthew nearly groaned aloud. But what good

would that do? "Honestly, sir, I don't think this is the place for me."

"Nonsense!" the old man barked. "You're the Earl of bloody Blodswell, and you are in the market for a wife. This is the perfect place for you."

"Sir, I'm not in the market for a wife."

One of Sir Ralph's bushy gray eyebrows shot upwards. "If you go around saying whatever it was to that chit, you'll find yourself leg-shackled to one anyway. Now there's the right way to go about all this business and the wrong way."

Matthew braced himself to hear Sir Ralph's version of the *right* way, God save him.

"Ah!" The baronet grinned as he looked toward the entrance. "There's the lady in question now."

Matthew turned to find Rhiannon Sinclair crossing the floor toward him. She was lovely from the top of her head to the bottoms of her feet. Her gown showed a scandalous amount of skin, which only made her seem even more beautiful to him than she had the first time he'd laid eyes on her. He feared she would look beautiful even if she was covered from head to foot in scratchy wool. Unfortunately, she drew more than one eye toward her as she crossed the room.

Matthew felt a small pain within his chest and reached up to rub it. What the devil was that? He hadn't felt anything like that in more than 625 years. But he didn't have time to pay it a second thought because Sir Ralph spoke in a low voice. "She's a diamond of the first water, she is," he sighed. "She'll draw a lot of attention this season. I'm glad you already claimed her."

"Claimed her?" Matthew choked. He'd done no such thing. Had he?

"Clearly, with whatever it was you said to the chit. You're a lucky man Eynsford decided to accept your apology, but rest assured by tomorrow morning all of London will know of your interest in the girl." Did the old man's eyes soften at the sight of the little witch? They did. Which didn't make any sense. Lovely as Rhiannon Sinclair was, she didn't possess a bit of charm in her body. In fact, she was a walking thunderstorm—abrasive and shocking. If Sir Ralph knew the truth of what she really was, the old man's rapt attention and obvious approval would wither away.

But Matthew doubted he could ever look at her differently, even knowing the power she possessed. The lady was nothing short of a siren. Rhiannon's lovely neck was exposed by her upswept hair. Matthew could almost see the tapping of her pulse at the base of her throat. He knew he could hear it. Her storm-laden scent, mixed with just a hint of gardenia, grew stronger as she approached.

Matthew tugged at his jacket, feeling somewhat comforted by the simple act of adjusting his clothing. It gave him something to do, after all. He really should step toward her to meet her halfway, but out of nowhere that little pup, Radbourne, stepped into her path and bowed low before her.

"Uh-oh," Sir Ralph grunted.

"Uh-oh?" Matthew just had to ask.

"Radbourne." The old man scoffed. Then he clapped Matthew on the shoulder. "A fortune hunter of questionable character. You should probably intervene, especially now that your encounter with the chit could very well tarnish her reputation. It could give you the opportunity to play the gallant."

Play the gallant, indeed. Damn it all to hell. Hadn't he already fallen on his own sword to protect Miss Sinclair's reputation? Letting them all assume he'd made an improper advance had been much easier than explaining the real reason why she'd slapped him.

Matthew froze as he watched the witch bestow a smile upon Radbourne, who looked amazingly similar to the Marquess of Eynsford. The two could pass for brothers, with the shade of their hair the only difference. They were obviously relations of some sort. Matthew had smelled the Lycan and his younger brothers the instant they'd stepped foot in the Pickerings' ballroom. But he hadn't realized the man was a fortune hunter. He looked as well turned out as any other man in the room.

Did Miss Sinclair possess a fortune? Did she need rescuing again? Matthew's thoughts evaporated the moment Radbourne lifted her hand to his mouth and pressed his lips against her gloved fingers.

Matthew's chest clenched again, nearly knocking him to his knees.

"Are you all right?" Sir Ralph asked. "Shall I call for a footman?"

"That won't be necessary," Matthew grunted as the pain receded. It was immediately replaced by something he didn't recognize when Radbourne lingered a bit too long over Miss Sinclair's hand. Then the beast tucked her hand into the crook of his arm and led her to the dance floor.

Miss Sinclair graced Radbourne with a smile unlike anything Matthew had ever seen, and red rage clouded the corners of his vision. He hadn't experienced an emotion like this in a very long time. What did they call it? He couldn't even put a name to it.

"Jealous, Blodswell?" Sir Ralph asked.

Jealous? Certainly not. He snorted in response.

But he *was* jealous, which was the strangest thing as he barely knew the chit. Matthew couldn't help but glower as Radbourne led Miss Sinclair into a waltz, his body scandalously close to hers. He watched closely as the young wolf held her hand in his. The bloody pup could probably feel the heat of her through his gloves. Damn his eyes. Matthew took a step toward them.

"I wouldn't do that if I were you," Sir Ralph said as he grabbed his arm.

Matthew gritted his teeth. "Do what, Sir Ralph?" he forced out.

The man chuckled. "Throttle the cad. You can't do that. Not here at any rate." He shook a finger at Matthew. "And no matter how much you might want to. Hell, I want to do it on your behalf. That fellow always did have a sense of entitlement. Never did like the whelp, nor his father. He's much more trouble than he has ever been worth, both him and his brothers who are following quickly in his dissolute footsteps."

Matthew fairly seethed as Miss Sinclair waltzed with the fortune-hunting, debauched Radbourne. Every smile she bestowed on the viscount made Matthew angrier. And his mood grew darker as he waited for the set to finally end.

Sir Ralph nodded toward the dancing pair. "Once he bows, you can go claim your dance with the lady. But do watch your tongue. It wouldn't do either of you any good if she slapped you again."

Five

Rhiannon knew quite well she was looking into the glinting eyes of a Lycan as Archer Hadley, Viscount Radbourne, led her around the floor.

"I believe he'll rip off my head if I don't relinquish you soon," Lord Radbourne said with a dramatic sigh. "Or at least make a good attempt at it."

"I doona ken who ye're referring ta, my lord," Rhiannon said succinctly, drawing on every lesson of decorum Aunt Greer had ever tried to drill into her head.

"Oh, *ye ken* exactly who I'm speaking of," he laughed, mimicking her accent to near-perfection. "That man hasn't taken his eyes off your backside the entire time I've had you on the floor."

Rhiannon felt heat creep up her face. "He most certainly has no' been starin' at my backside," she hissed quietly.

Lord Radbourne chuckled. "What *did* you do to deserve such devotion from the man? From what Cait tells me, you just arrived in Town last night. I can see how you could win hearts quickly, but twenty-four hours is rather fast, even for a beauty like you." His amber eyes twinkled with mirth. "It would take me at least a fortnight to fall in love with you." His eyes slid down her body languidly. "Well, maybe half that."

Rhiannon tripped over his toe. Or her toe. She wasn't certain which. But he just clutched her more closely to him and drew her back into the dance.

"Don't look now, sweetheart, but the unlucky earl is barely holding himself in check," Radbourne said.

He spun her so she could see Blodswell around his shoulder, and the man did, indeed, look as though he could consume her in one bite. After he killed her dancing partner, that was. The thought sent shivers down her spine as memories of a different night and a different vampyre flashed in her mind. To shake the image away, she turned her attention back to the dark-haired, amber-eyed Lycan.

"Are ye enjoyin' this evenin'?" Rhiannon asked, biting back a grin.

"More than you could ever know," Radbourne said. "I came tonight at Cait's request. To help your entrance into society. But with that dress, and..." his gaze slid down her again, before he drew his eyes up and grunted, "the rest of you, I needn't have bothered. The only reason your dance card is empty is because no one had time to pencil in his name before I stole you away."

"Are ye always so direct?"

He shrugged. "I assume so. Does it bother you?" He looked down at her as though the answer was suddenly important.

"No, I appreciate yer candor. I believe I could talk ta ye all night."

"Would that it were true." Radbourne sighed. Then the music stopped and he bowed low before her, his eyes narrowing slightly when he stood back up and said one word, "Blodswell."

Rhiannon glanced over her shoulder. There he was, the regal vampyre. He bowed low to her as well. She'd never been paid so much favor in her life.

"May I have this next dance, Miss Sinclair?" the earl asked.

If she refused, she wouldn't be able to dance with any other man the rest of the night. All things considered, that might be all right this evening. She hadn't come to husband hunt; she'd come to keep an eye on Ginny. Rhiannon looked to Radbourne for advice, but the Lycan merely winked at her.

"Please don't say no," Blodswell said quietly, "or everyone will assume my earlier breach of decorum was scandalous enough for you to give me the cut direct."

Breach of decorum. Is that how vampyres referred to turning delightful men into one of their kind? She'd like to give him the cut direct, among other things, but making another scene would hardly help Ginny. So Rhiannon smiled at the vampyre.

"Would ye mind if we took a turn about the room instead? I doona feel much like dancin' this evenin'." She glanced up at the ceiling, where a small storm cloud brewed. "Why canna I seem ta control myself around him?" she muttered to herself.

Unfortunately, both Blodswell and Radbourne heard her words. The latter looked the former over with more than a hint of disapproval. "Best of luck to you, Blodswell," the viscount offered before he turned on his heel to rejoin his brothers across the room.

Of course, Radbourne had no knowledge of her storms; at least she didn't think he did. So, the Lycan viscount must have thought she meant something entirely different than the storm cloud over their heads that threatened to erupt at any moment.

"*Havers!*" Rhiannon said as she fanned her face. "That wasna what I meant at all. Now the man will think I have feelings for ye."

The Earl of Blodswell took her hand and placed it on his arm, and then graced her with his most winning smile. "Well, you do, don't you?"

Rhiannon nearly tripped on her hem as his dark gaze momentarily disarmed her. The blasted vampyre shouldn't go around smiling at women like that. The female half of London would throw themselves in his path to catch a glimpse of that smile. It was foolish of her to forget the enchanting power of vampyres. She quickly shook her head to clear her mind. She should never have looked into his eyes. She didn't think he'd enchanted her, but one could never be too cautious when dealing with his kind.

"I suppose irritation and dislike *are* feelings, my lord."

Blast him. He smiled again. Rhi refused to look at him. Smiles and enchanted gazes might work on some women, but not her. She knew what he was about, after all. She glanced across the crowded ballroom and spotted Ginny at the far end with Aunt Greer who was glaring daggers at her. For a moment Rhi wasn't certain whose gaze was worse, Blodswell's or Aunt Greer's. But only for a moment. Aunt Greer, nasty as she was, didn't have the power to drain someone of their own free will.

"And why do you dislike me so, Miss Sinclair?" The earl's gentle, baritone voice brushed across her ear like a caress as they strolled the perimeter.

She kept her face focused on the couples dancing a few feet away, afraid to give him any opportunity to look in her eyes. "Do ye truly have ta ask that question? After what ye did ta Alec…"

"MacQuarrie aside, you didn't know my connection to your friend last night when you fabricated a husband and bolted through Hyde Park as though the watch was after you."

No, she hadn't. She'd been terribly embarrassed to have been caught having a temper tantrum, and *then* she'd realized what he was. "The watch would have been preferable," she grumbled.

Blodswell stopped walking and towed her closer to him. Rhiannon looked above his head to avoid eye contact, but she could tell he was frowning. "No one has ever taken an instant dislike toward me, Miss Sinclair. Not in hundreds of years. Pray tell me what I've done that offended you so terribly last night."

Rhiannon let her gaze settle on the dimple in his chin. "Ye're a vampyre," she said beneath her breath. Heaven help her if anyone other than Blodswell heard her words.

"And you're a witch," he returned just as quietly, bending slightly to speak softly in her ear. The hair on her arms stood up. "I've known several of your kind over the years, Miss Sinclair, and we've always gotten along rather amiably."

"Well, I've no' had the same fortune with those of *yer* kind." That was an understatement, but not something she wished to discuss with him. Rhi tugged her hand from the vampyre's arm. "And I'd rather keep my distance from vampyres, if ye doona mind."

"I'm afraid I mind very much. The Marquess of Eynsford has requested my presence in his home tomorrow, and I've given my word as a gentleman that I'll attend."

What did vampyres know about being gentlemen? The one in Edinburgh certainly hadn't been one. "Why would he make such a foolish request?"

"To smooth over the blow you dealt my cheek, not to mention my honor, earlier this evening, I would imagine," the earl explained as though she was a child.

Rhi begrudgingly had to admit that made sense, but she still didn't like it. Besides, she wasn't the only one in residence at Thorpe House. Rhiannon feigned a smile and curtseyed. "Well, then I hope ye and the marquess get along famously on the morrow. Good evenin', my lord."

❦

Addled. Matthew couldn't recall the last time he'd felt addled. But there wasn't another word for it. Every time Rhiannon Sinclair escaped his company he was more bewildered than the time before. She'd run from him three times now. It was almost enough to deal a fatal blow to a fellow's ego. By Saint George's teeth, he had only tried to help the lady. Chivalry was not necessarily dead, but Rhiannon Sinclair wanted none of it.

He watched as Lady Eynsford and her pack of wolves circled around the lady in question. She clearly didn't want any part of him or his help. What should it matter to him? He didn't know her. He didn't owe her anything. Yet as the bloody Viscount Radbourne pressed his lips to Miss Sinclair's fingers, Matthew had to stop himself from flying across the room and crashing his fist into the fortune hunter's face. But that was hardly gentlemanly…

Radbourne *was* a fortune hunter, wasn't he? Or so Sir Ralph had claimed. And why would Sir Ralph malign Radbourne if there was no truth behind it? If Miss Sinclair *was* in the possession of a fortune, he should make certain the *fortune hunter of questionable character* kept his distance from the lady. After all, Eynsford and his wife seemed to be blind to Radbourne's character flaws. The two men were most definitely related somehow. Matthew only wished he knew the particulars.

If Eynsford couldn't be trusted to ensure Miss Sinclair's best interests, Matthew probably should keep the lass in his sights. Besides, who better than a knight to rescue a damsel in distress, even if the damsel didn't know it?

"And you say *I'm* stubborn," Alec MacQuarrie muttered at his side.

Matthew hadn't even noticed the reborn Scot approaching him. He didn't even bother to glance at MacQuarrie, as his eyes were still trained on Miss Sinclair. "What are you going on about?"

"I specifically asked you to stay away from Rhiannon, and you ignored me completely."

At that, Matthew scoffed and finally did look his charge in the eyes. "I believe you have assumed a role unbefitting our relationship, Alec," Matthew scolded. He said the words low enough that the Scot was the only one who could hear them. He was certain he'd hit his mark when MacQuarrie's face colored.

Matthew softened his expression. The lady was an old friend of Alec's. He should be happy the Scot cared about *something*, considering the way he carried on with little regard for feelings or emotions now that he was a vampyre. "You should have seen her last night. She was so sad. And now…"

"And now what?" MacQuarrie glanced across the room at Eynsford's corner, toward the weather-disturbing witch and her friends, and winced when he saw Lady Eynsford.

Would the poor man ever get over the loss of the marchioness? Matthew doubted he would. He'd seen other vampyres suffer loss, and it simply made for centuries of anguish. He suddenly realized how fortunate he was to have never loved someone he would have inevitably lost in the end.

"And now what?" MacQuarrie repeated with more than an irritated edge to his voice.

Matthew shook away his maudlin thoughts and refocused his attention on the beguiling witch at whom Radbourne grinned wolfishly. How strange to be asking his charge for advice. But the man had socialized in these circles before his untimely death. "What do you know of Radbourne?"

MacQuarrie shrugged as he regarded the man in question. "I've bumped into him a few times in the past, but never in a ballroom. He doesn't frequent the upscale venues. Or consort with *ladies* as a norm."

"I hear he has pockets to let. Though he doesn't look impoverished at the moment." Matthew scratched his chin. Secretly, a small part of him wanted to find something to dislike about the man. Should he feel bad about that? He certainly hated the way Rhiannon Sinclair's gaze sought out the viscount. She wouldn't even look Matthew in the eye.

"No, but he is, if rumor is true, and it usually is." Then MacQuarrie frowned, his gaze intensified on Radbourne. "He looks amazingly similar to Eynsford, does he not?"

"I was thinking the same thing."

"I've never seen them together before," the Scot muttered. "I've never heard of any connection between the two families. But they could pass as brothers." He spit out the last as though the idea was distasteful to him.

"They're beasts of the same variety," Matthew explained. "There must be some familial ties somewhere down the line."

"Beasts?" Alec's head snapped in his direction. "What do you mean beasts?"

Matthew heaved a sigh. Why had he let that slip? "Not here. I'll explain about Lycans later."

"What the devil is a Lycan?"

"This isn't the place."

Alec grabbed a handful of Matthew's jacket. "You'll tell me here and now!" he hissed. "If Caitrin's in danger—"

"She's not," Matthew growled, extricating himself

from the Scot's hold. "Do try to remember you're in public, Alec."

"Are you saying Eynsford is a Lycan, whatever the devil they are?"

Matthew straightened his jacket. "We should head back to *Brysi* if you want to have this conversation now."

"But Cait!" Alec pressed.

"Is married to the man. Look at her," Matthew directed. "Does she seem unhappy? Does she look as though she's been injured? They've been married for months, Alec. More than one moonful, and she still seems to adore the marquess. I know it's painful for you, but it is the way of things."

Anguish stained MacQuarrie's face. "Promise me she's safe."

That was an easy promise to make. Eynsford treated his wife as though she was the most precious of treasures. "On my honor, I swear to you that Caitrin is safe with Eynsford."

Alec nodded tightly. "Thank you."

"I do believe we should take our leave, though." Matthew's gaze shot back across the room to land on Rhiannon Sinclair. What was it about her that intrigued him so? Hopefully, he'd find out tomorrow when he called on her at Thorpe House. Until then, he'd learn what he could about the insolvent Viscount Radbourne.

Six

THORPE HOUSE WAS A BIT OF A MADHOUSE, OR A doghouse, depending on one's view. Rhiannon wasn't quite certain what her view was at the moment. Shortly after breakfast, the Marquess of Eynsford had unceremoniously scooped Caitrin up in his arms, despite her halfhearted, giggly protests, and bounded for parts unknown. For a half second, Rhi had considered sending a shock to his hindquarters, the same way she had when he'd nearly mauled Cait at their wedding all those months ago. But as she was a guest in the man's home, she decided it probably wasn't the best idea.

She hadn't seen either of them since.

Rhiannon was far from lonely, however. Caitrin had the right of it when she said Eynsford's brothers were always underfoot. The twins, Grayson and Weston Hadley, bickered back and forth about one inane topic or another—from styles of cravats to the latest offerings at Tattersall's. Watching them was vastly entertaining until Lord Radbourne, from his position near the window seat, suggested the pair hie off to Gentleman Jackson's to settle their squabbles in more appropriate surroundings.

"And leave Miss Sinclair alone in *your* debauched presence?" Weston Hadley raised one dark eyebrow. "I think not."

"I'm in complete agreement." Grayson Hadley settled in beside Rhiannon on a dark green brocade settee. "I am sorry my younger brother's ineptitude about cattle has kept the conversation from you, Miss Sinclair."

"Sorry, sweetheart." Lord Radbourne smiled wolfishly at her. "Apparently the only thing they agree on is thwarting me."

"And I am *not* younger," Weston Hadley insisted as he sank into a nearby high-backed chair, casting an irritated glance at his twin. "We're the *same* age."

"Ah, but I beat you by a whole five minutes." Grayson Hadley leaned toward Rhiannon and whispered dramatically, "The runt of a litter typically is the weakest, both mentally and physically. You wouldn't believe how many arguments we've had over *that*."

Rhiannon couldn't help herself, and she laughed at the pair. "Oh, I believe you, Mr. Hadley."

"Mr. Hadley is so formal, and there are *two* of us. Please call me Gray instead." He winked at her.

A strangled sound escaped his twin. "First names already? Well, then, Miss Sinclair, I insist you call me Wes."

Gray chuckled. "Beat you again."

"Only because I'm better mannered than you," Wes returned.

Lord Radbourne rubbed his brow as though his

siblings gave him a headache. "I am very sorry, sweetheart. I should have left them at home. In the nursery." He shot them a quelling glance.

Wes snorted. "We could hardly allow you to keep Miss Sinclair to yourself." Then he graced Rhiannon with a charming smile. "Cait has told us very little about you, Miss Sinclair."

Including the fact that she was a witch. They didn't know about Cait, either. Her friend had confided that bit after the ball last night. Fortunately, Lord Radbourne hadn't noticed the cloud above them when Lord Blodswell intercepted them. That would have been difficult to explain. "There's no' much ta tell," Rhiannon hedged.

"I don't believe that." Wes leaned forward in his seat. "Well, how do you know Cait?"

Rhiannon pushed one of her curls behind her ear. "We've kent each other since infancy. Our mothers were close friends. We're like sisters of a sort." Coven sisters counted, didn't they?

"And how are you finding London?" Gray inquired. "Very different from Edinburgh, or so Cait has said."

"Complained is more like it," Radbourne put in with a good-natured grin.

At that moment Price, the aged butler, entered the parlor with a silver salver outstretched in one hand. "A gentleman to see you, Miss."

Rhiannon gulped. Only one gentleman had threatened to call on her today. She snatched the vellum card from the tray and cringed at the bold, block letters emblazoning the words "EARL OF BLODSWELL." Blast him. Why couldn't he leave her alone?

"Your devoted suitor?" Radbourne asked.

"The fellow from last night?" Gray slid forward on the settee. "He seemed rather… intense."

"Lord Eynsford asked him to come today."

Wes scoffed. "Then Dash should have to visit with the man." Which had been Rhiannon's first thought last night as well.

"If you don't want to see Blodswell, sweetheart, you can tell Price that you're not in," Radbourne suggested.

Rhiannon nodded. That did seem the best idea. "Yes—" But her answer was interrupted by a delighted squeal from the corridor.

"Lord Blodswell!" Caitrin's disembodied voice filtered into the parlor. "I'm so glad ye're here. Everyone has converged in my green parlor. Do follow me."

"What a pleasure to see you again, Lady Eynsford." Despite his words, Blodswell sounded far from pleased.

Perfect! Cait was absent all morning but arrived just in time to make certain the blasted vampyre was allowed to stay. Slight thunder rumbled overhead.

"Hmm," Gray mused. "Did you hear that? There wasn't a cloud in the sky when we arrived."

"Here we are," Cait practically sang as she and Lord Blodswell entered the parlor. All three Hadley men rose from their spots at the marchioness' entrance. "Oh, do sit." She gestured to her brothers-in-law. "Well, except for ye, Grayson." Cait frowned when he resumed his spot beside Rhiannon. "The marquess would like a word with ye."

"Me?" Gray rose again from his seat and stepped closer to Cait. "Why does Dash want to see me?"

"I really couldna say." She gave him a little push

toward the corridor. Then she glanced over her shoulder to the vampyre standing behind her. "Oh, my lord, why doona ye take the seat next ta Rhiannon since ye're already acquainted."

What exactly was Cait about? She knew Rhiannon didn't want to see the man. She'd told her so in no uncertain terms after the ball last night. The thunder overhead rumbled louder. At the sound, Cait raised one arrogant blond brow. *Watch your temper.* She didn't say it aloud. She didn't have to.

"Lord Blodswell, I believe ye met Lord Radbourne last evenin', and seated by himself over there is his brother, Mr. Weston Hadley. They are relations of Eynsford's. Archer, Weston, this is a friend of mine, the Earl of Blodswell. Do make him feel comfortable." Then she turned her attention to the poor butler still standing in the middle of the room. "And, Price, please do bring some tea and refreshments."

"Of course, my lady," the butler replied as he ambled out of the room.

Cait pushed Lord Blodswell a tiny bit toward Rhiannon and the green settee before taking her own spot in a seat next to Wes. The earl's dark gaze landed on Rhi, but she refused to meet it. "Miss Sinclair," he said as he settled in beside her, "how lovely to see you again."

Rhiannon could barely move. How was it possible that he took up nearly all the space on the settee? It hadn't seemed that way when Gray was seated beside her. She slowly raised her gaze to his face. Blast him, he was handsome in the daylight. She quickly looked away. "Thank ye, my lord," she croaked.

"Well, then," Caitrin began brightly from her

corner, "Archer, I received the nicest letter from your mother today."

Lord Radbourne grumbled something under his breath that Rhi couldn't hear, but Weston chuckled to himself. Blast those Lycan ears. What she wouldn't give to be able to hear their rumblings and grumblings.

"I was hoping, Miss Sinclair," Lord Blodswell said softly, "that I might take you for a ride in my curricle today. I believe you've seen Hyde Park, but it's entirely different in the light of day."

Rhiannon gaped at him. Was he mad? Vampyres couldn't go out in sunlight. What was he about? She was too curious not to find out. "What a wonderful suggestion, my lord."

❦

Matthew could hardly believe his luck. Had she actually agreed to go riding with him? And after she'd initially decided to have the butler tell him she wasn't home? Yes, he'd heard her. He'd also heard the pups as they tried to help her thwart him, which made him none too happy with the lot. He couldn't imagine what changed her mind, but he wasn't willing to take the chance she'd change it again.

He rose from his seat and offered her his hand. "Shall we then?"

"Yes, of course." She came gracefully to her feet, though her eyes never rose past his nose. What the devil was that about?

Matthew tucked her hand in the crook of his arm and smiled his thanks to Lady Eynsford. "Until later, my lady."

"Do enjoy yer afternoon, Lord Blodswell." Then the marchioness actually winked at him, which took Matthew a little by surprise. Caitrin Eynsford had clearly been his advocate that afternoon, but for her to admit it with that wink… Well, she was a formidable lady indeed.

Matthew led Miss Sinclair from the parlor and down the corridor toward the front door. "You doona truly intend ta take me for a ride in the park," she said matter-of-factly.

"I don't?" Matthew frowned at her as he continued down the hallway. Every encounter with the lady left him more confused. Hadn't he asked her to go for a ride, and hadn't she agreed? "What do I intend to do with you then, Miss Sinclair?"

"That's what I'm waitin' for ye ta tell me. Ye clearly have somethin' ta say ta me as I've seen ye more in the last three days than I've seen my own sister."

He wasn't sure what to say to that. She was the most beguiling creature, and he couldn't figure her out at all. "I assure you, I do intend to take you for a ride in the park." And he did. He'd come up with the plan early this morning for two reasons. One, the curricle would only accommodate two people so there would be no room for any stray Lycans to tag along. And two, if they were seen riding together, the *ton* would assume that whatever horrid thing he supposedly said the night before was all but forgiven and forgotten by the lady.

A footman opened the front door. Rhiannon stopped and narrowed her eyes at him.

"Are you all right, Miss Sinclair?" Matthew cocked

his head to one side. It was that or shake it violently to dislodge the lack of cohesive thought inside.

"Ye're really all right, goin' out in the light of day?"

Matthew would have been frustrated with her, but she looked so sincere that he couldn't bring himself to be so. "Would you rather stay here instead of going riding through the park?"

Her beautiful hazel eyes narrowed even more suspiciously. "Ye said ye wanted ta take me for a ride, but I doona see how ye could."

Matthew wasn't at all certain what she meant, but a part of him stirred at her mutterings. Still, taking her for a ride of a different sort was... not something a gentleman did, he berated himself. "Of course I can take you for a ride, Miss Sinclair." He gestured to his black curricle out front through the still open door. "But only if you'll walk through the doorway with me." Was she waiting for him to sweep her off her feet and abscond with her? That sounded delightful. He forced himself to be more sober.

She nodded hastily. "Fresh air would do me a bit of good." Then she took his outstretched hand.

Matthew led her into the sunlight, down Eynsford's stone steps, and out to his awaiting curricle. He helped her into the conveyance, paid the lad holding the ribbons to the matched grays with a shiny coin, and then slid into the box beside the witch. With a flick of his wrist, the horses moved into the traffic headed toward Curzon Street.

He caught her staring at him in amazement, and he turned to level his most charming smile at her. "There. Is that better now?"

She nodded. "How is it ye're able ta go out in the sun?"

Without thinking his actions through, Matthew took her hands in one of his and squeezed. The sunlight glinted off his ring. "Five wonderful women gave me a gift long ago that has made this existence bearable."

She looked down at their connected hands, and he knew the moment she put the pieces together. "That looks like Blaire's ring."

"Identical," he agreed with a nod, and then he grasped the ribbons in both hands as he directed the grays across Park Lane and through the gates of Hyde Park. Almost at once they came to a stop as there were so many people out for a ride this time of day.

"Ye were at Briarcraig Castle with Blaire when she met Lord Kettering."

Silently, Matthew nodded again. He wasn't certain what to say. He had very few fond memories of his time at Briarcraig, all culminating in the terrible night when Alec MacQuarrie lay dying at his feet. And he really didn't want to mention that situation again, not now that she seemed to be softening a bit toward him. He wasn't even certain why that mattered to him, but it did.

"I still canna believe our mothers trapped the poor man in that castle. It was unconscionable."

Matthew glanced at the witch beside him. She was staring at her hands with her head bent downward in shame. Was she feeling guilty for her mother's actions? "It's not your fault, Miss Sinclair."

"No, but it was my coven. My legacy. I hope the five of us never do somethin' so dreadful that our daughters are mortified on our behalf."

Daughters. Some day, she would have a child with some very lucky man. It was too bad he couldn't be that man, though he had no idea where the thought had came from. "As contemplative as you appear to be, I'm certain that worry is unfounded."

She lifted her head and stared at his nose. "That is kind of ye ta say."

"Why do you do that?" he couldn't stop himself from asking. "You never look at me."

Miss Sinclair scoffed nervously. "That's ridiculous. I look at ye all the time."

"No." Matthew urged his grays forward. "You look at my chin or my ears or nose, but you never look *at* me. Why is that, Miss Sinclair?"

She slid away from him and watched a couple, hand in hand, walking nearby.

"Are you not even going to answer me?"

"Caitrin says I doona need ta be afraid of ye, but I canna help it, my lord. I canna look in yer eyes. I canna take the chance that ye'll enchant me."

If the Serpentine had sprouted watery legs and walked away, Matthew couldn't have been more surprised. "A vampyre enchanted you?" His eyes scanned the column of her neck but saw no telltale signs that any of his kind had ever partaken of her life force. He ached to check every inch of her to look for bite marks.

She nodded, still looking out across the park. "I was inside my mind, watchin' the events unfold; but he had complete control over me. I couldna move. There was nothin' I could do."

And she thought he'd do the same to her. It wasn't as though he hadn't ever used the power before. He had. More times than he could count, but this was the first time he felt guilty for having done so. "I give you my word, Miss Sinclair, I will never enchant you."

Rhiannon nodded, but she kept her gaze averted to watch a happy couple yards away.

"Rhi!" some chit called from somewhere behind them.

Matthew glanced over his shoulder and spotted a girl fresh from the schoolroom with two older women in the same conveyance.

Rhiannon shifted on the bench, and her face lit with joy. "Ginny!"

∽✦∾

A young man maneuvered Ginny and Aunt Greer's barouche alongside Lord Blodswell's curricle. That was when Rhiannon noticed someone seated opposite her family on the bench—the formidable Duchess of Hythe. Rhiannon gulped.

The vampyre at her side tipped his hat in greeting. "Good afternoon, ladies."

"And just who are you?" Aunt Greer snapped.

Rhiannon closed her eyes out of mortification, and a strong wind whipped through the park. Lord Blodswell gently squeezed her hand again, and the wind receded. Rhi opened her eyes to regard her aunt with a scathing glare.

"Lord Blodswell, may I present my aunt, Greer Cooper, and my sister, Miss Ginessa Sinclair." She smiled weakly at the dragon of a duchess. "I'm afraid I've yet ta make yer acquaintance, ma'am."

The duchess' shrewd gaze narrowed on Lord

Blodswell. "You." She pointed a bejeweled finger at the earl. "I knew your grandfather, young man."

"Did you, Your Grace?" It looked as though he was trying to smother an amused grin.

The duchess leaned toward Blodswell's curricle. "I did, and I'm certain he would not have approved of your behavior last night. Your title is one of the oldest and most respectable in the kingdom."

Aunt Greer's expression softened as she eyed the earl. What was that about? Rhi had never known her aunt's opinion to change once she'd decided to dislike something or someone.

The duchess turned her icy eyes on Rhiannon. "And, you, Miss Sinclair, I am glad to make your acquaintance. The chits these days are too free with their favors. Back in my day, women behaved with a bit more decorum. I don't know what the bounder said to you, but I'm certain he deserved it. Has he behaved himself today?"

Rhiannon blinked at the duchess and managed a nod. "Perfect gentleman."

The old woman smiled wryly. "Just as I suspected. Men are like dogs, Miss Sinclair. They need to know their boundaries. I commend you on training yours so well."

Rhiannon choked, and again Lord Blodswell gently squeezed her hand. "He's not *mine*, Your Grace," Rhiannon protested, but the earl cut her off.

"I am hers to command," the earl returned.

The duchess ignored him and kept her light blue eyes leveled on Rhiannon. "You are staying with the Marquess of Eynsford and his wife, are you not?"

"Yes, Your Grace," Rhi said quietly.

"Splendid. I am hosting a soiree at the end of the week, and I'd like you to be my special guest. Bring Eynsford and his wife with you."

Rhiannon nodded. "Thank ye. I'm certain they'll be delighted." At least Cait would be, anyway.

The duchess glanced back at the earl. "And you'll be there, Blodswell. I want to see how well trained you really are."

He chuckled lightly. "I'll be happy to escort Miss Sinclair, if she'll allow it," he said as he smiled down at Rhi, his eyebrows arched in question. Finally, she allowed herself to look into his dark eyes. The obsidian depths held nothing that scared her. In fact, his black eyes twinkled at her, if that was possible. "Miss Sinclair?" he prompted, one corner of his mouth lifting.

She nodded, forcing herself to close her mouth. She must look like the worst sort of fool, staring into the man's eyes with her mouth hanging open.

Ginny clapped and giggled. "Wonderful! I canna wait ta see ye there!" She gasped and reached for her bonnet as her barouche moved forward. Ginny leaned over the side of the open carriage and called, "See ye at the end of the week!" as she waved frantically.

"Wait!" Rhiannon called. But the conveyance didn't slow or stop. She sighed deeply. Two minutes with her sister? Was that all she would be allowed?

"In a bit of a hurry, are they?" the earl asked as he stared down at her. A drop of rain landed on the sleeve of his jacket with a wet plop. He looked up at the sky. "There wasn't a cloud to be seen when we left Eynsford's," he lamented.

Rhiannon sniffed and forced her spine to stiffen. "My apologies."

"And what are you apologizing for?" His eyebrows arched in question.

She motioned to the air around her. "The weather, my lord," she whispered. "I canna always control it. But I'll try no' ta drench us both."

He chuckled. "I rather liked the last storm."

"The one here in the park? Or the one at the ball?" Rhi covered her face in shame. "That was a terrible day. I'm very sorry ye had ta see either of them."

"Your storms? Why on earth would you be sorry I saw them? I thought they were splendid." He looked down at her as though she'd lost her mind.

"The incident in Hyde Park was a temper tantrum," she admitted. "I was frustrated beyond reason over my sister. My Aunt Greer willna even allow me ta see her. My very presence would impede Ginny's successful launch into society, my aunt said. So I took out my frustration in the only way I ken how. I made a storm of epic proportions." She sniffed again. "I still feel badly about it."

Blodswell bumped her shoulder gently with his. "I still thought it was beautiful."

He thought what? "Beg yer pardon?"

"May I be quite frank with you, Miss Sinclair?"

She shrugged. "Of course."

"I have been alive for more than six-and-a-half centuries. I have seen a lot in those years. And done a lot. And left very few stones unturned. After a time, it does become a bit of a boring lifestyle. So, when I saw you here in the park, I was the one enchanted for once." He tweaked her nose with a crooked finger. "Thoroughly."

Certainly the man was simply trying to salvage her feelings. That raindrop must have made him feel incredibly sorry for her, for him to say such ludicrous things. No one liked a storm. No one liked things beyond their control. No one liked *her*. Aside from her coven, that was. "It's kind of ye ta say so."

"No, it's wrong of me to say so."

"I doona ken what ye mean." He was speaking in riddles, which was incredibly frustrating.

"Never mind," he said as he flicked his wrist and set his grays to moving.

Seven

IT WAS WRONG OF HIM TO HAVE THOUGHTS SUCH AS HE was about Miss Sinclair. Completely and horridly wrong. But she smelled of gardenia blossoms and sat close enough that his thigh touched hers in a most inappropriate way. In a most thrilling way. By anyone's standards, he was too old for the likes of her. Too jaded. Too much of a vampyre.

Matthew knew, deep down in his soul, that he had nothing to give to an innocent lass like the lovely lady who sat beside him. In fact, all he could think about was taking *from* her. He could hear the thrilling thrum of her pulse within her veins and could even see it beating beneath the thin skin at the base of her neck. He wanted more than anything to draw her to him and take from her. How on earth had they gone from an innocent ride to an all-out disaster within moments? Perhaps chaos simply followed her. Absurdly, he wanted to follow her, too.

"Are ye all right, my lord?" she asked quietly.

"Quite," he replied cryptically, although he wasn't. He wasn't at all. He was experiencing a hunger unlike any he'd had for centuries. In fact, his incisors picked that very moment to descend. It typically only happened when he was hungry or highly aroused. At that moment, he was both. He forced his lips into a grim line.

She leaned forward to look at his face. He allowed a half smile to twist his lips.

"Oh," she said quietly as she sat up taller and crossed her slender hands in her lap.

What the devil did "oh" mean? "Miss Sinclair," he began, about to tell her he would be returning her to Eynsford's with haste. He needed to set her at least ten paces from him. And do it quickly. He hadn't felt so out of control since he'd cut his vampyre teeth all those centuries ago.

The lady grimaced and cut him off before he could continue. She lifted her hand to her mouth, where she put the heel of that hand beside her lips, flatted her palm, and then blew a slow breath out of her perfectly formed lips. He shifted in his seat.

What made matters worse was that the horses suddenly had a mind of their own. A gentle wind lifted their manes and made their ears twitch, and soon they were moving off the well-worn carriage path in the middle of Hyde Park and across the green into the shelter of nearby trees. He tugged at the ribbons to no avail.

"No need ta fight it," she said quietly. "I have their heads." She blew another breath, and his pair stopped. Before he could even tell what she was about, Miss Sinclair vaulted from the curricle and landed in a tangle of skirts on the ground beside it.

"Why do I suddenly feel as though I've been manhandled?" he asked. He wasn't at all accustomed to losing control of any situation, much less one with a lady.

"Perhaps it's because ye have," she chirped. Then she walked away.

Where the devil was she going?

"Miss Sinclair!" he called to her retreating backside as he climbed down and followed her. And what a lovely backside it was. He caught up with her in three long strides. She couldn't outrun him. If he truly wanted to catch her, he could, he told himself. Then he grimaced. He truly wanted to catch her. "May I ask where you're going?"

She turned quickly to face him and tugged her bonnet free, dropping it to the green grass at her feet. "Do ye want ta drink my blood, my lord?" she asked blandly. Then she tilted her pretty little head to the side. "If so, let's just get it over with so I can stop bein' afraid of ye." She made a come-hither motion with her hand and pointed to her neck. "How bad can it possibly be? I'm certain Blaire allowed Kettering ta do it. I heard whispers about it on the wind."

Blast his responsive body. His teeth ached at the very thought. He turned to stare off in the opposite direction. "You have no idea what you're asking for," he said slowly. What was bad was that he was starving. He hadn't dined at *Brysi* or anywhere else since the moment he'd met her. For some reason, he wasn't thinking about blood. He was thinking about *her* blood.

"I'm askin' for ye ta help me."

He couldn't help himself; he looked at her again.

"And I'm fully willin' ta repay ye in kind. Ye do want me, do ye no'?" She tilted her lovely head and appraised him, her lashes slowly brushing her cheeks with each blink of her fetching hazel eyes.

He couldn't. Could he? No. He most definitely could not. "I couldn't, Miss Sinclair," he began. He'd love to, but he'd be the worst sort of cad if he did so.

"I'm no' good enough for ye, either?" A gust of wind blew against him, hard enough to get his attention.

Matthew shoved his hands into his pockets. It was that or grab her with them. The little witch dared to use his powers against him. That made him smile. "You are too good for the likes of someone like me." Blast it, but he heard Alec MacQuarrie's voice in the back of his mind with that admission.

"Oh, do that again," she chirped as she walked closer to him.

"Do what?" Gads, this was painful.

"Smile." She waited patiently, staring at his mouth. Then she made a face at him, sticking out her pointy little tongue. She looked so blasted ridiculous that he couldn't keep from smiling. From laughing out loud.

"Oh, nice," she crooned. Then she reached one hand up to brush the corner of his mouth with her thumb. "Do they hurt?"

"They positively ache right now," he admitted.

"Why right now?" she asked, a most dumbfounded look on her face. Had she no idea? She'd offered herself up to him like a lamb on a sacrificial platter. Yet he couldn't have her. He could only want her with a single-minded purpose.

Her hand still hovered, cupping his cheek. He turned his face, unable to avoid nuzzling her gloved palm. At least there was fabric between the fragile pulse that beat at her wrist and his most hungry teeth. Not that it would stop him. He inhaled deeply at the base of her hand, taking in the gardenias and the scent that was hers alone. She made him want to peel back her glove and sink his teeth into the delicate skin of her wrist, but that would be highly improper.

"Ye dinna answer me," she reminded him, her voice soft. She giggled lightly as his lips walked down the fabric of her glove toward her elbow. She moved to pull back, but he trapped her arm within his grasp and refused to allow it. Her mouth dropped open as she watched the path his lips traveled.

"They ache, Miss Sinclair, because I want you more than I have ever wanted anything in my life." He took a step, which brought her breasts close to his chest. If he moved one more inch, he would feel her clothing against his. Her heat against his. Her heartbeat against his lack of one. He took a step back.

"I propose a trade, Blodswell," she said.

"You will not *trade* anything, young lady." He frowned at her. Really what could she be thinking?

"Oh, posh," she scoffed. "We could do wonderful things for one another."

He had no doubt of it. That was the problem.

"No one kens what ye are, correct? Ye're out in society and no one is the wiser?"

"Until you, yes," he admitted. Well, and Lady Eynsford, but that went without saying.

She giggled. "Doona I feel special?" Her laughter

was nearly contagious, and he found himself wanting to join her. She laid her hand flat on his chest and looked up into his eyes.

"You *are* special, dearest. Never think otherwise."

"I need ye," she breathed on a sigh. Naked, unadulterated, unfulfilled lust unlike any he'd ever known swamped him. He all but fell to his knees. God, this slip of a girl could undo him. "Ta be respectable."

He forced some of the lust from the forefront of his mind and leaned back to look at her more fully. "I am quite respectable, thank you very much." Or at least he had been until she'd slapped him the night before.

"No," she griped, swatting at him playfully. "I need ye ta make *me* respectable."

He wanted to do no such thing. He wanted to make her as unrespectable as possible. Matthew sighed. "You seem quite respectable already." Aside from the temper tantrums and the storm clouds that hung over her head like an omen at times.

"No' ta my aunt. She hates me. And she willna allow me ta even see my sister. Because of the *taint* I bring with me simply because of what I am."

He could see the sorrow that statement caused within her in the way she avoided his eyes and with her downturned lips. "Your aunt is bound for Bedlam, dearest. She must be the most idiotic woman who ever lived. And I have met some spectacularly foolish people in all my lifetimes."

"My aunt hates me," she asserted again. "And she hates Caitrin. So, I willna gain any favor with her by stayin' at Thorpe House, but I doona have anywhere else ta stay."

"Certainly, you don't think you can stay with me." Oh, how he wished she could. But she'd be ruined. Permanently and completely.

"Oh, no. Nothin' so drastic. I just want ta borrow some of yer respectability. Well, the respectability of the Blodswell *title*." She tugged at the lapels of his coat with her two fists. "I need ye."

"To do what?" God, if she didn't spit it out, he'd go mad with wanting to hear it.

"Ta court me. Ta pretend ye're interested in me."

"I wouldn't be pretending," he said quietly. Her hazel eyes sparkled with his admission. "But I can't." He set her away from him and took a few steps back. "I simply cannot."

She sighed deeply. "But I can pay ye."

"I've no need of money, dearest."

But then she shoved her dark hair back from her shoulder and exposed the graceful line of her neck to him. "No' with money, Blodswell."

Good God! Did she know what she was doing to him? The scent of her was already driving him mad. Now he could see that little pulse furiously pumping beneath the delicate skin at the base of her throat. The wind, her words, and the sounds of a lifetime were replaced with the cadence of her heart. Was she trying to get herself ravished? Matthew closed his eyes and counted to ten. Then he did it again. Slowly.

He must have made some painful sound because she stood up straight and frowned at him. Then she tugged the fall of her hair back over her shoulder. Thank God. "Oh, never mind. I thought ye would do quite nicely. That duchess seemed so taken with ye. And my aunt stopped frownin' when Her Grace mentioned the age and respectability of yer title. But I can just ask one of Eynsford's relations. Of the three of them, certainly *one* is respectable enough for me ta use him."

Matthew immediately saw red. Blinding, red rage. He grabbed her arms and pulled her to him, and then he snaked an arm around her waist to hold her there while he tipped her chin up to force her to look at him. "You will not ask one of those lecherous beasts to partner you. Not for a dance. Not for a feigned courtship. Not for a buggy ride. Over my dead body."

"That would be a bit difficult, seein' as how ye're immortal and all," she acquiesced. "Ta be over yer dead body, I mean. That's no' likely ta happen." She laughed lightly. She didn't even squirm against him. She just let him hold her, his legs tangled in her skirts. She fit against him nicely, like she was made to be there.

"Yet you have the power to fell me unlike any other," he said quietly.

"Say ye'll do it, then? Please tell me ye will." Her hazel eyes widened hopefully.

Matthew sighed. If he didn't do it, she'd ask that damned Radbourne or one of his brood. Then she'd end up wearing someone else's mark. He couldn't allow that. He nodded quickly before he thought the better of it. "Very well, I'll do it. I'll pretend to court you. To make your aunt happy. I'll do my best to charm her and appear respectable."

"And ye'll allow me ta pay ye?" She shivered in his grasp. Yet he immediately sensed it wasn't a response to fear. It was to very real feelings she had while being held within his arms.

"I'll think about it," he grunted. Blast and damn. He'd think about it. And think about it some more. And dream about it. And wish for it. And it would consume him. And he'd be stuck dining on animal's blood because no one else would ever do, not now that he'd smelled her. Not now that he held her close.

"Think about it," she giggled. "I'll make ye want me."

He took her by the hand and dragged her back toward his curricle, grumbling under his breath, "Of that, I have no doubt." Reaching his conveyance, Matthew picked her up and set her on the bench. "Miss Sinclair, I think you would be the death of me, if I wasn't already dead."

"Ye willna change yer mind, will ye?" She looked at once worried.

Matthew shook his head. "I gave you my word." Then he slid into the curricle beside her and said, "May I have their heads now?" He gestured to his grays, who still seemed entranced.

She blew in the horses' direction, and both sets of gray ears twitched. "They're all yers." She giggled.

He shook his head with wonder. He'd just made a fool's bargain. And he was the damn fool.

Eight

THIS TRULY WAS ONE OF THE BEST IDEAS RHIANNON had ever had. She couldn't have held back a smile if she wanted to. The Earl of Blodswell was the perfect candidate to gain her aunt's approval. He was titled, handsome, wealthy… and from one of the oldest and most respected families in England. Surely Aunt Greer couldn't find fault with him.

Well, there was that little problem of the slap Rhi had delivered to the vampyre in the Pickerings' ballroom, but the Duchess of Hythe seemed to have smoothed that over rather nicely. Since the duchess seemed enamored of Blodswell's title, or perhaps just his *grandfather*, Rhiannon couldn't see her aunt disapproving of the earl. On the contrary, when the duchess had mentioned Blodswell's ancient title, Aunt Greer had actually smiled. That was a rare occurrence, to be sure.

Thank heavens for the Duchess of Hythe. Rhi nearly giggled to herself. Eynsford would never believe the thought had even crossed Rhi's mind, not considering the look of horror that had crossed his face the night before when he spotted the woman. And yet it was true just the same. Without the duchess' favor...

Rhi frowned. What *was* her aunt doing in a barouche with the duchess? The absurdity of that situation hadn't even crossed Rhi's mind until this very moment. She'd been so elated to see Ginny and then terrified of the formidable duchess that Rhi hadn't considered what odd companions the three of them made.

Havers! Aunt Greer must be better connected than Rhi had originally assumed. Not that the thought should make her unhappy. Perhaps her aunt truly did have Ginny's best interests at heart and was using her well-placed connections to ensure Ginny's success on the marriage mart. And then again, perhaps flying dragons would deposit a family of trolls at Carlton House where they would be invited in for tea with the Regent.

Actually, there was more likelihood of the latter happening than the former. Aunt Greer only ever had her own best interests at heart. If only Rhi could figure out how her sister played into their aunt's plans. And did the duchess have anything to do with the situation?

She glanced up at the vampyre beside her. Blodswell was glowering at no one in particular. What was that about? "Are ye all right, my lord?"

"Perfectly," he replied, keeping his eyes focused on the street before them.

But he didn't look perfectly fine. He didn't sound it either. He said he wouldn't change his mind, that he'd given his word; and Rhi had offered to pay him. Perhaps vampyres were simply moody creatures. That was certainly the case with the Lycans she knew. Rhiannon decided not to press the earl and instead watched the homes of Mayfair pass by as Blodswell directed his grays back to Thorpe House.

Before she knew it, the curricle had come to a stop in front of Caitrin's home. Blodswell quickly alighted from his spot, strode behind his conveyance and offered his hand to help her down. Once on firm ground, Rhi stared up into the earl's midnight eyes, something she would have never considered doing a mere two hours earlier. But he'd promised not to enchant her, and she believed him.

He seemed a very steady soul, different in almost every way from the tormented vampyre who'd taken control of her in Edinburgh. At once she felt a little embarrassed to have let those old fears color the way she saw Blodswell. The only thing they shared, it seemed, was the blackness of their eyes.

"Thank you, Miss Sinclair, for joining me today." The earl pressed a kiss to her gloved hand.

Shivers raced down her spine and settled in her toes. "Thank ye, my lord, for everythin'."

Something she didn't quite understand lingered in his gaze. "I find myself unwilling to relinquish you, dearest," he said. He looked most sincere as he said it, and almost pained by it.

Blodswell reached into his pocket, retrieved a folded note, and held it out to her. "Alec asked me to give this to you. He said you'd wanted to meet today," he glanced up at Thorpe House behind her, "but under the circumstances, it's better he not call on you here. I'm sure you understand."

Of course. What had she been thinking to even suggest such a thing to Alec? Rhiannon closed her hand around the note and nodded. "Is he all right, sir? I mean truly all right?"

"Your devotion to him speaks wonders for his character." He tipped his head in a slight bow. "I shall call on you tomorrow."

Then he launched himself back into his curricle and headed off before Rhiannon realized he hadn't really answered her question. She glanced at the folded note in her hand and then dashed up the steps of Thorpe House.

The kindly butler opened the door before she had even reached it and smiled warmly. "Welcome back, Miss Sinclair. Lady Eynsford is holding court in the green parlor."

Which meant Rhi would avoid the green parlor at all costs until she had read Alec's note. It practically burned a hole through Rhiannon's gloved hand, and she knew in her heart that the contents were not something she should share with Caitrin. She smiled at the aged butler. "Thank ye, Price. After I freshen up a bit, I'll join her ladyship."

Then she bounded up the steps before Cait could leave the parlor to intercept her as she had done with Blodswell that afternoon. Rhi rushed down the corridor toward her chambers and stopped in her tracks when she saw a very large, very male figure leaning against the doorjamb of her room.

Lord Radbourne pushed himself away from the wall and offered a slight bow. "I am glad to see you've returned in one piece, sweetheart."

Havers! The air rushed from Rhiannon's lungs. Was he lying in wait for her? And why? "My lord?" She took a hesitant step forward. "I thought ye were with Cait." What a stupid thing to say.

Radbourne's warm amber eyes drifted over her appreciatively. "I hope that doesn't mean you're avoiding me."

Rhiannon shook her head. "No, I just wanted ta freshen up a bit after the ride."

The viscount made a sweeping motion with his hand as though inviting her into her own bedchamber. "Please do wash the scoundrel's scent away."

Rhi gaped at the man. "I beg yer pardon?"

One of Radbourne's dark brows rose in mild amusement and he touched his nose. "Excellent senses, you know."

She did know, having spent a little time with Lord Eynsford and a whole lot of time with Lord Benjamin Westfield. A Lycan's sense of smell was unparalleled. Still, she hadn't found anything unpleasing in Blodswell's scent. "He's no' a scoundrel," she defended for no apparent reason. Where had that come from?

"No, he's worse than that." Radbourne stepped toward her, taking up most of the space in the corridor. "He's a creature who preys on the living."

Rhiannon sucked in a surprised breath. "Ye ken what he is?"

The viscount tucked a stray curl behind her ear. "I know a great many things, sweetheart. Until recently, I've not been acquainted with Blodswell, but I've known others of his kind. They're a dangerous breed."

"The same could be said of Lycans." Rhiannon found herself defending Blodswell once again.

"Touché." Radbourne chuckled lightly. "Yet Lycans enjoy the company of ladies for pleasure, not as a food source."

Rhiannon gulped. She couldn't exactly counter that point. Still, she had offered Blodswell a payment for his aid, and though he had said he wanted to take from her, he'd kept himself from doing so. That had to mean something, didn't it? That she meant more than his next snack, perhaps? Though part of her didn't think she'd mind so much being tasted by the earl. That thought should have scared the life out of her, but it didn't. How strange this day was turning out to be. "Well, his lordship behaved quite gentlemanly. Would ye like ta search for bite marks?"

Radbourne's golden eyes darkened, and a wolfish grin lit his face. "I'd like nothing better, sweetheart. Where shall I begin?"

Warmth engulfed Rhiannon. *Havers!* What a foolish thing to have suggested to the man. "I–I dinna—"

"Archer!" Cait called from the top of the staircase. "I wondered where ye had gotten off ta. Dash has been lookin' for ye."

"Has he indeed?" Radbourne smothered a smile. "In the same fashion he was looking for Gray earlier this afternoon?"

"Exactly," Cait replied haughtily. "And what are ye doin' blockin' Rhiannon from her room? I canna imagine yer mother raised ye ta accost young ladies outside their bedchambers."

The viscount laughed as he sidled past Rhiannon to face his sister-in-law. "There are a great many things my mother did not raise me to do."

Cait sighed. "As I am very aware. Now, off ta Dash's study with ye."

"As you wish, my lady." He dropped a kiss on Cait's brow. "A more lovely termagant, I've never met."

Cait batted him away. "Be off before I have Dash put you out with the hounds." As soon as they were alone in the corridor, Cait stepped closer to Rhiannon and grinned. "Tell me all about it."

Rhi closed her hand tighter around Alec's letter and shook her head. "All about what?"

"The ride, ye ninny, and doona leave out any details."

Oh, there were a great many details Rhi would leave out. "We saw Ginny, and Aunt Greer seemed impressed with Blodswell's title."

"As well she should be."

Rhi folded her arms across her chest. She wasn't certain she appreciated Cait's gaiety in regard to the earl. Though Rhiannon had decided she liked Blodswell much more than she had initially thought, Cait's wide-eyed interest in the situation made her a little uncomfortable. Hopefully, Cait would never learn of Rhi's deal with the vampyre. "Ye havena been peekin' inta my future again, have ye?"

Looking as though she was the epitome of innocence, Cait shook her head. "I said I would no'. But if ye doona want me ta peek, ye should tell me everythin' that happened. Otherwise, I could get so curious I might no' be able ta stop myself."

Rhi resisted the urge to roll her eyes. Cait would

get the same version she planned to bandy about Town and nothing more. "Well, it appears as though his lordship plans ta court me."

Cait's pretty blue eyes twinkled. "Well, of course he plans ta court ye. Blodswell is as smart as he is old. But do ye like him, Rhi? Tell me ye do."

In that Rhi didn't have to fabricate her answer. She nodded. "I do like him, Cait, and ye doona ken how surprised I am by that."

Cait threw her arms around Rhiannon's neck. "This is so wonderful."

Rhi pulled herself from her friend's embrace. "I fear I smell a bit like Blodswell's grays. Do ye mind if I change my dress and then meet ye in the parlor?"

Cait grinned as widely as Rhi had ever seen. "Of course, take yer time, and then ye'll tell me all about yer ride?"

Rhi stepped toward her chamber. "Aye, I'll tell ye all about the Duchess of Hythe who has requested our attendance at her soiree sometime at the end of this week. And she said ta bring ye and Eynsford."

Cait giggled. "Oh, I canna wait ta tell Dash!" Then she started back toward the staircase.

Rhiannon escaped into her chamber and tugged on the bellpull for her maid. Then she sank onto her bed and unfolded the letter she'd been hiding from her friend.

My dearest Rhiannon,

I am so glad to see you well. You are a welcome taste of the home I thought I might never see again. I would like to discuss some things with you, and

I am certain you have questions for me as well. If you can indulge me, I will send a carriage to pick you up this evening. Just sent a note to my rooms in Piccadilly, and I will make the arrangements posthaste. I look forward to seeing you again.

Eternally Yours,
Alec

Eternally yours? His eternity was certainly not in question. But the rest of his existence was. Rhi wanted desperately to talk with him. But, of course, he couldn't present himself at Thorpe House, not with Caitrin there. Or Eynsford, but that was another matter all together. Alec's plan did seem the best.

She bolted from her bed to the small writing desk in the corner of the room to jot off a quick response to her old friend. Hopefully, Cait would honor her word and keep from poking her meddling nose into Rhi's future.

Nine

DEAR GOD, WHAT A DAY! IF RHIANNON SINCLAIR wasn't occupying his mind, then trying to locate his errant charge was. MacQuarrie moved faster than Matthew could even track him. He'd started at *Brysi*, only to learn that Alec had recently left for parts unknown. Getting a sense of the Scot's location, Matthew arrived at Tattersall's, only to find the Scot has just departed.

He'd then made his way to Gentleman Jackson's, only to discover that MacQuarrie had vanished once again. He even spent a good part of his day waiting at Alec's bachelor lodgings, thinking the man would have to show his face at some point, but to no avail.

Back at *Brysi*, Matthew had finally dropped into an overstuffed leather chair and sighed heavily. Of course, he didn't need the deep breath, since his heart didn't beat, but those very human actions made him feel normal, more like a man and less like a creature of the night.

With that as a goal, he *should* have gone to White's instead of the vampyre haven, but some habits were

hard to break. He could have at least pretended to
nurse a whiskey over on St. James, played cards with
gentlemen, debated whether or not Lord Elgin was
a vandal or a hero, and appeared to the world as the
respectable Earl of Blodswell. Instead, he'd hied off to
his usual destination and found himself subjected to
dozens of brazen women, in various stages of dress,
who wanted nothing more than to share their bodies
with him.

A lovely young Cyprian touched his shoulder. He
looked up into the brightest blue eyes he'd ever seen.
"May I make myself available to you, my lord?" she
asked quietly. Her hand shook slightly on his shoulder.
She was obviously new to the club, as he'd never seen
her before.

A few days ago, there would have been no question to his answer. He could make her entry into the
world of pleasure better than she'd ever dreamed.
Yet when he looked at her now, he felt... nothing.
Well, he felt something. He felt sadness at the way
she was offering herself up to him as a way to survive
when she was obviously worth more than a tup and
a drink.

He took her hand in his and tugged gently, bringing
her around the chair and into his lap. She may as well
have been his younger sister, considering the lack of
lust he felt for her. "May we talk?" he asked quietly.
She shivered in his lap, so he gave her hand a brief
squeeze. She nodded. "Why don't you start by telling
me your name?"

"T-tillie," she stuttered and avoided his gaze entirely.

"Are you afraid of me, Tillie?" He wasn't that

terrifying, was he? She did approach him, after all. And she was in *Brysi* of her own free will. At least he thought she was.

"N-not really afraid, sir." She squirmed in his lap. But that had no effect on him at all. He felt nothing at having the chit in such close proximity to his nether regions, aside from annoyance at her twittering.

"Why are you here?" He crossed his arms over his chest, leaned back, and then looked down his nose at her. She carried the scent of the sea with her. Perhaps she was from the docks.

"Because you pulled me into your lap," she said quickly as she made a move to get up.

He stalled her movements with a harsh glance. "I don't mean *here*. I mean at *Brysi*. How did you come to be at *Brysi*, dear?"

"Oh, I walked." She pulled her dress to the side to show him her well-worn shoes.

"From…" he prompted.

"From…?" Her eyebrows rose as though she waited for him to finish the sentence.

Matthew heaved a sigh. Her mind was as vacant as an empty cupboard. He'd been afraid of that.

Tillie continued, "I have a cousin who lives here. And she sent word that there might be work for me." She smiled softly.

"And had you an idea before you arrived of the sort of *work* you'd be doing?"

She whispered her next comment, "My cousin says it's not really work. That it's much easier than the work I was doing at Madame Lefèvre's."

So she wasn't an innocent, no matter that she

looked like one or shuddered like a frightened waif. "Your goal was to move up in the world, then?" Talking to the girl was like speaking into a cave and then waiting for the sound to echo back.

"Actually," she began as she blushed furiously, "I'd hoped to get a bit of pleasure out of it."

Matthew's mouth fell open. He probably looked like an idiot at her confession. He'd not doubt it at all.

"I never enjoyed it before. You know… *it*?" She waited for him to acknowledge his understanding with a nod. "But my cousin, she said there's a great deal of pleasure with your kind. And I'd like to experience it." She began to swing her legs like a child on a park bench.

He pressed on her skirts to keep her legs in place. "Don't do that," he grunted. If it was pleasure the chit wanted, he'd give her pleasure.

Matthew bent to sniff the side of her neck. And that scent of the sea wafted up to meet his nose again. She didn't smell like gardenias. She didn't smell like a storm-laden night. She didn't have hazel eyes that sparkled at him. She wasn't Rhiannon Sinclair. She wouldn't do at all.

"They said to ask you to take me first. Because you're the best," she breathed quietly as she ran one practiced finger down the side of his jaw. He wanted to bat her away like a fly, but he just gritted his teeth instead.

"They?" Who the devil were *they*?

"The other girls," she explained. "They say you're better than the rest. They said sessions with you are remarkable and unforgettable."

He'd had no idea *they* felt that way. "Would you

care to elaborate?" To him, their encounters simply provided him with a meal and a warm body. And not always in that order. Of course, he took great care with them. Perhaps that made the difference?

"They say the pleasure is the greatest with you. That you care if the woman you're with is happy. That you are powerful and consuming." She crossed her dainty little hands in her lap. "And I want to be consumed." Then she giggled like a schoolgirl.

"Be careful who you say that to," he grunted, displeased with the gruffness he heard in his own voice.

"I've only said it to you." She pouted. "You do want me, don't you?"

Bloody hell! That was the second time he'd been asked that today. Matthew was absolutely starving. He could feel the need throughout his body. His teeth ached with the very thought of sinking them into a warm and willing body. Yet his incisors hadn't even descended when the chit sat down in his lap. He could typically make them come and go at will, unless he was overly aroused, as he'd been with Miss Sinclair. However, in *that* situation, he hadn't been able to make them recede. Neither his teeth nor his erection. Yet he couldn't even make them descend for this girl.

He nodded quickly. He should want her. He did want her. Or at least he wanted to want her.

She brushed her hair off her neck and leaned to the side. "You can have me," she said.

The image called to mind another girl in the park with the same offer. Matthew heaved another sigh. He couldn't take from Tillie. He couldn't have her at all. And not because of some gentlemanly honor, but because his blasted teeth wouldn't work.

She began to work at the buttons at the front of her gown. He grabbed her hands to stop her. "What are you doing?"

"Disrobing, my lord. You said you wanted me."

But, regrettably, he didn't want her at all.

"You may keep your clothes on, Tillie," he instructed. She moved to lift her skirts and straddle him instead. Matthew picked her up and set her on her feet. "No," he said, plainly and simply.

She tilted her head to the side and regarded him with vacant confusion. "Why not?"

Why not, indeed. Because at the forefront of his mind was a lightning-throwing, storm-cloud-bearing, hazel-eyed witch. And until he had her, no one else would do. He might even have to take her up on her offer of payment.

Damn it to hell, he'd be the worst sort of cad if he did. But what choice did he have? He'd die of starvation if he didn't take from her. He could take her blood without taking her innocence. But doing so would mark her forever. That thought made his hand tremble when he reached out to press a coin into Tillie's hand. "Some other time."

She harrumphed and thrust out her lower lip.

A tumbler made a clunking sound as it hit the side table next to him. "You're looking a bit pale, Matthew," Alec MacQuarrie said. He motioned toward the glass, which was full of dark red blood. "Drink up, my friend."

"Where the devil have you been?" Matthew demanded.

But his charge ignored him completely as Tillie batted her pretty blue eyes at Alec. "He didn't want me."

Good Lord, he'd never hear the end of it from the Scot.

"Then he's the worst sort of fool, miss." MacQuarrie soothed her as he dropped an arm over her shoulders and whispered something in her ear that made her blush furiously.

Matthew reached over and picked up the tumbler, raising it to his nose. He took a whiff. *Sheep's blood.* It wasn't his favorite fare, not by a long shot. One didn't drink sheep's blood if one could help it. But as his incisors refused to descend, he'd have to make do. He was feeling quite weak and tired. And a bit dazed. In all his 650 years, he'd never been unable to feed. Or perform, as the case may be. Yet, all of a sudden, drinking the blood of some chit he didn't even know made him feel a bit ill.

He downed the contents of the glass and motioned to a nearby footman for another. He couldn't starve. But he couldn't face the moral dilemma of taking from the innocent Miss Sinclair, either. He was damned if he did, and damned if he didn't.

"Why don't you take Tillie here abovestairs, Alec?" Matthew asked. Perhaps the younger man could perform. Matthew certainly couldn't. He harrumphed to himself. Bloody hell, when had he gotten old? "Take care to see that she enjoys herself, will you?"

"I'd like nothing more, but I have an appointment with a lovely lass myself," Alec chimed, much too jovially.

"I don't mind sharing," Tillie threw in for good measure, as she chewed on a fingernail.

"Ah, something to keep in mind for the future."

MacQuarrie chuckled. "But I'm afraid Miss Sinclair isn't that sort of lass."

"Miss Sinclair?" Matthew rose from his seat and glowered at the Scot. "*Why* are you seeing Miss Sinclair?" That damned note! Why the devil had he delivered Alec's letter without scanning the contents himself? Foolish honorable tendencies.

"That would be my business, Matthew." Alec MacQuarrie glowered back, his brows pushing together in annoyance.

How dare the damned Scot assume that posture with his elder? With his maker, for God's sake? And what if Rhiannon offered her neck to Alec the same way she had to Matthew in the park?

Within seconds, Matthew had MacQuarrie pushed up against the wall, his arm thrust under the Scot's neck. Alec's boots dangled off the floor. "If you touch her…" Matthew snarled.

Of course, the manly posturing was for show, since MacQuarrie didn't need to breathe air any more than he did. "Put me down, Blodswell," MacQuarrie grunted. "Please, oh, please, mighty master, benevolent knight errant," he added sarcastically.

Against his better judgment, Matthew released his hold on the infernal Scot.

Alec slid to the floor where he landed on his feet. "For the love of God. Rhi is an old friend." He adjusted his clothing. "I had no idea you had developed such strong feelings for the good witch in so short a time," Alec said low enough so only the two of them could hear.

"I don't have *feelings*," Matthew protested.

The Scot scoffed. "If those aren't feelings hanging all over your sleeve like badges, then I don't know what they are, Matt," Alec grumbled. "Just keep in mind that Rhiannon Sinclair is one lass you can never, ever have." Then Alec turned his back on Matthew, crossed back over to Tillie, tipped her chin up, and kissed her pouty pink lips quickly. "I'll return soon. Save yourself for me?"

The little Cyprian nodded, dancing on her toes in anticipation.

"Behave yourself with Miss Sinclair," Matthew warned to Alec's retreating backside. The blasted Scot just lifted his hand and waved Matthew off.

"If you want me, I'm certain he wouldn't mind," Tillie said quietly.

No, Alec probably wouldn't mind, not that it would matter. There was only one woman Matthew wanted. And wanted with a fury that was unparalleled. By God, if he ever had her, lightning wouldn't be the only product of their union. It would be fierce and furious and… delightful. But Alec was right. Matthew couldn't have her. He couldn't have her at all.

His gaze swept across the chit offering herself to him, and Matthew shook his head. "Another time, perhaps."

∼ॐ∼

Rhiannon could see very little out the windows of Alec's carriage. Occasionally the warm glow of a lamp from inside a stately home caught her attention, but she had no idea where she was headed. She supposed this was what happened when one agreed to meet a vampyre in the dead of night without asking for details, even if that vampyre was an old friend. She had no doubts about Alec's intentions, however. None whatsoever.

The coach slowed to a stop. A moment later, the door opened and Rhi found herself looking at Alec MacQuarrie's smiling face. "Welcome to the British Museum, Rhiannon."

The British Museum? Why in the world would he bring her here? Rhi looked up past Alec at the beautiful mansion behind him. "It canna possibly be open at this hour," she muttered as he helped her alight from the carriage.

Alec's black eyes twinkled. "If you know the right people, anything is possible." He led her to the grand front door and pushed it open as though he owned the place.

The inside was just as dark as the night sky, but that didn't seem to deter Alec in the least as he guided her down one corridor. "Would you like to see the marbles that have all of London in an uproar?"

Rhiannon stumbled a bit on her hem. "The Elgin marbles?" Even in Edinburgh there was some outcry over the ancient Greek sculptures.

"The very ones." Alec towed her a bit closer to him. "I was fortunate a few years back to see a private showing of the collection before it was acquired by Parliament. Anyone can see them these days, which I suppose is for the best; but the sheer number of visitors makes them difficult to enjoy at one's leisure."

Up ahead, the golden flickering of candlelight called to Rhiannon like a beacon. As they reached the threshold, Rhi had to catch her breath. The warm glow danced off the marble statues lining the walls, and it seemed as though she had been transported to another time and place. "They're from the Parthenon?"

"Most of them," Alec replied as they stepped farther into the large room. "Though some are from Propylaea and Erechtheum. Take a look around."

There was nothing else she could do. It was the most amazing display she had ever seen. A panel depicting an ancient battle scene caught her attention. "Is it foolish ta say I feel like I'm in Athens?"

"Not foolish at all," Alec assured her.

She turned her attention to look up at him. "Are ye sure it's all right we're here?"

Alec winked at her. "I've known the curator for years, and I can be very persuasive."

As soon as he uttered those words, Rhiannon felt as though marble suddenly weighted her to the floor. She swallowed slowly. "Ye dinna enchant him, did ye?"

Something dangerous flashed in Alec's eyes. "What do you know of that?" he demanded. "Blodswell didn't… did he?"

"No." Rhiannon shook her head. "And he promised he wouldna do so." Alec's features softened only marginally, so she laid a hand on his arm. "But I encountered a vampyre in Edinburgh who was no' so accommodatin'. I would no' wish the feelin' on anyone."

"When was this?"

"A few months ago. When Blaire and Lord Kettering returned from the Highlands."

A hard look settled on Alec's face, almost making him appear as though he were made of stone. "Damn it! Did he hurt you? Are the others all right?"

Realization hit Rhiannon, and she felt like the biggest fool. "He was the one who attacked ye at Briarcraig."

Alec nodded. "There were two of them. A man and a woman. She is responsible for what I am now. Honestly, Rhi, I don't remember it clearly. One moment we were looking at stars, and the next I was lying on the cold ground, barely able to nod as Blodswell stood over me. I literally felt the life drain from my soul." He looked a million miles away, his eyes focused on images Rhiannon couldn't see.

She touched a golden button on his waistcoat. "I am so sorry, Alec."

He shook his head, and a roguish smile settled on his lips. "Come now. I've always been a student of history. Think of how much of it I'll get to see now."

Rhi stared up at him. "Doona try ta downplay yer situation, Alec. I ken this change has ta be difficult for ye."

"Allow me to find a bright side to it all, would you?" He grinned at her.

"Fair enough," she replied, and attempted a smile.

"Blodswell has lived through so much. I can only wonder at what I'll see in my lifetime. Do you suppose future generations will look back on us now and think us quaint and wholly uneducated?"

Rhi shook her head. He was smiling in wonder, but there was an emptiness to his voice. If she didn't know him, she would have never realized he was lying though his fangs. "Doona pretend for my sake, Alec."

His smile faltered for just a moment.

"I am worried about ye."

He frowned, and a deep crease furrowed his brow. "I'm more worried about you. Rhi, how can you and…" He looked over her shoulder to avoid eye contact. "How can you and Caitrin stay in that house with those beasts?"

So he knew about Lycans now. Rhi sighed. "They're no' all that bad. No' really."

Alec's dark gaze leveled on her. "I don't know how you can even say that. They transform into vicious, drooling oversized wolves, and they've been known to hurt women and blame it on the power of the moon."

Not any women Rhiannon knew of, but she chose not to voice the dissenting opinion. In fact, Elspeth was delighted with her beast, who just happened to be Alec's best friend, even though he had no idea about his friend's monthly change under the light of the moon. Besides, he wasn't concerned about other women. He was concerned about Cait.

"She *is* fine. And she has seen that side of him. He doesna harm her. In fact, he would protect her with his life. I've no doubt about it."

"Blodswell promised me she was safe."

"She is. They're all like trained lapdogs around her." Rhiannon smiled, hoping he would do so as well. "Ye ken how she is. All of Thorpe House is at her beck and call. If she tells them to sit, speak, or roll over, they all do as she commands."

He didn't smile. "Be careful, Rhi. I don't want her fate for you or for Sorcha."

Sorcha, her youngest coven sister, was a bit obsessed with possessing a Lycan for her very own, but Alec didn't need to know about any of that. A gentle wind swept through the museum, making the candlelight flicker wildly, and smoothed Alec's dark hair from his brow. He smiled softly at the gesture and shook his head. "You've done that my whole life. I just never knew it was you."

"Done what?" she asked, pretending to be completely innocent of the use of her magic.

"I still worry for you, Rhiannon."

"Ye doona need ta worry about me. I've been takin' care of myself for as long as I can remember."

"Because Dougal Sinclair keeps his head buried in books instead of focused on his daughters."

Rhi bristled at the slight directed toward her father, no matter how many times she'd thought something similar. "He's researchin', Alec."

"He's been letting life pass him by since your mother died, and in the process he's left you to fend for yourself and for Ginny. You've taken care of everyone else for so long and done it so well that you now have a false sense of security. You think you can keep yourself safe from all the dark creatures who stalk the night."

All of this over Lycans? She had half a mind to tell him his best friend was just such a creature, but she held her tongue. There was no point in upsetting him more than he already was. "I think my lightnin' can deter just about anyone."

"How did your lightning work against that vampyre in Edinburgh?" he asked, his tone condescending as he crossed his arms over his chest and glared at her.

If he didn't watch his tone, she'd feel inclined to see how lightning worked on a vampyre in the middle of the British Museum. She sniffed and raised her nose a bit instead of answering.

"You can't protect yourself against something superhuman. Not something determined to have you." Alec frowned again. He was doing that quite a bit lately. "You should keep your distance from Blodswell, too."

Blodswell? Where had that come from? Rhiannon's heart clenched in her chest. Hadn't Alec defended the earl the previous evening? "Ye said he saved ye."

"He did save me." Alec took her shoulders in his hands and stared into her eyes. "But I don't want him to have the need to save you in the same fashion, Rhi. Go home. Go back to Edinburgh where I know you're safe. Keep an eye on Sorcha."

Rhiannon shook her head. "I'm here for the season, Alec. Ginny's here. I willna go home without her."

He winced a bit. "Then promise me you'll stay away from Blodswell."

But she couldn't do that, either. She'd made an agreement with the earl that very afternoon. "I'm no' afraid of him."

Alec grumbled something under his breath that sounded a lot like "stubborn witch," but she couldn't be sure. "He's honorable, Rhi. Legendary. Can you believe I actually studied the man's heroics in Harrow?"

She'd had no idea. Rhiannon shook her head.

"Richard the Lionheart bestowed the earldom on Sir Matthew Halkett. He was given the title Blodswell because blood gushed from his sword whenever he took it up. He was quite revered in his day. And I've gotten to know the man fairly well over the past few months. He is a knight in shining armor in every way. He's just the sort who could capture your heart and never give it back. I don't want that for you. You deserve better than a creature like him or me. You deserve a man of flesh and his own blood."

Rhi's mouth fell open. After that little monologue, she most definitely shouldn't mention her deal with Blodswell. Who knew how Alec would respond to that. "I promise ta be careful, Alec. That's the best I can do." Because vampyre or no vampyre, Lord Blodswell was who she needed. Rhi wanted to stay close to Ginny, and having Lord Blodswell at her side was the best way of ensuring that goal.

"Very well." Alec nodded. "But I'll hold you to that."

She smiled at her old friend. "I'd expect nothin' less."

He held his arm out to her. "Let's take a look at some statues, shall we?"

She slid her hand into the crook of his arm and smiled up at him. He hadn't changed. Not where it mattered. Thank heavens.

Ten

MATTHEW FELT LIKE THE WORST SORT OF FOOL FOR hiding in the foliage outside Thorpe House. But he had to see if Alec had brought Miss Sinclair home. He had no idea where they'd gone. But if they weren't back soon, he'd probably lose what was left of his mind. He paced back and forth from one end of the street to the other, his hands deep in his pockets one minute and running through his hair in frustration the next.

The loud sound of masculine laughter reached his ears from inside Eynsford's house. The wolves. All four of them must be inside. But then the door opened, and three of them came quickly tumbling out. One of the twins, Matthew wasn't certain which one, fell onto his backside in the walkway. Matthew stepped farther into the shadows as the pup got up, dusted himself off, and growled loudly. "That was completely unnecessary," he grunted.

The one who looked just like him laughed loudly. "It was worth being thrown out just to see you land on your arse on the ground," he hooted.

Eynsford stood in the doorway, glowering at the

three of them with unbridled hostility. "The next time I tell you to behave yourselves, you should do so immediately. Or it won't be just Gray's arse that's aching."

"But, Dash—" Radbourne began.

"*But Dash*," Eynsford mocked with a feminine tone to his voice. "Don't 'but Dash' me, Archer. You're just as bad as the other two. Now, go home, the lot of you."

"Can we come back tomorrow?" the twin who hadn't landed on his backside asked with a cheeky grin. "Or are we banished for a week like the last time Archer worried the devil out of you?"

"You may *attempt* to return tomorrow." Eynsford hid a grin behind that huge frown, Matthew could tell. He'd used that move himself a time or two. The marquess obviously had great affection for the younger men, even if he didn't want them to know it at the moment.

Matthew held still, hidden by the darkest of shadows as the Lycan trio walked past. But then Lord Radbourne stopped and said to his brothers, "Do you smell that?"

Blast and damn! Of course they smelled him. They had unparalleled senses.

The twins chuckled.

"Dash!" the viscount called just as the door was about to close.

Eynsford sighed loudly and replied, "What *is* it, Archer?"

"I thought you might want to know there's a blood-sucker in your bushes. Do have a good evening." Then he caught Matthew's eye and smirked before heading down the street with his look-a-like brothers.

"For the love of God." Eynsford groused. He descended his stone steps after the trio, but they were gone. "What about a blood-sucker?" the marquess muttered to himself, staring in the direction the other Lycans had departed.

Matthew figured he might as well make himself known. Eynsford would catch his scent in a moment anyway. "I believe he said, 'There's a blood-sucker in your bushes.'" Matthew stepped from the aforementioned foliage.

The Lycan stopped and tilted his head at Matthew. "And just *why* are you in my bushes?"

Lie? Or tell the truth? Eynsford could probably read Matthew as well as a copy of *The Times*, and if he couldn't, his wife could.

"Hiding, actually," Matthew confessed.

"Well, I had a feeling you weren't playing hide-the-slipper. But the question was—and still is—*why* are you hiding in my bushes?" Eynsford folded his arms across his chest, and a suspicious glint flashed in his amber eyes.

It was a bit embarrassing. Still, this was what happened when one hid in the bushes at a Lycan's home. It was a wonder he wasn't found out before now. "Waiting for Miss Sinclair," Matthew grumbled under his breath, knowing full well Eynsford would hear him anyway.

"Indeed?" the marquess narrowed his eyes on Matthew. "And there was a reason you couldn't present yourself at the door like a normal human being to call on the lady? Aside from the fact that you're not a normal human being at all, of course." He shook his head as though he could shake the absurdity out of it like a dog shakes water from its coat.

"I didn't want to pay a social call, actually," Matthew confessed. "I just wanted to be certain Miss Sinclair was all right. She went out to meet MacQuarrie." He shrugged.

"She did *what*?" The Lycan growled loudly and started back for his door. He glanced over his shoulder at Matthew. "Well, what are you waiting for? Don't just stand there. Follow, man, follow."

Matthew had been alive for more than six centuries and had never had anyone suggest he *follow*. But he fell in line behind the Lycan, regardless. The ancient butler took Matthew's greatcoat as Eynsford bellowed for his wife.

"Caitrin!" he called so loudly that the home nearly shook on its foundation.

She appeared from around the corner, a slight scowl on her beautiful face. "Why are ye bellowin' at me?" she asked, her dainty little hands on her hips as she glared at her husband. MacQuarrie would be relieved to see that she stood up to the overgrown wolf.

Eynsford was undeterred by her scathing look. "Blodswell just informed me that Miss Sinclair is out with *Alec MacQuarrie*." He grumbled the name as though it were a curse. "Were you aware of this?"

"Perhaps," she admitted sheepishly, her pert little nose rising as she scrunched up her face and folded her arms across her chest.

"*Perhaps*, Caitie?" Eynsford pressed.

"Well, Rhiannon dinna tell me, if that's what ye're askin'. And she's asked that I no' peek inta her future." Her shoulders lifted in a small shrug.

"However?" her husband prompted.

"I did anyway." That was all she said.

"You peeked into her future?" Matthew couldn't stay silent any longer. "Is she all right?"

The blond witch waved him off as though he were a pesky fly. "Of course, she's fine. She's with Alec, after all. He'd never harm her." She snorted the last, which earned an even louder snort from her husband.

"When will she be home?" Matthew asked.

The witch's eyes took on a vacant look, as though she saw pictures no one else did. "About twenty minutes, I'd wager." She looked within her own mind again. "And she'll be none too happy if she realizes the two of ye were frettin' over her outin'." She shot Eynsford a quelling look. "Ye ken what happens when she's no' happy."

The Lycan shivered lightly, which would have been an amusing sight if Matthew wasn't so concerned.

"What happens when she's not happy?" Matthew had to know.

"Her emotions go off like mad when she's nervous or upset. But she also has great control that no one is aware of." Lady Eynsford lowered her voice to a dramatic whisper, "She once zapped Dash with a bolt of lightnin' for gettin' too amorous with me."

He could just see Rhiannon doing something like that with her temper. A grin tugged at the corners of Matthew's lips. "What was that like?" he asked the Lycan.

"Jolting, to say the least," Eynsford admitted. He took a step toward Matthew. "Since Miss Sinclair is not yet home, I'd like to have a word with you."

"A word?"

"In my study," the Lycan barked. Then he led the way down the corridor to his private domain and motioned for Matthew to take a seat.

Matthew did so regretfully. He'd rather be in the bushes than inside the study with Eynsford. What the devil did the Lycan want with him?

The marquess gestured to a decanter of claret on his desk as he dropped into his large chair. "I'd offer you a taste, but I don't believe this is your vintage."

Matthew said nothing but regarded the wolf in gentleman's clothes with disdain. He'd never cared for Lycans as a breed. They tended to be loud, uncultured brutes for the most part. Still, Caitrin Eynsford seemed happy with hers. This one, to be precise. There was no accounting for taste.

The marquess frowned when his goading caused no outward reaction. "I thought you would present yourself this morning so we could talk," Eynsford said smoothly as he poured himself a tumbler of the dark red wine.

"About?" Matthew asked, his patience growing thin. He had nothing to say to Eynsford. He didn't owe the man a blasted thing.

"At the Pickerings', you nearly ruined Miss Sinclair."

"Ruination is a strong word. I surprised her, and she reacted. Nothing more."

Eynsford narrowed his amber eyes. "It can take less than that to ruin a lady's good name."

"Firsthand experience?" Matthew couldn't help himself from muttering.

The Lycan snorted as he leaned back in his chair. I asked that you present yourself at Thorpe House this morning so we could come to an understanding. I was far from pleased when you did not arrive."

Heaven forbid the beast be unpleased. Matthew leaned back in his own seat, mirroring Eynsford. "I arrived as requested."

"Only to present yourself to the lovely lady instead of me."

"Why on earth would I present myself to you?" The confounded Lycan was barking up the wrong tree.

"Since Miss Sinclair's father is not present, and wouldn't be present even if he was here in London, I'm standing in for him."

The idea was ludicrous that anyone of sound mind would ask the Marquess of Eynsford to stand in for him. "And he asked you to do such a thing, I assume?" Highly unlikely.

Eynsford's brows pushed together in annoyance. "He needn't ask me. I take it as my duty. Miss Sinclair is a guest in my home. My wife loves the lass like a sister. It's my honor to protect her."

"From fortune hunters or just vampyres?"

"From whomever I deem a threat." The Lycan growled low in his throat.

"Meaning me."

"Meaning you," Eynsford assured him.

Matthew snuffled. "Well, I can assure you her honor is safe with me." Much too safe. He'd drunk sheep's blood, for God's sake. Vile stuff that it was, he still hadn't gotten the taste out of his mouth.

"Indeed?" The Lycan took a sip of his claret. "What are your intentions with her then?" Eynsford sat back and regarded Matthew stoically.

To do her bidding without tasting a drop of her blood. Matthew sighed in annoyance, more at himself than with Eynsford. "I intend to court her." The man would find out soon enough as it was; and Matthew never prevaricated.

The Lycan choked on his drink, splashing the dark red liquid down his cravat. "Over my dead body," he said when he finally could breathe.

"That *can* be arranged," Matthew replied. He'd had enough of the young man's posturing. He'd been alive for too long to allow this pup to unman him. He'd been nothing but honorable, and he wouldn't let some Lycan bring him to heel.

"Why do you want to court Miss Sinclair?" Eynsford finally asked.

Because she was the most singularly intriguing person he'd ever met. And she was bloody gorgeous. And because he couldn't help himself from craving her. "The normal reasons." Matthew shrugged enigmatically. If he had to suffer through this interview, he'd make it as painful for the Lycan as extracting teeth.

"Blodswell," Eynsford growled in warning.

"Oh, bloody hell," Matthew said as he stood up to pace. "I'm doing it because she *asked* me to. I'd never, ever choose someone like Miss Sinclair on my own." Choosing her would drive him mad, and he'd always enjoyed his sanity. "Her emotions are all over the place. She's unpredictable."

The Lycan raised his eyebrows but said nothing more.

"She asked me. No, she *begged* me to allow her to borrow some of my respectability." When Eynsford wanted to break in, Matthew spoke over him. "And, by God, she needs it if she's hoping to have any influence at all over that aunt of hers. A reincarnation of one of Hades' Furies, if I've ever seen one."

"And is that why you'd like to help Rhiannon?" the Lycan asked softly, his voice a low rumble in the room.

"No, I'd like not to help her at all." He'd like to rush back to Derbyshire to preserve whatever sanity he had left. Chasing after Rhiannon Sinclair's skirts had him hiding in a Lycan's shrubbery and unable to drink life-sustaining blood. "But I'm obligated," he ground out. He had given his word.

"So you don't want to court her?" Eynsford certainly knew how to wring all the details out of a person.

Want? He wanted her like there was no tomorrow. He wanted to hold her, to taste her, to sink inside her, but not court her. That was much too tame for what he *wanted*. Saint George's teeth, she was dangerous to his very existence.

"No, I don't want to court her. Not at all. In fact, if I never saw her again, it would probably be for the best."

A gasp reached his ears from the doorway. Matthew had been so wrapped up in his own diatribe that he hadn't even heard the ladies walking down the corridor. How long had she been there? How much had she heard? All of it, if the wounded look on her face and the black storm cloud hanging over her head were any indication.

"Miss Sinclair," he began. But she turned and bolted in the other direction.

∽

Rhiannon could hear his footsteps behind her and knew he could overtake her at any moment, so she did the only thing she knew how. She glanced over her shoulder and socked him with a quick and well-placed bolt of lightning.

His footsteps stopped only momentarily as he cursed loudly and prolifically.

Then within a second, he had her by the elbow and was dragging her through a side door and out into the small courtyard.

"That wasn't fair," he said quietly, staring down at her, his black eyes filled with some emotion she couldn't quite name.

Fair? He could go hang. The storm cloud over her head broke and rain fell over them both, drenching them within seconds.

"Neither was that," Blodswell said as he blew the torrents of water from his lips.

"*That* I canna help. The lightnin' bolt, on the other hand, was all me. And ye deserved it, ye blood-suckin' excuse for a gentleman." The rain slowed to a drizzle, but it didn't stop completely.

"I've been called worse, Miss Sinclair," he said softly, his gaze avoiding hers.

She instantly regretted her words but refused to take them back. "Give me time, Blodswell, and I'll call ye worse things," she said, instead.

"I imagine you would," he groaned. "Would an apology help?"

"Would ye mean it?"

"No."

"Then why in the world would it help?"

He frowned a response, which only made Rhiannon's ire stronger.

"How could ye tell him I begged ye? Ye said ye wanted me, and I believed ye."

"Miss Sin—"

Rhi shook her head. "If ye dinna want ta help me, why dinna ye just say so, instead of lyin' ta me?" She groaned as the rain grew heavier and the mortification of the overheard conversation sank her spirits even lower. She had thought for some inexplicable reason that she could trust the blackguard. Some knight in shining armor he had turned out to be. Now she'd never be able to face Lord Eynsford again as long as she lived.

"I didn't lie!" he called to be heard over the thunder that rumbled above them.

Liars always claimed they didn't lie. Rhiannon glared at him. Besides, she'd heard him with her own ears.

"I didn't lie," he said again, this time softer.

But Rhiannon had heard enough. "I'll no' hold ye ta our bargain, my lord. Ye may go. I'm sorry I ever bothered ye." She turned her back to him so he wouldn't be able to recognize the real tears that ran down her cheeks along with the rain. "If ye doona want me, I'll no' force ye inta anythin'."

"That's just it, Miss Sinclair," he said quietly, as he came and stood within a hairsbreadth of her, his front to her back. "I *do* want you. I want you more than I've ever wanted anything."

That certainly wasn't what he'd said to Eynsford, was it? She spun back to face him. "Ye doona need ta lie ta save my feelings."

"You scare me, Miss Sinclair." The intensity of his dark gaze bore into her. "You positively terrify me."

"Ye're a dolt, Lord Blodswell."

A smile tilted one corner of his mouth. "In more ways than one," he agreed. "And it's Matthew. Call me Matthew."

"It doesna matter what I call ye, seein' as how I willna be callin' ye a blasted thing after tonight."

"May I call you Rhiannon?" he asked as he slid one arm around her waist, his hand flattening on her back like an open fan to draw her to him. "That's how I think of you."

Rhi pushed back from him, but his chest felt like a granite wall beneath her fingertips. "Let me go," she breathed quietly, but she was certain he heard her when he shook his head.

"I can't."

"Of course ye can. I ken ye doona want me," she cried.

Rhiannon squealed as his hands slid down over her bottom and raised her to meet him. The evidence of his desire pressed against her belly. His voice deepened, suddenly seeming to be almost as dark as his eyes. "Does it feel like I don't want you?"

Not giving her a moment to reply, he simply smothered her shocked gasp as he pressed his lips to hers. They were soft but demanding. Supple but strong. He took her mouth with amazing slowness that sucked the very breath from her body. Rhiannon felt lost in that instant, as though she were floating among the clouds. The scent of sandalwood enveloped her, and tingles raced across her skin.

She'd never felt so alive, so utterly wanted, so soft or feminine. She'd never had someone's complete and total attention, not as she did the earl's at that very moment. He was hers. And she was everything he was thinking about as his mouth consumed hers, absorbing her gasps and whimpers. He tasted her. He wanted her. He wanted more of her. She knew it and felt a supreme sense of power because of it.

When Blodswell lifted his head, amazement graced his features. "You've never been kissed."

"No' like that," she said, her breathing labored. Of course, that could be because he still held her bottom in his hands, his fingertips gently clenching and releasing her, pressing her tightly against the ridge of his desire.

His lips dropped to trail along the line of her jaw, sending delicious tingling sensations to places she didn't know she had. "I have tried so hard to be honorable with you," he said, his voice tortured and raspy. His lips pressed against a sensitive spot below her ear that made her belly flip. She squirmed in his hold, trying to press herself more firmly against him. The ridge of his desire moved against her belly as he groaned. It was a torturous sound. Much like the whimpers that were leaving her own mouth.

"I'm sorry," she gasped. "I dinna mean ta do whatever I did."

He chuckled as he lifted his head to look down at her. "The truth of the matter is, Rhiannon," he said, her name tumbling over his lips like water over the falls, "I want you so badly I can taste you. You're all I think about. In all my lifetimes, I have never felt this way. Not ever."

He teased her lips again with his own. She tipped her head back to meet him. When his tongue slid along hers, she gave back to him as much as she received. He pulled back with a harsh oath, but his eyes were still on her as he brushed a lock of hair from her face and looked down at her. He wanted to say something else, but she had no idea what it was.

Rhiannon lifted a hand to his face. "But those things ye said ta Dashiel," she started.

"Were because I am afraid of you, Rhiannon."

A powerful vampyre? That was the silliest thing she'd ever heard. "My gifts are no' that great, my lord." Certainly not in comparison to his.

"Oh, they are," he affirmed. He squeezed her lightly. "Look at me."

Rhi looked up into his obsidian eyes and saw something she didn't quite understand staring back at her. Then he smiled. His incisors were fully distended. But he didn't frighten her at all. In fact, she was intrigued. She stood on tiptoe to kiss the corner of his mouth and then licked across his extended tooth with the tip of her tongue.

Abruptly, he set her away from him and turned to face the other direction.

She wavered on her feet for a moment before she could gather enough wits to address him. "Did I do somethin' wrong?" she finally asked when he didn't turn back toward her.

"You do everything perfectly. That's the problem," he said quietly. "I can't offer you anything, Rhiannon. I can't offer to take you as my wife. I can't offer to give you a family. Because I can't do any of those things."

She wanted to ask why not, but she refused to beg him for his favor. He did look a bit tortured, however, standing there with his clothes sopping wet, his hair sticking out at all angles where he'd shaken it.

"But I can pretend." He nodded, as though coming to a decision. "I can *pretend* to court you, make your aunt happy, and then send you safely back to Edinburgh."

Her heart rejected his words. How could he kiss her like that and only want to pretend? "And that's all?"

"That's all I have to give you."

Rhi nodded briskly. She'd take it. For now.

⤜⤛

Matthew sank into a chair across from the Lycan and longed for the ability to imbibe the blood-red claret the marquess seemed to be quite fond of. It would be delightful to drown his problems in a bottle of spirits. He remembered that much from his previous life. But, unfortunately, he couldn't partake of the mind-numbing beverage. He could only smell it. And dream of it. Just as he could smell and dream of Rhiannon. He sighed loudly.

Eynsford chuckled softly across from him. "Blasted you with a good one, did she?"

Matthew rubbed the side of his neck. He was still smarting from that blast, which hurt like the devil. "She did," he grunted. He'd tried to sneak out of the courtyard after they'd made their arrangement, to avoid having to talk with anyone else, but Eynsford had come upon them and requested Matthew's presence in his study. Fortune was not on his side.

"As a recipient of one of her bolts of fury, myself, I offer you my deepest sympathies." He chuckled again. Blast and damn. The man was having a grand time at Matthew's expense. "Although mine was just a small one. By the sound of your curses, you weren't quite so fortunate."

"I assume you Lycans hear everything," Matthew groused.

"The whole damn household heard it, Blodswell." Eynsford tilted his head and regarded him with amusement. "It's not easy to miss a boom of thunder that originates indoors and the squeal of a man who has been hit by lightning."

"I didn't squeal," Matthew growled as he crossed his ankle over his knee. "I cursed. And my apologies to the rest of the household."

"Consider yourself fortunate that my brothers weren't in residence at the time." The Lycan was enjoying this way too much.

"Did you need me for something?" Matthew asked, noting the impatience that coated his own words. He didn't particularly care if he offended the marquess. In fact, he'd like to throttle the Lycan just for giving him such a difficult time.

"We didn't quite finish our conversation before you had to go chasing Miss Sinclair down the corridor." Eynsford's eyebrows pushed together. "Dreadful misfortune there, Blodswell. You should have stopped talking about five minutes prior to her arrival."

Matthew lifted his gaze quickly to meet the Lycan's and saw that Eynsford's eyes twinkled with merriment. "You knew she was there!" Matthew said as he jumped to his feet and began to pace. "And you let me continue on like an idiot."

"You were playing the idiot part so well, that I had no desire to stop you." Eynsford shrugged. "No doubt you would have heard her footsteps, too, if your mind hasn't been clouded with thoughts of how to get beneath her skirts."

Matthew stopped his pacing and spun to face the marquess. "I don't have any desire to get beneath her skirts." He attempted a careless snort, but it came out more like he was choking on his own lie.

"Certainly, you don't."

"And I don't appreciate you speaking of her virtue in such a cavalier way."

"You don't? Interesting." The Lycan let his statement linger in the air.

"You are a bloody nuisance, Eynsford. It's a miracle you talked your wife into taking your hand in marriage." Any other woman would have run quickly in the opposite direction. Of course, Lady Eynsford had probably thrust herself right into his path, knowing her own destiny. "Your wife is much too good for you." Two could play at this game.

"Oh, I'm quite well aware of that. But one cannot fight love at first sight."

"There's no such thing," Matthew grunted.

"I beg to differ," Eynsford said. "I was well and truly caught the first moment I saw her." He got a faraway look in his eye for a moment and then sobered and sat forward. "So, what's your plan with regard to Miss Sinclair?"

"For all intents and purposes, I plan to court her."

Matthew nodded as though by doing so he could reassure himself along with the Lycan.

"To court her? Flowers delivered at random? Sonnets to her beauty? Attempting to fill her dance card at the next ball?"

"Smelling that intoxicating scent day after day after day…" Matthew said quietly, though, of course Eynsford heard him.

"Scent? She has a scent?" He looked upon Matthew as though he'd grown two heads.

"A most delightful one," Matthew said begrudgingly. "Don't act as though you can't smell it." Though the thought of Eynsford putting his snout anywhere near Rhiannon made Matthew see red.

The Lycan shrugged. "My wife's scent is the only one I can smell. Or at least it's the only one that matters. What does Miss Sinclair smell like?"

"Gardenias," Matthew grunted.

"Beg your pardon?" The Lycan sat forward again to hear him better.

"I bloody well know you heard what I said. She smells like a bouquet of gardenia blossoms." And sin. She smelled like gardenia blossoms and sin. No. Heaven. She smelled like gardenia blossoms and heaven. For nothing as beautiful as she was could be sinful.

"Gardenias are used to soothe the anxious," Eynsford said. "It's no wonder Sorcha gave her that scent as her signature." Matthew must have looked flummoxed because Eynsford continued to explain. "Sorcha's the youngest of the coven sisters. She can control plants and their growth. She gave my Caitrin the scent of honeysuckles, which suit her perfectly."

"And I need to know this because?" Matthew prompted.

"*Because*," the Lycan said loudly, "Miss Sinclair is very special to my wife, as are the rest of them. They're one big family, and they're fairly charming once you get past the lightning, fire balls, and creeping vines, and never having a single secret that you can call your own." He took a deep breath. "But because these women are like family to my wife, I feel the need to warn you."

Matthew's hackles rose. He couldn't help it.

Yet the Lycan continued. "If you sink your teeth, or anything else, into the fair skin of Miss Sinclair, I'll gladly help those women plan where to hide your body after they kill you." He sat back and regarded Matthew stoically.

"That you'd leave such a monumental chore for five young ladies doesn't speak well of you, Eynsford," Matthew said. "A noble man might take me on himself, rather than simply coming in to help clean up the damage five ladies might do."

The Lycan laughed. He laughed until tears rolled from the corners of his eyes. "Oh, that was amusing, Blodswell." But then the Lycan sobered. "Those witches are a formidable force. It would be amusing to see you try to best them. Hence my warning. Take it as you wish. But do not cross that coven. Because if you cross that coven, you also cross me. And I'll not allow them to be hurt, not a single one.

"While you're plotting to *help* Miss Sinclair, keep that in mind. There will be no drinking of her blood. There will be no improper behavior. And there will be no interesting forays up her skirts. Unless, of course, you do the honorable thing and marry her first. And at this point, I'm not certain I'd give my blessing for that."

Marry Rhiannon. He couldn't possibly do such a thing. He'd live forever, while her days would end. She would grow older while he looked exactly the same. Eventually, he'd have to either leave her or take her from everything she knew so he could continue his ruse and appear human. And, while he wasn't a pauper and could care well for her needs, he would never be able to provide her with a family. Didn't all young women dream to cuddle babies in their arms?

"I have no plans to dishonor her. Nor do I plan to foray up her skirts, as you so indelicately put it. She has asked for my help, and I shall provide it. Then she will return to Edinburgh. End of story."

"End of story," Eynsford echoed.

"If you are done with your warnings of doom and gloom, I've business to attend to."

"Thirsty, are you?" the Lycan asked.

Eynsford had no idea how very thirsty he was. "Not at all," he clipped out. "But business does await."

The Lycan extended his hand. "I'm glad we understand one another."

As Matthew took Eynsford's hand, he wasn't at all certain they did. But he seemed to have permission to pretend to court the lovely Miss Sinclair. Of course, as long as he didn't drink her blood, throw her skirts over her head in a fit of passion, or otherwise embarrass her publicly, he had permission. Why did that have to be the parting thought? He wouldn't be able to get the thought of tossing her skirts over her head out of *his* head the rest of the night.

Matthew stepped out the front door and couldn't help but look up at Thorpe House, to the upstairs window. His eyes were drawn to the only one lit by the soft glow of a candle. There she stood, her face in shadow, half behind the curtain. He bowed quickly to her, threw her a winning smile, and turned to walk down the street.

A gentle breeze caressed his cheek, and he couldn't keep from reaching up to touch the spot. As he did, a tiny twinge of pain flashed within his chest. What was *that* about? Matthew frowned. It didn't hurt much. It was a bit uncomfortable, but mostly it was unsettling. He supposed he'd have to pay a call to Callista. Damn. He'd rather drink bilge water.

Eleven

MATTHEW STOOD ON THE COBBLESTONE STREET, frowning at the little cottage in Hampstead. In all of Britain, it was the last place he wanted to be. But he was here, so he might as well get this over with. Although, the ache in his chest *had* stopped. Well, mostly anyway. Perhaps it would be better to drop by another time. Surely the pain would subside all together and this little trip would have been for nothing.

The front door creaked open, and in the blink of an eye, Callista stood before him, her russet curls billowing over her shoulders. One sculpted eyebrow lifted imperiously. "Are you just going to stand in the street all evening?"

How long had she been watching him? "I didn't realize the hour, Callista. I should come another time."

"Where is your protégé? And why do you smell like sheep's blood?" Though she was shorter than him by at least a foot, she somehow seemed to be looking down her nose at him like a regal queen eyeing an insignificant squire.

Sheep's blood. Could that vile blood have caused this

dull ache? That didn't seem likely. Of course, having chest pains after more than six centuries didn't seem likely, either. "May I have just a moment of your time?"

Fast as a blur, Callista was back at her front door, holding it wide. "Do come in, Matthew. I don't have all night."

He followed her, though at a much more human pace. As soon as he crossed the threshold, the aroma of fresh human blood assaulted him. Like a hound on a fox hunt, Matthew followed the scent into a small parlor, which was swathed in black. Dear God, he was starving.

Callista appeared at his elbow, a goblet outstretched in her hand. "You look awful. Drink this."

He must look awful. He'd never known Callista to act the role of servant for any man, vampyre or otherwise. Matthew tentatively took the glass from her. Inside, the liquid was nearly the same dark red as Eynsford's claret. "Where did this come from?"

Callista frowned at him. "Gift horses and all that, Matthew. Drink the damned blood."

No one ever argued with Callista, not if he wanted to keep his head. So Matthew tossed the drink back and swallowed it in one gulp. And he instantly wished he hadn't. Bloody hell! He'd never tasted anything so revolting. "Good God," he rasped. "The sheep's blood was better. Are you trying to poison me?"

Callista's glower darkened. "What would be the point in that?"

She always had been calculating. And there was no good reason to poison him or kill him. None that he could think of anyway. "The blood is rancid."

Callista's frown vanished, only to be replaced with

a most quizzical stare, as though he was an oddity or anomaly of some sort. "There is *something* off about you."

Matthew wasn't sure whether he should be relieved that he wasn't imagining things or worried that something was most definitely wrong with him. "Do you know what it is?"

She shook her head and gestured to a chaise a few feet away. "But you should probably sit. I've never seen you look so terrible."

And that was saying something as she had found him slowly dying beside dozens of already dead knights in the Holy Land. "I look like I'm once again at death's door?" Matthew sat, staring up at her, hoping she had some wisdom that would help.

"So to speak."

Well, that was hardly reassuring. "You're right, of course. There is something wrong. I just don't know what it is. That's why I've come, Callista. I've never felt this way before."

"Felt what way?" She settled in beside him.

There were so many things now that he thought about it. "I couldn't feed today. The girl offered herself up to me. And nothing. No desire." He laughed derisively. "My bloody fangs didn't even distend."

"Am I to suppose that explains the sheep's blood?"

"MacQuarrie gave it to me to tide me over."

Her brow rose in reproach. "Shouldn't you be taking care of him, not the other way around?"

"I don't know that I'm fit to take care of anyone right now. I've been getting headaches. And there's a pain," he tapped his chest, "right here. It's slight and dull, but it won't go away."

Callista leaned forward and touched his chest. "Here?"

Matthew nodded, hoping beyond reason she could help. She was the oldest vampyre he knew. If there was something to be done, some precedent, Callista would know it. She cocked her head to one side and winced, but only for a second.

"What is it?" He pressed her hand more firmly against where his heart had once beat.

She scoffed as though the idea was ridiculous. "It's nothing."

"Tell me."

Callista stared deeply into his eyes, and for the first time in a very long while, she seemed to be completely sincere. "I'm not sure, Matthew. But I don't believe sheep's blood is the answer."

"It was a one-time occurrence."

"Well, I can still smell it on you." She scrunched up her nose. "I am concerned about all this. We've seen plagues sweep through and decimate human populations. I would hate for it to be our turn."

Matthew hadn't even considered that possibility.

"This girl that offered herself up to you. Was she attractive?"

Which one? There had been two. An image of Rhiannon Sinclair tossing her hair over one shoulder flashed in Matthew's mind. "There was..." But he'd really rather not mention Rhiannon to anyone. Still his teeth did distend when he was with *her*.

"There was what?"

Matthew shook his head. "The girl at *Brysi* was perfectly attractive."

Callista's black eyes narrowed infinitesimally.

"Come now. You've known me too long to mistake me for a fool, Sir Matthew," she said, reminding him exactly how long she had known him by referring to him by that name. "What is it you're keeping from me?"

If he didn't tell her, she'd still find out one way or the other. Alec MacQuarrie would probably blurt it out at the worst possible time. "There is a girl…"

"Yes, there are *many* girls," she said, her tone implying he was a complete simpleton.

"My fangs… They do work for her."

Callista froze, her gaze locked on his. "Indeed?"

Everything else worked for her, too, but Matthew would rather not divulge that. He nodded once.

"And have you taken from her?"

"No." He shook his head. "And I've promised not to."

Callista tossed her back and laughed. "More fool you." It seemed ages before she could control her mirth.

"I hardly find it amusing."

Callista put a hand to her heart and rose from her seat. "You had me worried, Matthew. And for no good reason. Take from the girl and be done with it."

The idea of sinking his teeth into Rhiannon brought other parts of his body to life. "I can't."

One delicate brow rose indignantly, and the mirth vanished from Callista's face. "You most certainly can."

Well, he *could*. There was no arguing that point. "What if it doesn't work? I can't take from the poor girl the rest of her life."

"Why not?"

Because it wasn't fair. He couldn't ask that from

Rhiannon. He had nothing to give her in return. He couldn't steal her future. But he couldn't say any of that to Callista. She wouldn't understand, and even if she did, she wouldn't agree. "I gave my word," he said instead.

"Then you will suffer the rest of your days, Matthew. Will your honor keep you warm during the day, do you think? I have a feeling this girl, whoever she is, would do a much better job."

"I have nothing to offer her."

Callista cupped his jaw with her hands. "You have yourself, my son." Then she patted his cheek with more force than was necessary, as though to abate any lingering sentiments of affection.

Matthew touched his ill-used cheek. "She's an innocent, Callista." Taking from Rhiannon wasn't the same as taking from one of the Cyprians who spent their lives at *Brysi*. However, his mother, for lack of a better word to describe his maker, had never seen the difference.

She threw up her hands in annoyance. "Then marry the girl if it eases your conscience."

Did she honestly think it was that easy? "She will want children."

"Then help yourself to the foundling hospital of your choice," she grumbled irritably. "You are making this more difficult than it needs to be, Matthew. Innocents and children. You are a vampyre. You need human blood. This girl calls to you for whatever reason. Have done with it already."

Matthew rose from his seat and tipped his head in Callista's direction. "Thank you for your wisdom."

"In other words, you'll do whatever the hell you want, like always."

He couldn't help the grin that spread across his lips. "It has been a pleasure."

Callista's brow furrowed. "I want you back here within the week, Matthew Halkett. And I want you looking like yourself."

Or she'd come in search of him. The threat was there, even if she didn't utter it. Matthew nodded tightly. "Until then, dear."

༄

Avoiding the all-hearing ears of a Lycan wasn't easy when one wanted to sneak out of the house. Rhiannon waited anxiously for the household to quiet, then very slowly opened her chamber door and peeked down the corridor. No one was moving about, and the corridors were dark; perhaps everyone had finally gone to bed.

Back home in Edinburgh, she had often slipped out under the cover of night to climb to the top of Arthur's Seat, where she could be alone to think. But finding time or space to be alone at Thorpe House was incredibly difficult. Not only were there servants everywhere, but Eynsford's Lycan brood was always underfoot. If they weren't lounging about, they were worrying the living daylights out of the marquess. Honestly, that part was quite humorous. She'd never seen the golden Lycan at sixes and sevens. But, still, if solitude was what one needed to find a balance within one's self, one could not find it at Thorpe House.

Her powers had been off-kilter ever since her arrival in London, and they weren't getting any better. Blodswell's appearance made it even worse. After that kiss, she wasn't certain she'd ever be herself again. She'd never felt so out of sorts in her life, and the majority of it centered on the earl.

Certainly, he was handsome beyond belief, but he also possessed something else that drew Rhiannon like a moth to a flame. Perhaps it was his confidence? She wasn't certain what it was, but from the very first moment, he'd had her powers, not to mention her heart, all aflutter.

On quiet feet, she tiptoed to the garden door and let herself out into the dark night. In London, there was no place like Arthur's Seat that she could take advantage of, but there was the park where she'd originally had her temper-fit and where she'd first met the earl. It should be quiet and vacant at this time of night.

Rhiannon tugged her cloak tighter about her body and raised the hood to cover her head. She had no fear of being alone in the night since she could create a fog so thick that no one could even see her, much less harm her. She inhaled deeply and continued into the night, her shoes barely making any sound on the cobblestones as she wound her way to Hyde Park.

When she finally reached the gates, she stopped to look up at the night sky and enjoyed the flicker of the bright stars. They often seemed to mock her with their winking and twinkling, but not tonight. Tonight, they hovered like beacons of hope.

What a ridiculous thought. Rhiannon silently berated

herself as she crossed to a park bench and sat down. Apparently, she'd been spending too much time with Cait, who had the most romantic of hearts. Rhiannon was very much the opposite. Of course, Cait's father had doted on her and made certain she'd lived a life that could foster hope and romantic imagination. Rhi's own sire had holed up in his study, rarely to be seen. And Aunt Greer… well, she wasn't the most nurturing of women.

The crack of a broken twig behind her caught Rhiannon's attention. She stood, closed her eyes, and spread her hands flat by her sides, and then she raised her palms as though she was lifting a heavy box onto a high shelf. As her hands rose, so did the mist. Fog was quite cumbersome, the weight of it a burden as she lifted it from the damp, night earth.

One would think it might be light and airy, but it held so much moisture that lifting and lowering it could be a trial. Yet she did so with ease, having done it many times before. She dusted her hands together. There. Now she could be alone with her thoughts. No one could see through the mist. No one would even know she was there.

She needed to practice, to prove to herself that her powers weren't out of control. That she was fully capable of wielding them all with the precision and dedication that was just part of her nature.

Rhiannon raised her index finger to her mouth, blew gently across it, and twirled her finger in the air. A small whirlwind appeared, dancing across the mossy earth with abandon. The circular bit of moving air behaving so precisely made her want to dance on her tiptoes with glee. She still had it. She could still wield her magic with deadly precision.

She clapped her hands together and the whirlwind came to an immediate stop, disappearing as quickly as it had arrived.

"Well done," a voice called from a few steps behind her. Rhiannon spun to find the Marquess of Eynsford standing in the shadow the moon cast from her body.

She crossed her arms over her chest. "What are ye doin' here?"

He made a tsking sound. "I could ask you the same question, lass. Isn't it time for all good little witches to be in bed?"

"If only I was a good little witch," Rhiannon murmured as she flopped onto the bench.

He sat down casually beside her. "Nice fog, by the way," he tossed out as he appraised the thick mass of swirling white. "Reminds me of the time I found you on Arthur's Seat." He nodded in appreciation. "Well done."

"I'm so glad ye like it," Rhiannon said. She'd only wanted to be alone for a little while. And already her peace was shattered. "Why did ye follow me?"

He shrugged nonchalantly and then tapped his ear. "Lycan ears. I couldn't help but hear you skulking around Thorpe House."

"I wasna skulkin'," she protested.

"Skulking. Creeping. Escaping." His eyebrows rose on the last as he regarded her with a question in his gaze. "Besides, Cait would never forgive me if I let anything happen to you. So, I followed."

"Ye smelled me through the fog," Rhiannon said as

she choked back a giggle. Of course, he did. Why did that seem so absurd?

"I'm glad you find my senses to be humorous." He shot her a quelling glance, but it only made her laugh more loudly. "You, Miss Sinclair, need to be more careful. If I found my way through your fog, other Lycans could as well."

"I'm no' afraid of Lycans." She squared her shoulders. "How many of ye are there anyway?"

"Enough that you should take care," he warned. Then he inhaled deeply. "Something tells me I will regret asking this, but what were you doing when I arrived?"

"Do ye always stick yer snout inta other people's business?" she quipped.

"When the person's safety is at risk, I have been known to do so," he replied, not even perturbed by her little barb. "My snout, my fangs, and my shaggy tail, if it's needed."

Rhiannon harrumphed and then decided to tell him the truth. After all, it didn't appear as though he would be leaving any time soon. So, she could either divulge her little practice session or she could give up the chance to have one. "I was practicin', if ye must ken."

"That little whirlwind was adorable," he said slowly, watching her face.

"Adorable?" She jumped to her feet. "I will have ye ken that I can create whirlwinds that will pick ye up off that bench and toss ye inta the next county."

He crossed an ankle over his knee and regarded his fingernails. "Prove it," he taunted.

"I doona have ta prove anythin' ta ye," she said, ready to stamp her feet in frustration.

"No, you don't. You need to prove it to yourself." He said this quietly, but it hit her like a ton of stone. "And since I have no plans to leave you out here alone, you can either go back with me now or get this *practice* out of your system. Personally, I've always enjoyed your magic. Cait's powers are fairly passive. I'm awed by the more active ones. Unless you're afraid to have an audience, of course." He let the last hang in the air.

Rhiannon stretched out her arms and made the circle of fog grow wider, allowing herself more space to work. She picked up a pebble from the path nearby and tossed it to him. He caught it without even looking. She pointed toward the stars. "If ye'll do the honors?"

Eynsford heaved the stone high into the air, and when it reached its highest peak, Rhiannon stuck out her index finger and shot a lightning bolt toward it, breaking it into a handful of tiny pieces that rained down around them.

"Nicely done," he said. "Try it again." This time, he retrieved a rock himself and tossed it high into the air. This second one exploded when the burst of energy from the tip of her finger scored it into pieces. "How do you do that without the crack of thunder pounding around us?"

She shrugged. "If I create a storm, I can create thunder. That little trick is just a bolt of lightnin'. It's no' enough ta cause thunder ta rumble."

He nodded as though he understood. And she imagined he probably did.

Rhiannon raised her finger to her mouth and blew and then spun the finger in a circle as she had earlier. The tiny whirlwind picked up the scattered pieces of stone and held them within its funnel. When the air stopped moving, it dropped them all onto the bench beside the marquess. He looked at her with astonishment.

"I had no idea you could achieve such precision."

"I canna remember a time when I couldna do that. I think I learned it when I was still in the cradle." She heaved a sigh.

"Then why the devil did you create such havoc at that ball? If you're capable of this," he motioned toward the pile of stones, "why did your powers go off so unpredictably?"

"A fatal flaw," she said quietly. "The more nervous I get, the harder my powers are ta control."

"And what makes you nervous?" He appeared to be thoroughly enraptured by the conversation.

"Things beyond my control," she admitted. "My life in Edinburgh is very ordered and normal. Well, normal for me."

"And nothing about London is ordered. I understand." He coughed into his hand before he continued. "Does Blodswell have anything to do with this?"

"I doona ken." And she didn't. She had no idea what role he would play in her life going forward. "He has promised ta help me. Ta make me appear more respectable. Since he has an enviable title, more money than anyone I ken, and fits well within society if he chooses."

"Yes, I had thought to offer one of my brothers for your use, but none of them fit that description." He grinned with what was obvious pride.

"And ye'd no' have them any other way."

"Exactly." He smiled at her as he tossed one of the stone fragments into the fog. "What else can you do?"

"Magically?" she asked.

"No, as in personally." He rolled his eyes dramatically. "Of course, I mean magically. I don't need to know about your embroidery or your watercolors. Those things bore me to death."

"Me, too, which is why I canna do them." She laughed lightly. "But I can make storms, lightnin', thunder, snow, rain…"

"Can you make rainbows?"

She nodded. "I can place them in the sky as though they're meant ta be there."

"I thought as much." He motioned toward her fog. "If you're done practicing for the night, I'll see you home."

Was she done? She assumed she was. Besides it wasn't fair to keep him from the comforts of his bed to watch over her. Rhi shrugged. "I suppose so."

"Do me a favor," he said as he directed her back toward his home in Mayfair, "and try not to sneak out more than once a week. I do like my sleep. I can give you a place to practice at Thorpe House. I want to see more of your powers anyway. They're interesting."

"Ye are truly interested in my powers?" Certainly, he was just trying to save her feelings.

"Of course I am. I can already envision the merry chase you'll lead Blodswell on. Be sure to use plenty of lightning. And that fog would be fun for a man to lose himself in, but he can smell almost as well as a Lycan, so don't assume it will protect you from him."

He chuckled. "Oh!" he cried dramatically. "Do you think you could shoot the buttons off his waistcoat with that lightning? Without causing permanent harm, of course?"

"I'm certain I could."

He laughed even more loudly. "I would pay money to see that." He chuckled all the way back to Thorpe House.

Rhi shushed him as they stepped through the door. He tried to look repentant but failed. Cait sat up in the oversized chair where she had been curled up, waiting, her dressing gown covered by a thick lap quilt. "Is everythin' all right?" she asked.

Eynsford scooped her up in his arms and spoke softly to her. "Everything is fine, love. She just needed some practice."

"See ye in the morning, Rhi," Cait called quietly over his shoulder, before something he did made her giggle, and he dashed up the stairs with her.

Could she knock Blodswell's buttons off his waistcoat? She'd have to try it and see. That thought made her giggle. She was a formidable witch. She just needed an opportunity to prove it to herself every now and again.

Twelve

RAUCOUS LAUGHTER FILTERED DOWN THE CORRIDOR from the breakfast room. Rhiannon shook her head at the sound, unsure what else to do. Lycans were most definitely a different breed. They seemed like overgrown lads with endless amounts of energy and no control over the amount of havoc they wreaked. In fact, the sounds emanating from belowstairs seemed more fitting for a seedy, dockside pub in the wee hours of the morning than an immaculate home in Berkeley Square.

Despite her reservations about dining with Eynsford's rowdy pack, Rhiannon continued toward the breakfast room. Just before she reached the threshold, the room went silent. They must have heard her approach. Rhiannon stepped into the room to find the three Hadley men sitting at the table, not a morsel of food anywhere in sight. The lot of them leapt to their feet at her entrance, and Gray—at least she thought it was Gray—toppled his chair over in his haste. She stifled a giggle.

"Good morning, sweetheart." Lord Radbourne tipped his head in greeting.

"Morning, Miss Sinclair," the twins said in unison.

Rhi smiled at the trio. "What a surprise ta see all of ye here this mornin'." It wasn't a surprise at all, but her comment sounded better than her thoughts, which were about why they had to make her breakfast a rowdy affair.

"The food's much better here," Gray admitted as he righted his chair.

"As is the company." Radbourne winked at her. He held out the chair beside him and Rhiannon slid into the offered seat. Then he gestured for a footman. "Coffee for Miss Sinclair, please."

"Thank ye."

All three Hadley men resumed their seats, and Rhiannon looked to her side to find the viscount grinning at her. "Radiant as sunshine."

"Ye are doin' it up a bit brown, my lord," she chided him.

Radbourne feigned a wounded heart by pressing a hand to his chest. "Ah, the unkindest cut of all."

Rhiannon rolled her eyes. "I believe ye have missed yer callin', Lord Radbourne. Ye should have been a thespian."

"Archer," he insisted. "If you're going to berate me, sweetheart, you should at least call me by my Christian name when you do so."

"I hardly think that would be proper."

Radbourne chuckled. "Nothing proper is worth doing."

"Here, here," Wes agreed with a grin.

"I'll keep that in mind, Archer." Rhiannon grinned at the scoundrel. She just couldn't help it. The viscount was charming in a roguish sort of way.

A cough sounded in the doorway. "Oh, for the love of God," the Marquess of Eynsford grumbled from the threshold. "What the devil are the three of you doing here? Didn't I toss all of you out last night?"

"You said we could attempt to return this morning," Wes offered from his seat beside his twin. "Price *did* admit us."

Eynsford's dark golden brows rose. "I shall have to have a long conversation with my butler in that case." Then his eyes landed on Rhiannon, and the marquess smiled. "Good morning, my dear. So sorry to subject you to this unruly lot so early in the morning."

Rhiannon grinned in return. "Actually, I quite enjoy them." And she did. Having only been raised with a sister, Rhi found the Hadley men and their highly improper interactions fairly amusing, even if they did inhale every morsel of food there was to be had.

Radbourne puffed out his chest at her comment, preening in his seat.

Eynsford sighed as though he suffered the never-ending punishment of Sisyphus, and then he strode farther into the room. The marquess took his spot at the head of the table and narrowed his eyes on the viscount beside him. "Archer."

"Dashiel," Radbourne returned with the same smug tone to his voice.

"Caitrin informs me your mother wishes to see you."

The viscount shrugged. "Your wife is meddlesome."

"Something you knew the first moment you met her. Pray do not change the subject. Lady Radbourne wishes for you to visit her."

"My mother will be quite disappointed then, will she not?"

The twins chuckled, and Eynsford's gaze swung in their direction. "Something one of you would like to say?"

Wes looked down at his empty plate.

Gray shook his head. "And deal with Archer's wrath? I'll hold my tongue."

Eynsford's eyes scanned the room, finally settling on the empty sideboard along the far wall. "Did you eat *all* of my food?"

"Cook is preparing more," Wes informed him cheerily.

"You do have your own lodgings," Eynsford grumbled.

"Yes, but we enjoy it here much more." Gray smiled at the marquess. "Besides, I wanted to entice Miss Sinclair to take a turn about the park with me today."

Wes' mouth fell open in surprise. "You lout! *I* had planned to entice Miss Sinclair with a ride in the park today."

Eynsford cleared his throat until all attention focused on him. The marquess' amber eyes twinkled with mirth. "Well, Rhiannon, you have two gentlemen vying for your attention this afternoon. They are nearly interchangeable and bookends of each other. Might I suggest the flipping of a coin to decide your fate?"

"I say," Lord Radbourne's voice rose above the din of the twins' outraged responses, "as the oldest, I trump both of them."

Rhiannon wasn't certain what to say. She'd never had so much male attention in all her life. No one had ever fought over spending time with her in

Edinburgh. Of course, here she was a novelty, and somewhere in the back of her mind, she knew their fascination with her would soon wane. Being sought after was nice, though none of the men in the breakfast room held her interest the way Lord Blodswell did. She found herself wishing desperately that the earl was beside her.

"Mornin'," Cait nearly sang from the doorway.

All four men came to their feet as Cait bustled into the breakfast room. Eynsford dropped a kiss on her brow. "Morning, Caitie."

She turned her attention to the table. "Ye all are lookin' so dashin' this mornin'." Then she walked the perimeter of the table before sliding into a seat beside Rhiannon. "We are goin' shoppin' today."

"We are?"

"Mmm," Cait agreed with a nod. "We need ta find somethin' new and expensive for the Duchess of Hythe's soiree."

At the head of the table, Eynsford groaned. "Hythe?"

His wife graced him with a beatific smile. "Did I forget ta tell ye, Dash? Her Grace has invited us along with Rhi ta attend a soiree at the end of the week."

"Us?" Gray sat forward in his seat.

"Well, no' all of us," Cait amended. "But I'm sure ye gentlemen will find somethin' ta keep yer interests for one evenin'."

"Tell me you're not really going to make me call on the Duchess of Hythe," Eynsford grumbled.

Caitrin shot him a cheeky grin. "Well, ye doona have ta escort me, Dashiel. I'm sure Lord Blodswell willna mind havin' Rhi on one arm and me on the other." She ignored the low growl emanating from her husband, gestured to a footman for a cup of coffee, and turned her attention back to Rhiannon. "I'm thinkin' somethin' green ta match yer eyes. What do ye think?"

Rhiannon was fairly certain her eyes were hazel.

"I think," Lord Radbourne cut in, "you lovely ladies will need someone to carry your boxes. Might I offer my assistance?"

❧

Bond Street was an experience. Cait had shuffled Rhi in and out of more than a dozen shops and did not appear to be tiring in the least. Rhiannon was glad to have Radbourne's company. He did make the excursion more enjoyable simply by needling Cait. No one ever did that, not if they knew what was good for them; but Radbourne, or Archer as he'd insisted Rhi call him, didn't seem concerned in the least. Then again, the man didn't know he was accompanying a pair of witches, either.

Just as they were about to step into a tiny dress shop, Cait narrowed her eyes on the Lycan. "Archer Hadley, ye are excused for the rest of the day."

A wolfish grin settled on his face. "Who will carry your boxes, Lady Eynsford?"

"A footman." Her brow rose imperiously. "They are paid ta do such chores, after all."

Archer turned his stare to Rhiannon. "I do believe the marchioness has tired of my company." He waggled his brow flirtatiously. "Pray say I haven't done the same to you, sweetheart."

Rhiannon laughed. There was nothing else to do. "No' ta worry, good sir. I quite enjoy yer company."

"See," Archer said to his sister-in-law. "You're the only one annoyed with me."

"Doona forget yer mother. She's quite annoyed."

"How can I," the viscount grumbled, "when you're constantly reminding me of the fact?"

Cait rolled her eyes.

"Ah, Miss Sinclair," came a warm voice behind Rhiannon. Just the sound of it made shivers race across her skin.

She glanced over her shoulder to find the Earl of Blodswell's black eyes focused on her, and she nearly sighed. "My lord," she breathed out, the memory of their kiss still fresh in her mind.

He looked more pale than she remembered, a bit haunted. Before she could wonder at that, his gaze lowered to her lips and Rhi's cheeks warmed. "What a pleasant surprise." Then Blodswell glanced at her companions. "Lady Eynsford, Radbourne."

"Lord Blodswell," Cait gushed. "I had a feelin' we'd see ye today."

"Did you?" The earl's eyes twinkled. "Well, how fortunate for me. Are you just beginning a shopping excursion?"

Rhiannon shook her head. "I am hopin' that it's come ta an end."

Cait grumbled something unintelligible under her breath. Whatever it was made Lord Radbourne choke on a laugh, and his face turned slightly red.

Rhi leaned toward the viscount. "Are ye quite all right, Archer?"

Beside her, Lord Blodswell stiffened, and his eyes narrowed on the viscount. "One wouldn't think to find you escorting ladies down Bond Street, Radbourne."

Archer shrugged. "Well, one wouldn't think to find your kind walking around in broad daylight either, Blodswell. How *do* you do that?"

"Archer!" Cait reprimanded.

"By putting one foot in front of the other," Blodswell replied dryly. "Much easier with two feet than four."

"This is hardly the place, gentlemen." Cait glanced over her shoulder at the other shoppers bustling up and down the street. More than one curious glare was pointed in their direction.

"Some beasts simply cannot be taken out in polite company." Blodswell sighed dramatically. Rhi suppressed a giggle at Archer's hangdog expression, which couldn't be further from what he was feeling, if the ire in his eyes was any indication.

"You think this is humorous, do you, Rhiannon?" Archer asked, his eyebrow arched playfully. "That the good night-dweller is offended at the very idea of Bond Street going to the dogs?" He grinned widely. Blodswell stiffened beside her and crossed his arms over his chest.

However, Archer's self-deprecating humor was infectious. And Rhiannon found herself pinching her lips closed to keep from laughing aloud.

"Ye had better behave yerself!" Cait scolded the Lycan.

"Or what? You'll make me run back home? Or simply put me on a leash?" He pretended to weigh his options. "That leash idea actually sounds like my idea of a good time."

Cait's face reddened, but Rhiannon wasn't entirely certain why.

"There are some things that should not be discussed with such frivolity," Blodswell said crisply. He shot Cait an apologetic glance, which made her blush even more. *He* knew why Cait was flustered all of a sudden? Why didn't Rhi know?

"Archer Hadley!" Cait finally bit out. "I *will* tell Dash if ye keep this up."

Archer appraised his fingernails with little concern for her outburst. But he suddenly leaned forward and kissed her forehead. "My apologies about the leash comment," she heard him mutter to her. "I had no idea you and Dash played that way…" He let the rest trail off, an unrepentant grin on his face. "My behavior is not usually this poor. From this moment forth, I'll tuck my tail and heel when you ask."

"A likely tale," Blodswell muttered.

"At least I have the courtesy of not showing up smelling like…" Archer leaned close to the earl and sniffed dramatically, as only a wolf could possibly do. Then he finished with a shudder and the word "livestock."

Blodswell advanced toward the viscount, taking one large step, but Rhiannon slid between them. "Doona listen ta him," she said softly. "He's only tryin' ta provoke ye."

"I do not smell like sheep," he grumbled.

"I never said anything about sheep," Archer taunted from behind Rhiannon.

Archer yelped when Cait smacked the back of his head. She pointed her index finger down the street. "Ta the coach with ye."

"I hope you have a whole litter just like the Hadleys one day," he teased Cait.

"And have ta raise two sets of ye? First ye and yer brothers and then a litter of my own? The fates would never punish me that way." She shoved his shoulder and pushed him down the street. Rhiannon turned to follow them. "Oh, no, you doona even think it!" Cait cried as she spun around. "I just remembered that I need some ribbons."

"Ribbons?" Surely, ribbons were not that important. They could wait.

"Yes, green. Green ribbons. I canna do without them. I need them for yer dress. For the Duchess of Hythe's soiree."

Rhiannon sighed heavily. "Then let's go and find ribbons."

"No, no. I have ta take Archer home before Blodswell does him bodily harm." She shoved the viscount's shoulder again when he made a move to protest. "Lord Blodswell, would ye be so kind as ta escort Rhiannon inta Grafton House? The line's always so long. I should return before ye're even helped."

"I would be honored," he said quickly as he offered Rhi his arm and raised his brows in invitation.

"But," Rhiannon protested feebly.

"But, nothin'," Cait called over her shoulder, already crossing the street. "I'll be back in a trice. But if ye get started without me, the green must match yer eyes. Otherwise, there's no point ta it. So, do take yer time."

Rhiannon groaned aloud as she took Blodswell's arm. "They're no' green, they're hazel. How on earth am I supposed ta find ribbons that match my eye color?"

Blodswell peered down at her, his midnight eyes twinkling. "You do have the prettiest flecks of green in your eyes. I imagine I could help with the chore of finding the right color, dearest."

"Chore indeed. I wish Blaire was here so she could set Cait ta rights."

"I can just imagine the sparks that would fly with those two in the same room," Blodswell chuckled.

"I keep forgettin' ye have met Blaire. And her husband, for that matter." She looked up at him as he led her casually down the street toward the shop Cait had indicated. He was tall enough that she had to tip her head back to look at his face.

"Blaire is a rare treat. Full of fire and passion. And I have known James for a very long time." He avoided her gaze. The creation of vampyres was a touchy subject, after all.

"Ye made him, did ye no'? Like Alec?" Blodswell stiffened again beside her. "Why *is it* that ye keep doin' that?" she finally choked out. The man was maddening. He could go from charming and sweet to rigid as a board within moments.

"Doing what?" he asked, his brow furrowing.

"Ye pinch yer lips together like ye're biting back an oath."

"I do no such thing." He straightened his shoulders.

"Aye, ye do. Ye did it when Archer was here. And ye did it again when I mentioned James and Alec." She stared him down. She'd never been as good at intimidating people as Blaire, the battle-born witch, was.

"You wouldn't understand," he said with a shrug. "It doesn't matter."

"Blodswell," she sighed, ready to give up and walk back to Thorpe House, ribbons or no ribbons.

He stopped and spun her toward him. "That's just it," he finally said, looking as though a small war was going on within him. One he was losing. If that was possible. "You call me Blodswell or my lord or whatever else crosses your lips. But it's anything and everything but my name. I have asked you to call me Matthew. But for some reason, you let Alec's and even *Radbourne's* given name fall across your lips like the sweetest of kisses."

~

Kisses? Bloody hell, now all he could think about was kissing her. Matthew's incisors descended, right there on Bond Street in broad daylight. Damn it to hell, this was not good. "I need to go back to my coach, Miss Sinclair." He swallowed hard, willing his eyeteeth to retract. But they failed to take heed. He shook his head in dismay. In all his years, this had never, ever happened to him.

"What's wrong?" she asked as she reached up to touch the side of his face. "Ye're lookin' extremely pale, Blodswell."

"Matthew," he grated out as he took her hand in his, spun her around, and nearly dragged her in the opposite direction to his coach. Thank God, his driver had stayed put.

"What are ye doin'?" Rhiannon whispered, in an apparent attempt to keep inquisitive eyes from watching them.

But Matthew couldn't answer her. He couldn't let anyone catch a glimpse of his distended fangs. Reaching his conveyance, he pulled the door open. "Come on. In with you," he said impatiently, glancing over her shoulder to make sure they hadn't caught anyone's attention. Feeling relatively safe, he looked at his driver. "Thorpe House, but take the long way."

When Rhiannon just stood there gaping at him as he held the door open for her, Matthew lost what little sanity he had left. He picked her up and put her inside with his own strength. He barely noted that she didn't fuss or complain. She went fairly willingly, for someone who was being tossed into a coach. He'd live to regret this, he was certain of it.

She sat back against the squabs in the dim confines of the carriage as he rapped on the roof and the carriage lurched away. She didn't say a word. Not a single word. She just tipped her head at him and regarded him with worry on her face. She reached one hand toward him. He caught it in the air and lowered it to her lap.

"No need to worry, dearest. I'll be all right in just a moment. I only need a moment." He stared out the window so he could avoid looking at her.

"Can I do anythin' ta help?" she asked, her voice soft.

She could stop smelling like gardenia blossoms. She could stop her heart from beating so he wouldn't have to hear the gush of blood in her veins, beating a staccato rhythm that called to him unlike anything ever had before. She could close those hazel eyes and stop blinking those long, long lashes at him. She could… let him taste her.

"I don't believe so," he finally said as he leaned his head back against the squabs and closed his eyes. He stopped his inhale. He didn't need to breathe. Yet the scent of her still hung in his mind like drapes over a window. He couldn't see past it. He couldn't move it aside. He couldn't do a damn thing.

"How long has it been?" she asked, as she began to remove her gloves.

"Beg your pardon?" He wasn't even certain what she'd asked.

"How long has it been since ye've fed, Blodswell?" she asked quietly. She worked the button free at her wrist and pulled her fingers free one by one. He could see the tattoo of her pulse beneath the delicate skin at her wrist. And it made his mouth water.

He wasn't sure. It could have been days by now. Days since he'd taken any real sustenance. His blasted teeth wouldn't work in any other situation. But they worked for her. Every part of his body worked for her. He tugged his jacket down to cover his lap.

"Not long," he lied. "Why do you ask?" He rolled his head on the seat to look at her without even raising it. He hadn't the strength. He was nearly a shell of a man, enchanted beyond belief by a weather-born witch who held everything he wanted in the world.

She reached to cup the side of his face. All he had to do was turn his head and he could sink his teeth into the delicate veins in her wrist and take from her.

Instead, he took her hand in his. "You don't know what you do to me," he groaned.

"Does it hurt?" she asked.

Oh, God, it hurt so much knowing he wanted her, needed her, had to have her but couldn't. But that wasn't what she meant, was it?

"Why have ye no' fed? Tell me the truth, Blodswell."

"Will you stop this bloody torture if I tell you? Will I have some peace?" Even as he said it, he knew there would be no peace for him. She didn't torture him on purpose. She just… existed, and her mere existence was all it took.

Rhiannon sat up taller and appeared slightly offended. "I havena done anythin' ta ye."

But she had. She'd somehow enchanted him, and even now he wasn't sure how she'd done it. And she'd asked him to court her, even if it had been a pretense in the beginning. "You haven't called me Matthew," he grumbled, as he couldn't bring himself to tell her the rest.

She sighed as though dealing with an unrepentant child. "Very well, I'll call ye Matthew. But I certainly doubt that's what has ye so tied up in knots."

"I am indeed tied up in knots," he admitted.

"Why is that, Matthew?"

Matthew. She'd said it. She'd said his name. He'd imagined that when it fell from her lips it would flow from her mouth like water over a dam. Like a gentle rain falling from the sky. But it hit him like thunder. Like lightning. Like Rhiannon.

"Say it again?" he urged, taking her face in his hands as he gently pushed her hair back from her temples.

"Matthew," she breathed. "What has come over ye?"

"I have not fed because I can't, dearest. And to be quite honest, it's driving me mad." More than mad. But that was as good a description as he could come up with.

"Are ye broken?" Her face lit with a hopeful smile. "My coven sister, Elspeth, once healed a broken wolf. He's her husband now. But if ye're broken, I could take ye ta her. She can heal ye."

"It's so kind of you to offer, Rhiannon."

She shivered lightly when he spoke her name. So, it affected her as well? Thank God he wasn't the only one.

"But I'm afraid it's not something that can be healed. I need to feed. That's all."

"But ye said ye canna? Has this happened ta ye before?"

"Never."

"In all yer years, this has never, ever happened?"

"Never," he repeated.

"What's causin' it now?" She looked perplexed.

"You are," he said quietly as he bent and pressed his lips to hers quickly. Her blasted heartbeat quickened; he could hear it in his head. Matthew pulled back, breaking off the kiss.

She leaned closer toward him. "Are my *powers* somehow the cause? I ken when ye are around, my powers go off without me even havin' any control. If they've affected ye, I'm very sorry." She placed a hand on her heart.

"Quiet, Rhiannon," he shushed her.

"But," she protested mildly, confusion clouding her face.

He had to tell her. Or go mad with the knowledge. He took a deep breath. "I want you." He smiled, allowing her to see his descended incisors. Her innocent little hand reached up, and she touched one with the pad of her thumb. Like a madman, he immediately turned and nipped her finger. Not hard enough to hurt her and only for a second. But enough to cause a drop of blood to well up on her thumb. She moved to pull her hand back, but he grabbed her wrist and stared at the essence of her. The heady aroma reached his nose. And his whole body stiffened.

"Do ye want it?" she asked innocently, and offered her thumb to him.

What had he done? He'd harmed her. To feed his own selfish needs. "I am so sorry," he grunted out. It was all he could do to talk.

"Why? It doesna hurt."

"It was very, very wrong of me." So wrong. He'd never forgive himself.

But, once again, that innocent little hand rose toward him. She dragged her thumb across his lower lip, smearing her blood where he had to taste it. So, he did. He closed his eyes because he couldn't look into the deep fathoms of hers anymore, not and feel like he was doing the right thing. He drew his lower lip between his bottom teeth, and the flavor of her washed over his tongue. She tasted like no one he'd ever had. She slipped over his senses like a silky coverlet, sliding across him like the softest of summer breezes. God, if he ever truly partook of her, he'd never be able to draw his teeth from her skin. He drew her thumb into his mouth and sucked it as hard as he could. The small wound would never appease him, but he had to taste her further.

"Something is happenin' ta me, Matthew," she whimpered. "Something I doona understand." Her confusion drew him from his storm-filled haze.

"Rhiannon," he groaned, reaching to draw her into his lap. Of course, she'd gotten his passion and his feelings in return the moment her finger had crossed his lips and they'd made that connection. "I am so sorry," he whispered.

"What *is* that?" she asked, her head falling back on his shoulder as she relaxed into him. She pushed her thumb back up to his lip, and he gratefully took it in. She took his hand, which rested on her thigh, moved it over to her abdomen, and then slid it down. "That, Matthew. What is that?"

"Tell me what you feel?" He led her gently as he gathered her skirts into his hands and pushed them higher and higher until he could slide his hand beneath them. All the while, he went back and forth between drinking from that tiny well that was the prick on her thumb and speaking softly to her.

"My belly is all aflutter. And there's this thump, thump, thump…" She gasped as he drew deeply on her thumb. Her desire and passion mixed with his.

He'd never been so hard in his life. He could explode any moment. She wiggled her bottom in his lap. "Be still," he chided. If she didn't, he'd lose his mind. Then he touched her heat, softly, with the back of his crooked index finger. Her curls were wet, her pulse pounding. "Here?" he asked, as he touched that little nub of desire.

"Aye!" she cried as she buried her face in his shoulder.

"I can make it better," he soothed her. He drew deeply on her thumb, her blood not much more than a memory, that tiny well drying up. But the connection between them was still there. He stroked his thumb across her, strumming her higher and higher. He couldn't resist arching into her bottom. He wanted to sink his incisors into her pretty little neck while he sank into her everywhere else. He wanted to consume her. But instead, he just sucked at that little spot on her thumb as he stroked her and watched her face, her mouth hanging open, small pants sliding past her lips to mingle with his.

He slid one finger into the silky warmth of her, just before her eyes flew open and she stared at him as he brought her to completion. Thunder may have crashed as she cried out for him, milking his finger as he continued to take her higher and higher, wringing every drop of pleasure from her.

Finally, when she'd settled in his lap, he let her pull her finger from his mouth and wrapped his arms around her, holding her close as she came back down from that storm-laden mountain of pleasure. She trembled in his arms.

"Matthew," she sighed as he raised a hand to wipe the hair from his brow.

"Yes, dearest?" She wiggled in his lap, making him wince in pain at the sensation of her sliding across the evidence of his unfulfilled desire.

"Will ye marry me?" she asked quietly.

"I think I'm supposed to ask that question." He chuckled and then kissed her forehead as he tugged her skirts back down. He'd never felt pleasure like he had just experienced with her. And that came with no more than a drop of her blood. It was her. Not her blood. Not her body. It was her. This enchanting, weather-born witch.

She was his.

He'd never thought of himself as selfish before, though he must be. It was a very good thing that he could never die, because he would surely be sentenced to hell for refusing to give her up. And he wouldn't, couldn't give her up after that. The fact that she seemed to need him just as badly was the only balm to his conscience.

"Well, are ye goin' ta?" Her words broke him from his thoughts.

Matthew looked down at the pretty witch still in his arms. "Am I going to do what?"

She bit her lip as though contemplating whether or not she should say whatever was on her mind. Then she sat a little straighter. "Will ye ask me already?" She turned, burying her head in his chest in embarrassment. "Ta be yer wife," she clarified, her voice muffled against his shoulder.

He didn't even bother to bite back the smile that graced his lips. The fires of hell would never lap at his feet. He'd adore her all the years they had together. "Rhiannon," he said slowly, nudging her to look at him. "Pray tell me you will be my wife."

"Soon?" Her hazel eyes glinted up at him.

"Why the rush, dearest?" They had the rest of her life, after all. She wiggled in his lap again, letting him know she felt his desire beneath her bottom.

"Because we could make a most lovely storm together. And ye're too honorable ta take from me without marryin' me first... And I'm worried about ye."

Matthew brushed his lips against hers. "No need to worry about vampyres, my beautiful witch. I've existed centuries and look no worse for the wear."

She regarded him with a dubious expression.

Perhaps he looked worse than he thought. She was right, of course. The faster they were properly married, the better. "I'm not acquainted with the Archbishop. I'm not certain we'd be granted a special license." Then there was the little matter that he hadn't stepped foot in a church in centuries, even before the Reformation.

Rhiannon's face fell. "I forgot we are in England. It would be so much easier if we just went ta the church and said our vows. Back home, the vicar, Mr. Crawford, wouldna be happy about another irregular ceremony, but I ken we could have convinced him ta forgo the banns. He'd bluster about it, but he'd perform the ceremony."

When she said *soon*, he had no idea she meant today. "Three weeks isn't so long to wait." Not when one had lived centuries, anyway.

Her brows drew together, and she ran her soft fingers along his jaw. "Ye doona expect me ta watch ye starve while we wait for the banns, do ye? I willna do it, Matthew."

He closed his eyes to block out her beseeching gaze. "We don't have a choice, dearest. I'm the lowest of cads to even take you as my wife. You deserve more than I can ever give you. But I will not dishonor you by taking your innocence or anything else before we're wed. I simply cannot."

She leaned her head against his shoulder. "Well, I simply willna wait three weeks. I willna watch ye suffer in pain."

"It appears, Rhiannon," he opened his eyes to make his point, "that we are at an impasse."

She sat up straight and grinned as though the most brilliant idea had occurred to her. "Perhaps Lord Eynsford kens the Archbishop. I'm certain he'd help us obtain a special license." She grinned unrepentantly at him.

If Eynsford knew what had transpired between them already, the Lycan would not only help, he'd *demand* a special license. Matthew frowned. He'd really rather not have anyone learn what had transpired between them. He wouldn't see Rhiannon's name tarnished, not even by those who loved her. She was so young, how could she understand… Exactly, how young was she? Matthew's mouth went dry. "Dearest, how old are you?"

"Almost twenty."

Damnation. He was a bloody cradle robber. He shook his head. "A special license wouldn't do us any good, Rhiannon. You're not of age. We'll need your father's permission."

Matthew's heart sank a bit. What if Mr. Sinclair wouldn't grant his blessing? They should probably refrain from mentioning the whole vampyre secret to the man.

"Stupid Sassenach laws," she grumbled under her breath.

Her frown only endeared her to him more. Matthew tipped her chin up with the crook of one finger. "He won't refuse me, will he?" Her answer mattered more than his next drop of blood.

Rhiannon shook her head. "If he can be bothered ta read a letter, he'll give ye his blessin'."

Matthew would make certain the man read the letter. He'd have someone hand-deliver it within the next two days, and that someone wouldn't leave Edinburgh without Mr. Sinclair's reply.

"It's better this way, lass. We'll send him a letter. We'll have the banns read by your Mr. Crawford in your home parish, and after your father sends his permission and the three weeks are up, you'll be mine 'til death do us part."

She thrust out her lower lip. "We could ride for the border."

Matthew sighed. Refusing her was one of the most difficult things he'd ever done. "And ruin your reputation in the process? No, dearest, I won't have it. We'll do things the right way." He rapped on the roof of the carriage and called for the driver to take them to Thorpe House.

"I doona want ta go back yet." Her hazel eyes beseeched him to reconsider their present course.

"Three weeks isn't so long, Rhiannon. Not when you've lived as long as I have." Matthew tugged her to his side and smiled when she rested her head on his shoulder. He felt complete with her there. Even without ever having partaken of her body, he knew he couldn't live without her. Not now.

"It feels like a lifetime," she complained softly.

And though he protested otherwise, Matthew silently agreed. Three weeks did seem like a lifetime away. "Say you'll do it for me, lass. I've never actually taken a wife, and I'd like to go about it the right way."

She cocked her head to see him better. "Ye've never had a wife before?"

"Until you, I never saw a reason to take one, not a real one anyway. Fictitious Countesses of Blodswell fill Debrett's, but they were never women of flesh and blood. Figments of my imagination to pull off my ruse."

She looked a bit relieved to hear his confession. "Ye could take me home with ye, and then I wouldna have ta worry over ye anymore."

"You believe I could abscond with you and no one would be the wiser?" He chuckled at the very thought. Eynsford's band of Lycans had their eyes on her, even if she wasn't aware, as did Alec MacQuarrie. Even if she wasn't being watched, Matthew's honor wouldn't allow him to do what she asked, no matter how much he wanted to.

"Ye will be all right? I mean, ye need ta feed, do ye no'?" She looked so concerned for him. He hadn't had anyone feel strongly about his needs or his health in a very long time. He chose to use the services at *Brysi* just for that reason, so that no one *would* care. It was a business transaction, his feeding. He traded pleasure for the life-giving essence.

"I will be fine." He tried to mollify her and hoped his words were true for his own sake.

Suddenly, Rhiannon sat forward, her eyebrows drawing together. "Will ye take from someone else ta tide ye over?" Was that jealously he saw in her pretty hazel orbs? What an unexpected boon that she didn't want to share him. He had no desire to be shared.

"Oh, lass, even if I could, I wouldn't," he admitted as he touched his forehead to hers and kissed her quickly to alleviate her worries.

"So, from now forward, I will be your only source for what ye need?" She looked extraordinarily pleased by that thought, and a quirky grin played around the corners of her mouth. She was so damned adorable.

"Is that all right with you? That I'll need you so much?" She wasn't a cow he'd keep in the pasture to provide his milk. She would be his wife. His everything.

"That ye'll need me?" She gasped and looked at him as though he'd grown two heads. "I think it will be nice ta be needed." She sighed out the last, leaning more heavily into his side. "I have never even been *wanted* before. Much less needed."

"I want you. And I need you. And I—" He gasped as pain erupted in the center of his chest.

She was on her knees before him within seconds, her hands clutching his. "What is it, Matthew?" she cried.

"I don't know," he grunted out, unable to avoid the pain in his chest. It pulsed and pounded.

"What can I do?" she asked. "Is it because ye need ta feed?" she cried out. She began to unbutton the bodice of her dress, drawing it away from her shoulder. "Take me, Matthew," she urged. "Please."

But before he could even respond to tell her that wasn't the problem, or he didn't *think* it was the problem, the coach rolled to a stop and the door was flung open. Then one masculine arm wrapped around Rhiannon and tugged her from the coach.

Matthew reached for her, but within seconds, she was gone. Bloody hell, what the devil was happening? He forced the pain to the back of his mind and did nothing more than grunt when two hands jerked him by his jacket lapels and pulled him bodily from the coach as well.

Thirteen

ONE FURIOUS LYCAN AND ONE LIVID VAMPYRE STOOD outside Thorpe House, sizing each other up. Rhiannon almost giggled at the absurdity of the situation. She took a step toward Matthew but then realized Alec MacQuarrie was holding her arm in a vicelike grip. So *his* hands had hauled her from the coach? No one would ever believe that MacQuarrie and the Marquess of Eynsford would work together. How annoying to have them united in thwarting her.

She raised one finger and pointed it at Alec. Light flared from her fingertips, barely touching him as she warned him with a bolt of energy. He jumped back, releasing her arm.

"If you ever grab her like that again, you won't have to worry about where you'll get your next meal. Because you will find yourself with a wooden stake through your chest, Alec," Matthew said quietly, but they all heard him, even her, when she caught his mumble on a quick breeze and brought it to her ear.

Alec picked at a piece of lint on his sleeve, avoiding

his maker's scolding glance completely. But he almost looked chagrined.

"Ye need no' worry, for he might find himself blown by the wind to the next county if he ever takes it upon himself ta manhandle me again," Rhiannon clarified loudly. Then she turned her attention to the infuriating marquess. "And what has come over ye, Dashiel Thorpe?"

But Eynsford paid her no heed; his amber eyes remained trained on Matthew. "March right up the steps, Rhiannon. I'll deal with you in a minute."

She gasped at his tone. Did he think he could speak to her in such a fashion?

"And straighten your dress while you're at it," the marquess ordered as though she was one of his unruly brothers.

Rhiannon rose to her fullest height, prepared to tell him just that, when she realized her dress hung open at the shoulder, where she'd bared it for Matthew when he was in distress.

Alec reached up one hand as though to cover her shoulder. He obviously was not thinking about his actions, because he braced himself when a blast of wind nearly knocked him from his feet. "I was helping!" he protested loudly. He looked so put out that, if he'd been a two-year-old, she'd have expected him to stomp his feet.

"Keep your hands to yourself," Matthew warned quietly. "Are you all right, Rhiannon?" he asked again, his eyes focused on Eynsford.

"Of course, I'm all right! I was perfectly fine until these two big oafs who canna even stand the sight of each other took it upon themselves to rip me from your coach."

"Rhiannon!" Eynsford growled. "In. The. House."

Alec bent and said quietly in her ear, "We heard you ask him to take you, lass." He said it with a look of sorrow on his face, as though someone had stolen the last crumpet at teatime.

"Is that all?" she whispered back to him, as though the other supernatural beings couldn't hear their hushed conversation.

"Well, we heard a lot of grunting from Blodswell first and then your offer," Alec returned softly.

"And just what are ye doin' here anyway? Ye despise Eynsford and yet ye banded together with him over *this*?"

Alec winced, and Rhi almost felt sorry for him. "We were concerned for you. I warned you to stay away from Blodswell."

Rhi's eyes flashed from Alec to Eynsford and back. Thunder rumbled over head. Did they think she was a featherbrained child who couldn't make her own decisions? "Ye both were worried for my virtue?"

They nodded in unison, though Eynsford still had his eyes leveled on Matthew. Much ado about nothing, all of it. She couldn't *give* her virtue to the earl, if she begged him to take it from her. "Well, ye have no need ta worry about me. Lord Blodswell is the most noble of men." That was dashed inconvenient at the moment. They should have fled London and ridden straight for Gretna Green. She wasn't part of London society. What did she care what they thought about her? She just wanted to take care of Matthew, and now she had Alec and Eynsford to deal with instead. "Too noble," she grumbled to herself.

Eynsford raised his brows in question at Blodswell. Or jest. Rhi wasn't certain which it was. "Too noble, are you?"

Matthew's dark eyes shot toward Rhiannon. "Perhaps it would be best, dearest, if you did go in the house."

She glared back at him. She wasn't about to leave. This was about *her* after all. "And let the three of ye pummel each other in the name of my virtue? I think no'." She squared her shoulders. "This has gone on quite long enough. Alec MacQuarrie, ye're a dear friend, and I appreciate yer concern; but there's no need for it. And as for ye, Dashiel Thorpe, if ye harm one hair on my fiancé's head, I'll make sure Cait has ye sleepin' in a doghouse for a fortnight or longer."

"Did you say 'fiancé,' Rhi?" Alec's face contorted with unveiled rage.

Thunder crashed in the sky, which had quickly turned to gray. Oh, dear. She was getting even angrier than she'd first thought. How dare they behave as though they knew what was best for her? She stomped her foot, and lightning struck nearby with a loud clap of thunder immediately following. At least it wasn't raining. She'd be hanged before she'd cry in front of these men.

"Aye, my fiancé, and ye owe him an apology. Both of ye." She blasted the supernatural meddlers with a gust of wind in warning.

"Rhiannon, this isn't necessary," Matthew protested. "They had your best interest at heart, I'm sure." He turned back to Eynsford. "As you can see, Miss Sinclair is perfectly fine. No harm done." But he still rubbed at his chest. He still wasn't himself.

Something was most definitely *wrong*. She just wished she knew what. He had been much too quiet during this whole episode. He was in pain. She could see it in his eyes, and he'd just been jerked from a coach by a wild Lycan and his blood-sucking lackey. That was hardly conducive to Matthew's health.

She started toward her vampyre. He still looked too pale by half. "What can I do, Matthew?"

"You can get your little witchy derrière inside my house," Eynsford barked.

The sky darkened even more as she brushed past the marquess. "I am no' above blastin' ye with a bolt of lightnin', Lord Eynsford." Rhi reached Matthew and tenderly touched his jaw. "Join me in the parlor?"

He shook his head. "I have a letter to write to your father." He glanced over his shoulder at Alec. "Among other things. I'll call on you first thing in the morning."

"Promise?" She knew his logic was sound, but she hated having to wait until the next morning to see him. Still, she had need of Cait's advice.

"On my honor."

Rhi cast an indignant look at Eynsford as she started up the steps of Thorpe House. Then she shot one last blast of wind toward Matthew and the marquess, which brought their quietly spoken words to her ear. "Pardon me, Blodswell," Eynsford growled. "But you *smell* like you did more than ride in your carriage with the lass."

Lycans could smell... *that*? She'd die of embarrassment. She'd never be able to look Eynsford in the eyes again. Who would have thought *that* had a scent, for heaven's sake?

"We'll be married as soon as the banns are read."

"See that you are."

The front door opened, and Price held it wide for her to enter. "Miss Sinclair," the old butler intoned. "Lady Eynsford would like for you to join her in her private study." Then the ancient man closed the front door, shutting out the conversation of the vampyres and Lycan.

Rhiannon sighed. "Thank ye, Price." She did need Cait's advice, but she didn't appreciate being summoned. Most likely the seer had already seen the events of the afternoon, and Rhi would really rather not discuss the particulars. What had transpired between Rhiannon and Matthew was private, even from the all-seeing eyes of a clairvoyant. Or it should be, at any rate.

Still, there was no getting away from Cait's summons. Her friend would find her sooner or later, and Rhi would prefer not to stoke Caitrin's ire. The all-seeing witch didn't possess any powers that could do harm, but she could sulk like a queen and make everyone around her completely miserable. It was generally better to just do whatever Caitrin asked. So, Rhiannon found her way to the Seer's private study that was just across the hall from her husband's.

At her entrance, Cait looked up from her desk and dropped her quill beside a sheath of foolscap. "Ah, there ye are." Then she sprinkled a bit of sand on the paper. "Ye wanted ta see me?"

Cait rose from behind her dainty Queen Anne desk and grinned. "Have ye set a date?"

Rhi frowned at her friend. "Ye kent what would happen when ye abandoned me on Bond Street, did ye no'?"

Cait shrugged unrepentantly. "Aye. But ye dinna ken, and that's all that matters. Now tell me, Rhi, are ye happy?" She towed Rhiannon to a small, golden brocade settee in the far corner and then pulled Rhi down beside her.

Happy wasn't quite the word. She was *anxious* to have Matthew all to herself, to look across him at an altar and become his wife. At the same time she was *concerned* about his well-being. He certainly didn't look like himself, not like the debonair gentleman she'd met in Hyde Park in the middle of her storm. And then there was the episode of him clutching his heart in the carriage and the expression of agonizing pain he had worn in that terrifying instant.

"Blaire said vampyres are the strongest of creatures."

Cait giggled. "Ye better no' let a Lycan hear ye say such a thing. They can be very sensitive."

But Lycans weren't immortal, were they? No, vampyres were most definitely stronger. "I'm worried about Matthew. He seems as though he's in pain. And he needs ta feed, and…"

"Ye'd like ta be his meal."

Rhiannon was certain she'd never blushed so fiercely if the warmth of her cheeks was any indication. "I-I just want him ta be all right."

Cait's icy blue eyes danced. "That's no' all ye want, but I'll let ye leave it at that for now."

"It doesna matter what I want. He willna let me help him." Rhiannon balled her hands into tight fists.

"And ye'll just let him make that decision, will ye? Hmm. That doesna sound like the Rhiannon Sinclair I've kent my whole life."

Rhi glared at her sister witch. "Well, what am I supposed ta do? Barge on over ta his home, bash my way in, and force my blood on him? I'm no' Blaire, ye ken."

Cait's eyes settled on her lap, and if someone didn't know her, they might have mistaken the marchioness as being demure. "I think, Rhi, that ye should do whatever is in yer heart. It's the best advice I can give."

The way her friend said the words sent a shiver of fear down Rhi's back. "Ye ken what will happen. Tell me, Cait."

Her friend simply shook her head, still not meeting her eyes. "Ye ken I canna tell ye."

Never before this moment had Rhi so hated the rules that went along with Cait's powers. If Rhi had just the tiniest of clues about what the future had in store, she would be able to make decisions so much easier.

"Cait," she began imploringly.

But her friend's lips tightened stubbornly. "I told ye ta follow yer heart, Rhi. I canna say more than that."

The wind rushed from Rhi's lungs. That was no help at all. Her heart told her to use every ounce of the seductive powers she possessed to make Matthew take whatever amount of her blood he needed. Her heart told her to convince her vampyre to race for the Scottish border and be done with all of this

English nonsense. Her heart told her that she had very little time.

✎

Scots were notorious for blustering. Matthew had known more than a few over his lifetimes. But Alec MacQuarrie might be the very worst blusterer of his countrymen. As the two of them had sat across the coach from each other, the Scot had done everything but pull the hair from his own head.

"I know you're my mentor, my maker, or whatever you want to call yourself, and you're supposed to be guiding me along this thorny path, but that's complete bollocks! I asked one thing of you. Just one. And could my one measly wish be granted by the great and legendary Sir Matthew Halkett? Apparently not. Apparently it was too much to ask you to keep your damned teeth off Rhiannon.

"Dozens of girls line the halls of *Brysi* waiting for your illustrious return. You could have any number of them or all of them for as long as you want. But that wasn't enough, was it? No, you had to go and do the *one* thing I asked you not to.

"Even then you couldn't stop there, could you? Oh, no! You had to get yourself betrothed to the lass. So her entire life will be ruined." He slammed his fist against the side of the coach.

"Do watch your strength," Matthew warned. "One more hit like that, and the whole conveyance might crumble to splinters."

"Would you prefer I hit you instead?"

"You are more than welcome to give it a try,

Alec; but I've been winning fights longer than you've been alive."

"How *could* you?" the Scot finally asked, and it sounded as though the question tore away at part of his soul.

Matthew took the momentary silence to calmly reply, even though deep down he agreed with most of the Scot's assessment of the situation. "I hardly think marrying me will ruin her life."

Alec glared at him. "Then you'd be wrong."

Matthew frowned at his protégé. "Hypocrisy does not look good on you, Alec."

"Me?" the Scot sputtered.

"Yes, you. You're so convinced I'll ruin Rhiannon's life, and yet you drool over Eynsford's wife like a lovesick schoolboy. If the marquess was to meet with an unfortunate and untimely end, can you honestly tell me you wouldn't knock down the door at Thorpe House and abscond with the lass?"

Alec's jaw tightened. "I would never subject Cait to what I've become."

Until now, Matthew had never thought himself willing to subject a woman to what he was, either. "You might feel differently if it was only *her* blood you could drink, my friend."

"I beg your pardon."

"I can't feed," Matthew admitted, watching his charge closely. "My fangs won't distend for anyone but Rhiannon. Nothing else tastes right. Not the detestable sheep's blood you gave me. Not the fresh human blood Callista forced on me. But just one drop of Rhiannon's blood is like the sweetest heaven I've ever experienced."

"Ever?" Alec narrowed his eyes on Matthew. "In your 650 years, Rhi's blood is the best you've ever tasted?"

"I find it's hard to remember anyone else." Matthew leaned back against the squabs. "Put your fears aside, Alec. I will not ruin her life. We have a bond, a connection I can't explain. I'll make certain her whole life is filled with nothing but joy."

"And how long will her life be?" Alec folded his arms across his chest. "Will you turn her so the two of you can enjoy eternity together?"

The thought of Alec's suggestion lifted Matthew's soul tenfold. How wonderful to share *forever* with Rhiannon. But he would never ask that of her. This sort of life wasn't for the meek. "You know I live by a code. You were dying, so I saved you. I don't make a habit of turning perfectly healthy people into vampyres."

Alec's frown deepened. "You said you saw Callista?"

Matthew nodded.

"You must have truly been worried. What did she say about all of this?"

Matthew would rather not repeat all of what his maker had said. Her words would most likely set Alec off once again. "She suggested I marry Rhiannon."

Alec snorted. "So you're simply following her directive."

"I've never been accused of following Callista's directive before. No, I'm doing what society and decency dictates, Alec. Rhiannon Sinclair wants to be my wife. I need her to survive. I would never take from her unless we were truly married."

"Noble to the last."

"The last isn't upon us yet. Now I could use your advice."

"Mine?" True surprise rang out from Alec's voice.

"I need to have a letter delivered to Mr. Sinclair asking for his daughter's hand. I don't know the first thing about the man, but you do. Suggestions are welcome."

Alec snorted. "If you could convince Dougal Sinclair to give a damn, it would be a miracle."

Matthew's mouth fell open. He'd never heard Alec say such a thing about anyone… Well, about anyone who wasn't the Marquess of Eynsford, in any event.

The Scot must have noted his surprise, because Alec hastened to explain. "I don't believe him to be a villain, and I think he *does* love his daughters. At least he used to. He just seems to have forgotten they exist. When his wife died, I think most of Dougal Sinclair went with her. To say he was neglectful would be a compliment."

Matthew stared at his friend. Rhiannon had been neglected? That explained so much about her. Why she seem so independent at times, yet still so starved for attention. What was it she'd said that very afternoon? She'd never been wanted before, much less needed. The thought of his sweet witch having been ignored sent a jolt of pain where his heart used to be.

"Poor Rhiannon," he muttered.

Alec shrugged. "So if you're asking what to put in your letter, a simple, 'I'd like your permission to marry Rhiannon. Please have the banns read this coming Sunday' should suffice."

"That's it?"

"You'd probably want to have your man wait for a reply, perhaps even pay the good vicar, Mr. Crawford, a visit as well to ensure everything is handled appropriately. Sinclair is a bit absentminded. He might not remember to send a reply if you don't have someone looming over him to demand action and a response."

"In that case, I should probably go myself."

"I would if I were you." Alec nodded tightly. "But if you hurt her, I'll…"

Matthew speared him with a glare. "I'm relieved to know you think so highly of me."

"Considering my wishes in regards to your current situation, my opinion isn't what it once was."

Matthew inclined his head. "I do hope, Alec, that you never find yourself in *my* situation. It is so difficult being lofty when your pedestal crumbles to ash."

Fourteen

"IF YE TUG ON THE BODICE OF THAT GOWN ONE MORE time, ye will find yerself with a torn neckline, Rhiannon Sinclair," Cait hissed as they walked out of her chambers. "There's no magical spell that will give the inches ye think ye're lackin'."

"I would argue that the good lady is not lacking a thing," Lord Radbourne said drolly as he looked up at them from the bottom of the stairs. They cut a dashing profile, the viscount and Cait's marquess. Rhiannon wasn't certain how anyone missed that they were brothers. But, evidently, society was either blind or chose to overlook it.

"You look lovely, sweetheart," Lord Radbourne said as he tucked Rhi's hand into his elbow and smiled down at her. "And thank you for allowing me to escort you to the Duchess of Hythe's soiree."

"Thank ye for offerin'. I have no idea what could be keepin' Matthew." She hadn't seen him since their last awkward parting, when they'd both been forcibly ripped from the coach by an overly protective vampyreling and a wolf in gentleman's clothing.

"Whatever it is, it must be important," Archer tossed in. "Or else the man is just a fool for leaving you to your own devices."

Cait shot Eynsford a glare. "Do ye ken where he is, Dash?"

Eynsford shrugged but refused to meet her eyes. "I'm certain I don't care where he is," he said enigmatically.

"I'm worried about him is all," Rhiannon said quietly.

"No need ta be worried, Rhi," Cait soothed. "He has been alive a very long time. He kens how ta take care of himself." She turned to her husband. "Right, Dash?"

"Mmm-hmm," the marquess said noncommittally.

"I'm just surprised he offered ta escort ye and then dinna bother ta explain."

"He did send a note, Cait," Eynsford reminded them both. "He was unavoidably detained."

"By whom?" Rhiannon asked.

"It's probably not a *whom*. It's probably a *what*." Dashiel took Cait's hand and started for the door. Radbourne handed Rhi inside the coach gallantly and then settled in beside her, with Cait and Eynsford across from them.

"You're just being generous by claiming that, Dashiel," Radbourne scolded playfully. "It very well may be a *whom*. Don't they need all the *whoms* they can get to avoid that dreaded thirst?"

"I'm fairly certain it doesn't work like that," Eynsford grunted, shooting a glare at his brother.

"Do you plan to let him bite you?" Radbourne asked candidly of Rhiannon.

Cait gasped from across the coach. "That is none of

yer business, Archer Hadley!" She pressed her hand to her forehead. "If I must be punished for my misdeeds, why must it be in the form of three Lycans who cannot control their tongues?" she breathed.

Radbourne shrugged innocently. "Don't tell me you're not curious, too." He grinned down at Rhiannon.

"Doona judge him," Rhi said softly. "Ye doona ken him well enough ta judge him." She stared out the window at the busy road they traveled.

"I wasn't judging. I was simply curious." He took a deep breath and then forged ahead. "It's not as though we Lycans don't have some odd mating rituals of our own."

They did? Like what? Rhi turned her attention back to the other occupants inside the coach.

Radbourne winced as Eynsford kicked him in the shin. Hard. "Behave," he said. Just one word. Behave. Then the viscount closed his lips. Tightly.

Rhiannon tugged at the bodice of her gown again and sighed deeply. She would have cried off on the night's festivities if not for the fact that Ginny would be there. Rhi desperately needed to talk to Ginny, to find out how she was doing. None of her correspondence to her aunt's house had received a reply. Not a single letter. Not a word.

Matthew was supposed to let her borrow some of his respectability, but how could he if he wasn't even present?

"Ye think ye'll be all right tonight, Rhi?" Cait asked quietly as the coach stopped and the men stepped out. "If ye feel like yer emotions will be goin' off at odd times, tell me and we can take our leave early. I'll plead a headache. It's no' so far from the truth in these settings."

That situation was highly probable. All the witches were well aware that Cait was tormented by the futures of strangers when she was surrounded by a number of people like she would be at the soiree. Eynsford was the only one who could quiet her world, but he couldn't keep his hands on her every moment.

"I'll be sure ta tell ye if I feel the sudden urge ta…" she almost said, *Fill the punch bowl with hail*, but she realized just in time that Lord Radbourne was at her side. "Flee," she said instead.

Cait giggled. "Please do."

Radbourne led Rhiannon inside and suffered through introductions with her. He was charming and social, but he wasn't Matthew. "If ye would like ta go ta the card room, Archer, ye need no' worry about abandonin' me. I see my sister right over there," she told him.

"If you're certain," Radbourne remarked as his eyes found a small parlor off the edge of the ballroom.

"No faro," Eynsford warned as his brother started in the opposite direction.

Radbourne made no indication that he'd heard his brother's words. However, Rhiannon didn't have time to think upon any of that. She'd caught Ginny's attention, and her sister was waving madly, motioning for Rhi to come her way. But before she could even take one step in the girl's direction, Aunt Greer took her sister in hand and tugged her to her side. Ginny winced at the woman's grip.

Before she could even think, Rhiannon raised her finger to send a spark toward the woman. But just before she could fling it, Eynsford's hand closed around her finger. "Don't even think about it," he warned.

"Unhand me," Rhiannon whispered.

"I will, as soon as you promise not to shock the stockings off that woman. Save it for a later date." He made it look as though he was simply taking her hand to lead her about the room.

Rhiannon nodded. "I'll hold it in."

"Don't hold it in, lass. You'll explode. Just make a conscious choice when it's a good time to use it." He raised an eyebrow at her.

She nodded again. He released her hand and let her move toward Ginny.

"Call if you need anything, Rhiannon," he warned.

That was about as probable as the Duchess of Hythe flipping her skirts up for her butler. It might be nice in theory, but it most likely would never happen.

The young woman playing the pianoforte had the worst musical abilities of any young lady in all of Britain, Rhiannon thought. Mating cats carried a more melodic tune, and Rhi winced as the girl hit another sour note. Her aunt had always tried to get her to learn the finer arts like embroidery, the piano, and other social graces, but Rhiannon had failed miserably. Evidently, her lack of upbringing carried over. Because she was not above eavesdropping, she suddenly found as she walked up behind a potted palm that rested directly behind her aunt and her brood of marriage-minded mamas.

"Her father is fairly plump in the pockets," Aunt Greer said to the group. "Not that you can tell it by the other daughter, Rhiannon, of course. That gel never was one for the finer things in life. She's not made to marry. I can't particularly see it. Ginessa, on the other hand, is a dear girl with a lot of potential. Why, I have only just begun to work with her and look how far she has come. She's nothing at all like her sister."

Rhiannon swallowed hard. How dare her aunt discuss such private matters?

Her aunt continued as the other women listened on. "Ginessa will marry to better herself. I've no doubt of it. She'll never be fooled by a handsome face. A woman can love a rich man as easily as she can love a poor one, and she can have a much better time doing it." She drew in a deep breath and continued. "Heaven forbid, but if my Harry should pass, I'd marry for money the next time."

Rhiannon snorted. She thought Aunt Greer had married for money the *last* time. It was too bad for her that her husband kept such a tight rein on the purse strings. Her aunt's only hope at happiness was getting a piece of Ginny's dowry to see her through her husband's tightfistedness. Rhiannon was well aware of that fact.

Some noncommittal comments came from the small circle of friends.

"No man has ever been lured to the altar by competent needlework."

Rhiannon looked through the palm fronds to her sister, who sat expressionless beside her aunt, obviously miserable.

Aunt Greer leaned over to whisper in Ginny's ear. Rhiannon caught the words and brought them to where she could hear them as well. "Do you think you could draw Mr. Finchley out onto the balcony?"

"Why on earth would I want ta do that?" Ginny returned.

"If you can get yourself compromised, this would be so much easier," her aunt hissed. "He's an honorable man. Just put yourself in his path and plead heat exhaustion. He doesn't have a title, but he has more blunt than half of Yorkshire. You could do worse."

Ginny rolled her eyes and then yelped as Aunt Greer pinched her on the back of the arm. Rhiannon would shake the earth if that woman hurt her sister. Her aunt wouldn't even have warnings of the winds before they knocked her coiffure out of place.

The Duchess of Hythe ambled into their circle and dropped heavily into a chair. "You haven't seen the Earl of Blodswell about, have you?" she asked absently.

"He is supposed to be escorting that niece of mine," Aunt Greer said. "But I just saw her on the arm of Viscount Radbourne as she arrived." She lowered her voice to a conciliatory whisper. "I had a feeling it wouldn't be long before the earl dropped her."

The duchess' eyes narrowed at Aunt Greer, but she didn't speak. Yet another sour-faced woman did. She scrunched up her nose and said dramatically, "In all honesty, I am still a bit in shock over the Pickerings' ball."

"As am I," Aunt Greer sighed. "I have tried so hard through the years to be a guiding force in that child's life." She brushed at a fake tear. "But there's only so much one can do."

"The Earl of Blodswell." The sour-faced woman

sighed as she said Matthew's name. "I would love to make a match like that for my daughter. So handsome and so noble."

If she only knew how noble.

"Indeed," her aunt snipped out. "It's quite unfortunate he was so taken with Rhiannon."

"Unfortunate?" the duchess chimed in. "In what way is it unfortunate?" Oh dear, the older woman's eyes glittered with mirth.

"Of course, by now, the girl has done something to turn his attentions from her. It was only a matter of time." Her aunt clucked her tongue. Rhiannon had heard that cluck her whole life. It was a harbinger of remorse, when that tongue clucked.

"I heard he called on Miss Sinclair and took her on a ride though Hyde Park. Did you know?" the sour-faced woman asked.

Aunt Greer nodded tightly. She looked none too pleased about the fact.

"I don't believe there is a more fortunate girl in all of Mayfair. However did she capture his attention?"

With lightning bolts and thunder, actually. Rhiannon's heart grew heavier as she listened.

Aunt Greer avoided the woman's question completely. "Mr. Finchley seemed quite taken with my dear Ginessa."

An old, slender woman scoffed. "Mr. Finchley is inconsequential."

Inconsequential? They spoke of men as though they were pieces on a chessboard.

"He's abominable," added another matron with a shudder. "The stories I've heard."

"Quite," agreed the slender woman. "And they are not fit for repeating, Minerva."

The sour-faced woman leaned closer to Aunt Greer. "Did you see Lord Blodswell in the park?"

Ginny sat forward in her seat. "We did, Lady Higgenbottom. He has a very nice curricle."

"Your sister was his guest." The sour-faced Lady Higgenbottom turned her full attention on Ginny, like a hawk about to snatch a baby bunny from its burrow. "Has he called upon *you* at all, Miss Ginessa?"

"Why on earth would he do that when he has the oldest daughter's attention?" the Duchess of Hythe chimed in. "Miss Ginessa will have her season, I'm certain. But the oldest girl, that one is a diamond of the first water. She'll make a brilliant match this year. I'd wager on it."

Tears pricked at the backs of Rhiannon's eyelids. No one ever took up for her. Aside from her coven sisters, that is.

Aunt Greer's face reddened as the duchess continued. "I do like that girl. She has quite the spine. Blodswell is in possession of one of the finest estates in Derbyshire. His fortune is unparalleled. Rhiannon Sinclair will fit quite nicely into his life."

"Well, before you know it, he'll have turned his attention from Rhiannon," Aunt Greer said waspishly. "You can mark my words."

"I sincerely doubt that," the duchess intoned, looking down her nose at Aunt Greer without even getting up. "He has never attended a single event. Not until the Pickerings' ball. He does not typically take ladies for rides in the park. And he certainly does *not* accept invitations to soirees such as mine. Yet your oldest niece seems to have enticed him to do all of that. You should be proud of that girl. Very proud."

Aunt Greer sputtered. She didn't even like Rhiannon. Certainly she wouldn't feel any pride over Matthew showing an interest in her older niece. In fact, Rhiannon was quite certain she detested the very idea.

"You do know it's ill mannered to stand behind the potted palms and listen to other people's conversations, don't you?" a voice asked from beside her. Rhiannon jumped. Radbourne simply crossed his arms and looked down at her.

"I thought you were off to the card room," Rhiannon whispered to him.

"It appears as though there's much more fun to be had in the foliage." Radbourne shrugged. "I think I'll stay here with you. I like listening to simple women get their just deserts from old stalwarts like the Duchess of Hythe. It makes my heart sing."

Rhiannon couldn't keep the corners of her lips from twitching up in a grin. Radbourne's droll sense of humor was a bit contagious. "If the duchess would just shove Aunt Greer in a cupboard and keep her there the rest of the night, this soiree could be salvageable," Rhiannon said, trying not to giggle.

"There are two young Lycan gentlemen who have been known to accomplish such feats," Radbourne teased, nodding toward his brothers, who stood talking with other men across the room. "And I hear they work cheaply."

"Did they sneak in?" Cait would be appalled since none of the Hadley men had actually been invited.

"They've crashed parties with security much tighter than Hythe's."

"And they work cheaply, ye say? I wonder how much they would charge ta stash my aunt away." She smiled. She couldn't help it. The very idea was ludicrous.

"They might do it for the beauty of that smile. They have been motivated by less." He held his hand out to her. "Come along. Let's get you out of the foliage. This is not where you belong, Rhiannon." He raised his eyebrows at her.

"Ye have no idea where I belong." If he knew what she was, he might not even want to speak to her, just like Aunt Greer. Just like her father.

"I understand more than you think," he said, as he put her hand in the crook of his elbow and tugged hard enough to get her moving. "Let me get you some punch, sweetheart."

Rhiannon stared up Radbourne. "What do ye ken about Mr. Finchley? Is there somethin' dreadful about him?"

"Harold Finchley?" the viscount frowned. "He hasn't approached you, has he?"

"No, but my sister..." she started to explain.

Radbourne shook his head. "Tell her to stay far away from the man."

"What is it about him?"

"You're not going to stop asking until I tell you, are you?"

Rhiannon shook her head. "I need ta ken."

"Very well," Radbourne sighed. "From time to time, he has kept many a mistress." He held up his hand in defense. "Not that I judge the man for that.

I've been known to dally myself. But Finchley has a reputation for not treating the women well."

"Doesna treat them well? Ye mean he doesna buy them baubles or expensive clothes?" After all, that's what mistresses wanted, wasn't it? Certainly, whatever Mr. Finchley did couldn't be worse than that. Her aunt couldn't possibly want to shackle Ginny with someone worse than that, could she?

"I mean," the viscount lowered his voice to a near whisper, "he's been known to hurt them, to misuse them. I'd rather not say any more."

Rhiannon agreed with a nod of her head. "I understand." And she did. Queasiness settled in her stomach. "I doona think I want any punch, Archer."

He agreed with an incline of his head. "Well, if I return you to Dash frowning, he'll have my head. Why don't you dance with me, Rhiannon?"

Rhi allowed him to tug her toward the middle of the room where other couples were just lining up across from each other for the next set.

"This should make you smile again. I dare you to frown during a quadrille." Radbourne winked at her.

Rhiannon giggled. "Do ye think ta tease me out of my mood?"

He waggled his brow dramatically. "If that doesn't work, I'll have to come up with something else."

She was of the opinion that he meant every word he said, which was a little intimidating. As they joined the other couples on the dance floor, Rhi realized that two of the men in their set were Wes and Gray Hadley. She shook her head.

"Ye ken, Cait is no' goin' ta be happy that they

crashed the soiree. She's tryin' terribly hard ta fit in here in London."

Radbourne chuckled. "Cait worries for no reason. She's married to a powerful man, and though Dash is less daunting than the late marquess, the name Eynsford still has the power to strike fear in most hearts. Half the people in this room are probably terrified of her. The other half are terrified of the duchess."

"Oh, and which one are *ye* terrified of?"

Radbourne glanced around the room as though making sure no one could overhear him. "Both."

The idea was absurd, and Rhi couldn't help but laugh. "I doona believe that for a moment."

"No?" He smiled slowly at her. "Her Grace has no need for weapons as she possesses the sharpest tongue in all of London."

"And Cait?"

"Knows my mother." He shuddered dramatically.

Just then, a violin struck the opening chord of the dance, and Radbourne bowed before Rhiannon. Then there was no more time for talking. The jaunty song did make it difficult to frown. In turn, as they traded partners, she danced with each of the Hadley men and a shy Welsh earl who couldn't quite meet her eyes.

As soon as the quadrille came to an end, Radbourne led Rhiannon toward the refreshment table, but they had to stop in their tracks when the Duchess of Hythe planted herself in their path. "Miss Sinclair and…" She stopped and lifted a quizzing glass to her eye. "Radbourne, is it?" She sounded none too pleased at the recognition. "I don't recall your name making my guest list." She peered over their shoulders and narrowed her eyes. "Nor those of your unruly brothers."

Rhiannon took a slight step forward. "Lord Radbourne offered ta accompany me this evenin', Yer Grace."

The old woman's icy blue eyes refocused on Rhiannon. "And where exactly is the Earl of Blodswell?"

Rhiannon had no idea where the Earl of Blodswell was exactly, so she shook her head. "Detained."

"Detained?" the duchess frowned.

"Out of town, I believe."

"My dear girl, we should have a conversation." The old woman reached for Rhiannon's arm while her eyes made a dismissive trail across Lord Radbourne. "You are not needed, my lord. You and your unruly brood may stay for now but don't make me regret my generosity."

"Thank you, Your Grace," Radbourne muttered with none of his usual mirth.

An instant later, the duchess, moving much quicker than Rhiannon would have given her credit for, towed Rhi down a long, winding corridor. "There are too many ears in there."

Too many ears? What in the world did the woman want to say to her?

They finally stopped at a small study, and the duchess waived Rhiannon in before her. "Sit, sit," the woman directed.

Rhiannon sat in an overstuffed leather chair. "I confess, ye have me a bit worried."

The duchess paced a small path in front of the

grate. "Do you know who Lord Blodswell *really* is, Miss Sinclair?"

Rhiannon could do nothing but gape at the old woman. Certainly, the *duchess* didn't really know who Matthew was. "I-I beg yer pardon."

The woman's icy eyes twinkled. "I can see that you do."

Fifteen

MATTHEW WINCED AS HE STEPPED OVER ALEC MacQuarrie's threshold. He generally was impervious to temperature, but the Edinburgh air was particularly frigid and he couldn't hold back a shiver.

"S-sir," MacQuarrie's stoic butler stammered, "we were no' expectin' ye." He held the door wide for the two gentlemen to enter.

Alec waved the man off. "Please start a fire roaring in my study, Gibson. And have a room prepared for Lord Blodswell."

"Of course, sir." The butler scampered off in the direction Alec had indicated.

Matthew's next step was a bit wobbly, and he soon found himself leaning on his protégé's arm for support. "Why the devil you felt it was necessary to make the trip, Matt, I'll never understand," the Scot complained. "You can barely walk, let alone run."

Matthew would rather not acknowledge the truth in Alec's words, so he grunted instead of actually speaking.

Alec narrowed his black eyes. "You're not in any condition to even *see* Dougal Sinclair. He's more than a bit self-absorbed, but even *he* would know something was wrong with you. When did you last feed?"

Matthew couldn't even remember. He shrugged. "I had the merest of drops from Rhiannon."

"And before that?" Alec barked.

"Something you gave me. Something Callista gave me. I'm not certain."

Alec growled low in his throat as he towed Matthew down the corridor toward a room from which a warm glow seemed to emanate. "You'll be the death of me."

"I already was," Matthew replied dryly.

"Not amusing."

The two of them entered the study that radiated warmth. Alec led him to a large leather chair that was soft with wear, and Matthew closed his eyes, letting the heated air wash over him.

"All I've got here is some whiskey," Alec complained. "Let me find *something* for you to drink."

"No!" Matthew's eyes shot open. "I'll be all right. Just give me a moment."

Alec frowned. "You look the furthest thing from all right, my friend. I'm perfectly capable of acquiring someone for you."

That fact, Matthew didn't doubt. Ever since Alec had been reborn, he had taken to the vampyre lifestyle with gusto. Most of their kind were charismatic, but Alec had taken his charisma to a whole new level. "I told Rhiannon I wouldn't take from anyone else."

His friend's mouth fell open. "What a foolish thing to have said. Have you looked in the mirror, Matt? You need blood."

"Just give me a moment to recover from the journey, and you can take me to Mr. Sinclair's home." Matthew closed his eyes again, drawing all of his energy together.

Alec grumbled unintelligibly, more grunts and groans than actual words, and then he stalked from the room. Matthew didn't expect him to understand. In fact, he had a hard time understanding the situation himself. What he did know was that nothing satisfied him the way Rhiannon Sinclair did.

He'd be fine. He just needed to collect his power and get a tiny bit of rest, and he'd be fine.

❦

Alec stalked into the corridor and then up the staircase to his chambers, which hadn't been occupied in months. He'd probably given poor Gibson an apoplexy by showing up unannounced, but he hadn't had much of a choice, not with Matthew's condition. Alec was sadly inept to handle this situation, which was more than a little frustrating. But he hadn't been a vampyre long enough to know what to do for Matthew.

He had no idea how to make this situation any better, especially if the damned knight wouldn't even take sustenance. He'd originally come along on this little excursion as an emissary of sorts, to introduce Matthew to Dougal Sinclair. Now he wasn't sure if it was a miracle that he'd come to ensure his maker's safe return or a hindrance, as he had no idea *how* to ensure his maker's safe return.

After pacing the length of his chambers several

times, Alec finally dropped onto his four-poster and closed his eyes. How could he get Matthew to partake of the life-giving elixir that he needed so badly?

A scratch sounded at his door.

"Come," Alec called, as he lifted up on his elbows.

Gibson pushed the door open and stepped over the threshold. "Mr. MacQuarrie," his butler began, his expression more stoic than normal. "I've put Lord Benjamin in the green parlor."

Alec scratched his head. *Benjamin Westfield?* Good God! Speaking to Ben Westfield was the very last thing he wanted to do. Now or ever. He'd successfully avoided his oldest friend ever since he'd been reborn because he had no idea how to explain his current situation. "I'm not at home, Gibson."

The butler shuffled his feet nervously. "Well, sir, the problem with that is, I sent for his lordship after ye arrived."

"Why the devil would you do that?" Alec bounded off the bed and was before his servant in the blink of an eye.

Gibson did, in fact, blink at him, as though trying to figure out how Alec had moved so quickly. "I–I, well, Lord Benjamin asked me ta contact him if ye were ta return home."

Alec frowned at his butler. "The last time I checked, Gibson, you work for me, not Westfield." In fact, Gibson had never liked Ben and had taken special pleasure in tormenting the Englishman in the past.

"He was worried about ye, Mr. MacQuarrie. Beside himself with worry."

Ben must have put on quite the performance to

have swayed Gibson to his cause. "I don't suppose you can send him away?"

His butler shook his head. "Ye ken how persistent Lord Benjamin can be."

Yes, Alec knew. In their younger days, every spot of trouble the two of them had gotten into had always been of Westfield's making and even so, he was able to convince Alec to join him time and time again. "I suppose there's nothing to do then."

Gibson released a breath of air. "Thank ye, sir."

Alec begrudgingly left his chambers, descended the stairs, and made his way toward the green parlor in question. Immediately, he was assaulted by the scent of a darkened forest. It was a scent he'd never smelled until his recent association with Lycans. What the devil!

He stepped into the parlor to find his old friend Benjamin standing behind an emerald settee where his very expectant wife sat with a protective hand resting on her belly. Alec's eyes flashed from Benjamin to Elspeth and back. The woodsy scent had only intensified at his entrance. "Jesus Christ," he muttered under his breath.

"Well, that's a fine welcome." Benjamin frowned at him.

"Heard that, did you?" No one other than a Lycan would have picked up his words. Alec's stomach dropped. He'd first met Ben Westfield at Harrow when the two of them were twelve years old. Since that time, the two of them had been nearly inseparable. So how had Ben hidden the fact that he was a werewolf for fourteen bloody years? Had their friendship been *that* one-sided?

"I've been worried about you, Alec."

Alec ignored his friend's words and focused instead on the red-haired witch still sitting on his settee. Were witches simply enamored with Lycans? Is that how he'd lost Caitrin? Because *Còig* witches were fated to marry the beasts? "Lady Elspeth, you look well, considering."

Her green eyes darkened with concern. "Considerin' what exactly, Alec MacQuarrie?"

Considering she'd thrown in her lot with a slobbering, snarling, howling wolf. How long had she known the truth? Before she married Ben? Sometime after? "Considering your condition, love," he answered instead.

"We know about Briarcraig," Ben said without preamble. Ben always did cut to the chase. Was that impatience also a trait of Lycans? "We know what happened there."

"Do you, now?"

Elspeth Westfield nodded fervently. "Blaire and Lord Kettering told us everythin'."

"So there are no secrets between us, then?" Alec finally met his oldest friend's eyes. "Nothing you want to tell me, Ben? Nothing you want to confess?"

Ben shook his head, confusion in his hazel eyes. "What do you think I'm keeping from you, my friend?"

Alec closed the parlor door tightly behind him. He had no desire for any of his staff with their prying ears to be privy to this conversation. "Well, you both have secrets, don't you?" He turned back around to face his guests. "You're a Lycan, are you not? And your beautiful bride a witch…" A *healing* witch.

The truth of that nearly knocked Alec to his

knees. He'd been so consumed with his worries over Matthew that he would have never considered tracking down his old friend or his healing wife. What a fool he'd been. And how fortunate that Ben had come in search of him.

In the space of a heartbeat, Ben was at his side, keeping Alec from stumbling backwards. "Are you quite all right?"

Alec shook him off and straightened to his full height. "As all right as a man can be when he discovers his oldest friend has lied to him his whole life."

Ben glowered in response. "Who told you? Eynsford? That prick?"

"Benjamin!" his wife chastised, though Alec couldn't determine if the rebuke was for his friend's language or the fact that Ben had derided the marquess.

Alec shook his head. "I can smell it on you. But your deception of more than a decade is inconsequential at the moment." He turned his attention to the fiery-haired witch. "I need your help, Elspeth. Rather, my maker needs your help."

"Maker?" Ben barked.

"What's wrong with him?" Elspeth struggled to her feet.

"Sit right back down, Ellie," her husband ordered.

She paid him no attention. "Has he been injured?" The sweetest concern radiated from the witch. "I thought yer kind was able ta heal themselves."

"Elspeth!" Ben growled low in his throat. "You are carrying our child."

Her eyes flashed to her husband. "I doona even ken Lord Blodswell, Benjamin. I have no affection for the man. If I can heal him, it willna do our daughter any harm."

Alec shook his head at his friend's luck in finding such a lovely selfless lady as Elspeth. She didn't refer to Matthew as a creature, a monster, or even a vampyre. She'd called him a man. He didn't even think of himself as such any longer. "He hasn't been able to feed."

Elspeth's eyes widened at the admission. "That is a curious problem. What have ye tried?"

Alec shrugged. "I've given him sheep's blood and he's consumed fresh human blood, but it was no use, the only…" He let his voice trail off. If he told them about Rhiannon, would Elspeth still be willing to aid them?

"The only…?" she prompted, touching his sleeve.

"We've come to Edinburgh so Blodswell can formally ask Dougal Sinclair for Rhiannon's hand."

"Rhi?" Elspeth's green eyes twinkled with glee. "Truly?"

Alec was so disarmed by her expression of happiness that he nodded. "*Her* blood is all that quenches his thirst, it seems."

"Meant ta be," Elspeth muttered to herself. "Take me ta him, will ye?"

Alec opened the door and directed the lady to his study, with Ben quick on their heels, grumbling protests the whole way. As soon as they stepped over the threshold, Elspeth gasped at the sight that met them—Matthew in a heap in the middle of the floor.

"*Havers!*" She rushed forward. "Benjamin, ye and Alec pick him up."

Her husband raced to do her bidding, lifting the earl by his armpits while Alec picked up his feet. "Where to, MacQuarrie?" Benjamin asked.

"First chamber on the right at the top of the stairs."

The two men took off toward the guest chamber Ben had used himself more times than once. Elspeth followed the pair and quietly watched as they placed Matthew on the large bed in the middle of the room.

"Ben," the witch began softly, "will ye retrieve my special valise from the carriage?"

"Of course, lass," her husband returned, as his hazel gaze rested on Alec, almost like a wayward pup who hopes his owner will forgive his misdeeds. As Alec turned his attention to Matthew's lifeless form, lying in the middle of the bed, Benjamin made his exit.

Elspeth gently touched Alec's arm, which caused him to glance down at her. "I willna let harm come ta him," she vowed.

"Why do you care so much, my lady?"

Her green eyes sparkled with affection. "Because I adore ye, and I can tell he means a great deal ta ye, *and* I have a feelin' he's meant for Rhi."

"I thought Cait was the Seer."

She grinned up at him. "Ye ken much more about our coven than I would have ever thought, Alec." Then she sighed, looking more serious than usual. "Doona be angry at Ben. They're forbidden from discussin' the nature of who they are. He couldna tell ye."

Alec didn't want to think about that, not now anyway. "Just help Blodswell. Please."

Elspeth squeezed his arm. "That is what I do best."

◈

Matthew's eyes shot open. He'd never felt quite so alive. He glanced around a dark blue room illuminated by a plethora of beeswax candles. A beautiful red-haired woman stepped forward, and the glow from the candles made her appear to be an angel.

"Welcome back ta the land of the livin', Lord Blodswell," the lass crooned.

"Wh-who are you?" he croaked, his mouth parched. But he knew the answer in his soul. She was one of Rhiannon's sister witches. "You're the healer."

She grinned at him. "And ye hold the loyalty of two of the men I hold most dear."

"Do I?"

"Lord Kettering and Alec MacQuarrie."

He smiled back at her, without even meaning to. "When you save a man's life, he tends to be loyal to you. Like a stray pup you feed. He tends to feel beholden to protect and keep you, even when you've no need of it."

"Oh, ye have a need of it." She sat on the edge of the bed and touched a hand to his head. "I'm afraid my fix is temporary, my lord. My powers can provide ye a bit of energy for a while, but it is no' a substitution for real sustenance."

Real sustenance. "I promised I wouldn't."

She smoothed a hand along his jaw, a healer's touch if he'd ever felt it. "I've kent Rhiannon my whole life. I'm certain she wouldna want ta see ye like this."

"I'd like to make sure she doesn't."

The fiery-haired lass rolled her eyes. "That wasna what I meant. Ye canna hide yer condition from her.

I'm certain if she kent the extent of yer circumstances, she would offer a bit of her blood ta save ye."

"We should be married first."

An expression of genuine admiration settled on her face. "I doona think Kettering and MacQuarrie are loyal ta ye simply because ye saved their lives, but because of who ye are, my lord."

"I need to speak with Mr. Sinclair."

She nodded. "Indeed ye do. I had my husband drag him from behind his desk and deliver him here. Mr. Sinclair is currently pacin' the length of Alec's library, waitin' for ye ta wake."

"I seem to owe you for much, my dear." Matthew realized he didn't even know the name of his guardian angel. "Your name, lass?"

"I'm Lady Elspeth Westfield."

"Well, Lady Elspeth, I will be forever in your debt."

She rose from her spot and gestured for him to rise. "All I ask, Lord Blodswell, is that ye return safely ta London and love Rhiannon with all yer heart."

Matthew nodded. There was no reason to tell Lady Elspeth he didn't possess a heart, but he would *care* for Rhiannon until the end of her days.

"Then get on with it," she ordered lightly. "Ye have Mr. Sinclair's attention, which is more than most can ever boast. So, go take advantage of it."

Matthew rose from the bed and smoothed his jacket into place. "Will you direct me to the library?"

"It will be my honor."

He followed the healing witch from the guest chambers, down a flight of stairs, and then to the library on the lower level.

She smiled one last time before pushing him lightly through the open door. "Good luck."

True to Lady Elspeth's description, Matthew found a slender, gray-haired man with wire-rimmed spectacles pacing the floor of the library. "Mr. Sinclair?" he said softly.

The old gentleman stopped mid-pace and faced the doorway. "Ye're Blodswell, are ye?"

Matthew nodded. "Thank you so much for seeing me."

"Westfield dinna give me much choice in the matter," Rhiannon's father complained as he pushed the glasses up the bridge of his nose. "Now, who are ye and what do ye want with me?"

At least the witch's husband hadn't divulged the nature of his visit. A man should do things the proper way. Matthew stepped forward and offered Rhiannon's father a smile. "I am Matthew Halkett, the Earl of Blodswell, and I have come from London to ask for your daughter's hand."

The man's gray brow rose slightly. "Greer said she'd find a husband for my Ginny, but I never expected a fellow ta come all the way from London. A letter would have sufficed, young man."

Matthew wasn't sure which was more amusing—that the man thought him a young man or that he thought Matthew wanted to marry Rhiannon's sister. "You misunderstand, Mr. Sinclair. I've come on behalf of your daughter Rhiannon."

The man's brow rose even higher, which would have been comical under different circumstances. "Ye want ta marry Rhi?"

"Very much so."

Dougal Sinclair shrugged. "Fine by me. Do ye need anythin' else, or might Westfield allow me ta return home?"

All Matthew's amusement vanished. Shouldn't the man want to know something of him? If he cared for Rhiannon? A bit about his character? "Is that all?"

The man's eyes darkened. "Is this about her dowry?"

Matthew nearly swallowed his own tongue. "Her dowry?"

"If ye marry her, it's yers. Is that what ye want ta talk about?"

He didn't care if she had a dowry or not. Matthew had accumulated more wealth over the years than most men could even dream of. He shook his head. "I just assumed you'd want to know something of me. Ask me questions. Ensure your daughter's future."

Dougal Sinclair laughed. "Rhi is a smart lass. She can take care of herself. As for yer character, I'm certain if ye get out of line, my daughter will have the ability to shock ye back ta where ye should be."

So that was it? Matthew supposed he should be relieved it was so easy to convince the man of his suit, but he wished Dougal Sinclair seemed more concerned about his daughter's welfare. "Well, thank you. Will you see that the banns are read?"

"Oh, aye, aye. I'll see Mr. Crawford."

"Indeed," boomed a voice from the threshold. A large, forest-scented man with light brown hair stood just inside the library. A Lycan, there was no doubt in Matthew's mind. "How about if we stop off at the vicar's before my carriage returns you home, Sinclair?"

Rhiannon's father scowled at the man. "Ye doona trust me ta go on my own, Lord Benjamin?"

The Lycan shook his head. "Oh, I have no doubt, you'll mean to, Sinclair, but life has a way of getting in the way. Best to speak with Crawford while the events are fresh in your mind." Then the man looked at Matthew. "Benjamin Westfield," he introduced himself.

Ah, Lady Elspeth's husband. Matthew nodded thanks to the man. "I had the pleasure of meeting your wife."

"And the pleasure of turning my closest friend," Westfield muttered so softly only Matthew could hear.

"You are mistaken. It was not a pleasure. Simply a necessity."

Westfield's eyes narrowed briefly before he said quietly, "Take care of Rhiannon *and* Alec, or you'll have me to deal with."

Again Matthew nodded. "You have no need to worry," he returned, *sotto voce.*

"I'll see to things on this end." Westfield said loud enough for everyone in the room to hear. Then he gestured toward the corridor. "Come along, Sinclair. We've a busy night ahead of us." The door closed softly behind them.

"All this time, and I never knew," Alec said from behind him as he stared absently at the door the Westfields and Dougal Sinclair had just walked through.

"Some things are better left unsaid," Matthew replied as he turned around to look at Alec, who stood with his shoulder braced against the wall. "When one is not fully human, one must take care to protect one's self. Not to mention the family and friends of said individual." Matthew sighed deeply. "Would you have told him what you are of your own volition?"

"Tell him I'm not a man. Absolutely not."

"Your manhood is not in question, Alec," Matthew bit out.

"My humanity is," Alec snapped in return.

All of a sudden, the front door opened without even a knock. A girl slipped through the crack and shut the door behind her like a gust of wind. In her haste, she barely stopped to look around her before she spun and barreled directly into Alec MacQuarrie's chest.

"What the devil?" Alec bit out as he reached out to steady her.

But the pretty little sprite paid not the least little bit of attention to his friend's bark. Instead, she giggled and pushed herself closer to him, wrapping her arms around his waist as she laid her head on his chest. "I heard ye were home," she said, inhaling deeply with her nose pressed against him.

For some reason, Matthew suddenly felt like an interloper.

"Are you daft, Sorch?" MacQuarrie said as he took her by the shoulders and pried her arms from around him. "You can't go bursting into someone's home. Or accosting men without warning."

So this was Sorcha, the little witch who could control nature. She was absolutely enchanting. And obviously was Alec's worst nightmare come to life.

"I dinna *accost* ye, Alec MacQuarrie." Her breaths were finally starting to slow. The witch must have run all the way up the drive. "I *hugged* ye. Even ye should recognize a *hug* when ye get one."

"What do you mean, even me?" Alec said, his tone clipped and biting.

She continued as though he hadn't spoken. "Where is Elspeth? She's why I'm here. Mrs. Niven is having her sixth bairn, and it's no' goin' well." The wood sprite dashed toward the nearest parlor and looked inside, then sighed deeply. "She's no' here, is she? I came all this way for nothin'."

"She and Benjamin just left," Alec informed her. He was still frowning. Interesting. Very, very interesting. The littlest witch exuded happiness, which made Matthew want to smile along with her. But not MacQuarrie. He looked like he wanted to bolt from the room.

"I made a tonic ta help Mrs. Niven, but it's no' doin' much."

"Is there anything I can do?" Matthew asked. The youngest of Rhiannon's coven sisters nearly jumped out of her skin when he spoke. MacQuarrie stepped closer to her.

"*Havers!* I dinna ken ye had a guest." She smiled brightly and tossed her dark hair over her shoulder with an impatient gesture. Then she elbowed Alec in the ribs. "Did ye leave yer manners in London?" she hissed at him. "Introduce me."

Alec sighed deeply, but he made a sweeping gesture and said, "Matthew Halkett, the Earl of Blodswell, this is Miss Sorcha Ferguson."

"Oh, ye're the earl who…" She let her voice trail off. Then she cocked her head to the side, smiled softly, and said, "Kettering."

"Yes, Kettering," was all he supplied. He had

turned Kettering into a vampyre. The witch could obviously fill in the rest.

She pointed to the man who sulked beside her. "And Alec?"

A single nod was the only response he gave.

But the wood sprite giggled, rushed toward Matthew, bounced up on her toes, and quickly kissed his cheek. "Thank ye for savin' his life."

That was the first time he'd been thanked for turning MacQuarrie.

"I doubt that it was the right decision some days," Matthew teased as MacQuarrie tapped his Hessians on the tile floor. "He can be a bit surly."

But the little witch just grinned and stepped closer to Alec. She leaned into his side and rooted against him until his arm finally landed around her. She placed a hand on his chest. "He's no' surly. Just misunderstood." She giggled. "Though I hear he does bite now. So, I suppose we should all be careful." Yet she leaned farther into him anyway.

"Westfield is the mutt who bites, and here I am getting the grief," MacQuarrie said testily, as he tried to shake Miss Ferguson from his side.

She narrowed her eyes at him and let him move away. But she said, "So, ye ken what he is, now?"

"How long have *you* known?" Alec asked.

"Me? I have always kent." She shrugged.

"And you couldn't be bothered to tell anyone?"

"Would it have changed yer friendship with him if ye had kent all along what he was?"

He didn't answer her, instead just picking at a loose thread on his jacket.

"Did it hurt yer feelings when ye found out ye were the last one ta ken?" A grin played around the corners of her mouth.

"Of course, my *feelings* are not hurt," he choked. "Men do not get *hurt feelings*."

"I beg to differ," Miss Ferguson taunted.

"I beg you to stop quibbling with me," Alec returned.

Matthew smothered a laugh in his closed fist.

"Did El say where they were goin'?" Miss Ferguson asked, as though she suddenly remembered her mission.

"To the vicar and then to the Sinclairs'," Matthew supplied.

"Why on earth would they go to the vicar?" the young lady asked, her eyebrows drawing together.

"The earl has asked Rhiannon to marry him. That's why we're here. He's so noble he felt he needed to get her father's permission. He did. And now Ben is helping Sinclair remember to have the banns read."

"Oh, that's so romantic," Miss Ferguson said, a dreamy expression crossing her face. "Do ye love her? Please tell me ye do. She needs ta be loved. She always has." The witch expelled it all in one quick breath.

"I have a great affection for her," Matthew said, suddenly defensive of his feelings under her penetrating stare.

"Ye have ta *love* her. It's the only way." She sighed deeply. "I wish I could tell ye. But then it might never happen."

Matthew shook his head quickly and glanced at MacQuarrie. "Do you know what she's talking about?"

Alec shrugged. "I never know what Sorcha's prattling on about. I don't think she knows either, most of the time."

The young witch punched Alec's shoulder. "I do ken what I'm talkin' about. But I canna tell ye the secret. It wouldna be right. Ye have ta find out on yer own. When it happens, ye'll ken it's right."

"Don't you have somewhere you're supposed to be?" Alec crossed to the door and opened it. "Come along, sprite. I'll see you home. Then I'll retrieve Elspeth and take her to Mrs. Niven's. I don't like for you to be outside at night in the dark. Particularly not alone."

Miss Ferguson giggled. "I'm standin' here with two vampyres who could have me for dinner at any moment. And ye think I'm scared of what's out *there*?" She laughed loudly this time. "That is humorous, Alec."

"You're safe from me," Matthew tossed out. He couldn't bite her if he wanted to. But MacQuarrie licked his lips and looked down the girl's dress as though he'd just discovered there was a woman standing in his entryway. A flesh-and-blood woman. "Him, I'm not so sure about." He pointed toward Alec.

The little sprite dashed out the door calling over her shoulder. "I doona need an escort," she yelled. "My brother is in the carriage." She waved all the way down the drive. After the coach started away, she poked her head out the window and yelled, "I feel safer and safer the farther I get from the two of ye," she teased, laughter coating her words.

"You should." Alec mumbled so low that Matthew could barely hear him. But he did. The man sighed deeply. Then he glanced down at his lapel, where a perfect red rosebud bloomed before their very eyes. He grinned.

"That's the first spontaneous smile I've seen out of you since you were reborn," Matthew said, watching his protégé closely in the wake of the littlest witch.

"Sorcha has this way about her..." he began. But his words just trailed off, the thought left unfinished.

Sixteen

"Who is Lord Blodswell. I mean who is he really?" Rhiannon sat forward in her seat, staring at the Duchess of Hythe.

The old woman chuckled. "Why the most eligible peer in all of the kingdom."

Was that what the duchess had meant? Rhi breathed a sigh of relief. She didn't know what she'd have done if the powerful woman had uttered the word "vampyre."

The duchess pulled her chair closer to Rhiannon's and tapped her chin, her gaze swinging from the top of Rhi's head to the bottoms of her feet.

"Your Grace," Rhiannon began.

But the lady suddenly jumped to her feet and crossed the room to pour two glasses of some amber liquid. She quickly downed one, refilled her glass, and held the other out to Rhiannon.

Rhi's fingers trembled slightly, she was embarrassed to see. At least none of her powers were going off. Yet. She sniffed the glass. "What is it?" she asked hesitantly.

"Liquid courage," the duchess exclaimed. "I have never been able to stomach the ratafia served at these things. But if I made brandy available to everyone here, I'd have people frolicking on the lawn before the night was over." For some reason, that idea seemed to please the duchess. She motioned for Rhiannon to drink.

The amber liquid made her nose water as she bit back a gasp. "Thank ye," Rhiannon choked out.

"Your aunt is not a nice woman," the duchess began.

The statement was certainly not news to Rhiannon, but it wasn't wise to admit as much. "What makes ye say that?" she asked with caution.

The duchess chuckled. "You are too kind, dear girl. That woman is determined to see you fail this season."

Rhiannon already knew that, but she found it terribly interesting that the duchess was aware of it, too. She raised the glass to her lips again. The next sip wasn't quite as painful as the first, and a warm flush spread across her skin.

"Well, I refuse to allow it," the duchess said. "I refuse to allow that lady to ruin your chance for success. And success you shall have, dear girl, or I am not the Duchess of Hythe. And the last time I looked in a mirror, I saw myself quite clearly. Yet I see *her* even more clearly."

Thank heavens, someone finally did. "I appreciate ye takin' an interest in my success."

The duchess smiled, which was still a surprising sight. "You remind me of my granddaughter."

"Do I?" Rhi touched a hand to her chest. The admission from the duchess was the very last thing she'd expected.

The old woman nodded. "Indeed. Madeline will come out next year, my dear. She's a plucky thing, just like you. And I'd hate to imagine her all alone in Town. I'd want someone to take an interest in her success. To help her navigate the waters that are the *ton*. But most importantly, I'd want someone to squash anyone who tried to hurt her chances."

"Like Aunt Greer," Rhi muttered, remembering all the awful things her aunt had said.

"Do not give Greer Cooper another thought, my dear. She will *not* be allowed to stomp on your success. I will not have it. I will formally take you under my wing as of this moment. You should consider me to be your mentor. Your taskmaster. Your confidante, if you so choose."

She waved her hand around in the air in an all-encompassing motion. "I know that you have Lady Eynsford to rely upon, but I think you need more if you hope to catch a man like Blodswell." She stared directly at Rhiannon from her perch on the edge of her chair. "You do plan to catch him, do you not?"

Well, he bit my finger and sucked a drop of my blood while his other hand did amazing things beneath my skirts. No. That would never do. Rhi raised her glass and drained it dry. "I do plan ta catch him, Yer Grace." She nodded emphatically. A bit too emphatically, as the spirits had already gone to her head. The duchess poured another glass and held it out to Rhiannon. She wrapped both hands around it and brought it to her lap.

"Splendid!" The duchess clapped. "I have waited for years to see the good earl take his tumble."

"Ye have?" Blaire felt like a spectator at a sideshow.

"I knew his grandfather, you see." The duchess got a dreamy look in her eye. Matthew's grandfather? That meant she'd really known Matthew. Oh, dear, how well had she known Matthew? Certainly, they hadn't… Had they? Rhi gulped another mouthful of the brandy.

"They look like they could be twins," the duchess continued. "Those dark eyes, that dark hair. That carefree stance."

She'd been appraising Matthew's stance? Oh, dear. "He does have a nice stance," Rhiannon mumbled.

"Indeed, he does," the duchess breathed. "Unfortunately, it wasn't meant to be, not between his grandfather and me. I could barely talk the man into looking in my direction. Much less into showing me more of his *stance*." The duchess giggled.

"Exactly how much of his stance did ye see, Yer Grace?" Rhiannon jumped to her feet. But she immediately sought the soft padding of the chair once more when the room moved around her.

"Not nearly enough," the duchess sighed. "He was too much of a gentleman to show me more of himself, no matter how much I wanted it." She got a faraway look in her eye. "Oh, but I did want to know more of him. All of him. Every little piece." She stared back at Rhiannon suddenly. "Although I doubt that any of his *pieces* were little." She laughed a throaty laugh, full of mirth and humor.

If anyone had told Rhiannon she would be discussing Matthew's endowments with the Duchess of Hythe, she'd have said they were bound for Bedlam. Yet here she sat, doing just that.

"How is it going with Blodswell, dear? Tell me the truth. I may be able to help." She leaned forward, all of her attention focused on Rhiannon, who felt a bit like a butterfly under a glass.

Rhiannon's tongue felt thick in her mouth. But she forced the words out. "That bloody gentleman thing, Yer Grace," she started. Then she felt heat creep up her face as she realized she'd just cursed at the Duchess of Hythe. "Beg yer pardon," she muttered, pressing the back of her hand to her forehead. If she could just collect her wits. The duchess took her empty glass from her. Where had all the brandy gone?

"That bloody gentleman thing, indeed," the duchess chirped, glee coating her words. "I say it's time to take the bull by the horns, dear girl." Her eyes twinkled. "Or by one horn, at least." She lowered her voice to the point where Rhiannon had to concentrate hard to hear her. "If you want to catch the man, choose an appropriate part of his body to grab hold to."

Rhiannon cackled. She couldn't help it. The sound simply erupted. And evidently it was contagious because the duchess joined her. The duchess was deep in her cups. And Rhiannon was well past foxed herself. And, suddenly, everything was incredibly humorous.

"Need I explain what part that is?" the duchess asked, her eyes glassy from the drink.

"I doona believe so, Yer Grace. I believe I understand." Did she? Maybe she'd understand more tomorrow when the edges of her world went back to being round instead of square.

"Seduce him." That was all the duchess said. But

then she repeated it. "Seduce the man. He will fall. I guarantee it."

"I doona really want ta cause his fall," Rhiannon stuttered out. She wouldn't do Matthew harm. Not on purpose.

The duchess raised her eyebrows and said slowly, "Cause him to *fall in love*, dear."

"In love?" Rhiannon parroted.

"In love," the duchess confirmed with a nod of her head. "With you. Despite your aunt's meddling ways. And your predisposition to wreak havoc."

"Ye ken about my havoc-wreaking? I canna help it. It just happens."

"Let it," the duchess said. "Let it happen. Then the good earl will feel like he needs to save you. Who cares if he's saving you from yourself? It will give him a purpose in your life. Aside from getting beneath your skirts, which will be his primary goal. The thwarting of havoc-wreaking can come second."

The duchess took Rhiannon's hand in her own and tugged her to her feet. The lady had much more strength and purpose than Rhiannon did at the moment, so she went willingly when the woman tugged her down the corridor and back into the crowded ballroom. The duchess kept Rhiannon at her side as she crossed to stand directly in front of Archer Hadley.

"Radbourne," the woman said sternly, immediately drawing his attention from the conversation he was involved in. He held up one finger to his compatriots and begged their pardon.

"Are you all right, Miss Sinclair?" the Lycan asked.

"Oh, posh," the duchess said with a breezy wave of her hand. "She's fine."

"Then why on earth is she having a hard time standing on her own two feet?" Radbourne growled. Such a lovely growl it was.

The duchess' eyes narrowed at him. "You will suit my purposes quite nicely," she sang. She pressed Rhiannon's hand onto his arm and stepped back. "Quite nicely," she said, clapping her hands.

An announcement at the entrance vaguely broke through the drink haze that clouded Rhi's mind. "Oh, Lord Blodswell has finally arrived. And he has that lovely Mr. MacQuarrie with him." She leaned closer to Rhiannon and said conspiratorially, "I could look at that man all night without an ounce of remorse."

"Your Grace," Archer began, an admonishment hovering on his lips. But the duchess was already abandoning them to go and greet her newest guests. Perhaps she wanted to admire Matthew's stance a little more.

"Do ye plan ta ask me ta dance?" Rhiannon asked quietly of Archer, but she was certain he could hear her.

"I don't think you could walk across the room, much less dance," the viscount clipped out.

"Try me," Rhiannon whispered.

Archer's eyebrows rose. Then his eyes narrowed. "Try you?" he asked. "You should know better than to toss out an invitation like that, Miss Sinclair. Particularly when you're foxed."

"What makes ye think I'm foxed?" she asked. She was upright of her own volition. So what if she leaned a little too heavily on his arm?

"You forget that we Lycans can smell odd things like brandy, particularly when you have been dipped in it."

"Dipped?" Rhiannon giggled. "It went in me, no' on me. It's all the duchess' fault. She kept fillin' the glass."

"She's a bad influence on you." But he looked as though he was biting back a smile. "You wanted to dance, did you? Then dance you shall."

He swept her across the room and onto the dance floor before she could take a deep breath. A waltz began and he drew her close to him, scandalously close. But wasn't that the purpose of a waltz? To tempt societal discord? Or tempt an earl. Or a viscount, as the case may be.

"Do ye find me likeable, Archer?" Rhi asked, her tongue still thick and unwieldy. Thank heavens Radbourne was such a good dancer, because he supported them both with his quick movements.

"No, I do not find you likeable at all, Rhiannon," he muttered.

She forced her lips into a pout.

"However, if you hold your mouth in that shape for one second longer, I will feel compelled to kiss you," he warned.

Her gaze flew up to his, where she found him smiling, his amber eyes twinkling.

"You do tempt me, Miss Sinclair," he said softly.

"Tempt ye ta do what?" Her mind was still muddled from the drink. She'd have to remember not to ever drink anything the Duchess of Hythe put in her hand again.

"Tempt me to do anything I want with you. Particularly when you are foxed, your guard is down, and you are in my arms instead of Blodswell's. You are aware he just arrived?"

"Aye, I heard the announcement. But the duchess gave me ta ye. So, I assume I'm yers for the moment."

He inhaled deeply, growled low in his throat and, in one sweeping motion, led her off the floor and out a door that exited into the garden. She stopped moving long before her head did, and she clutched the lapels of his jacket to steady herself.

"Mine for the moment," he said softly as he brushed a lock of hair from her forehead.

"It appears that way." Rhiannon's thoughts were beginning to clear, thanks to the cool, crisp air in the outdoors.

"Feeling better, now?" he asked as she loosened her clutch on his clothing and stepped back.

"Much," she replied. "Thank ye."

"For what?"

"For bein' who ye are," she replied.

"And just who are you, Miss Sinclair?" he asked, appraising her closely. Rhiannon opened her mouth to speak, but a voice from behind her broke through her thoughts.

"She's my fiancée, that's who."

❧

Matthew had cursed his need to appear human when he'd seen Radbourne sweep Rhiannon out the side door into the garden. He wanted to fly across the room and jerk her from the viscount's arms the moment the waltz had begun, but MacQuarrie's restraining hand on his arm had stopped him. But once Radbourne had absconded with her, there was nothing Alec could do to hold him back. Matthew was across the room in a trice and out into the garden, where he saw Rhiannon in the Lycan's embrace.

Decapitation would be too good for the wolf in gentleman's clothes. Perhaps evisceration would be better. It would certainly bring Matthew more satisfaction.

"She is my fiancée, and I solidified that fact just earlier today. So, I would appreciate it if you could remove your hands from her person."

"If I do that, she very well may topple over." Radbourne sighed.

"Why on earth would she do that?" Matthew bit out. "What have you done to her?"

"It wasn't me," Radbourne chuckled. "The Duchess of Hythe is the responsible party. The old dragon got her foxed. I just brought her out to get some fresh air."

"Air? Is that what you're calling it?"

Radbourne straightened his shoulders. "When that's what it is, yes. Air."

"It's no' his fault, Matthew," Rhiannon sighed. "He was helpin'."

"Helping himself to your person," Matthew grunted at her.

"If I'd wanted her person, I could have had it. I can be quite charming when I choose."

Rhiannon smiled. "That's true." Then she laughed. "He can be very charmin'." She spun to face Radbourne. "Would ye mind leavin' us for a bit, Archer? I have some things ta discuss with Matthew."

"I don't think this is a good time for you to be alone with anyone," Radbourne began.

"I was alone with ye. And I am no worse for wear." She held her arms out to her side and spun in a slow circle, but she teetered when her dress caught on the toe of her shoe. Radbourne reached for her, but Matthew was faster. He caught her to himself and pulled her away from the Lycan.

"What have you done, lass?" he asked. "Had I not arrived, you'd be at the mercy of a pack of wolves."

"They're trainable." She giggled.

"So are bears, but I wouldn't leave you with one of those, either."

"See here, now. There's no need to throw stones," Radbourne growled.

"I'll throw the biggest stone I can find right at your thick skull," Matthew countered.

"Stop!" Rhiannon cried. "Would ye just stop it? Both of ye?" She faced Radbourne. "Thank ye so much for takin' care of me, but I'm feelin' ever so much better and I have some things I need ta say ta my intended."

"I'll take my leave," Radbourne clipped out. "But if you need me, just yell. I'll hear you."

"Of course, you would," Matthew said caustically.

The Lycan bowed quickly to Rhiannon and took his leave.

Rhiannon reached up to touch the back of her hand to Matthew's forehead. "Are ye well?"

"As well as can be expected, thanks to your coven sister, Lady Elspeth."

"Ye met Elspeth?" his witch cried. "How is she?"

"She's as big as a house and ready to deliver very

soon. I met her husband, too. Nice fellow." He took Rhiannon's hand and led her farther into the shadows of the darkened garden so they could talk. That's all he wanted, to talk. And maybe to hold her close to him for a moment. Just a moment. Then he'd take her back to the soiree.

"Did ye see my father?" she asked tentatively.

"I did."

"And?" She stopped and faced him.

"And he gave his blessing for our union. He's having the banns read. All is as it should be."

She twisted a lock of hair around her finger. "Did he seem concerned about me?"

He hadn't. Not a bit. Not even when Matthew suggested it. "He was quite concerned," Matthew lied. "And he put me through an inquisition that would rival that of the Spanish if I had a desire to compare them. He wanted to know everything about me. But, in the end, he finally agreed." He wouldn't look her in the eye. She would see the truth if he did. She would see that her father didn't worry about her, not at all. "And I met Miss Ferguson," he volunteered more cheerily.

"How is Sorcha?"

"Utterly charming. There were some interesting dynamics between her and Alec."

"Between Sorcha and *Alec*? Ye must be mistaken."

He shrugged. "Perhaps I am."

"Did ye feed while ye were gone?" She walked slowly toward him until she had to tilt her head back to look up at him. The gardenia scent of her washed over him, and Matthew's incisors immediately descended. Of course, they would choose now to descend.

"No," he admitted. He couldn't if he'd wanted to. But he didn't want to. He was saving that pleasure for her. For them to share.

"How long can ye go without dyin' of thirst?" she asked as she walked deeper into the shadows of the empty garden. "Can ye wait three weeks for the banns ta be read?"

"Probably not. But I will make do." How, he wasn't certain. But he would.

Rhiannon hitched herself up onto a low garden wall with a short hop. Then she began to tug her gloves from her hands, finger by finger. What lovely fingers she had. "Come here," she sighed. "I havena seen ye for days, and ye insist on stayin' way over there," she said as she laid her gloves on the ledge beside her and crooked a finger at him, beckoning him forward with a coquettish motion.

"Rhiannon," he protested, but his feet moved forward of their own volition. "You are more than a little bit foxed. And I'd be the worst sort of cad if I took advantage of your inebriated state."

"A cad?" she breathed as she parted her thighs, grabbed the lapels of his jacket, and drew him to her. He all but fell on her, he was that enraptured by her. Oh, holy hell. The lady would unman him. "What if my fondest wish is ta be taken in a darkened garden by a cad?"

"*I* am a gentleman." He wasn't certain if he was reminding her or himself. But her mouth hovered inches from his, and he couldn't resist closing the gap. She tasted like brandy, hot and spicy. She tentatively opened her mouth when he pressed her. Then he swept inside. She met him, her tongue brushing his, her head tilting so he could consume her.

"I doona want a gentleman," she breathed against his lips as she cupped the back of his head and drew it down to her. Rhiannon tilted her head to expose her neck. "I want ye. All of ye. Right now."

"What has come over you?" he asked, between frantic kisses he pressed to her throat.

"Ye havena come over me. No' yet," she breathed. Bloody hell.

❧

Rhiannon could feel the heat as it crept up her neck. But she couldn't give up now. He needed to feed. And she was the sole person who could fill that need for him.

His indrawn breath when she pressed her lips to the side of his jaw was nearly her undoing. She had no idea how to seduce a vampyre. But she would give it her all. "I want ye," she breathed against his skin. He groaned and lowered his hands to where they spanned her waist. Then he tugged her closer to him. Rhiannon reached down and gathered her skirts in her hands, lifted them above her knees, and drew him closer to her, her legs wrapping around his waist and her feet locked behind him.

Matthew groaned as he raised his head and cupped her face in his hands, tilting her chin up until she stared into those dark-as-night eyes. "Rhiannon, there are people who could stumble upon us at any moment. We have to stop."

"Do ye *want* ta stop?" she breathed.

"God, no. I want it to go on forever and a day."

"Good, because I will be sorely miffed if ye stop me now." She drew his mouth back down to hers.

She took his hand and raised it to cup her breast. The gentle swell of it filled his palm as her tongue conquered his mouth. The ridge of his manhood was *right there* at the apex of her thighs, hard and unyielding in its voracity. And she wanted it.

He jerked his lips from hers. "We cannot do this here," he bit out. He leaned his forehead against hers. "Rhiannon, I'm a gentleman. Please don't prove me wrong. I'll be unable to resist you."

"Good," she bit out as she tugged at the fall of his trousers. He batted her hands away, until she caught one of them and pressed it toward her center. She knew she was wet, and she was completely unashamed. When his hand cupped her heat, she arched into it. "Please," she begged against his lips.

"Not yet," he groaned. Then his hand began to unlace her gown with quick and efficient movements. With a gentle tug, one breast popped free. He stared down at her, his gaze more feral than anything she'd ever seen. Then his hand encircled her breast and brought the aching peak to his lips. When his mouth closed around that turgid flesh, Rhiannon's head fell back, her mouth dropped open in ecstasy. She quickly bared her other shoulder and offered herself up to him as though she was a feast for a starving man. Perhaps she was. Of course, she was.

Matthew went back and forth between her breasts until the ache between her thighs became a thumping pulse that demanded satisfaction. She ran her fingers into his hair and tugged. He looked up at her, desire clouding his vision. His fangs glimmered in the moonlight. "Please," she whispered.

"Yes," he breathed in response. Matthew's hand found her center and began to sweep across that little nub of pleasure that had brought her so much rapture the last time. She locked her feet more tightly about his waist, holding him pressed close to her. She tugged at the fall of his trousers again, and he allowed her to expose him to the night air. But he was well hidden within the layers of her skirts, as was his hand, which still worked to bring her to a fevered pitch. He slid one finger inside her as his thumb strummed with that frantic rhythm, the one that nearly matched her pulse.

"Take me, Matt," she breathed against his ear, and then she gently sucked his earlobe into her mouth and bit down gently. His own mouth was dangerously close to her shoulder, and she pulled his head until his lips began a slow walk toward her pulse. "Please, Matt," she cried, the pleasure his hand provoked reminiscent of that last time he'd brought her to completion. She didn't want to topple over that precipice without him. "Please," she begged.

Her hips rocked in time with his movements as his teeth gently abraded her neck with a soft bite, not hard enough to break the delicate flesh there. His thumb pushed her farther and farther into the pleasure he had to offer. Then, just as she was about to explode with the ecstasy of it, his teeth pierced the skin of her neck. She cried out, her sound echoing on the night air as wave after wave of pleasure rocked her body.

She quivered around his finger that stilled inside her as she let her head fall back, let him sup on the meal that was her, and let him find his release. He swallowed, his body wracked with pleasure as he took from her, and hers was just as fulfilled as he gave back to her. He grunted, drinking his fill of her. Then when her body stopped fluttering, he pulled his teeth from her skin, licked gently across the wounds to close them, and sighed long and hard.

"Did I hurt you?" he asked softly by her ear, not even looking her in the eye.

"Quite the opposite," she breathed, happy to be wrapped in splendor in his arms as they both fell back to earth.

But footsteps on the gravel path drew his attention. "If you take one more step in this direction, Radbourne, I *will kill* you," Matthew called out.

The footsteps stopped.

"She is fine. I will return her to the soiree in due time," he said. The footsteps started away. "It appears as though you have a protector in the mutt," Matthew grunted as he helped her restore her clothing.

"Did ye…?" she started, wondering if he'd found his pleasure but uncertain how to ask.

"I did," he confirmed with a nod. "A fact that brings me great shame because I have not been that out of control since I was a green lad."

"It brings me pleasure that I was able ta do that," she giggled.

"Of course, it does," he chuckled as he moved back to look her in the eye. "You're all right?"

"I'm no' made of glass, Matthew. I willna break,"

she teased. Then she groaned a complaint as he
unlocked her feet from behind his back and turned to
adjust his trousers.

He appraised her from head to toe, once they had
righted her clothing. "You look as though you have
been tupped on a garden wall, lass," he lamented.

Rhiannon stifled a grin. "Do I look like I enjoyed it?"

"Did you?" His gaze was penetrating.

"That's for me ta ken and for ye ta find out, my
lord," she sang as she spun away from him. He ran to
catch up with her. She could hear his footsteps behind
her, but then they stopped.

Seventeen

J<small>UST AS</small> R<small>HIANNON</small> <small>DISAPPEARED AROUND A HEDGE</small>, Matthew found himself surrounded by a pack of wolves. Oh, they looked like men to anyone else, but they were wolves, nonetheless.

The moonlight glinted off the Marquess of Eynsford's golden hair, and he growled low in his throat. "We had an agreement, Blodswell."

"Did we?" Matthew clasped his hands behind his back, forcing himself to appear composed in front of the unruly pack.

"You were not to take a drop of her blood unless you were married. That was the deal we made," the marquess reminded him.

Oh, *that*. Matthew silently dared Eynsford or any other man to resist the temptation Rhiannon presented. He needed her more than he had ever needed anyone, and she had offered herself to him for the taking.

"I smelled blood as she raced past," Viscount Radbourne snarled. "She was safer with me."

Matthew suppressed a snort. Radbourne was more put out about having heard Rhiannon's gasps of pleasure moments earlier than he was about her lack of blood. "As she's my fiancée, I'll determine in whose company she is most safe."

"One would think that as her fiancé," Eynsford grumbled, "you'd have accompanied her this evening instead of sending your regards."

"It couldn't be helped." Matthew folded his arms across his chest. Truly, Eynsford's devotion to Rhiannon was admirable, but Matthew didn't have to explain himself to the marquess or his pack or any other well-meaning Lycan, for that matter. He'd had his fill of their breed this evening.

"You'll have to do better than that," one of the twin Lycans barked.

Well, that was the outside of enough. It was one thing to deal with Eynsford's arrogance and Radbourne's pomposity. But it was something else entirely to let one of their young pups speak to him as though he was a recalcitrant page in need of a reprimand. Matthew glared at the marquess. "Westfield has just given me notice. So call off your dogs."

Eynsford appeared taken aback by the statement, shaking his head as if in disbelief or disgust. "Westfield?" he growled. "Which Westfield?"

There was some underlying situation Matthew didn't quite understand, nor did he care. "Lord Benjamin."

Eynsford seemed to suck in a relieved breath of air, but then his brow furrowed anew. "Benjamin? Where did you see *Benjamin* Westfield?"

Matthew straightened his jacket and said, "Edinburgh," as he removed a gardenia-scented piece of lint from his sleeve.

"But you said…" Eynsford took a step closer to Matthew. "I thought you met Rhiannon in London."

"I did."

"Then when were you in Edinburgh? When exactly did Westfield give you notice?"

Ah, so these Lycans were unaware of the extent of vampyres' powers and abilities, or of their speed at the very least. Matthew bit back a smile. "About an hour ago."

Eynsford's eyes widened in surprise as the truth began to sink into his thick Lycan skull. "I had no idea."

"Clearly." Matthew rose to his full height. "Your devotion to Miss Sinclair is admirable but unnecessary, Eynsford. The lass' father has given me his blessing. The banns will begin to be read on Sunday. She will be my wife before the next full moon. So Rhiannon does not need you to protect her from me."

One of the twins snorted at that statement. "All of London needs to be protected from you. Miss Sinclair included."

Before Matthew could respond, the verbose twin rose off the ground, his feet dangling in the air. It took his brothers and the marquess a moment to realize someone had actually lifted the reckless pup from the garden path by the scruff of his neck and still held him in her grasp.

"Callista!" Matthew growled. "Put the man down."

"Don't you mean dog?" His maker snarled, tightening her grip on the Hadley twin.

"Put him down!" Matthew ordered again. "What if someone saw you?"

"Then I'd help them forget." Callista thrust the man from her grasp and he tumbled into the hedge a few feet away, gasping for breath. Then she slowly folded her arms across her chest as the other Lycans closed in around her. "Pathetic, all of you."

"I beg your pardon," Radbourne bit out.

Callista's gaze traveled up and down the viscount. "Handsome, I'll grant you that. But pathetic all the same."

Matthew winced. There wasn't a way this evening would end well. Still, he could hope the participants could see reason. "Callista, I have this under control."

Her black eyes flashed to him. "You, I will deal with later." Then she turned her attention to the four Lycans in their midst, their fallen member having just found his feet. "I haven't the time to deal with male pride and posturing at the moment. So allow me to end the debate, gentlemen. *I* am the strongest creature here, and none of you come close to matching me, except perhaps the gallant knight over there, who for some reason humors the lot of you by allowing your inane interrogations."

"Humor?" Eynsford echoed.

Callista scoffed as she narrowed her eyes on the golden-haired marquess. "And I thought Lycans had excellent hearing. Yes, *humor*. Are you having difficulty understanding the meaning of the word, my lord? Shall I define it for you?"

Eynsford growled low in his throat.

"Callista!" Matthew called. "Stop this now."

After a dismissive sweep of her eyes, his maker glanced back at the marquess. "Do you know who this man is?" She gestured toward Matthew.

"Of course. He's the Earl of Blodswell. Who are you?"

"He's my creation," she clipped out. "He's worth all of you and more. He is a noble vampyre of the Griffinic order. And yet you berate him and question him as though he is someone to be feared or reviled." She paused for dramatic effect, as she was wont to do. "And it has come to an end."

"Noble?" Radbourne grumbled. "I hardly think a man taking liberties with a young lady can be described as noble."

In a flash, Callista was before the viscount, her razor-sharp nails wrapped around his throat. "You will hold your tongue. Is that understood?" Then she shoved him back toward his brothers.

"Does being his maker mean she's his *mother*?" one of the twins mumbled. "Looks rather good for her age."

"Do you think he lets his mother fight all his battles?" his look-alike added, *sotto voce*.

Matthew rubbed his brow. Any chance that the evening would end peacefully had just come to an end. Callista had never been known for her patience. And sarcasm tended to chafe her pride more than a bit. Of course, the pups had no way of knowing that, no way of knowing what kind of wrath they provoked.

Callista turned a sultry gaze on the second loquacious Hadley twin, entrancing him completely within seconds. She gestured the young Lycan forward with the flick of her finger. "Such a charming young man."

Matthew stepped between the two, keeping the foolhardy wolfling from reaching the vampyric temptress. "I *let* them interrogate me because they care for my human lass. They are worried for her, Callista. That is all."

"Worried about *you*?" She tossed her head back regally, sending her russet curls billowing over her shoulders. "That's the most amusing thing I've heard this century."

"I'm glad Rhiannon has those who care for her welfare." Her father certainly didn't, nor did her aunt, from what he'd seen. Annoying as he found Eynsford and his pack, they *did* have the lass' best interest at heart, no matter how misguided they might be.

"Human sentiments," she complained. "I'll have that word with you *now*, Matthew."

Matthew agreed with a nod. As always, there was no arguing with Callista. He glanced back at Eynsford. "Make sure Rhiannon gets home safely."

It took only that fraction of a moment when he wasn't watching his maker for Callista to grasp the twin she had originally beckoned forward. She held the young man by his jacket. "Insolence is so ugly." With a pointy fingernail, she scratched a mark on the Lycan's face from his ear across his cheek to his mouth. "Perhaps that will remind you to watch your tongue in the future."

Matthew groaned. "Good God, Callista!"

She tossed the now scarred Lycan toward his brothers. "Consider that a warning for all of you."

The young man yelped in pain and clutched at his cheek, as though waiting for the injury to heal. It wouldn't do any good. Lycans *could* heal themselves, and the pain and blood *would* recede momentarily, but this Hadley twin would wear Callista's mark until the end of his days.

Eynsford grasped the wolfling by the arm and began

to pull him from the group. "Let me see it, Wes." Then he glanced back at Matthew, a warning in his eyes that this encounter, this unprovoked attack would not go unanswered. "Archer, go extricate my wife from whatever she's doing and gather up Miss Sinclair in the process. Gray, call for the coaches and be quick about it."

Both the viscount and uninjured twin rushed to do Eynsford's bidding.

"And, you, Blodswell, I'll expect you in my study first thing in the morning." Then the marquess began to lead his injured pack member into the safety of the darkness.

"Watch your tone, my lord," Callista warned to the man's retreating back. "You do not dictate to Blodswell or any of our kind."

"I'll be there, Eynsford," Matthew called after the Lycan, hoping to keep the situation from becoming even more explosive. "And please tell Rhiannon I shall see her soon."

The marquess and scarred wolfling disappeared around a hedge, and Matthew could hear the pair make their way toward the front of the house. He raked a hand through his hair as he glared at his maker. "Was that necessary?"

Callista shrugged. "It'll make it easier knowing which one is which in the future. Besides, I didn't care for his impudence. As though you'd need me to fight your battles." Then she rose to her full height, which was still more than a foot shorter than Matthew, and speared him with her haughtiest stare.

"However, if *you* had behaved properly, they

wouldn't get such foolish ideas. Whoever heard of a vampyre allowing those drooling beasts to question him in such a fashion? Completely absurd, all of it. The evening's events can all be laid solely at your feet, Matthew."

"*My* feet?" he echoed in outrage.

"Of course, *your* feet. Who else is responsible?" Callista smoothed her filmy gown back into place as though she hadn't a care in the world. "At times like this, Matthew, I cannot quite believe you are my creation. First it was innocent chits and the desire for fatherhood. And now, *now*, it's cavorting with Lycans?" She spit out the last word as though it left a bad taste in her mouth and once again met his gaze. "Have you descended into madness?"

The innocent chits and foundlings she had been all right with. Fraternizing with Lycans had been too much for her to understand. "My intended is a guest in Eynsford's home, dear. I did not seek out Lycans of my own accord."

"Well, I should hope not." She scrunched up her pert little nose as though she smelled something rancid. "Why is your *intended* staying with Lycans? Is her discernment so flawed?"

"Her lifelong friend is Eynsford's wife."

One of Callista's sculpted brows shot upwards. "So poor judgment begets more of the same? Is that it? None of this speaks well for your bride, my son."

Matthew shook his head. "Do leave Rhiannon out of this."

Callista reached up and smoothed her hand over Matthew's jaw. "Well, you haven't left her out of it, have you? Your color looks better." She brushed a motherly kiss to his chin. "You smell properly of *human* blood tonight. Tell me, have your difficulties ended? Or have you finally partaken of your intended?"

Matthew could still taste Rhiannon's sweetness on his tongue. He shouldn't have indulged. He should have waited. Yet her passion had swept over him, and as he'd pierced her tender neck, he'd only barely kept himself from taking her innocence. "We'll be married as soon as we're done with the banns."

"Three weeks?" Callista scoffed. "Do you intend to go three weeks without the chit's blood? Or do you, oh noble knight, intend to be very naughty in the interim?"

"I won't discuss this with you." Especially, as he had no idea what to say. He wanted to be strong, but he wasn't sure if he was strong enough, which was something he was loathe to admit to anyone, most especially Callista.

"Had you visited me, my excursion into Eugenia Hythe's garden would have been unnecessary. I told you I wanted to see you by the end of the week."

"I was in Scotland."

She shrugged. "Then you should have visited beforehand." She started toward the garden path. "How is Eugenia these days?"

"A dragon of the worst order."

Callista laughed. "Good for her. I knew she had it in her. I should love to pay her a visit sometime."

Matthew scrubbed a hand across his face. Why did she torture him like this? She knew paying a visit to her old nemesis would be disastrous. He didn't believe she would actually go through with her threat. She just did these things to put him on edge. "Go home, Callista. Please do not make this evening any more difficult."

A rustling in the nearby hedges caught both Matthew and Callista's attention. "Who's there?" his maker called.

A soft patter of slippers headed toward the main house. Dear God. Who had been spying on them? And what had she heard? Matthew started in the direction of the sound at the same time that he tossed, "Go home, I beg you," over his shoulder to his maker.

In a matter of seconds, he caught up to a dark-haired girl just as she reached the door leading back into the ballroom. Before she could escape to the safety of society's ever-watchful eyes, Matthew grasped her shoulder to spin the chit around to face him. But she slipped out of his hands and into the crowd before he could even see her face.

෴

A shower of little pebbles rained against Rhiannon's bedchamber window. If she had been asleep, the sound most certainly would have woken her up, but she'd already been awake, wondering at the strange events of the last few hours. Lord Radbourne rushing her and Caitrin from Lady Hythe's soiree. The anxious expression Archer and Gray Hadley had exchanged in the short carriage ride. The fact that Eynsford hadn't escorted them home and she hadn't seen the marquess ever since their return to Thorpe House. The fact that her inquiries had all gone unanswered.

Another stream of pebbles hit the window before Rhiannon could pull back the drapes. She wrenched the fabric back and pressed her face against the cold pane. Standing beneath her window, Ginny shivered in a long coat with a blue-and-green Sinclair plaid wrapped around her neck. Rhiannon unlatched the window and yanked it heavenward.

"Ginny!" She nearly fell out of the window. "What's wrong? What are ye doin' here?"

Her sister shook her head. "I escaped Aunt Greer's because I need ta speak with ye."

Rhiannon released her hold on the drapes and raced from her chamber, down the steps, and to the front door. She tugged on the handle only to find it locked. Poor Price had already gone to bed at this late hour.

Rhi leaned toward the handle and whispered, "*Fosgail.*" A satisfying click came from within the door, and Rhiannon hauled it open.

Ginny raced inside and threw her arms around Rhiannon's neck. "Oh, I'm so glad ta see ye," her sister gushed.

Rhiannon tightened her hold around Ginny, not remembering the last time she'd been able to embrace her sister in such a fashion. "I'm glad ta see ye, too. What are ye doin' out at night like this? Aunt Greer'll have yer head." She pulled back slightly to see her sister's face.

"Oh, Rhi, there's so much ta tell ye that I doona even ken where ta begin."

Rhiannon didn't even care. They were together with no evil aunt waiting in the wings to pull them apart. Ginny could start wherever she wanted and talk all night. "Come ta my room, and ye'll have ta just tell me everythin'."

Ginny allowed Rhiannon to tow her up the flight of stairs and then down the corridor to her chambers. Once safely behind the door, Rhi took her sister's coat and plaid, then gestured to the bed. "Sit there, like we used ta."

Ginny obeyed the request, falling in a heap on Rhi's bed. "Aunt Greer. Mr. Finchley. Lord Steven Patterdale. And, and the garden. And Lord Blodswell. And some woman. The duchess. And my stupid gown, and—"

Rhiannon couldn't make any sense of her sister's ramblings. Though she did pick up on a few names she was quite familiar with. "Gin, just start at the beginnin'. There's no rush."

Her sister gulped and sat up straight. "Aunt Greer kept tryin' ta get me out on the balcony with Mr. Finchley. But I doona like Mr. Finchley. He's nice enough, I suppose, or at least I thought he was; but he smells a bit like the inside of Papa's slippers and now I doona even think he's nice." She made a sour face. "But Aunt Greer got heated in the ballroom and dragged me outside ta get a breath of fresh air. Then I turned around and she was gone, but Mr. Finchley was there." She sucked in a steadying breath.

Rhiannon's ire began to build, and thunder rolled in the distance. How dare their aunt put Ginny in that sort of situation? Of course she had been in the garden herself, in a most compromising position with Matthew, but that wasn't the same thing.

Ginny's breath constricted in her, though. "And he tried ta kiss me and wouldna let go of me. And I was pushin' at his chest and then…" Ginny closed her eyes as a tiny smile graced her lips. "…he fell back-wards. When I opened my eyes, Lord Steven stood over Mr. Finchley, and he was rubbin' his knuckles as though he'd just sent the blackguard sprawlin' across the balcony."

Rhiannon hadn't met Lord Steven, but he had suddenly become one of her most favorite people in London. "What happened, Gin?"

Her sister glanced down at her coat as though she was still in her ball gown. "My bodice was loose and my hem ripped, and I looked a mess, I'm sure."

Thunder rumbled overhead. Mr. Finchley would be lucky to walk away from the lightning headed in his direction.

"Doona get angry, Rhi," Ginny begged. "Lord Steven took care of me. We went farther inta the garden so no one would see and he helped me fix my hem."

"And the bodice?"

Ginny turned scarlet. "I—well…"

Rhi rubbed her brow. "Oh, Ginny." She released her breath, ignoring the little part of her conscience that screamed she knew exactly what being ravished in the garden felt like and she shouldn't make judgments about her sister's choices. But she *was* the older sister, and she *had* taken care of Ginny for so many years that it was too difficult to let that part of her fade away without a fight. "What if someone had seen ye? Ye canna go around kissin' gentlemen in the garden."

Ginny began to sob.

Rhiannon cursed herself for being the most

hypocritical and caddish sister in existence. "I'm sorry, Gin, doona cry."

Her sister shook her head. "Th-that was the worst part." Ginny gulped for air. "I-I did see someone."

Rhiannon's heart sank. "*Havers!* Who was it? What did they see? Does Aunt Greer ken?"

Ginny would be ruined by morning.

"Lord Blodswell!" Ginny spit the name out.

Matthew? She must have misheard her sister. "Did you say Lord Blodswell?"

Had flames resided in Ginny's eyes, they would have scorched Rhiannon, and her face was way too flush. If Ginny had seen her with Matthew, Rhi would die of mortification.

"I thought he liked ye, Rhi. The scoundrel."

Havers! She had seen. "He does like me."

Ginny gritted her teeth. "I saw him, Rhi. In the garden and some woman kissed him right out in the open."

Rhi's blush refused to abate. "I-I," she stammered hoping inspiration would fill in the rest of the sentence. It didn't.

"Ye're much prettier than she is," her sister continued, defending her with every breath. "Which can only mean the man is blind. He ought ta be strung up over the Thames and dunked in the river hourly."

Rhi sat back a little, staring at her sister. "Ye *saw* the woman Matthew was with?"

"Matthew?" Ginny blinked at her. "Oh, ye mean Lord Blodswell. Aye, I saw her. Fiery-haired witch." She flushed a bright red. "I dinna mean that. Witch, I mean."

Rhiannon shook the insult off. Ginny had apparently spent too many days under their aunt's roof. But that was neither here nor there at the moment. Someone had kissed Matthew in the garden? And it wasn't her. Well, it had been her. But there had been someone else, too? Rhi's head began to throb. "Do ye ken who she is?"

Ginny shook her head. "I've never seen her before. But he kent her well. They were arguin'. I doona ken about what, and then she touched his face and kissed him."

Had Thorpe House collapsed on top of her, Rhiannon would have been less surprised. "He's supposed ta call on me in the mornin'."

Eighteen

"MY BROTHER'S FACE IS SCARRED!" EYNSFORD'S FIST smashed down onto his desk, and Matthew heard a faint crack in the wood. He wouldn't trust the furniture to handle the added weight of an ink pot.

Standing in the threshold of Eynsford's study, Matthew clasped his hands behind his back. "Brother?"

"I… uh…" If possible, the marquess' face grew even more purple, which did not bode well for his health. "You heard me. Shut the damn door."

Matthew closed the heavy door behind him and leaned against it, not anxious to take a seat across from Eynsford when he looked so enraged.

"Weston should have healed," Eynsford growled. Then he traced a path from his ear to his mouth with his finger as he continued, "But he's got a scar from here to here."

Matthew nodded in understanding. "I'm sure he does." In fact, he'd have been surprised if Weston Hadley *hadn't* been left with a scar after his encounter with Callista. "Your bodies do not react well to interactions with ours. The mark may fade a bit."

"Who the devil was that monster?"

Matthew shrugged. What else could he do? "She told you the truth of it. Callista found me dying in a heap with other dead knights and she saved me."

The marquess scoffed. "I can't imagine her saving anyone."

"She does take a bit of getting used to. She, uh, can be formidable and doesn't appreciate anyone questioning the superiority of vampyres."

"She's a malevolent bitch."

Matthew agreed with a nod of his head. "She can be." He sighed. "I *am* sorry about your, uh, brother. It was too late before I realized what she meant to do."

Eynsford scowled at him. "I didn't mean to reveal that bit. I'd appreciate it if you'd keep that information in your confidence."

That the Hadley men were his brothers? Matthew had suspected the truth, but he would never tarnish the marquess' name. At least he assumed the marquess' name would be blackened by the truth. "Your father...?"

Eynsford sighed. "Which one? The bitter old marquess who raised a bastard son he detested or the dissolute viscount who allowed him to do so?" He leaned back in his seat and folded his arms across his chest. "I didn't even know I had brothers until a few months ago. Cait sought them out."

Yet the camaraderie among the four men was unmistakable. "You seem as though you all grew up side by side."

"The bonds are tighter than I ever could have imagined."

Matthew smiled. He was familiar with that feeling. He shared it with Kettering and MacQuarrie. He even had it with Callista, though he thought it wise not to mention his maker at the moment.

Eynsford raked a hand through his golden hair. "So Wes is permanently scarred? His mother is going to kill me."

"It should lighten some," Matthew offered again, though he knew that wasn't the answer the marquess was hoping for.

"Enough about my relations." The Lycan sat up straight in his chair. "Did you really return from Scotland yesterday?"

Matthew answered with a nod. "I met with Mr. Sinclair. He gave me his blessing to marry his daughter. And Benjamin Westfield promised to have their vicar read the banns."

"You said Westfield gave you notice. What did you mean by that?"

"I suppose most would interpret it as a threat."

Eynsford threw his head back and laughed. He laughed until tears streamed down his face. Then he wiped them from his cheeks and gestured to the overstuffed leather chair across from his desk. "Sit."

"I am not certain what is so amusing," Matthew said as he dropped gingerly into a chair.

Eynsford shook his head. "They do like to hand out threats. Don't take it personally. I've been on the receiving end of more threats from Westfield men than I can count."

Somewhere in the back of Matthew's mind, he thought it might just be possible that Eynsford deserved each and every threat he'd ever received. "He just wanted to make sure I would take care of Rhiannon and MacQuarrie."

The smile vanished from Eynsford's face. "MacQuarrie," he grumbled under his breath. Then he heaved a sigh. "I suppose I should tell Rhiannon you're here, but you know what often happens to the messenger."

"He gets shot?" Matthew supplied, not following the marquess at all.

Eynsford nodded as the tinkle of feminine voices rose up from the corridor to meet them. "There they are now." The marquess winced. "I should warn you," he began, but Matthew was already up and walking toward the door.

Matthew stopped briefly. "Warn me about?" he asked.

The Lycan scratched his head. "Never mind," he grunted. Then he said something beneath his breath that sounded like, "You'll find out soon enough anyway."

Matthew opened the door quickly and stepped into the path of the oncoming ladies. Rhiannon, her sister, and Eynsford's wife all stopped short and regarded him with disdainful expressions that would have felled a lesser man.

"God be with you," Eynsford said from behind him.

The three women assumed nearly identical poses. All three crossed their arms beneath their breasts, squared their shoulders, and if looks could kill, he would have been dead thrice over.

"Good morning?" he attempted. He probably sounded like the worst sort of fool.

"Is it?" the youngest of the three asked.

"Of course it is for him, Ginny," Rhiannon bit out. "He's a *man*, after all."

What the devil was that supposed to mean?

Eynsford's hand shoved him the rest of the way out of his study and into the corridor. His smothered "Best of luck to you, Blodswell" was little comfort as Eynsford shut the study door, leaving Matthew alone to face the three lovely women, all of whom apparently held him in great contempt for some reason.

"Were you on your way out?" he asked, appalled to discover his voice trembled a little when faced with the trio. He'd been alive for more than six centuries, and three small lasses had him ready to drop at their feet and beg for their favor? What rubbish.

Rhiannon looked the other two women up and down, and then shot a glance down her own body. "Does it look like we're dressed ta stay at home?"

In fact, now that it came to his attention, the three of them were wearing full-length pelisses. The ladies were obviously headed out. Why that fact had escaped him moments before, he had no idea. Aside, of course, from the fact that Rhiannon's heartbeat, which he could hear in his head beating its frantic little rhythm, had the majority of his attention. His ever-increasing desire to once again taste her gardenia-scented body held the rest. One would think that after just having a taste of her the night before, he would be satisfied. But that was not the case.

"I am at your disposal should you need an escort," he offered. He finally met Rhiannon's gaze, which flashed like the lightning he knew she barely held at bay. She was that angry. She was very, very angry. If only he knew why.

"I believe we can find our way across Town, but thank ye for the offer," Rhiannon clipped out. But beneath all that anger in her fierce gaze, he sensed a measure of hurt as well.

"Might I have a word with you before you go, Rhiannon?" he asked casually.

"Might ye be boiled in a cauldron of oil, Lord Blodswell?" the youngest one said. She looked quite pleased with herself. That one wasn't even a witch, though she'd obviously been raised by one.

He sighed heavily in exasperation. Lady Eynsford locked arms with Rhiannon on one side and her sister on the other. Then they charged down the corridor, forcing him to scurry to the side like a rat in hiding to keep from being run over.

"Perhaps later, then," he called to their retreating backs.

When the women had disappeared out the front door, Matthew sagged against the wall, closed his eyes, and tried to rein in his errant thoughts. What on earth had made Rhiannon so angry? The night before, she'd found pleasure while he shared in her life force. And today he was a pariah. What could possibly have changed?

The door to Eynsford's study opened slowly, and the Lycan pushed his head out, glancing left and right down the hallway. "Are they gone?" he whispered dramatically.

Matthew nodded.

"Thank God," Eynsford sighed, and his shoulders

drooped in relief. "I don't know what you did, but you have until they get home to undo it. Because, if I have to spend another morning with my wife shooting mental daggers at me simply because I have bollocks, I'll have your head." He jabbed a finger at Matthew as he talked. "And I don't give a damn how strong your maker is or how many scars she might inflict upon me as recompense for any harm that could befall you. It would be worth it."

Then a smile broke across the man's face. He was enjoying Matthew's discomfort. Oh, yes, he was.

"What did you do?" the Lycan asked.

If only he knew. Matthew shrugged. "I have no idea." He touched his own ear. "You didn't by chance overhear anything, did you?"

"Whispers," Eynsford offered in way of explanation. "Just sounds like hissing to me, and my thoughts have been occupied with Weston's disfigurement this morning."

Disfigurement was a slight exaggeration, though Matthew held his tongue.

"You've clearly done something."

Clearly. Though he had no idea what it could be. "I would say that the fact that I'm breathing has irked them, but since I really don't need to breathe to live, that wouldn't hold water."

Eynsford grinned broadly. "Oh, it's not the breathing that offends them. It's your very existence." The man chuckled all the way back into his study. He laughed until Matthew would wager that his side hurt from the merriment.

❧

Rhiannon settled back against the squabs of Eynsford's plush coach and bit back the tears that threatened to fall. "How *could* he?" she moaned instead. She turned to face her sister. "Ginny, are ye certain he kissed her? Ye couldna be mistaken?"

"I am completely certain," Ginny said, the truth in her tone achingly familiar. "Well, *she* kissed *him*, but he liked it."

"How do ye ken he liked it?" Cait asked, her tone frantic. She'd been beside herself all morning, ever since breakfast when she'd learned about what had happened the night before.

"He dinna stop her," Ginny said.

Cait groaned and flopped back against the seat. "I canna believe I was so wrong about him. Why dinna I see it?"

"Cait, all ye have ta do is look inta the future ta see if there's any truth behind what Ginny saw. Perhaps she was just mistaken." Of course, Cait could. What good was such a power if one could not use it?

"That would be lookin' in the past," Caitrin grumbled. "I doona have that power." Then she shook her head vehemently. "Besides, I have interfered enough. Ye never would have fallen for him if I hadna forced it."

"Ye dinna force anythin'," Rhiannon corrected. As though Cait could force her into somewhere she didn't want to be. Cait's was a passive power after all, while Rhiannon's was quite active. More active than she wanted it to be most days.

Cait massaged her forehead. "Oh, I did," she groaned. "I thrust ye inta his path at every opportunity."

She threw her hands up in defeat. "And now look what has happened. Ye have fallen in love with the scoundrel, while he's out kissin' other lasses."

Rhiannon sat forward. "Cait, look inta my future, just this once," she prodded. "And tell me what the outcome will be."

"No." Cait turned to look out the coach window, quite effectively dismissing them all. "I willna participate in this debacle of a courtship. No' anymore."

"This debacle of a courtship just happens ta be my life," Rhiannon charged. "And since ye *did* thrust me inta the path of that man, ye owe me."

"Which probably caused the problem in the first place. I kent better than ta interfere with the future, but ye looked so happy in my vision. I wanted it so badly for ye."

"Cait, please," Rhiannon begged.

"Canna ye see what my interferin' has already caused, Rhi?" Cait shook her head. "It's all my fault, and I willna compound the mistake by makin' another one." She clamped her lips together tightly.

Rhiannon knew at that very moment she was done for. Cait had decided not to participate. And there would be no swaying her from her decision.

"Where are we goin'?" Ginny asked quietly from her side of the coach. "I should probably get back ta Aunt Greer's house. I've been gone all night. She must be frantic with worry."

Or thoroughly perturbed that she couldn't control Ginny's every movement. The latter was more likely.

"I need ta talk with the Duchess of Hythe," Rhiannon said.

"Why on earth would ye want ta talk ta her?" Cait countered.

"She offered last night ta be my mentor," Rhiannon mumbled, hating to tell them all the truth of the matter. But she was desperate.

"She did?" Cait couldn't have looked more shocked if Rhiannon had just hit her with a bolt of lightning.

"She did," Rhiannon affirmed with a nod. "She likes me."

"She doesna like anyone," Ginny announced.

Just then, the coach stopped in front of Hythe House and Cait pushed the curtain back to peer cautiously outside. "Ye doona expect me ta go in there, do ye? I would sooner have someone string me up by my toenails than drop in on her Her Grace unannounced. It's simply no' done." She looked at Rhiannon as though she'd gone mad.

The coach door opened, and Rhiannon bounded out. She turned back to Ginny and Cait and said with a smirk, "Ye may stay in the coach, or ye may join me. But if ye decide no' ta accompany me, I willna fill ye in on the details later." Their own yearning to know what was going on would be their downfall. She was certain of it.

They both scurried out behind her, just as Rhiannon had assumed they would. No one would miss the tale that was about to unfold.

Rhiannon squared her shoulders as the butler opened the door and looked down his long, crooked nose at her. "Miss Rhiannon Sinclair for the Duchess of Hythe, please," she said, happy to hear it when her voice didn't tremble. Well, only a small bit.

"Her Grace is not receiving at the moment," he said, his eyebrows drawing together in the fiercest look she'd ever seen.

But Rhiannon refused to be cowed. She pushed through the door, sliding directly beneath his arm and into the foyer. She stood proud and tall. "I'd appreciate it if ye would tell the duchess I'm here anyway."

He closed the door, nodded once to her in deference, and walked slowly down the corridor. As soon as he was gone, Rhiannon opened the front door and ushered Cait and Ginny inside.

"She's finally done it. She has finally gone mad. I kent all those year spent out of doors would be her downfall," Ginny whispered to herself, her eyes closed tightly.

The clunk of the butler's shoes heralded his return to the foyer. "The duchess will see you in her sitting room."

Cait reached over and grabbed Rhiannon's arm, hissing in her ear. "Ye have been invited inta the duchess' own sittin' room?"

"If ye swoon, I swear I willna catch ye," Rhiannon warned sternly.

"And the ladies may—" the butler began.

"They may accompany me," Rhiannon blurted before he could relegate them to a separate room in the house. When he opened his mouth to protest, she raised her nose a little higher in the air and glared at him.

"Very well," he clipped out. The three women fell into formation behind him as he weaved through corridors and up stairs.

He finally stopped and scratched lightly at a door. A formidable grunt was the response.

"She's not at her best in the morning," he said smugly as he stood aside and ushered them over the threshold. Then the door closed behind them, almost like a harbinger of an upcoming storm. Oh, dear.

The duchess reclined on a large, overstuffed chair, a cup of chocolate resting in her hands. She narrowed her eyes at Rhiannon, who curtsied quickly, with Caitrin and Ginny following in her wake. "Good mornin', Yer Grace," Rhiannon began.

"I don't believe I can remember the last time someone disturbed me at this hour of the day," the duchess said, her tone biting.

Rhiannon took a deep breath. "Ye did say I could call on ye," she reminded the duchess.

"I meant at a decent hour." She raised her brows at Rhiannon, who simply crossed the room to take a chair across from her.

Rhi didn't care if she hadn't been invited to sit. She did so, regardless. She heard Cait groan behind her. "I find myself in a bit of a fix." There was no better time than the present to jump right in. "I'm in need of yer counsel."

"Indeed," was all the duchess said.

"It's about Lord Blodswell," Rhiannon clarified.

A light began to shine in the old woman's eyes. "Do tell," she said.

"Well, ye do remember last night when ye told me what I should do ta win Lord Blodswell?" She didn't want to say it out loud, not with Caitrin and Ginny standing nearby. She shot them a pointed glance, and they ambled together over to the window, where they pretended to admire a large oak tree.

"Continue." The duchess waved a hand at her.

Rhiannon continued in hushed tones. "Well, I did. And… we… well… we… we *did*, Yer Grace." Rhiannon felt the blush rush up her cheeks at her confession.

The duchess laid her cup on the nearby table and faced Rhiannon. "You *did*?"

"Well, we dinna… ye ken… we dinna… do *that*. But we did… Well, we did somethin' else."

The duchess smiled and clapped her hands together, which was quite unexpected and made Rhiannon jump. "I am very proud of you," the duchess exclaimed. "Exactly how far did you…?" Her eyes beseeched Rhiannon to continue.

"Oh, blast and damn," Rhiannon finally bit out, burying her head in her hands. "I'm still an innocent. But no' by much." She said the last between the heels of her hands, which rested against her cheeks.

The old woman's eyes twinkled with glee. She reached forward and patted Rhiannon's knee. "I am so happy. That man will take a tumble. And I will be there to witness it all." Rhiannon wasn't certain if the duchess was talking to herself or to Rhiannon. So, she just waited, her heart in her throat, for the woman to continue. "He has asked you to marry him, has he not?" she asked for clarification.

"He has. And he has sought my father's permission."

"And?" the duchess prompted.

"And he received it. The banns will be read." Rhiannon held up her thumb and index finger, and pointed to the inch of space in between. "But I have a small problem."

"You have the man ready to drop at your feet and declare his everlasting devotion, Miss Sinclair. You have him by the bollocks, as one with less dignity than myself might say." Cait giggled from across the room but turned it into a cough against her closed fist.

"I might have had him by the bollocks at that moment, Yer Grace. But as soon as I left him, he moved on to another." She bit back the tears that threatened to spill over her lashes. Oh, dear, the duchess would never forgive her if a storm cloud ruined her good Aubusson rug.

"Moved on to whom?" the duchess barked. "And how do you know this?" She sat all the way forward, as though ready to bound from her chair, though with her considerable girth, "bound" might be the wrong word.

"Ginny," Rhiannon called to her sister from across the room. "Come and tell Her Grace about the lass he was with."

"So, you didn't see this assignation, Miss Sinclair?" the duchess wanted to know. She regarded Ginny with her nose in the air. Even from her lower position, she appeared to be looking down at the girl.

"No, Yer Grace," she sighed. "Ginny did." If Rhi had seen it herself, she would have felt the need to cleave the lightskirt into two pieces with a lightning bolt.

The duchess motioned impatiently for Ginny and Caitrin to sit. "Out with it, gel. I'm not getting any younger while you stand there."

"I was in the garden, and I saw Lord Blodswell with a lady. She stood up on her tiptoes and kissed him."

Ginny drew in a deep breath, as though she needed fortitude. They all needed fortitude.

"*Where* did she kiss him?" the duchess asked.

"I… in the garden," Ginny stammered.

"Where on his body, gel?" the duchess demanded, stamping her foot in frustration. Ginny wrung her hands together nervously.

"On his face. She petted his face, and then she kissed him. And he didn't pull away. And then she asked him if he planned to be really naughty. Or at least that's what it sounded like." Ginny was fighting to remain composed, Rhiannon could tell.

"What did this ladybird look like?" Her Grace's eyebrows drew together so deeply that a vee formed in the loose skin between her eyes.

"It was dark—" Ginny began.

"Oh, I certainly hope it was, after what your sister was doing with him in the garden," the duchess said as she cast a wicked glance at Rhiannon. "For which you are to be commended, my dear." She patted Rhiannon's knee. "Did you see her features at all?" The woman turned her icy eyes on Ginny.

"Well, her eyes were dark. I canna be sure of the color. But she has red hair. Well, reddish brown," Ginny clarified. "And it wasna pinned up properly. It hung down her back like a wanton."

The duchess harrumphed and Rhi hoped the woman didn't wonder what Ginny knew of wantons.

"And she dinna wear gloves. Her hands were exposed, and she had long, pointy fingernails."

The duchess nodded as though that meant something to her. "A tiny little thing, was she?"

Ginny nodded. "Aye, and she had a voice like a siren and a smile so wicked it made me want to shiver."

"Callista," the duchess sneered. "She sounds just like Callista."

"Who is Callista?" Rhiannon asked.

"Who *was* she," the duchess corrected. "I knew a woman like that back before I married Hythe. Callista de Burgh exuded sensuality in everything she did. I've never seen such confidence in a woman. She had half the men in Town falling at her feet."

"Well it canna be the same woman," Ginny said. "She'd be old now."

The duchess' brow creased with annoyance. "Of course it's not the same woman, Miss Ginessa. And she wouldn't be *old*. She'd be my age. Please refrain from opening your mouth unless you have something helpful to add." Then she refocused her attention on Rhiannon. "What I meant, Miss Sinclair, was that I am familiar with that sort of woman."

Had Matthew always cavorted with that sort of woman? Rhiannon leaned forward in her seat. "Was Lord Blodswell's grandfather enamored with this Callista?"

The duchess shook her head. "I said she had *half* the men in Town falling at her feet. The other half, my Hythe included, were more discriminating."

Rhiannon released a breath, not that Matthew's actions five decades earlier really meant anything at this point. Still, the duchess' answer brought her a bit of relief. "So *yer* Lord Blodswell had more discriminatin' taste?"

The duchess shrugged. "Well, he was fond of her.

In a very brotherly sort of way. He most definitely was not part of the throng who followed her from room to room, however."

"What has this ta do with anythin'?" Ginny asked. "It's the *current* Lord Blodswell ye need help with, Rhi."

The duchess narrowed her eyes on Ginny. "The two of you may go." She gestured to Cait and Ginny absently, motioning her hand toward the door. "Our planning will go better without interference."

"I canna go home. No' without a reason for bein' gone when Aunt Greer woke up," Ginny said quietly to Rhiannon.

The duchess sighed as though dealing with Ginny would try even Job's patience. "You may wait in one of my parlors, Miss Ginessa, and then I'll escort you myself to Cooper House. By the time I'm through with your aunt, you will have gained not only her forgiveness, but also her favor. Now, go." She motioned toward the door again.

"Rhi, will ye be all right?" Cait asked softly.

"I do not gobble up debutantes, Lady Eynsford. Pray keep Miss Ginessa company somewhere, anywhere else, for the time being."

As soon as the pair exited the private sitting room, Rhiannon found herself completely alone with the Duchess of Hythe, who looked more alive than Rhi had ever seen her.

"I do have an idea," the duchess began. "How daring are you, Miss Sinclair?"

Nineteen

MATTHEW DROPPED INTO THE SEAT BEHIND HIS mahogany desk and closed his eyes. The pounding in his head had only intensified, beating like an African drum, ever since he'd left Thorpe House. He placed both hands on his temples, hoping to massage the pain away, but to no avail.

"You look nearly as bad as you did in Edinburgh." Alec MacQuarrie's voice came from the threshold.

Matthew opened one eye to glare at his protégé. "It's just a headache."

"I didn't think we were supposed to get those."

Matthew scrubbed a hand across his face. Apparently, he was to have no peace. "Trying to sort out women can give any man a headache."

Alec chuckled. "Good to know." He pushed himself from the doorjamb and walked farther into Matthew's study. "I'll just indulge in *Brysi*'s offerings and wash my hands of the whole lot."

"That's a wonderful plan." But not for Matthew. He didn't want to wash his hands of Rhiannon. Even if he could partake of another, he had no desire to do so. He wanted to bask in her mischievous hazel gaze. He wanted her soft lips to trail up and down his skin. He wanted to strip her of every stitch of clothing and hold her in his arms for all eternity.

What he didn't want to ever see again was the scathing, hurtful glare she'd cast in his direction before scrambling out of Thorpe House.

Alec folded himself into a chair across from Matthew. "So what is it you're trying to sort out? How she can stomach to surround herself with those dogs?"

Matthew snorted. He wasn't all that thrilled with *those dogs*, either. Eynsford could have been a tiny bit more helpful this morning. Blasted Lycan. "Honestly, I don't have any idea, Alec."

His friend's eyes settled on Matthew. Concern and devotion filled their dark depths. Confiding in Alec might be the very best thing. After all, the Scot had known Rhiannon most of her life. His insight could be most useful.

Matthew sat forward, leaning his elbows on his desk. "She was happy to see me last night." More than happy. He'd gone to bed smiling at the memory of her gasps echoing in his ears. "And then this morning at Thorpe House, she looked at me as though I'd killed her best friend."

Alec's brow rose with amusement. "I'm assuming you *didn't* kill her best friend since Sorcha's safely tucked away in Scotland."

And he'd thought Alec could be of some use. Matthew scowled at the Scot. "Never mind. Forget I said anything."

"No, no, no," Alec protested. "Go on. Rhi wasn't happy to see you this morning."

Matthew shook his head. "I would have thought it had something to do with Weston Hadley's injury, but she made some comment about me being a *man*, as though it were the vilest of curse words."

"That sounds like Blaire more than Rhiannon."

"Something happened. I'm just not certain what."

"You thought it might have something to do with some injury?"

"Callista scarred one of the Hadley twins last night in a temper. If Rhiannon was upset about it, I'm sure she would have just told me so. Even still, I don't think she'd be angry with *me*. It's not as though I inflicted the gash."

Confusion crossed Alec's face. "Are you saying she actually scarred the dog? But you told me Lycans could heal themselves just as we do."

Matthew nodded absently. "They do with any normal injury, aside from something that kills instantly anyway. Broken neck, that sort of thing."

"But Hadley didn't heal?"

"He *healed*," Matthew stressed. "But he'll wear Callista's mark across his face 'til the end of his days. But as I said, I don't think that's what Rhiannon is angry about. It wouldn't have anything to do with me being a *man*."

"Go back," Alec said. "If Hadley has healed, why does he wear Callista's mark?"

"Because it was inflicted by vampyre flesh," Matthew explained, then added when he saw Alec's eyes flash with delight, "and, no, you may not go about disfiguring Eynsford, his pack, or any other Lycan. The last thing we need is a war on our hands."

"Just a little scar?" Alec asked, the gleam still present in his eyes.

"No scarring Eynsford. It might bring you a bit of satisfaction in the moment, but you'll have a lifetime of moments afterward when you'll regret the action."

"So you say." Alec slumped back in his seat.

Matthew resisted the urge to roll his eyes. "Do you think Lady Eynsford would thank you for it? I was on the receiving end of her scathing glare this morning too, and I'd rather not repeat…" He let his voice trail off as an idea struck him. The clairvoyant Caitrin Eynsford *had* been furious with him too, hadn't she? "Do you suppose they're not angry with me for something I've done, but for something I *will* do?"

Alec shrugged. "You're sure you haven't done something to deserve her ire?"

"I've done nothing." Matthew frowned. "Nothing at all. Good God! What awful thing do you suppose I'm going to do?"

"Scar Eynsford?" Alec put in hopefully. "Or sever one of his limbs perhaps?"

Matthew glared at his friend. "You've been exactly no help, Alec. Thank you so much for visiting."

What did Rhiannon think he was going to do? What future crime had Lady Eynsford seen? *He's a man after all.* Rhiannon's words echoed in his mind. That wasn't even a usable clue. That could mean a million things, because he *was* a man after all.

◦⋙✦⋘◦

Rhiannon didn't think she'd heard the Duchess of Hythe correctly. "I beg yer pardon?"

The old woman cackled with glee. "How else are you to find out what you're up against, Miss Sinclair?"

Rhiannon shook her head. "If I was discovered, I'd be ruined."

"A risk worth taking. Do you love him?"

A tear streamed down Rhiannon's cheek, just as a deluge pitter-pattered against the window. At least the rain had transpired outdoors rather than in. Rhi swiped at the traitorous tear as she nodded. "That's why this hurts so much, Your Grace."

The duchess offered Rhi a handkerchief. "Of course it does. And that's why you'll want to find out what he's up to. The sorts of places he frequents. The sort of people he calls friends. Until you enticed him into polite society, Miss Sinclair, no one had seen neither hide nor hair of him. But he must go places, see people. After the bloom is off the rose, he'll return to those pursuits. It's the way of men. And once you've said 'I do,' it's too late to back out. No, no, it's best to know up front what sort of scoundrel you've given your heart to."

Matthew hadn't even waited until their vows were said before he'd returned to those pursuits, had he? Rhiannon twisted the handkerchief in her hand. "I wouldn't know the first thing about following him. I've never been very good at subterfuge."

Her Grace grinned. "Recruit that Radbourne fellow to go along with you. He seems willing to do your bidding. And if anyone is adept at hiding, though in his case from creditors, it's Viscount Radbourne."

"And if we're caught?"

"I have a feeling Radbourne never gets caught. Take it from me, Miss Sinclair, that fellow knows how to stay hidden in the proverbial shadows. And you need to know what you're getting yourself into with Blodswell. You've given the man your heart. It's time to find out if that was a wise decision. And if you discover his sins are darker than you can bear, it is better for you to learn such details before you say your vows. It's not too late for you to reclaim your heart, after all."

Rhiannon nodded. She knew the duchess was right. It was better to know what she was getting herself into with Matthew than to let her heart lead her.

"Good girl." Her Grace patted Rhi's hand. "Now, go on with you and send that sister of yours up. We'll have to get our story straight before we head over to Cooper House."

After Rhi departed from the duchess' personal sitting room, the Hythes' butler led her to a small parlor done in soft pinks and yellows, where Cait and Ginny sat across from each other in matching chintz chairs. When Rhiannon entered, Ginny bolted from her seat.

"What did she say?"

Rhiannon shrugged. Ginny was the last person she'd tell her plan to. Heaven forbid her sister put the same featherbrained plan in motion with Lord Steven as her target. "She said she's ready for ye ta join her so ye can decide what ta tell Aunt Greer."

Ginny crossed the floor in a few strides and threw her arms around Rhiannon's neck. "I am so sorry about all of this."

Rhi was sorry, too. She patted her sister's back. "No' ta worry, Gin. One way or the other, things will turn out."

"That dishonorable, skirt-chasing blackguard. I'd like ta slap that smug expression from his face."

Rhi pulled out of her sister's embrace. "Ye doona want ta keep the duchess waitin'."

Ginny agreed with a quick good-bye to Cait and a kiss on Rhiannon's cheek, and then she quit the room.

Cait folded her arms across her chest and frowned. "I'll expect ye ta tell *me* the truth."

As though anyone could ever lie to Cait and get away with it. "Of course, but I'd rather do so in the privacy of yer carriage."

"Well, then," Cait hooked Rhi's arm with her own, "let's take our leave already."

If Rhiannon's heart wasn't so heavy, she would have laughed. Cait hated being kept in the dark about anything. They waited patiently as the Eynsford carriage pulled in front of the steps, and then Cait rushed Rhi into the conveyance and shut the door behind them.

"All right. Let me hear it."

"Ye are a mite impatient, Caitrin."

The seer narrowed her pretty blue eyes. "I am waitin', Rhiannon Sinclair."

Rhi nodded. "Very well. Her Grace said I should follow him for a sennight. See where he spends his time and with whom. That if I canna deal with what I find, then I should cry off before it's too late."

Cait frowned and fell back against the squabs with a harrumph. "I doona think that's a very good idea, Rhi."

"Why no'? I might learn who this woman is. What she means ta him."

"I think we already ken what she means ta him. She's a willin' lass. Besides, I've *seen* some of the places he and Alec haunt, and I wouldna want that vision for ye."

Rhi leaned forward on her bench. "What sort of places?"

Cait's frown darkened, and she folded her arms across her chest. "For heaven's sake, Rhi. The man is a vampyre. The sort of places he goes are no' fit for anyone's eyes. I wish *I* hadna seen that feeding trough that doubles as a gentlemen's club."

"Gentlemen's club?"

"Oh, no." Cait shook her head. "I willna say one more word about it. Just stay clear of the place and no followin' Blodswell. I had no idea the duchess was goin' ta fill yer head with such nonsense. I thought for sure she'd tell ye ta cut yer losses and find a man who is truly deservin' of ye."

"She asked me if I love him," Rhi said softly.

Cait groaned aloud and closed her eyes. "It's all my fault."

"It's no' yer fault, Cait. So doona blame yerself. I think Her Grace is right. I should learn all I can about Matthew. If I am ta marry the man, I should ken the whole truth of who he is. I need ta ken if I can live with all of it."

Cait's pained expression spoke her blatant disagreement more clearly than if she'd used actual words.

The coach slowed to a halt. "I'll ask Archer ta go with me. I promise I'll be safe." Rhiannon tried to assuage her friend's worry.

The coach door opened and Lord Radbourne poked his head inside, a charming grin upon his handsome face. "Did I hear my name?"

Cait rolled her eyes. "Ye must be hearin' things, Archer. No one was talkin' about ye at all." Clearly her friend thought she could talk Rhiannon out of her plan.

Rhiannon sighed. She wasn't about to be managed so easily. "I *was* talkin' about ye, my lord. I'm hopin' ye might be willin' ta help me with somethin'."

"Your wish is my command."

Cait pushed past the viscount as she exited the coach. "We'll just have ta see what your brother has ta say about it." She started up the drive as quickly as her slipper-shod feet could take her.

Before Rhiannon could follow her friend, Archer climbed into the coach and sank into the seat opposite her. He rapped on the roof to get the carriage moving, smiled roguishly at her, and said, "If I'm going to have the pack alpha snarling at me for the rest of the week like some dog who has lost his bone, you had better fill me in on your plan. I need to decide if time spent with you is worth the pop on the nose I'll get when I next see Dashiel. Where are we going?"

Rhiannon looked out the small window to see Cait standing with her hands on her hips. "She's goin' ta be so angry," she mumbled. Then she gave Radbourne her full attention. "I'm no' entirely certain where we're goin'. But I'm almost sure we'll know it when we get there."

"Why does that frighten me?" He gave a mock shiver.

"Ye are no' required ta accompany me. I'm certain I can find Matthew on my own." She refused to look Radbourne in the face when she said the last.

"Have you lost him?" He didn't even crack a smile.

"No, I havena *lost* him." She shook her head with dismay.

"You haven't lost him, yet you feel the need to find him?" His eyes narrowed at her as though by doing so he could peer at her innermost secrets.

"I'm simply… interested." She shrugged her shoulders in what she thought was a nonchalant gesture. To him, it probably just looked foolish.

"I already knew you were interested, considering your betrothal and how close you two became at the Duchess of Hythe's soiree." He held up two hands to fend off her sputtering protests. "I know it's not appropriate to discuss, but you nearly got yourself ruined. You'd run headlong into trouble with every turn if you didn't have someone looking after your best interests."

"And ye have taxed yerself with that job, Lord Radbourne?" she returned hotly.

His brows rose as he chuckled. "Oh, so we're back to formalities now, are we?"

"Ye doona ken me well enough ta judge me," she said softly as the most mortifying of tears slipped down her face. She swiped at it with the back of her hand. The pitter-patter of raindrops hit the top of the carriage.

"Now you're going to be a watering pot? Good God, you women do know how to tug at a man's heartstrings." He groaned deeply, switched sides in the carriage, and then drew her head to lie on his shoulder. He didn't embrace her or otherwise touch her but let her sniffle against the sleeve of his coat until she was done. "Now do you want to talk about what has you so upset?" he asked gently.

Gone was the snide, devil-may-care viscount. In his place was Archer Hadley, and she wasn't too sure how to process that.

"My sister caught Matthew in the garden with a lass at the duchess' soiree," she said quietly, hating the very thought of saying the words out loud. As though that would give them credence.

"Was this before or after *I* caught *him* with *you* at the soiree?" He didn't have a bit of smile in his voice, but Rhiannon was afraid to look at his face.

"After," she replied.

"So, you believe he had a tryst with you and then went on to have another with some other unsuspecting female?" She heard the smile in his voice this time. The blackguard. She poked him in the side.

"I doona think she was unsuspectin'," Rhiannon said. "She was suspectin'."

He actually chuckled out loud. Even more gloom settled over Rhiannon. The rain began to fall harder on the roof of the carriage. "Sweetheart, he's just a man. And I can tell you from experience that he cannot do what he did with you and then do it again five minutes later." He paused as though mulling something over in his mind. "Well, I can, but I doubt Blodswell can."

"Ye can do what?" She sat up to look him in the eye. "I doona understand."

"Never mind," he said as he coaxed her head back onto his shoulder. He took a deep breath before continuing. "As much as I hate the very idea of helping the man, have you asked Blodswell what the situation was with the other woman in the garden?"

"No," she admitted.

"Of course not. That would be much too direct for those of you who wear skirts, wouldn't it? Just once, I'd love to find a woman who will speak to me directly, question my every move, and challenge my very existence." He sighed.

"The duchess said I should follow him," she admitted. "Watch and see where he goes."

He snorted. "Absolutely not. We will do no such thing. We will simply go and ask the man." He tapped the roof with his fist. "Upper Brook Street. Blodswell House." Then he glanced back down at Rhiannon. "We will take the bull by the horns."

"The duchess said somethin' about that, and knowing which horn to grab, but I wasn't sure what she meant…" She let her voice trail off.

He coughed into his hand to smother a laugh. "The duchess is much naughtier than I ever expected. The next time she attempts to eject me and my brothers from one of her soirees, I might just let on that I'm aware of her mischievous side."

"Leave me out of it, if ye do," Rhiannon requested. That was all she needed. To be on the outs with the Duchess of Hythe, her only ally aside from her coven sisters. "Are ye sure we should do this? I mean, go ta Matthew's home."

Archer's amber eyes sparkled with mirth. "After what you *have* been doing with the man, visiting his home is nothing. Besides, you're with me."

Which really wasn't much better than being alone, at least not in society's eyes. In fact, it might be worse. "I shouldna even be with ye. I do still have a reputation."

The coach slowed down and came to a stop. Archer lifted the curtain and glanced out. The rain still poured. She was still feeling melancholy, so of course it did.

"Are you ready?" he asked.

Was she ready? No, she would never be ready to face Matthew and simply *ask* him what had happened with that other lass. What a ridiculous notion. She shook her head in the negative.

"Chin up, Rhiannon," he teased. "It's not as bad as you think. When you ask direct questions, you might just get direct answers."

She squared her shoulders. She was a weather-born witch. She had years and years of a prosperous magical legacy at her disposal. And here she sat, cowering like a homeless waif? What rubbish.

"I'm ready," she said.

He stepped out of the coach and ducked his head against the pouring rain. He moved to shuck his coat and cover her head, but she dodged him.

"I love the rain," she explained, raising her arms to catch the droplets in her cupped hand. She inhaled deeply, using the weather imbalance to upright the emotions that had roiled within her only moments before.

"Have you finally gone daft on me, Rhiannon?" he asked, taking her chin in his hand and forcing her to meet his gaze. "Rhi, are you all right?"

"Better," she sighed. Then she hopped up on

her tiptoes and quickly kissed his cheek. "Thank ye, Archer. But ye can go now. I'll be fine." She started toward Matthew's door.

Archer followed close on her heels, but she spun quickly, raised her hand, and shoved him back with a blast of air. He stumbled under the onslaught. "What the devil?" he cursed.

"My apologies," she said, feeling lighter than she had all day. "Thank ye for accompanyin' me, but this is somethin' I need ta do on my own."

"You're soaking wet, Rhiannon," he complained, looking around as though he still wanted to know where that blast of air had originated. "Let me take you home."

"I have my nerve up, now, Archer. But thank ye all the same." She dismissed him by turning her back as she rapped on the door of Matthew's town house.

His butler opened the door and gazed down at her. "May I help you?"

Certainly, she looked like a street urchin with her hair stuck to her head and her dress dripping with rain. But she raised her nose up in the air and asked for Matthew, regardless.

"His lordship is not in residence at the present time," he said. He closed the door in her face. *How dare he?*

"*Now* are you ready to go home?" Archer called to her.

"No, I am no' ready ta go home," she replied.

He sighed heavily. "How much longer until you give up?"

"Oh, ye doona ken me very well, Archer, if ye think

I might give up." Evidently, he found her to be weak. Of course, if you paint the portrait, you must play the part. Well, the part of a weak, little Scottish lass wasn't a character she was willing to portray. Not anymore.

"This is nonsense. The man isn't home, and you're drenched. Get back in the coach, Rhiannon."

But she shook her head. "There is no' a thing in the world ye could say that will dissuade me. So be off."

"You really mean to stand here in the rain and wait for the man?"

"No. I plan ta sneak inside and wait for him."

Twenty

RHIANNON CREPT BACK UP THE STEPS OF MATTHEW'S home. She pressed her ear to the door and was relieved not to hear anyone moving about on the other side. Then she cracked the door and peered inside, looking left and right. No one was in sight. She stuck an arm out the door and motioned to Archer that all was well. Hopefully, he would leave. Somehow, she doubted that, though.

She glanced down at the floor, which was quickly becoming a sopping wet mess, thanks to her drenched skirts. Rhiannon pulled her hem above the floor and dashed up the staircase as fast as her feet would take her. Most town homes had bedchambers abovestairs, didn't they? She certainly hoped so.

She tiptoed around until she found what had to be the earl's master chamber. She didn't know what she had expected, but certainly not the rich opulence that met her eye. Large furniture pieces in dark mahogany stood sentinel in the room, with the focus being a massive four-poster bed. Various knickknacks and bric-a-brac were tossed about, and Rhiannon stopped briefly to glance at them. But what she needed most was the fire. She was still dripping and cold. Thankfully, a small smoldering fire still warmed in the grate. She poked at it, bringing new life to the flames. Within moments, she had a nice blaze going. Now what to do about the water?

She shook her skirts, only to sling more water across the floor. "He'll think one of the Lycans has been in here shaking water from his fur," she mumbled. She couldn't do much at this point, aside from letting her clothes dry. But she might be warmer if she let them dry hanging by the fire. Matthew wasn't there and might not be for hours. So, it was reasonably safe to remove her garments quickly and hang them across a pair of chairs that sat near the grate. She got down to her chemise, which was so wet that it was completely transparent, and she tugged it over her head as well.

When all her clothing was arranged to her satisfaction, she slipped under the counterpane of Matthew's bed to warm herself. She'd only stay long enough to dry her clothes and don them, and then she would sit and wait for him to arrive. She would take Archer's advice and ask some very direct questions, and she wasn't leaving until she had Matthew's answers. Who was that woman he kissed in the garden? And what did she mean to him?

Rhiannon had never expected a love match. She always assumed she'd end up married to a Scotsman who was more enamored with her dowry than her person. That was the way of most marriages, after all; and she had resigned herself to the fact. But then

Matthew had found her in Hyde Park in the middle of a storm… Rhi shook her head. No matter who her husband was destined to be, Matthew or some nameless Scot, she would expect faithfulness.

She ran through various scenarios and conversations in her head, trying to decide the best way to approach him. But finally boredom overtook her and her lids grew heavy. She'd rest for only a moment. By then, her clothes should be dry. Yes, only a moment. No longer than that…

❧

Matthew arrived home to discover his household all aflutter. He glanced anxiously around, expecting to find that a tragedy had happened within his doors, like his butler being tied up and the house ransacked. Or one of the maids being caught with a footman. He'd actually interrupted that very thing the week before, but he'd chosen not to begrudge them their affections.

He realized the butler was safe when the man approached him, wringing his hands. "Lord Blodswell," he began, his voice cracking with the effort to speak. He was obviously overwrought about something.

"What is it, Hughes? Has something happened?" Matthew tossed his coat and hat to the man, despite his mumbled protests. "Out with it," he snapped. He truly didn't have time to listen to one old man blather about missing silver or stores from the cellar that had gone missing.

"Lord Blodswell, I don't know how it happened," the man began again, his gaze dancing around the room as he looked everywhere but at Matthew.

"Exactly what are you referring to?" Matthew said as he smacked his gloves against this palm with irritation.

"She knocked on the door, sir." He pointed toward the offending portal as though it had sprouted wings and would fly away. "And I told her you weren't home. Then I dismissed her."

"Her?" Matthew questioned.

"She looked quite bedraggled, all wet and all, so I didn't invite her in." He danced from side to side, still nervous, obviously. As well he should be.

"A wet woman showed up at my door, and you did not allow her entrance?" Matthew asked. That sounded very ungentlemanly.

"It was raining, sir, and I'd watched her out the window. She just stood there with her hands cupped, trying to catch the rain. I believed she was a bit mad." His breathing began to steady.

A madwoman, reveling in a rainstorm? A smile tugged at his lips. That could only be one person. She'd come to him, despite the fact that it was horribly improper. Despite the fact that she'd obviously been angry at him for something or other that very morning, which he still didn't understand. Matthew reached for his hat.

"I believe I know who you're referring to," he said. "Dark hair that's long enough to wrap around your finger? Hazel eyes that flash like lightning?"

"I didn't get a good look at her eyes, sir." The butler still looked positively green. "I saw the rest of her, though," he murmured. At Matthew's shocked expression, he hastened to clarify. "Not that I was trying to, you see. She didn't even know I poked my head in. I just went up to check on her at his insistence." Hughes pointed toward the sitting room, where two booted feet rested over the end of his settee. Matthew ambled into the room.

"What the devil?" he murmured. Radbourne was asleep on his settee. "How long has *he* been here?" The butler began to speak, but Matthew held up a hand. "Wait. You mentioned a girl."

Matthew stopped and crossed his hands in front of him, determined to wait for Hughes to collect himself.

A muffled voice from the couch said, "Rhiannon's in your bed." Matthew spun to face Radbourne and saw the Lycan burrow his face deeper into a pillow on the settee, his eyes still closed.

"I beg your pardon?" Matthew asked.

Radbourne sat up slowly with a belabored grunt, swinging his feet to the floor as he righted his clothing.

"Why are you here?"

"Protecting Rhiannon's virtue," the Lycan said with the smallest hint of a smile on his face, as though he knew a secret no one else did. "Though I have decided to give up that pursuit, if you'll grant me some answers. Then I'll take my leave."

Matthew massaged his forehead in frustration. That pounding within his head was returning. With force. "I think I'm the one who deserves the answers."

Radbourne scowled at the butler. "You may go," he said.

The man turned on his heel and fled. So much for loyalty.

"Pray tell me what's going on?"

"Your butler didn't like me," Radbourne said.

"I don't particularly like you, either," Matthew admitted.

"Yes, I know," Radbourne chuckled. "I prefer it that way." He gestured to a plate with nothing more than crumbs left. "He did feed me, though, so I think you should keep him."

"Keep who?" God, it grew more and more absurd.

"The butler." His eyes narrowed at Matthew. "Have you been drinking?" Then he shook his head.

Matthew wished he could have a drink at that very moment, something to soothe his frayed nerves. He simply leveled a glare at Radbourne. "That is the most idiotic question I have ever heard."

"I do aim to entertain," the viscount said, a look of pride on his face.

"Why are you here, Radbourne?" Matthew asked again, dropping into a chair across from him. He gave up all pretense of being a gentleman. There was no point with this rabble.

"I accompanied Rhiannon," Radbourne said, dabbing at biscuit crumbs on the platter with his finger and licking them off. "Fabulous cook, by the way," he said.

"I wouldn't know." Matthew inhaled deeply. "Rhiannon was here?"

"*Is* here. Do you listen at all?" He had the nerve to look offended by Matthew's discomfort.

"Radbourne, I swear before God," Matthew said as he jumped to his feet, "if you keep talking in riddles, I will have to dispose of you."

"*Dispose* of me? Couldn't you come up with something better than *disposal*? Like evisceration? Strangulation?

Extinguishment? Eviction?" He made a job of dabbing at the biscuit platter again.

Matthew growled. Radbourne growled back. Good, he finally had the Lycan's attention.

"What *is* this about Rhiannon?" Matthew held up a hand to stall the viscount's answer. "Pray give me the information I need in some way that might make sense."

"Rhiannon was angry at you this morning." The viscount waited, licking crumbs from his finger. At the rate they were going, Matthew would have to call for more biscuits.

"Yes, she was."

"Her sister saw you kissing a woman in the garden." The Lycan looked somewhat pleased by that.

"I did no such thing," Matthew protested. The only woman he'd kissed in the garden was Rhiannon. She was the only one he wanted to kiss. Forever.

"She thought you did. So she set up some hare-brained scheme to find out what you were up to. She came here. That butler of yours shut the door in her face. It was pouring rain." The Lycan pretended to mull it over. "Perhaps you should sack him after all. It wouldn't be a bad idea."

"Where is Rhiannon?"

"I'm getting to that," Radbourne snapped. He narrowed his gaze at Matthew. "You made her cry."

So *that* was what all the rain was about. It looked like a torrent had hit Mayfair, but the rest of the city was bone dry.

"She bade me farewell, sneaked into your house, dashed up your stairs, and is, at this very moment, asleep in your bed." His gaze danced toward the main corridor. He sighed deeply, came to his feet, and looked Matthew in the eye. "You will do right by her."

"I will," Matthew said.

"Then I shall leave you to it." He started for the door.

"So, why were you asleep on my settee?" Matthew called to his retreating back.

"I couldn't just abandon her," he said with a shrug. "How else was I to pass the time?" At the last moment before he stepped through the door, he turned back to Matthew and said, "Treat her well, Blodswell. She deserves better than you. But you're what she has chosen."

Matthew was damned glad of that. He watched Radbourne through the window until he disappeared.

Matthew ran a frustrated hand through his hair. Rhiannon was in his bed? He'd only been gone a short while. She was probably pacing the floor by now, waiting to clock Matthew over the head with a heavy object when he came through the door.

The butler poked his head around the corner of the corridor. "Is all well, sir?"

"I'm not completely certain," Matthew admitted.

"The gentleman," the butler soured over the word *gentleman*, "said he would chew me to bits and bury me outside if I called the watch."

"You believed him?" Matthew felt a grin tugging at the corners of his lips.

"I did, sir," Hughes admitted.

"Smart man," Matthew mumbled as he started for the stairs. He took them two at a time, slowing only when he reached his doorway, where he slowly and silently turned the knob and slid into the room. He tiptoed over to the bed, taking in the general disarray of his space. Her clothes were hung about on his furniture, and a hint of gardenias hovered in the air. He absently petted her gown as he passed a pair of chairs. The dress was still wet. The poor thing must have been freezing. He noticed her chemise and raised his eyebrows, glancing back to the bed where her bare shoulders peeked out from beneath the counterpane. She *was* naked. He scrubbed a hand across his mouth. Dear God. Her stockings hung from the bedpost.

He looked down at her where she was turned on her side, her little hand pressed beneath her cheek. She was the most beautiful woman he'd ever seen. Her hair lay around her like a tangled mass, perfect in its disarray. The heat of the room made her cheeks rosy. He reached down to stroke her face. But he drew his hand back at the last moment.

She was everything he'd ever wanted. She was wind, rain, hail, and storms. She was also love, devotion, kindness, and heart. His own chest hurt a little when he thought of the heart he used to have. If he had one, he'd give it all to her. Instead, she had to settle for a shell of a man who would never grow old and never give her children, but who, in his selfishness, would allow her to be in his life. He couldn't *not* have her in his life.

She wore his mark. Two little pinpricks from where he'd bitten her the night before rested at the soft place between her neck and shoulder, marking her forever as his. She was part of him. A twinge of pain hit his chest, and he absently rubbed at the area. She closed her mouth in sleep, snuggling in closer, mumbling a little to herself as she settled back down.

She was beautiful. She was more than he'd ever dreamed of. And she loved him.

She blindly reached out for something, causing the counterpane to shift and expose the side of her breast. Holy hell, she was stunning. If there was one person he could love, it would be her. But he didn't have a heart anymore. That little twinge struck his chest again, but this time it was more of a pulsing pain. He bent over double. Vampyres weren't supposed to experience pain. They weren't supposed to experience love, either.

The pain hit him even harder, and he dropped to the floor, blindly reaching for Rhiannon and missing as he fell. He grunted with the force of it, trying to drive the pain from his body. His chest swelled before his gaze as he lay there on his back. Then he exhaled.

Bloody hell, he *exhaled*.

Matthew reached for his chest, still rubbing at the ache that was ebbing. If he was dying, he didn't want to go without telling her. "I love you, Rhiannon," he said softly, from his place on the floor beside the bed. Breathing and talking were a bit difficult, and he worked to modulate one while he did the other. He held a hand up to his mouth and felt the humid air that he exhaled. Then he heard his own heartbeat in his head. Thump. Thump. Thump.

How could it be? He was a vampyre. He couldn't have a beating heart.

Rhiannon leaned her sleepy head over the side of the bed and looked down at him, brushing the heavy mass of her hair from her eyes in frustration. "I love ye, too," she preened, her voice sleepy and unfocused. "Why are ye on the floor?"

"I'm not certain, love," he gasped out, finding it easier and easier to talk and breathe at the same time. It seemed as though he had to do both of them. "It just seemed like the best place to fall." He eased up on one knee and covered his heart with his hand. His toes and fingers were pulsing with his awakening.

She cupped his face in her hand. "What is it, Matthew?" she asked.

He leaned close to her, his mouth inches from hers, and breathed against her lips. She flinched. "What was that?" she asked as she scurried back across the bed, clutching the counterpane to her chest.

He crawled onto the bed and grabbed her foot, stopping her retreat. "Stay," he said. "I don't know what's happening. But I have a feeling you're part of it. Did you put a spell on me? To make me come to life?"

Rhiannon frowned a bit as though remembering something. Then she shook her head. "If I could have done that, I would have done it when I first met ye, Matt," she admitted. Then she scooted closer to him, and he tugged her hand to lie upon his chest. She smiled when she felt the steady rhythm of his heart. Then she pressed her ear to his chest. The proximity of her head to his nether regions had him instantly growing hard. He urged her to sit up.

"I want to try something," he said. She nodded her agreement and sat still. He kissed across her jaw and down the side of her neck. Then he nibbled on the tender skin there, making her giggle. He sat back and lifted his lip in a sneer. "Do you see fangs?"

"Not a single one," she said with a shake of her head.

He was aroused, and she was naked, and he was hard, and she was letting him kiss her, and his teeth wouldn't work?

"Yer heart is beatin', yer teeth won't work, and ye're breathin' because ye have to and no' because ye want to." She tilted her head at him. "Ye ken what this means? Ye've become human."

"That's impossible," he harrumphed. He'd never heard of such a thing, not in all his years.

Her hazel eyes twinkled mischievously as she pointed to the tent of his trousers. "Typically, when ye're like that, yer teeth descend, but they have no'." She colored prettily when she realized what she'd said. "Ye think maybe ye just need more motivation?" she tried.

Matthew groaned as she scooted closer to him in the bed.

Twenty-One

RHIANNON'S HEART SOARED AS THE REALIZATION THAT the *man* before her truly did love her. He wouldn't be like this if he didn't. However, he wasn't as easily convinced that his situation had changed. But after he'd spent more than six centuries as a vampyre, she supposed she could understand his reluctance. So she'd just have to go about proving the truth to him and had no qualms at all about using her womanly charms to do so. She tugged the counterpane from her shoulder and bared the tops of her breasts to his gaze. He lovingly traced a path along the line of the blanket with the tip of his index finger. "Teeth yet?" she asked.

"Not yet," he said, but he was already tugging her counterpane lower. He gasped as he tugged the linens from her breasts, baring them both to his gaze. He reached for her, his eyes hungry, his hands eager.

Very gently, Matthew pushed her back to lie on the pillows on his bed as he brushed her nipples with this thumbs, squeezing her breasts gently in his hands as he did so. "Teeth yet?" she asked.

"Not yet," he said, his voice a little more choked than the last time. He bent his head and took her nipple between his lips, gently rolling the turgid flesh and abrading it with the tip of his tongue. Rhiannon closed her eyes to the onslaught of feeling. Then he sucked the trembling peak into his mouth and had her gasping with pleasure and reaching for his head to draw him closer.

"Teeth yet?" she asked between breaths.

He smiled slowly at her as he bent to take her other nipple in similar fashion. "No, love," he said, just before he drew that aching peak into the warm haven of his mouth.

"This is disturbin'," she gasped as he moved up to look into her face, her sweet breath brushing across his cheek.

"This is bloody brilliant," he said before his lips touched hers. He gently coaxed her mouth open with his tongue, sliding it along the seam of her lips. She opened to him. The pulse between her thighs intensified. "My heart is beating like mad," he said softly.

"Mine, too," she admitted. Then she giggled at the absurdity of the comparison.

"What's amusing, you little witch?" he asked as his hand walked down her belly and his fingers slid into her curls. He dipped a finger inside her and brought her own moisture up to slide around that little nub of pleasure she hadn't even known existed before him.

Her mouth opened of its own accord, her answer to his question eclipsed by her moan of pleasure as he built a fire within her. Then he stoked it with his teeth and tongue and lips on her breasts, the pleasure of which nearly tore her asunder.

"Matthew," she gasped out.

"Yes, love," he asked, sounding awfully calm.

"Will ye take me already?" she pleaded.

"Take you where?" he asked playfully as he tugged the boots from his feet. "You want me to take you back to Eynsford?" He unbuttoned the fall of his trousers and pushed them down and then settled his hips firmly between her thighs. He was hot and hard and probing at her tender flesh. "You have only to ask…"

She smacked his shoulder. "Ye ken that's no' what I meant." He began to tug his shirt over his head and she helped him.

"I'm a gentleman, Rhi," he teased. "Stop trying to get me naked."

He pressed at her center, sliding through her wetness to probe at her softly. Yet he still didn't slide inside her.

"Ye're already naked," she charged. "So the damage is done. I have corrupted the gentleman. So be it marked on this date." She wrapped her legs around his waist and tugged him forward.

"So be it marked on this date that the man lost his heart to a witch and found it all at the same time." A tear rolled from her eye as he said the words.

"Mark it however you like," she urged. Then he finally slid inside her. He moved slowly, taking small plunges that drove her wild as he looked into her eyes. She felt small nibbles against the side of her neck and flinched slightly.

"Teeth?" she asked.

Then he pressed home and stilled within her, allowing her time to adjust to his size and the small amount of pain that had come with his entry. "No teeth," he confirmed, obviously fighting to stay still within her. He looked down and brushed the hair from her face.

"Yer eyes," she said as she cupped his cheek. Any lingering doubts she had vanished as she looked up into his soft green eyes.

"I'm inside you, and you want to discuss my eyes," he teased as he began to move, stealing her breath once again.

"Later," she grunted as the pleasure welled within her. His hand slid down to her curls, where he caressed her center, taking her to new heights as he moved inside her, hot, hard, and heavy. He tilted her hips so she could take more of him, though she hadn't known that was possible.

All the while, he murmured words of love in her ear as he brought her higher and higher and finally allowed her to topple over that precipice. He followed immediately, coming home deep inside her as she pulsed around his length.

Matthew untangled her legs from around his waist and rolled to his side, and then he tugged her to lie on his shoulder. He pressed little kisses into her hair, his breathing as labored as her own. She reveled in the feel of his breaths moving in and out of his chest and his heart beating beneath her cheek.

"Teeth yet?" she asked, knowing the answer but asking it anyway.

He bit his teeth together, making a clacking sound. "Not a single one. And I had no thoughts at all during that about drinking your blood. In fact, it makes me a little uneasy, the very thought."

His stomach growled loudly below her ear, and she sat up to look at him. "Your guess is as good as mine," he laughed.

Rhiannon shook her head. "No, my guess is *better*. Ye need real sustenance. Lord Kettering downed an entire table of food. The meal could have fed half of Edinburgh."

∽

Matthew pushed up on one elbow to look down at his witch. What she'd just said made no sense at all. "What's this about Kettering?"

She stared up at him as though truly seeing him for the first time. "When his lordship came after Blaire, he'd changed. Just like ye have." She shrugged against the pillows. "In fact, I never met him while he was a vampyre."

Matthew was well and truly breathing, because the wind had just been knocked out of him. "James transformed? Like I have?" It was too much to comprehend. For over two hundred years he'd known Kettering. He'd known him since he was a child, in fact, at a neighboring estate. He'd saved him from an untimely death. How was it possible that James had *changed* and not told him? He glanced down at his signet ring, identical to James'. He could still sense James' presence. And Alec's.

Rhiannon blinked up at him. "Ye dinna ken."

"No." He'd had a letter from his old friend, containing a magical signet ring, which he'd in turn bestowed upon Alec. That same letter detailed a final battle with an old foe. And he'd received other letters since. James and Blaire had retired to his estate in Derbyshire and looked forward to seeing him soon. His old friend had gushed about the happiness he'd found with his bride and his eternal wish that Matthew could find the same *peace within his heart* someday. Was *this* what he meant? "Human?" he muttered to himself.

"Lord Kettering said it was his love for Blaire that made his heart beat again." She smiled. "And it was yer love for me that made yers beat again. Ye really *do* love me."

Of course he really did love her. He loved her with his whole heart. He loved that she smelled like gardenia blossoms. He loved that she stood in the middle of her own storms. He loved how she made him feel. "I do."

"Then why," she lightly smacked his shoulder, "were ye kissin' someone else in the garden last night?"

Where did she get such a foolish idea? His conversation with Radbourne popped in his head. "If Lady Eynsford saw that, then her powers are faulty."

"It wasna Cait. My sister saw ye in the garden last night with some other woman, and ye kissed her."

Callista. That's what all the fuss was about? How utterly ridiculous. Matthew scrubbed a hand across his face. "I don't remember kissing Callista. I suppose it's possible. But—"

The color drained from Rhiannon's face. "Callista?" she echoed.

Matthew tucked a lock of hair behind Rhiannon's ear. "*If* I kissed her, it was in a very brotherly fashion. She was in a snit last night, and I'm afraid she ended up scarring one of Eynsford's pups."

"What the devil are ye talkin' about?" Rhiannon sat up to face him and clutched the counterpane to her chest. "I want ta ken why ye were kissin' her, since I ken ye *do* love me."

Matthew leaned forward and kissed the very tip of her nose. "She's my maker. She's the one who saved me that awful night in the Holy Land. She plucked me from a pile of dead knights, men I had known and fought with side by side on the battlefield. I wouldn't be here without Callista."

A range of emotions played across Rhiannon's face. "The Duchess of Hythe mentioned her. She said yer grandfather was fond of her."

He couldn't imagine how Rhiannon and Eugenia Hythe had landed on that subject. He was almost hesitant to ask for fear of her answer. "How exactly did that come up in conversation?"

"Ginny described the woman she saw ye with, and Her Grace said it reminded her of someone she kent when she was younger."

"And my fondness for Callista?"

Rhiannon nibbled her bottom lip as though she was trying to decide whether or not to answer him. Finally she said, "The duchess told me that Callista had half the men in London fallin' at her feet. So I asked if yer grandfather was one of them."

"Sneaky lass." He grinned at her. Who knew jealousy could make one's eyes sparkle? "You could have asked me. I would have told you I am *fond* of Callista, but that's all. She's like a mother to me in a strange sort of way."

Rhiannon gulped. "Are ye sure?"

At that Matthew fell back against his pillows, laughing. He'd known Callista for more than six centuries, and in all that time, never had he desired her. He knew she was beautiful and mortal men desired her, but he'd never been part of their numbers. Seeing her in that light would have been impossible. She was Callista. His maker. His oldest companion. His friend.

"I hardly find it amusing." Rhiannon sniffed, looking down on him.

Matthew tugged her back down beside him and curled his arm around her waist. "You are beautiful when you're jealous. And when you're angry. And," he softly kissed her, "every moment in between, Rhiannon."

She wrapped her arms around his neck and sighed. "Are ye goin' ta do that every time ye want ta distract me?"

He couldn't help himself. He laughed again. He could well imagine laughing with her the rest of their lives, just like this. And he hoped to never repeat the previous day. "Do you know how I spent yesterday, dearest?"

"Nay."

Matthew scoffed at his own foolishness. "Sitting in White's, wracking my brain, trying to figure out why you were angry with me, to no avail. I had convinced myself that you must be angry with me for something I had yet to do. That Lady Eynsford had foreseen it and told you whatever future sin I would commit."

She looked appropriately apologetic. "Cait would never do that. She lives by a code and willna reveal the future ta others."

"Indeed?"

"Aye. Though she has bent it from time ta time. She saw ye in my future, so she placed me in yer path every opportunity she could."

A memory flashed in Matthew's mind. "Did you know that the first time I met your seer, she was traveling with Alec and hadn't yet married Eynsford, though he had marked her?" He caressed the spot on Rhiannon's neck where his own mark was visible.

"Cait never mentioned it ta me." Her eyebrows narrowed. "He'd marked her? What does that mean?"

Could she be any more charming? He chuckled. "Lycans have this odd mating ritual where they bite their lover."

She looked positively disturbed by that. "And drink their blood?" she gasped.

"No, they just get overwhelmed with passion. A lot like vampyres, but in a totally different way, if that makes any sense." He gently rubbed across the tiny teeth marks on her shoulder and smiled at her. "Remember how I marked your neck when you were experiencing pleasure?"

She shivered lightly. Of course, she remembered. "I thought ye were just drinkin'," she said with a sheepish grin. "So, Cait had been marked before she married Eynsford? Interesting." He could almost see the information working through her head.

He smiled as the memory settled more firmly in his mind. "She knew instantly what I was, but she wasn't afraid. And when we parted, she said that I would learn a lot more about her kind. She knew even then, didn't she? That I was destined to find you causing a storm in Hyde Park."

"I think she did."

"She even told me to enjoy the fair weather while I could," he lamented. She knew. She'd seen all of this, months before it happened. Matthew was certain of it. Cheeky witch. He'd have to properly thank Lady Eynsford for her meddling. His stomach grumbled again. He truly was hungry. He sincerely hoped Radbourne hadn't finished off all the biscuits there were to be had.

"Ye need food."

"I'm afraid I do. Though the last thing I want to do is leave this bed. I want to stay here all night wrapped in your arms."

Rhiannon grinned and then kissed his chest. "We could raid the stores in the kitchen and bring all our bounty back up here."

Matthew rolled her beneath him, kissed her quickly, and gave her a look he hoped promised her sensual delights to come. "Excellent plan. You stay here, and I'll be right back."

❦

Well, he wasn't *right* back, but Rhiannon doubted Matthew had ever spent any time in a kitchen and would be completely lost trying to locate food. She grinned to herself and tugged the counterpane up to her neck, imagining him making quite the mess for his cook in the morning—pots and pans all askew, cupboards open, flour scattered about the place. Then a strange thought occurred to her. Did Matthew even employ a cook? After all, a vampyre would have no use for such services. But he did have servants, and they would need to be fed. So there must be some food around, which was a good thing as she'd completely missed dinner herself.

She turned on her side and slid her hand over Matthew's vacant spot. It was still warm. He was warm. He was alive! And he was hers. She must be the luckiest lass in the world. Never in her wildest dreams had she ever imagined that her true love would be an actual knight in shining armor. Not that she'd seen him in armor. Perhaps later.

"For my lady," Matthew said from the threshold, carrying a tray laden with a mound of biscuits.

Rhiannon rose up on her elbows. "Matthew, do ye have chain mail?"

"Chain mail?" His green eyes danced. "I leave you for a few moments and when I return, you want to know if I own chain mail?"

She giggled. "Well, ye are my knight. I thought I might like ta see ye in yer armor."

"You do, do you?" He grinned as he sat on the edge of the bed and placed his tray between them. "Well, your knight is starving, and all I could find are these biscuits. Apparently, Hughes has a sweet tooth."

"Hughes?"

"My butler," he explained as he popped an entire biscuit in his mouth and began to chew, a look of wonder on his face.

The butler was that sour man who'd greeted her at the door. "Oh."

He turned his gaze to her. "I know he was less than kind to you tonight. I'll sack him first thing in the morning, if you'd like."

Rhiannon shook her head. "I'm sure he thought I was a bedlamite."

"He did say something to that effect," Matthew admitted. "But I won't allow anyone to treat you ill. Not your father. Not your aunt. Not my butler. You are mine, Rhiannon, and I love you."

She didn't know what to say to that, and a lone tear trailed down her cheek. Matthew brushed it away with his thumb.

"I've waited more lifetimes than you can imagine just for you."

Her heart melted. To keep any more tears from spilling, she grinned unrepentantly. "What dreadful luck ye have. I was fortunate and found ye on my very first lifetime."

He chuckled, and Rhiannon doubted she would ever tire of that sound. Matthew and happiness all rolled into one. Then he sobered a bit. "We're going to have to get you back to Eynsford's, you know."

She shook her head. "Ye said we could stay in this bed all night."

"I know I did, and it was foolish of me. Only Radbourne and Hughes know you've come here. I believe we can actually trust the viscount, and as I pay Hughes' salary, I am certain he will hold his tongue."

He was still so concerned about her reputation. She knew she should appreciate the fact, but she couldn't help thrusting out her bottom lip in a very childish pout.

"Yep." He winked at her. "Still beautiful, even when you do that."

Twenty-Two

As soon as his carriage door closed, Matthew pulled Rhiannon into his lap. He hated returning her to Eynsford's, but knew it was the best course of action. Soon she would be his wife and he wouldn't see scandal attached to her name. The ride would be short, so he would have to enjoy the next few moments.

"Did ye ken yer eyes are green?" Rhiannon snuggled closer to him.

Matthew snorted. He hadn't given his eyes a second thought. He wasn't sure if he had ever known their color when he was alive. It wasn't as though he stood around peering in mirrors in those days. "Are they?"

"Lord Kettering's are blue."

They had been centuries ago. So, it was true. James had transformed, too. He still wasn't sure what to make of that. "After we're married, I'd liked to spend our wedding trip in Derbyshire."

"I doona care where we go as long as I'm with ye."

Matthew kissed the top of her head. "I think you'll like Halcourt."

"Will I?"

"Mmm," he replied, "My chain mail is there."

She giggled against his chest.

"And Blaire and James are at the neighboring estate. We have so much to catch up on."

"Ye're upset he dinna tell ye." She pulled slightly away from Matthew so she could look in his eyes.

What was the point of lying about it? "I am." He nodded. "After all we've been through together, I can't believe he wouldn't tell me about the most important thing that ever happened to him."

"Perhaps he wanted ta tell ye in person," she suggested.

Perhaps. Matthew grunted noncommittally. He supposed he should give James the benefit of the doubt, but his friend's silence still grated a bit.

"Perhaps he just wanted ta enjoy the beginnin' of his new life with Blaire."

Well, now that Matthew could understand. As soon as Rhiannon was his, they'd leave for Derbyshire, and he might not let her out of his chambers for a fortnight. They could eat biscuits in bed, and he'd even don his old chain mail. He smiled at the absurdity of it.

The coach rolled to a stop, and Matthew slid a protesting Rhiannon from his lap. "I know, dearest, but it's for the best."

He opened the door, ready to help her out, but noticed that every window of Thorpe House was glowing with candlelight. Did that mean the entire household was awake? Apparently so. The front door opened, and Caitrin Eynsford stepped through the threshold with a fiery glare.

Matthew knew he couldn't throw Rhiannon to the wolves, and quite frankly, that was what he would be doing as soon as they walked through the door. Directly behind the lady stood her formidable blond wolf of a husband and his three Lycan half brothers. "Perhaps I should speak to them first," Matthew suggested as Rhiannon put her hand in his and stepped onto the walkway.

"There's no need," she said with a smile. "Ye may be mortal now, but I'm still a witch. And a rather powerful one at that." Her eyes twinkled with laughter. God, he loved her. Here she was ready to face the wrath of the righteous and he was the one who was nervous. "A well-placed bolt of lightning can change a man's temper in a mere moment."

"Can you place one right between Eynsford's eyes?" Matthew whispered as he regarded the scowling marquess.

"Good evenin', Cait," his witch said with a giggle as they walked up the steps. The seer's blue eyes were as icy as her demeanor.

"Where have ye been?" Lady Eynsford hissed with her hands punched against her hips.

"As though ye doona ken..." Rhiannon muttered to her friend as she walked by her with little more than a glance in her direction. The marchioness wasn't at all used to being treated with so little tender handling, if her affronted expression was any indication.

"I told ye I wouldna look inta yer future," the blonde said as she reached for Rhiannon's arm and snatched her close to look into her eyes. What she saw staring back at her must have startled her, because the seer immediately let Rhiannon go. Then her eyes filled with tears.

"Oh, Cait," his witch said, as she drew her coven sister in for a hug. "Doona cry. Ye'll force me ta join ye, and then we'll all be a soppin' wet mess."

Matthew looked up at the sky, which was suddenly darkening. "Perhaps we should move this inside," he suggested.

"Perhaps you should return to your own home," Eynsford returned from his place behind his marchioness. He reached out to stroke his wife's shoulder, and she turned her head into his hand like a cat.

"Inside with all of ye," Lady Eynsford finally said with a grand sweeping motion of her hands. The Lycans all immediately moved to her bidding. Only then could Matthew see someone behind the crowd.

"This is all your fault," came the accusation from the back of the corridor.

❧

The last thing Rhiannon had expected to find was her Aunt Greer at Eynsford's house, waiting like a hawk that wanted to devour a defenseless mouse with its eager beak and talons. "If you had never come to London, this would never have happened." Greer raised a wadded handkerchief to her nose and sobbed into it. "Now I will have nothing. And it will be your fault!"

"Do ye ken what she's talkin' about?" Rhiannon asked as she leaned close to Cait.

"It's Ginny. She's run off," Cait whispered back.

"She did what?" Rhiannon cried.

"Are ye all right?" Cait asked quietly, appraising Rhiannon's body from top to bottom.

"Aye, I'm fine," Rhi, said, brushing her concerns into the background. How could Ginny run off? Had Aunt Greer done something to her? "What happened?" she demanded of her aunt. "Please start at the beginnin'." Matthew's solid fingers closed around her own, reminding her of his presence.

"I had plans," Aunt Greer sneered. The Lycans all had dispersed to parts unknown, aside from the marquess, who kept a comforting hand on Cait's shoulder. "And then *you* had to come to London." Her aunt jabbed a finger in Rhiannon's direction with every word.

"Aye, ye had plans ta set Ginny up with someone with bags of blunt, with no' a care for his common sense or decency," Rhiannon shot back.

Greer rolled her eyes. "That's how one advances in society," she said as though she was speaking to the most ignorant of children. "One must forget all preconceived notions of love, devotion. One must find a wealthy, marriage-minded man of noble blood and make a good match."

"That's not a good match by any stretch of the definition," Rhiannon tossed back with a laugh. "Where has Ginny gone?"

"She has gone for Gretna," Cait said quietly.

"With whom?" Rhiannon hoped it wasn't that dreadful Mr. Finchley.

"*Lord Steven*, of all people!" her aunt shrieked at the top of her lungs. "Can you believe it? She had to choose a second son who hasn't a farthing to his name. I had her all set up to marry Mr. Finchley."

"Ye had her set up ta be *ruined* by Mr. Finchley," Rhiannon shot back. "No' married. There's a difference, ye ken?"

Her aunt's scathing glance moved across her and Matthew. "Yes, I'm aware there's a difference between ruined and married. Ruined would be what you are. I never expected better of you, but I always wanted more for Ginessa. I wanted a home with opulence that she could be proud of."

"That she'd have ta share with a man who wanted her for nothing more than a dalliance and an heir!" Rhiannon said. "Everyone knows Mr. Finchley has more than one mistress. And more than one of them has been mistreated."

"She would have to endure his attentions but for a short time," her aunt tried to explain. "Then she could do whatever she wanted."

"Let me tell ye this," Rhiannon started, pointing her finger at her startled aunt as she advanced at her.

Matthew's arm circled about her waist and drew her into his side. "Rhi," he began. When she fought against his hold, still trying to approach her aunt, he said, "Stop," his voice direct and biting.

Everyone in the room stopped moving and looked at him.

He turned and faced her aunt. "How much?" he asked.

Aunt Greer pretended to appear confused by his question. "How much what?" she asked softly, sniffling in her handkerchief.

"How much had he promised to settle on you when the match was made?" Matthew asked.

"I don't know what you're referring to," Aunt

Greer said, her back bristling, but her face colored. She was lying.

"How much had he promised to settle on you in exchange for your niece?" he asked again as he folded his arms across his chest and peered down at her with a stony glare.

"You make it sound like I planned to sell her."

"Exactly," Matthew bit out. "How much? I'll match it."

"No, Matthew," Rhiannon started, tugging on his arm.

"How. Much?" He repeated the words slowly, as though his patience was growing thin.

"He'd promised five thousand pounds," her aunt grumbled.

"I canna believe ye would sell yer own niece," Rhiannon spit out. "Ye should be ashamed."

"Matches such as this are made every day," Aunt Greer tried to explain. "You would know that, dear, if you'd been prepared for the season the way your sister was. We had no hopes of an advantageous match for you, with you being what you are… But Ginessa, she had prospects…"

Matthew's tone was biting when he replied, "Rhiannon is not your concern." He clucked his tongue at Aunt Greer. "I'm tempted to tell you that I'll pay the amount to you in one lump sum. But I believe I'll make it a trust, one which you can only withdraw from if certain conditions are met."

"Conditions such as?" It was sad that her aunt seemed so willing to beg.

"If my future wife, the future Countess of

Blodswell, ever tells me that anything you have said or done has made her unhappy, I will stop all payments. In fact, I would like for her to tell me you've performed random acts of kindness in her company as well." He leaned forward as though Aunt Greer was addled. "You will be nice to your nieces, *both* of them, from this day forward. If you meet my conditions, the trust will pay an annuity to you. Fail, and you get nothing."

Her aunt sputtered.

"Do you accept?" he barked. Rhiannon saw Eynsford hide a grin beneath his hand.

"I accept," she replied quickly. Then she turned to Rhiannon. "You know, dear, I am so happy you found a wealthy earl to marry."

"I'd imagine ye are," Rhiannon said dryly.

"I knew you would make a brilliant match all by yourself. That's why I spent so much of my time on Ginessa. You were always destined for greatness." Aunt Greer's eyes sought out Matthew's, as though looking for approval. He just scowled.

Rhiannon exhaled loudly and shook her head. She shot a glance at Matthew. "She need no' lie ta me. Yer dictate may need some adjustments ta keep me from castin' up my accounts."

Matthew chuckled. "I'll see what I can do."

Like a dog with her tail between her legs, Aunt Greer departed Thorpe House. Rhiannon sagged against Matthew in her aunt's wake. He'd been so strong. He'd handled her aunt with such efficiency. "Thank ye, for that. Ye dinna have ta pay her."

He grinned down at her, his light green eyes

twinkling in the candlelight. "It's a small price to pay for that termagant to behave herself around you."

"Shall we?" Eynsford gestured with his arm that they should retire to the closest parlor.

"After you, dearest." Matthew placed his hand at the small of Rhi's back and gently directed her into the room, which was adorned in white with golden accents.

She settled on the brocade settee, relieved when Matthew took the spot beside her. She leaned against him and rested her head on his arm. It would be like this forever. The two of them side-by-side facing whatever came their way.

Eynsford dropped into a chair across from them, the twin of the seat Cait had already assumed. A glare that could halt an army focused on Matthew. "Now that it's just us, Blodswell, I'd like an explanation from you."

"Dash," his wife soothed, "take a good look at his lordship."

"And what exactly am I supposed to be looking for?"

"Does he seem different at all?"

The marquess grumbled, "Most men seem a little smug, Caitie, after…"

Cait cleared her throat. "That is certainly no' what I mean." Then she flashed a smile in Rhi's and Matthew's direction. "He is different in almost every way. If ye look, I'm sure ye'll notice it."

Matthew didn't even stiffen beside her; he seemed as relaxed as though they were enjoying a lovely picnic in a meadow.

Rhiannon caught Eynsford's eye and knew he would never tell the difference. He didn't have a clue what to look for. "He's human," she explained. "As human as ye or... All right, we're bad examples. How about as human as the Duchess of Hythe?"

Eynsford intensified the stare he cast in Matthew's direction. Then he closed his eyes. "I can hear it. His heartbeat. At least I can hear four different hearts in this room. I don't know which belongs to him." The marquess' golden eyes flashed open. "How is this possible?"

"Love," Cait explained. "It's the most powerful magic there is."

Her husband leaned back in his chair. "Of that, I am well aware, Caitie. I just had no idea it was *this* powerful."

At that moment, the Hadley men all burst into the room. "Brilliant handling of the old harridan." Gray beamed at Matthew.

Rhiannon noticed then that he looked quite different from his twin. She gasped and rose from her spot. "Wes! What happened ta ye?"

The Lycan touched the red, swollen mark on his face. "Does it make me look dangerous?"

"What?" she squeaked. Dangerous? Was he mad?

Matthew tugged her back down beside him. "Callista," he reminded her.

He had said Callista had scarred one of Eynsford's pups, hadn't he? But she'd had no idea he meant *this*. Right across his face! Poor Wes would never look the same. He was still handsome, but now... "Well," she said as brightly as she was able, swallowing heavily to remove the lump in her throat, "I suppose it does make ye look more dangerous."

Wes' brown eyes twinkled. "I think so, too."

"The swelling will go down," Matthew put in quietly.

Rhiannon glanced up at her knight. "I canna believe she did that."

He sighed. "She's capable of much more than that, dearest."

"So," Gray began as he leaned against the wall, looking at Matthew. "Love brought you to life?"

Matthew nodded. "It did."

"Hmm." Wes frowned. "Do you figure that would work on Lycans? That if we found the love of our life we'd stop changing, howling at the full moon, and all that?"

Radbourne sighed. "Have you met our brother, Wes? Do you think it's possible for a man to love a woman more than Dash does Caitrin? *He* still sports a tail and claws every full moon."

Wes shook his head. "You've got a point there, Archer." Then he grinned. "What a relief. I'd hate to just be a *normal* man." He threw an apologetic glance at Matthew. "No offense, Blodswell."

Matthew chuckled. "None taken, Mr. Hadley. After more than six centuries, I'm quite looking forward to being a *normal* man."

Twenty-Three

MATTHEW STEPPED THROUGH THE ENTRANCE OF *BRYSI*. How foreign the club seemed now. He glanced around at the dark walls and wondered how he'd spent so much of his life in this dreary place. He made his way into the main parlor and immediately noticed the blue-eyed Tillie.

The sultry Cyprian batted her eyes at him from across the room. Then she crossed the floor, pouting as she did so. "Are you ready to have me now, my lord?"

Matthew frowned at the chit. "I'm looking for my friend Mr. MacQuarrie."

She ran a finger down his chest, stopping to unbutton his waistcoat. "He's abovestairs. Shall I take you to him?"

Matthew removed her hand from his waistcoat and scowled at the girl. "I'll just wait here for him, shall I?" At least he'd found Alec. He had hoped the Scot would be at his rooms in Piccadilly, but that had proved to be false.

Tillie heaved an indignant sigh and stalked from the room. "Suit yourself."

Thank God, he'd never have to step foot in this establishment again. Matthew sank down into an overstuffed leather chair he had sat in many times in the past. His life had irrevocably changed in a way he had never imagined possible. How could he ever explain it to Alec?

"Blodswell!" the Scot boomed from the threshold, sans shirt. At least the man had donned his trousers. "What the devil did you do to make the chit cry?"

Matthew stared at his one-time protégé who now would have to face this world without him, without his guidance or insight. "We need to talk, Alec."

"I'll say. It's bloody difficult staying in the mood when a chit burst through your chamber door in tears."

Of the crocodile variety, Matthew was certain. The girl had been annoyed when she walked away, not distraught. "Do forgive me for interrupting your tryst."

In the blink of an eye, Alec was before him. "What happened to you?"

Had he ever moved that fast himself? It didn't quite seem possible anymore. Matthew sighed. "We need to talk."

Alec dropped into a chair across from him, horror splashed across his face. "You're different. Your eyes are... green," he sputtered in disbelief.

Everyone seemed so intent on his eyes all of a sudden. "Something has happened," he confirmed. "Something magical. Something I didn't know was possible."

"Is your *heart* beating?" Alec asked incredulously. "I can hear it."

"If you will just listen, I will try to explain."

Alec clamped his lips closed, though confusion still clouded his eyes.

"To be honest, I'm not sure how it happened. I only know the why."

"What happened?" Alec bit out.

Matthew rose from his seat. This wasn't nearly as easy as he had thought it would be. He began to pace a small path before his friend. "I'm human."

In a flash, Alec had him pinned against the wall, his hands around Matthew's throat. Something he never could have done before. "What did you say?"

"Put me down," Matthew said calmly.

In utter confusion, Alec removed his hand from around Matthew's neck and let him slide back down the wall.

"You're taking this badly."

Alec's black eyes lit with anger. "How am I supposed to take it?"

"With hope, perhaps," Matthew suggested, catching his breath. "If it could happen to me, if it could happen to Kettering, it could happen for you, too."

"Kettering?" Alec asked. "He's *human*, too?"

"So Rhiannon says, and I have reason to believe her." Matthew rose to his full height and tried to straighten his jacket. "It was love, Alec. Pure love that made my heart beat again. For the last little while, I'd felt twinges and pain. But tonight, when I looked at Rhiannon, I fell to my knees from the pain because it was so strong. I thought I was dying, but then air filled my lungs. And I *had* to breathe. I can feel the blood flowing through my veins. I am human once more."

"Love?" Alec barked. "Your true love?"

"Yes," Matthew replied, staring at his friend with every ounce of sincerity he possessed.

"Then how does that help me?" Alec roared. "Tell me, Matt, how *does* that help me, if my one true love married another, loves another?"

"Then she's not for you," Matthew began, but he closed his mouth when he saw the rage in Alec's eyes.

"It means I'm bloody doomed," Alec whispered. Then he dropped back into his seat and raked a hand through his hair. "I don't even know what I'm doing. You haven't told me half the things I need to know. And now I'm all bloody alone in this world."

"You know everything," Matthew assured him. "I've taught you everything, Alec. The rest comes with time."

"Well, I have plenty of that, don't I?" Alec shot him one last withering glance and stormed from the room.

❧

Rhiannon was in a daze as she dressed and went through her morning ablutions. The evening's events played out again in her mind. Matthew was human. Ginny had run off with Lord Steven Patterdale. And her aunt had to be nice to her. It was hard to believe all of it had happened in such a short period of time.

She made her way to the breakfast room, not surprised in the least to find the Hadley men quarreling with each other like children. Rhi shook her head at the sight. Once again, the three of them had devoured every morsel on the sideboard.

"Cook is making more," Wes told her cheerily.

"I suppose I'll just start with coffee then." She

motioned to a footman to fill a mug for her as she slid in a seat beside Archer. "I do want ta thank ye for goin' with me yesterday. Ye were right. Askin' a direct question is the best way ta go about things."

The viscount winked at her. "I thought it might be. I might wish things had turned out differently, Rhiannon, but I never had any doubt that Blodswell cared for you."

From the threshold, Price tapped on the door. "Miss Sinclair, pardon me for interrupting your breakfast, but the Duchess of Hythe is here and demanded I find you."

There was nothing to eat anyway. Rhi rose from her seat. "Of course, Price. Where did ye leave Her Grace?"

"The white parlor, ma'am."

She nodded to the old man. "Thank ye." Then she glanced back over her shoulder at the Hadley men. "*Behave* while she's here." She punctuated her statement with a glare of warning.

"Did you hear that?" Gray asked with mock incredulity.

Rhiannon graced him with a smile. "If ye behave, ye might no' have ta crash the next event the duchess holds." Then she quickly escaped to the white parlor before any of the Lycans could retort.

The Duchess of Hythe paced the floor in a fashion that did not seem very ducal. When her icy eyes landed on Rhiannon, she sighed. "Well, I hope you had more luck yesterday than I did."

Rhiannon nodded. "Aye, Yer Grace. Matthew— er... Lord Blodswell—confided the nature of this kiss to me."

The old woman actually smiled. "And you're satisfied with his tale?"

"Aye." More than satisfied.

"Well, that is good news. So the wedding is on?"

"As soon as the banns have been read."

"Well, that ought to give us enough time to get everything in order."

"In order?"

"Yes," the duchess replied as though Rhiannon had three heads. "You'll be married at St. George's, of course. I imagine Lady Eynsford will host your wedding breakfast. But we need to get a stunning gown that will have all of the *ton* talking. And we want to do this before news of your sister's Scottish wedding reaches everyone's ears."

Rhiannon gulped. "Ye ken about that already?"

The duchess snorted in a very unladylike way, but she was a duchess and above reproach. "I was there when Lord Steven arrived. I was returning your foolish sister to your aunt when she leapt in the Patterdale carriage. I saw the whole thing with my own eyes."

Oh, heavens, Ginny! Rhi closed her eyes and hoped her sister had made a wise decision. "Aunt Greer had wanted to marry her off to Mr. Finchley."

The duchess chuckled. "I know. Who do you think told your sister to bolt with that Patterdale boy?"

Rhiannon choked on a laugh. "Ye dinna?"

"Of course I did," the duchess replied imperially. "The young man was deeply besotted. And your sister very much the same way. He's not the sort I would want my Madeline to marry, but he'll be fine for Ginessa."

Rhi gaped at the woman. "What is wrong with Lord Steven that ye wouldna want yer granddaughter ta marry him?"

"Well, nothing's wrong with the boy, except he had the misfortune of being a second son," she answered. "Had he been born first, I would have had no objections to him at all."

That was it? "I see." Rhiannon giggled. Ginny had no need for titles. And if the duchess thought Lord Steven had a fine character, then all turned out well. Or mostly.

"Laugh if you want to, Rhiannon, but things being what they are, we should circulate the news of your betrothal and the ball I'm hosting for you afterwards all about Town. Everyone will be so eager for an invitation that they won't pay one whit of attention to your sister's surprising elopement."

"That's a wonderful idea," Cait said from the doorway. "I will, of course, help in any way I can."

"Perfect, Lady Eynsford." The duchess nodded at Cait.

"I propose we start with a breathtakin' gown," Cait gushed, walking farther into the room.

"Guest list first, my lady," the duchess said grandly. "We are in a hurry to get invitations to the right people by the right time."

Cait acquiesced with a bob of her head. "Ye are correct."

"Of course I am." The duchess dropped onto the settee. "Now you should call for tea."

As Cait rang for Price, Rhiannon stepped closer to Her Grace. "Can I make a request?"

"What request?"

"For the guest list, will ye include Lord Radbourne and his brothers? I've become quite fond of them."

The old woman laughed. "Very well, Rhiannon. Besides, they'd sneak in anyway. That's why I never invite them to anything. I want to see what scheme they'll come up with next."

Twenty-Four

THREE WEEKS SAILED BY. RHIANNON NEVER WOULD have believed time could move so quickly. But between Caitrin and the Duchess of Hythe, her wedding had turned into quite the social event. Rhiannon barely had time to see Matthew as she was shuffled to one fitting or another. But today that would all change. Today she would become the Countess of Blodswell, and she and Matthew would belong to each other until the end of their days. She wondered if he was bothered that his days *would* end now that he was a man, that she'd cost him his immortality.

She stared at her reflection in the mirror, contemplating the pomona-green gown Cait had insisted on as she swore it matched the flecks in Rhiannon's eyes. Rhi stepped closer to the mirror and shook her head. She didn't see one fleck of green, not one. Not that it mattered; arguing with Cait was a lost cause. Especially as Her Grace had been in complete agreement.

"I doona ken," Cait sighed from behind her. "Somethin' is just no' right."

Rhiannon spun to face her friend. "No' right? What do ye mean by that?" Had something happened? And on her wedding day of all days.

"My, ye are a bundle of nerves." A wicked smile and a mischievous glint in Cait's eyes did not bode well. "I was just thinkin' yer flowers doona look right, a little droopy in the heat."

Cait walked to the bedchamber door and threw it open.

Standing in the corridor, Sorcha grinned. Then she bolted into the room and threw her arms around Rhiannon's neck. "Oh, ye are so beautiful! That dress, it matches yer eyes."

Rhiannon couldn't quite believe it. How had Sorcha made it all the way from Edinburgh? Tears formed in Rhi's eyes, which apparently *did* have some green in them somewhere even if she couldn't see it.

"Watch yer emotions," Cait warned. "Ye doona want it overcast. What will Lord Blodswell think?"

Sorcha pulled out of their embrace and handed Rhi a handkerchief. "Cait's right. Ye canna have splotchy cheeks before ye say 'I do.' Ye have ta smile grandly and be the happiest bride there ever was."

"How?" Rhiannon shook her head. "How are ye here?"

"I always have a way of gettin' what I want." Sorcha dropped across Rhiannon's bed. "As soon as I met Lord Blodswell and kent ye were goin' ta marry him, I started pesterin' Papa. He finally agreed ta come with me." Then she frowned. "El's sorry she canna be here, but with the bairn…"

"I'm just so glad *ye're* here, Sorch. I've missed ye so much." Rhi swiped at a tear. "Did my father come with ye?" It was too much to hope for, but she asked it anyway.

Sadness flashed in Sorcha's soft brown eyes as she shook her head. "But he did send his love." Then with more energy than an eight-year-old, Sorcha bounded off the bed. "What can I do? Did ye say somethin' was wrong with the flowers? I can fix whatever it is."

Cait shook her head. "The flowers are fine, ye goose. It was just somethin' ta say before I surprised her."

"Oh, so I doona get ta do anythin' ta help?"

"Ye can help by sittin' next ta the Duchess of Hythe durin' the ceremony. The woman terrifies Dash and the others."

"Really?" Sorcha giggled. "I canna wait ta meet her then."

"Well, ye'll do so soon because we need ta get Rhi ta the church before Blodswell thinks she left him standin' at the altar."

"His landau is out front," Sorcha said cheerily. "I'll ride with both of ye and send Papa on ta the church."

"Dash and his brothers are already there," Cait explained, smoothing out Rhiannon's skirt with her hands.

"Eynsford has brothers?" Sorcha rushed to ask. "Are they wolves, too? Can I meet them?"

"Ye'll never hear the end of it now that ye've told her," Rhiannon laughed.

Cait shrugged. "She would have found out anyway." She smiled that faraway smile that she so often wore when she thought no one was looking. "It's a secret, so doona go blabbin' it around," she warned Sorcha.

The littlest witch's eyes narrowed at Cait. "Ye ken somethin' about my future?" Sorcha cried. "Do I get a Lycan of my very own?" She clapped her hands together with glee.

"Doona start this again, Sorch," Cait warned. Then she pushed a curl behind Rhiannon's ear. "Oh, ye are so beautiful."

"What about Blaire?" Rhiannon asked hopefully, "Is she here, too? Matthew wants very much to speak with Lord Kettering."

One of Cait's dainty blond brows rose. "I can tell ye this. Ye ken how overprotective Benjamin is with El?"

Rhi nodded. It was still a sore subject with Caitrin, Lord Benjamin's protective, sometimes overbearing nature with their healing witch.

"Kettering is just as bad with Blaire."

"How can ye say that? Ye havena even met him," Sorcha declared. "He is a perfectly nice man and a very handsome one, too."

Cait tossed her head back. "*That* he may be. But I have seen the future, Sorcha Ferguson, and Blaire willna leave Derbyshire for another seven months at least."

"Seven months?" Sorcha asked. "They've been married *three* months. Are ye sayin' she's expectin'?" She nearly bounced on her toes with excitement.

"Indeed."

"Well, that was quick," Sorcha gushed. "Blaire must be so ecstatic."

Cait shrugged. "She's no' had the best time of it so

far. Queasy stomach and all that, but she'll be fine in a month or so. *Then* she'll be ecstatic."

"So we can go visit her then." Sorcha beamed.

"I'll look in on her in a few days," Rhiannon put in. "Matthew's estate borders Kettering's. I'll make sure she's all right."

"From what I've seen, Kettering is a mother hen." Cait rolled her eyes. "As though *Blaire* was breakable. Completely ridiculous. When Dash and I have our first, I will no' allow him ta circle me like a herding dog with a flock of sheep."

Rhiannon giggled. Lord Eynsford already watched Cait's every move. She just didn't realize it because she loved him so much and wanted him there. And she hoped Matthew would hover over her if they had children. She smiled at the thought.

"Well," Sorcha interrupted her reverie, "shouldna we be leavin'?"

"Absolutely," Cait said, holding the door open wide. "It is time."

Rhiannon turned back to the mirror for one last glance and pinched a little color to her cheeks. "Alright, I'm ready."

❧

It had been so many years since Matthew had stepped foot in a church that he'd quite forgotten what they looked like inside. Of course, so much had changed since then, the Reformation being the obvious standout. He stared up at the large arched ceiling above him, which was so different from the Catholic churches of his youth.

A hand clapped him on the back. Matthew looked over his shoulder into the smiling face of the Marquess of Eynsford. "Any sign of them?"

The Lycan grinned. "They'll be here. It's still early, Blodswell. How are you holding up?"

Matthew shook his head. "Magnificently. I never imagined I'd be standing here, Eynsford. I never imagined my life would take this turn. I'd never dared dream for such a thing."

The marquess squeezed his shoulder in a sign of solidarity. "Call me Dash. You'll be part of this mad family now, you know. This coven is like nothing I've ever seen."

But Matthew had seen many generations of this coven. From his very first meeting with *Còig* witches, he'd respected the tight-knit bond that connected the Scottish lasses. "They are amazing together."

"Lord Eynsford!" the Duchess of Hythe barked from her spot in the front-row pew. "Take your place. The bride is here."

Matthew turned on his spot to see Rhiannon in the prettiest green dress with not one, but two coven sisters smoothing her skirts. She met his gaze and smiled beatifically. He caught his breath at the sight. He could hardly wait to hold her again, to never have to let her go.

The rector cleared his throat. "Are we ready, my lord?"

Rhiannon nodded, as anxious as he'd ever seen her. Sorcha Ferguson pressed a bouquet of gardenia blooms into Rhi's hands. Eynsford reached Rhiannon's side and offered her his arm. Matthew remembered thinking all those weeks ago that someone would have to be mad to let the Marquess of Eynsford stand in for them. But he had a feeling the Lycan was more a part of Rhiannon's circle than her own father. It was more fitting this way.

But, at the very last moment, the doors of the church opened and Alec MacQuarrie looked in across the threshold. He shot Matthew a look of consternation at the very thought of crossing through the portal and into the church, but then he shrugged and reached behind him. Quite unceremoniously, he dragged a man forward by the lapels of his coat and shoved him through the doors. With a sheepish grin and a wink at Rhiannon, he shut the door behind the man.

"Papa!" Matthew heard Rhiannon exclaim as a smile broke across her face. Matthew had begun to think Alec wouldn't fulfill his request and have the man to the church on time. But this would make Rhiannon's day complete. He wanted her to have everything she needed, and she needed for her father to give her away. So, he'd sent Alec on a last-minute mission to collect the man. After all, he no longer had the speed needed to make the trip himself on such short notice, and he certainly couldn't remove his soon-to-be father-in-law's memory of the unorthodox mode of travel, which probably involved being slung over MacQuarrie's shoulder. But Alec could.

The man struggled to right himself after Alec's shove and pushed his spectacles up higher on his nose with his index finger. His gaze landed on Rhiannon, and his mouth fell open. "Ye look just like yer mother," he said as he stood peering at her with his head tilted to the side.

"I dinna ken ye were comin'," his witch said, her voice heavy and filled with emotion.

"Wouldna miss it for anythin'," he replied as he drew her hand into the crook of his arm and stood ready to walk his daughter down the aisle.

Matthew turned back to face the clergyman, "We are ready, Mr. Hogsdon."

Lady Eynsford and Miss Ferguson scampered to their seats on either side of the duchess.

Rhiannon's father led her down the aisle, his hand covering hers on his arm.

"Who gives this woman in matrimony?" the clergyman asked.

Rhiannon wiped at a tear as her father said, "I do, with great pride." He leaned in to kiss her cheeks and placed her hands in Matthew's.

Matthew had a feeling that hadn't been suggested to the man. It was a good thing he'd finally come up to scratch. He smiled at his bride. His heart so filled with love and happiness that he thought it might actually explode.

"Lady Eynsford asked me to recite a line from the 'Song of Solomon.'" The rector's voice grew louder. "'I found the one my heart loves.' And looking at Miss Sinclair and Lord Blodswell, that certainly seems the case for them. Let us begin."

Never had a Bible verse meant so much. Matthew took a steadying breath.

"Do you, Matthew Jonathan Halkett, take Rhiannon Moira Sinclair to have and to hold from this day forward, for richer, for poorer, in sickness or in health, to love and to cherish until death do you part?"

She beamed up at him, her pretty hazel eyes shimmering with happy tears. "I do," Matthew said, feeling it in every corner of his heart.

The rector turned his gaze to Rhiannon. "And do you, Rhiannon Moira Sinclair, take Matthew Jonathan Halkett to have and to hold from this day forward, for richer, for poorer, in sickness or in health, to love and to cherish until death do you part?"

"I do," she breathed.

The rector looked out at the small assemblage of friends and family. "Then I now pronounce you man and wife."

Matthew took Rhiannon in his arms and held her close, as if he didn't want to ever let go.

⁂

From his spot against one of the pillars outside St. George's Church, Alec waited so he could hear every word of the wedding ceremony. He'd closed his eyes and listened to the heartfelt vows and wistful promises Rhiannon and Matthew exchanged. After the rector pronounced them man and wife, the pair had started for the exit, their party consisting of witches and Lycans following closely behind them.

The happy couple stepped into the cheerful sunlight, which explained more than words the joy Rhiannon must be feeling. Alec offered a slight bow in greeting. "Congratulations."

Rhi threw her arms around Alec's neck and kissed his cheek. "Alec, thank ye so much for comin'. And for bringin' my father."

Alec drew her away from him and smiled. "I wouldn't

miss it for the world, lass." He leaned close and whispered in Rhiannon's ear. "Your father remembers a very peaceful ride in Blodswell's fine coach." He rotated his shoulder and clutched at it as though in pain. Then he grinned unrepentantly. "That's not exactly how it happened, though."

A warm wash of air brushed Alec's cheek, nearly startling him until he realized it came from her.

"You're welcome," he grunted.

Matthew reached out his hand to Alec. "I am glad to see you, my friend. You will be fine without me, you know."

Well, he'd have to be one way or the other, wouldn't he? But Alec feigned a look of nonchalance. "Of course I will. Do take care of her."

Matthew agreed with a nod. "Until the end of my days."

Alec kept from wincing. Matthew's days would eventually come to an end, but *his* never would. He nodded good-bye to his one-time mentor as the Blodswell landau door opened to take the earl and countess away. Then he started off toward Conduit Street, until he heard his name called.

"Alec." Caitrin Eynsford's lilting voice halted him.

He glanced over his shoulder to see the blond witch standing alone by one of St. George's pillars. Fool that he was, Alec appeared before her in the blink of an eye. "Cait."

She beamed up at him, like she always had in the past. "We are hostin' a weddin' breakfast at Thorpe House. I'm certain Lord Blodswell would like ye ta come."

And watch her rule over Eynsford's home? Watch

Rhiannon and a very human Matthew stare into each other's eyes, love and adoration overflowing at every turn. Alec shook his head. "I don't think that's a very good idea, Lady Eynsford."

Cait frowned at him. Whether because of the use of her title or his refusal to attend her breakfast, he wasn't certain. "All is no' lost. Doona give up hope, Alec," she finally whispered.

"Hope for what?" he asked, though he had a fairly good idea what she would say next.

"Ye can still find happiness too, ye ken?"

Alec scoffed. "I'm not like Kettering or Blodswell, Cait. My heart isn't dormant waiting for my one true love to bring me back to life."

"Alec," she started, but his glower caused her to swallow whatever else she was going to say.

"I don't have a heart, Caitrin," he said more forcefully. "I didn't have one when I was reborn. It's not waiting to be repaired. I don't know what you think you've seen for me, but my future does not lie down Blodswell's path. Whatever fanciful ideas your mind has spun, you can just forget them."

"Ye do have a heart, Alec," she whispered. "I ken ye do."

He shook his head. "You're mistaken. I gave my heart away some time ago and never did get it back." Then he tipped his hat in farewell and resumed his walk toward Conduit Street, ignoring Cait's order for him to stop, ignoring Sorcha Ferguson calling his name, ignoring the Duchess of Hythe, of all people, murmuring what "a fine leg that Mr. MacQuarrie has."

He couldn't get away fast enough. From Conduit

Street, he'd summon a hack and try to forget this world, sampling instead the sins to be found at *Brysi*. After all, *this* world had nothing to offer him. Not anymore. He'd already lost everything that meant anything to him.

Twenty-Five

RHIANNON COULDN'T REMEMBER EVER HAVING SO many eyes focused on her. She wasn't even certain how the Duchess of Hythe had managed to squeeze so many people in her ballroom for the celebration. Rhi touched Matthew's arm beside her. "This is overwhelmin'."

He leaned closer and kissed her brow. "There are even more people here than there were at Eynsford's."

"Cait's probably ready ta throw a temper tantrum at havin' been outshone," Rhiannon laughed.

He pulled his watch fob from his pocket and glanced at it quickly. "We can make our farewell soon enough."

"And then we head off for Derbyshire?"

Matthew winked at her. "Where I'll don my chain mail, and you'll wear," his voice changed to that of a naughty whisper as his hand slid around her waist to hold her close, "as little as possible." He kissed the tip of her nose.

Rhiannon giggled. "I canna wait, Sir Matthew."

"This display of affection is nearly nauseating," Lord Radbourne said as he strode past them.

"It will be yer turn soon enough," Rhiannon called back.

He shuddered dramatically. "Now you sound like Cait, Lady Blodswell," he teased. He bowed dramatically at them both and swept himself into the crowd.

"Has Lady Eynsford seen his future?" Matthew asked.

"No' that I'm aware of." She shrugged. "But he'll find someone just for him. He's a good man, despite all the trouble he causes."

"The whole lot of Hadleys needs a guiding hand," Matthew groused. "They need to go straight back to the schoolroom and start all over."

"Speakin' of trouble," Rhiannon started. She pointed to the entry where a small ruckus was brewing.

"What's that?" Matthew asked, pulling her into his arms as he looked over the top of her head toward the source of the noise. "Oh," he breathed.

"What is it?" Rhiannon craned her head to see better, but with no result.

Matthew cursed lightly beneath his breath. "It's Callista." He sighed. "I knew I would have to speak with her eventually. But I'd hoped to avoid it as long as possible. I just wonder what she thinks of all this. I can't feel her presence anymore. There's no connection between us."

"Do ye think she can feel the disconnect between ye now that yer heart beats?"

"I would imagine she can," he said with a shrug.

"Her Grace wouldn't turn her away at the door, would she?" Rhiannon asked.

"Doesn't appear to be," he murmured. "Though I almost think it would be better if she did."

The band struck a chord, and he tugged her playfully toward the dance floor. "Dance with me, Rhiannon."

She couldn't help but laugh. "I've already danced with ye twice," she protested as he pulled her toward the center of the room.

"And you're my wife," he teased back. "I'll dance with you as often as I like."

"A gentleman would never do something so scandalous as to dance with his wife all night, forsakin' all others."

"'Til the day I die," he shot back.

Matthew pulled her into his arms, and the world settled for Rhiannon. Not a single lightning bolt went astray. No storm clouds choked the retiring room. Not a single item had fallen in Her Grace's cleavage, much to the woman's dismay. They had about three minutes to stare into one another's eyes. But out of the corner of hers, Rhiannon spotted the Hadleys all exiting the room, heading for the garden. Eynsford followed not far behind. Cait tried to dash past the dancing couple, but Rhiannon immediately caught her and drew her to a stop. "What's goin' on?" Rhiannon hissed.

Cait wrung her hands together. "It's that woman," she whispered back. "She had the nerve ta laugh at Wes' scar. And now the twins and Archer are all herding her outside. Dash has gone ta intervene, but he's just one man."

"Do ye ken the future?"

"That's just it!" her coven sister cried. "Dash had his hands on me when she arrived and still had them on me right until the moment he saw his brothers with that woman. I dinna see a thing. And what I can see now doesna look very comfortin'."

"I'll be right back," Matthew said, bending to kiss Rhiannon's forehead.

"No, Matthew!" Rhiannon cried, tugging on his arm. "Yer human!" she hissed at him.

Matthew took her shoulders in his hands and made her face him. "I'll be fine. I don't think she'll hurt me." He stroked up and down her arms as he glanced anxiously toward the garden door.

"That's just it," she said. "Ye're no' thinkin' at all!"

Matthew disentangled himself from her grasp and followed the way the Hadleys had gone.

Rhiannon waited no more than a moment before she followed as well. "He willna want ye ta go out there," Cait warned.

"He's human. He can be harmed. I canna stay in here and do nothin'."

Cait nodded solemnly, linked her arm within Rhiannon's, and fell into step beside her. There might only be two of them, but just having Cait there made it all seem better. But, truth be told, Rhiannon would rather Matthew not be involved at all.

"I assume it's impossible for Matthew ta stay out of this, seeing as how he was involved with the last encounter."

"He's no' responsible for that woman's actions," Cait reminded her.

The pair of them stepped out into the dark night, which was much darker than Cait had expected. Heavy clouds, not even of Rhiannon's own making, covered the sliver of moonlight she'd expected to light their way. But the sound of feminine laughter some-where down the path drew Rhiannon farther into the garden, with Cait following in her wake.

The Hadley twins had Callista backed into a dark corner, where she was evidently pleased to stay for the moment. Rhiannon wasn't certain what made Wes and Gray think they could win against a vampyre of her age and strength. They would most likely be proven wrong. Dead wrong.

To help matters, Rhiannon cleared the darkened sky, pushing the clouds back until the stars twinkled and the moon lit the clearing where they stood.

She found Matthew in the throng of male bodies. He said softly, "Callista, I believe it's time for you to take your leave. Come. I'll see you to your coach."

She placed her hand in Matthew's but didn't follow when he tugged her arm. "So sad, what they all have done to you," she said quietly.

"Sad?" Wes bit out. He pointed to the scar that now streaked across his face. "*This* is sad, madam," he bit out.

"That is but a consequence of your youthful follies," she replied, laughing beneath her breath. The very sound made the hair on the back of Rhiannon's neck stand up. "Follies you seem destined to repeat." She motioned toward Gray with her pointy fingernails. "I can make you a matching set again. Would that be helpful?"

Archer growled low in his throat.

"Oh, such savage creatures," Callista crooned. She shot a glance at Cait. "How do you stand to bed one of the beasts, Lady Eynsford?"

"You've done enough damage, Callista. It's time to

go home." Matthew motioned to the path, indicating that she should precede him.

"Do you plan to escort me, Matthew? You and I need to discuss a few things, regardless. I have need of your company."

"Over my dead body," Rhiannon said, stepping into the light.

"That, my dear, can be arranged," the vampyre sneered. There was pure hatred for Rhiannon in her gaze. The animosity and irritation she felt because of the wolves was obviously fodder for her playful side. But Rhiannon, on the other hand, was a different matter.

"Callista!" Matthew barked. "You and I both know you will do no such thing. If I have to pick you up and carry you out of here, I will."

"You and who else?" she asked softly. "You are not the man I created." She pointed one long red finger-nail at Rhiannon and beckoned her closer. "Come here, my dear. I have a wedding gift for the two of you." She turned to Matthew. "If I kill her, Matthew, I can bring her back to life. Don't worry. It worked for you for a very long time."

She patted his cheek hard enough that a slap rang out. But when she turned back, Rhiannon saw it. She saw that little hint of pain in the woman's eyes. She was hurting. She already missed Matthew, and he wasn't even gone. Theirs had been a friendship of more than six hundred years. Matthew had said himself that she was almost like a mother to him.

The Lycans all advanced upon Callista at once when she threatened Rhiannon. There were four of them, all determined to do good on this night.

Rhiannon created a gust of wind that blew around the clearing and then put enough force behind it that she physically pushed each of the Lycans back, away from the vampyre. Their astounded curses barely registered as she pushed Cait back as well and removed Matthew from Callista's reach. Rhiannon raised her hands by her sides and lifted them flat toward the heavens until a heavy layer of fog hung between the clearing and the Lycans and Cait. Through the mist, she heard the Hadleys curse as they struggled to find their way out of the fog. Then Rhiannon stepped closer to Callista.

Callista could move with so much speed that no one could even see her, yet when her body coiled for motion, Rhiannon called quickly to the heavens and shot six heavy spears of ice into the ground at the woman's feet. Matthew could do no more than gasp as he watched, helpless, as Rhiannon stopped the vampyre's advance.

Callista looked down, astounded to find herself trapped in a web of icicles that had sliced through her gown and into the earth. She narrowed her eyes at Rhiannon. "Do you think that will stop me?" she asked directly.

"No, but I have more. And ye can either accept that I will win this battle, or ye can continue." Her voice didn't quiver, not even once.

The vampyre jerked her skirts free of the heavy spears with more than a little effort and torn fabric. But before Callista could fully remove the last icicle, Rhiannon spun her finger in the air as she blew across it, and a whirlwind erupted around Callista. The woman shrieked as that one stake held her fixed to the ground and the swirling wind spun her around and around, until her legs were tied up beyond a point she could escape from within her skirts.

"Callista," Matthew tried again. "It doesn't have to be this way."

The vampyre's gaze swung toward Matthew again, and Rhiannon saw more than a hint of pain within the depths of Callista's eyes this time. If the woman had a heart, it would certainly have been breaking. "I made you," she cried.

"You did, and I will thank you until the day that I die," Matthew said, his tone sincere, his hand over his heart.

"But you *will* die," she said softly.

"Yes, I will. But I will also live. And love. And have children. And I will still be your friend."

"Not with *her*," Callista spat toward Rhiannon.

Rhiannon peered down at her fingernails, trying to appear bored and unconcerned. But Callista moved in one last feeble attempt to win. She jumped forward as much as her trapped skirts would allow and reached for Matthew. That was when Rhiannon had finally had enough. She closed her eyes and brought down the biggest bolt of lightning she had ever summoned. The bolt shot through the air as though in slow motion, moving in a zigzag pattern until the glowing spear of energy stopped just above Callista's head.

"What shall it be?" Rhiannon asked. She pointed toward the hovering bolt of lightning and said, "If ye survive this, I'll have the winds bring me a wooden stake next. I willna let ye harm anyone else."

She saw the moment when Callista gave in. When

the vampyre gave up the attitude of superiority. When she let go of all the hatred. When she allowed herself to feel the hurt. She dropped to the ground in a tangle of skirts.

Rhiannon sent the lightning bolt back from whence it had come and kneeled down to peer at the woman who had once saved her husband. Because that was all she was in that moment. A woman. "There comes a time that every mother must pass her child's safekeepin' over ta someone else. In this case, it's me. Have I proven I'm worthy of him?" She tilted her head and waited for the vampyre's response.

A sniffle met her ears, which nearly made Rhiannon want to grin. But she forced herself not to.

"He'll be safe with you?" Callista asked cautiously.

"Always," Rhiannon replied with a nod. "I love him."

"I do, too. In a very different way than you do, of course," she explained.

"Of course," Rhiannon agreed, still biting back that smile.

"I refuse ta be nice ta those beasts," Callista groused as she motioned toward the fog.

"That battle is their own to fight," Rhiannon laughed. She extended a hand to Callista and helped her rise.

"I would ask you to dance with me, Callista, but you look as though you've been caught in a windstorm. And there are the oddest tears in your gown." Matthew obviously bit the inside of his cheek.

"Will you take me home?" she asked, instead.

"Of course, we will," Matthew said as he leaned over and slid his arm around Rhiannon. She leaned into him, accepting his strength. She lowered the fog. Cait and Dash stood in a close embrace, and the Hadleys all looked a bit dazed by the entire event.

"We could hear but couldn't see," Archer said.

Rhiannon just nodded.

The Lycans all grumbled as they turned and dispersed back into the dark. But she heard Archer exclaim, "I knew there was something odd about Lady Blodswell. Thank God, you found a normal lass, Dash."

Rhiannon covered her mouth to keep in the explosion of laughter that threatened. Cait certainly couldn't be called normal.

"Ye ken ye canna tell anyone about the odd weather…" Cait began.

"Who would believe us?" the twins asked in unison.

Matthew tucked a stray lock behind Rhiannon's ear. "I'll take Callista around to the front. Do you mind saying our good-byes to the duchess?"

"Of course no'." Rhiannon smiled at him one last time.

She made her way back inside the ballroom and located the Duchess of Hythe whispering something in Sorcha's ear. It could only have been Her Grace's distraction that kept Sorcha from joining the others in the garden, which was a blessing. Rhiannon crossed the floor, nodding and smiling at people as she passed.

"Rhi," Sorcha gushed as soon as Rhiannon reached them, "I've had the most marvelous time."

"This little friend of yours," the duchess began, "is probably the cheeriest gel I've ever met."

Rhiannon agreed with a nod of her head. "She is indeed."

"She simply must meet Madeline and help bring the girl out of her shell a bit more." Her Grace focused her icy eyes on Sorcha. "Do you have plans to be in Town next season?"

"I hadna thought about it." Sorcha shrugged.

"Well, think about it. I'm certain I can get you attached to an earl of your own, given enough time."

An *earl* of her own was the last thing on Sorcha's mind, unless that particular earl was a Lycan. Rhiannon winked at her friend, knowing they shared that private joke. Then she smiled at the duchess. "I do hate ta leave so early, Yer Grace. But Blodswell is already havin' our carriage brought around."

"In a hurry to get you home, is he?" The old woman's eyes crinkled when she smiled.

"Indeed. We are startin' for Derbyshire this evenin'."

"At night?" The duchess' hand flew to her chest. "With highwaymen about?"

"I am certain we will be safe." No highwayman could withstand a jolt of lightning, should one be so foolish as to stop her coach. Rhiannon leaned forward and kissed the woman's cheek. "Thank ye for everythin' ye've done for me."

The duchess squeezed Rhiannon's hand. "It was my pleasure, Lady Blodswell." Then dismissing Rhi, Her Grace turned her focus back to Sorcha. "I am planning a house party this summer, Miss Ferguson. I do hope you'll come. Madeline could use a girl her age in attendance."

"That is very sweet. I'm hopin' Cait—Lady Eynsford—will ask me to stay with her."

The duchess rolled her eyes heavenward. "Miss

Ferguson, Hythe's family seat in Kent borders Eynsford's. The marquess and his wife are, of course, invited to whatever festivities I have planned this summer. But you should stay with me."

Rhiannon started for the exit, grinning to her ears. The Marquess of Eynsford would *not* be happy to learn his summer had already been planned for him.

❧

Clutching Rhiannon's hand in his, Matthew looked across the dark coach at Callista. She hadn't said more than two words since they had started their journey to Hampstead. In his heart, he knew this would be the last time he would see his old maker.

"You are welcome to visit anytime, you know," he said, knowing she would never take him up on his offer.

Callista nodded once.

From the window, he saw her cottage come into view. Matthew tugged his signet ring from his finger and leaned forward on the bench. "I want you to have this," he said, placing the ring in her hand.

She looked down at it, disdain in her dark-as-night eyes. "I don't want your ring, Matthew."

But she'd be so much happier if she'd take it. "Don't you miss the sun warming your skin? The joy of a cloudless day and the birds chirping?" His ring had allowed him, for all these years, to still live in the world of humans. It was one of the reasons his outlook on the world was so different. If she'd just take that chance, her life could be more than it was.

Callista sighed, turning the ring over and over in her hand. "I can feel the life within it."

Matthew settled back against the squabs. "Enjoy it, Callista."

She shook her head, leaned forward, and dropped the relic back in his hand. "I never wanted any of your rings. Not the first time you offered one. And not now. Give the heirloom to your children." Her glance briefly touched Rhiannon.

The coach stopped before Callista's quaint home, and Matthew grabbed her hand before she could exit. "But you would get so much more from it than anyone else. Please."

Finally, the old twinkle was back in her eyes. "Alas, I have no use for it. I live in the world I was meant to, Matthew. And now you shall have to live in the one meant for you." She looked again at Rhiannon. "I am trusting you to take care of him, Lady Blodswell."

"Yer faith is no' misplaced," Rhiannon said quietly. "I love him."

For the first time that evening, Callista smiled. "I know." Then she opened the carriage door and vanished into the night so quickly that Matthew couldn't see where she'd gone.

❧

For some reason, Rhiannon grew more anxious the closer they came to their destination. She'd never run an estate before. She'd managed Sinclair House, but only because her father had been too preoccupied to do so. What lay in store for her at Halcourt?

"There's nothing to worry about, lass." Matthew smiled down at her.

"Why do ye think I'm worried?"

"Because," he kissed the tip of her nose, "your brow creases when you're worried."

The carriage came to an abrupt stop, and Rhiannon couldn't quite believe they'd arrived. The driver opened the door and lowered the steps. Matthew exited and then offered his hand to help her climb from the conveyance.

"So this is it," Matthew said, pride exuding from his voice.

Sunlight bathed the Tudor mansion in a warm glow. Halcourt was sprawling, and wings had been added since its original construction, making it appear a patchwork home. Rhiannon's breath was almost taken away. "It's beautiful." And it was. It had seen the same history Matthew had. She could feel him radiating from every stone, every board in the estate.

"It's all yours." He beamed down at her, guiding her to the massive front door.

Before they reached the steps, the door opened and a middle-aged man dressed in black stood before them. "Lord Blodswell," the man greeted, "and Lady Blodswell, welcome home."

"Thank you, Lynch." Matthew's hand at the small of her back urged Rhiannon over the threshold. "My wife will want a bath brought up to her chambers."

A bath sounded heavenly. Washing the travel dust from her skin.

The butler nodded. "Of course, sir, but..." his voice trailed off.

But Matthew paid the servant no heed at all. He scooped Rhiannon up in his arms and dashed for the stairs. "Water, Lynch!" he called back over his shoulder.

"Yes, sir," the butler called back, and scurried into action.

"Put me down, Matt," Rhiannon laughed as he jostled her all the way up the stairs. "The servants will think you canna keep yer hands off me."

"They would be correct," he grunted as he stepped into what she assumed was the earl's chamber and slowly dropped her to her feet, allowing her to slide slowly down his body. "I've spent days in a coach with you and still can't get enough of you. I never will," he said as he tore at his cravat. Through the connecting door, the splash of water could be heard as servants filled a bathing tub. "Off with those clothes, wife, or I'll not be held accountable for what I do to them."

"Promises, promises," she taunted as she spun away from him and dashed for the door that led to her chambers.

He caught her within seconds and then stole her breath when he wrapped one arm around her waist and cupped her breast with his free hand. "Welcome home," he breathed against her lips.

"Do ye give all yer visitors such a welcome?" she gasped back at him as his hands began to bunch her skirts around her waist. His fingers prowled toward her heat as he hefted her against the door and wrapped her legs around his waist.

"I've waited like a perfect gentleman to wed you."

"Ye bedded me before ye wed me, sir." She fought to keep from shattering apart at his questing fingers as he stroked across her center. "How quickly ye've forgotten."

"I've forgotten what it feels like to be inside you," he grunted as he worked the falls of his trousers and freed himself and then probed at her center.

"Thank heavens I'm here ta remind ye." She cried out as he thrust home. He'd taken her numerous times after the wedding brunch and even in the coach. But there was nothing like having him surge inside her in their own home.

"'Til the day we die," he grunted as he filled her once again, clutching her bottom in his hands and taking all of her weight upon himself as he lifted and lowered her, matching his thrusts.

She couldn't help but giggle as she taunted him. "Only a gentleman would be so careful with my skirts as he tossed them up around my ears."

"There are times when I'm a gentleman," he said as he slowed his strokes. "This isn't one of them."

He hit that spot, the one that drove her mad. She gasped and clutched him more tightly. "Doona stop," she cried out, her head falling back against the door in pleasure. Within moments, he sent her over that precipice. And then he followed. He leaned his head into her neck until he could catch his breath. She tugged his hair until he leaned back to look at her, his lids drowsy.

"This breathing thing is quite a hindrance, love," he said on a sigh. Then he chuckled as he lowered her to the floor and kissed her quickly. He stepped back and let her skirts fall. "Let's get cleaned up and I'll show you around."

"If ye hadna felt the need ta devour me, I'd already have seen it," she quipped back at him.

"You love it when I devour you." He winked at her as he opened the door to his chamber. The butler shifted there on his feet. "Yes, Lynch?" Matthew stepped closer to the servant.

The man swallowed. "Well, sir, Lord and Lady Kettering have been awaiting you in the blue parlor all morning."

Rhiannon's bath was forgotten in an instant as her heart leapt in her chest. "Blaire's here?"

"Thank you, Lynch," Matthew sighed. His teasing countenance immediately changed to seriousness. "Will you please bring tea, in that case? We'll be down in a moment." The butler scuttled off to do his master's bidding.

"There was a time I was so in synch with James that I would have known he was here." He blew out a harsh breath.

Rhiannon gently touched Matthew's back. She could see the strain of his features and wished she could make this easier. "We should go see them," she said softly.

His charming smile slid right back into place. "Of course we will. As soon as we've cleaned up."

"Ye're delaying the inevitable," she reminded him as he helped her disrobe. "Let him explain," she suggested.

He pretended to be much more interested in helping her bathe and dress than in seeing his old friend. But finally Matthew offered her his arm and then escorted her down an unfamiliar corridor. How long would it take to learn the layout of this place? Before she could contemplate the décor or possible changes that should be made, Matthew led her downstairs, opened a door, and directed her inside.

Blaire rose from her spot on a divan beside Lord Kettering and smiled more radiantly than Rhiannon had ever seen. "There ye are!" her friend gushed, rushing forward and embracing Rhi tightly, almost too tightly. The battle-born witch wasn't always aware of her strength. "I'm so sorry, we were unable ta come ta London, but…"

Rhi kissed Blaire's cheek. "It's all right. Cait explained."

"Did she?" Blaire stepped closer to James Maitland, Baron Kettering. "It's impossible ta keep secrets from her."

Rhi smiled. "So true," she agreed. "She said, in fact, that Lord Kettering was just as dotin' as Lord Benjamin."

Blaire laughed and slid an arm around her husband's waist. "As well as I ken Cait, I'm certain *dotin'* was no' the word she used."

How true. Rhiannon linked her arm with Matthew's. "I'm hopin' mine will be the same when the time comes."

"I'm certain," Lord Kettering began, his low voice reverberating around the room, "knowing Matthew as I do, you have nothing to worry about, my lady." The baron stared intently at his old friend. "How are you, Matt?"

❧

Matthew met Kettering's gaze and sighed. He'd known James for more than two centuries. He'd seen him grow from a child to a man and from man to vampyre. And he still couldn't quite believe his old friend had managed to keep his transition a secret. "The same, apparently, as you are, James."

James raked a hand through his hair. "I knew you'd be upset." He closed his blue eyes that were as clear as the summer sky, just like they had been all those centuries ago. "I didn't know how to tell you. Surely you can see that."

"Apparently."

James pinned Matthew with his gaze. "I had no idea such a thing was possible."

"Neither did I."

James frowned. "For all I knew, the… possibility of this life wasn't an option for anyone else, and it hasn't been from anything I've ever seen or heard." He shook his head apologetically. "I've known you all of my days, Matt. I've seen the genuine smile you have when watching children at play or couples walking hand in hand. I couldn't tell you that all of that was possible for me, but not for you."

Rhiannon squeezed Matthew's arm, and he looked down at his beautiful witch. "And yet it was." He supposed he could see James' point. Telling MacQuarrie had been gut wrenching in so many ways. James had known Matthew much longer. Saying the words would have been even more difficult.

His heart lifted a bit. There was no reason to start this life with hard feelings. James had always been his friend, and being neighbors and married to witches of the same coven, they always would be. "Think nothing of it, James." He finally smiled at the baron. "I suppose we will navigate these waters together."

James gave a sigh of relief and stepped forward, clasping Matthew's hand in his own. "Like we always have."

"Like we always have," he agreed. Though this time it would be different. This time they each had found love strong enough to make them breathe again, with wives who loved them just as much in return. This time they were men with actual futures ahead of them, including children and grandchildren. No, this time would be different in all the important ways.

About the Author

Lydia Dare is a pseudonym for the writing team of Tammy Falkner and Jodie Pearson. Both are active members of the Heart of Carolina Romance Writers and have sat on the organization's Board of Directors. Their writing process involves passing a manuscript back and forth, each one writing 1,500 words after editing the other's previous installment—Jodie specializes in writing the history and Tammy in writing the paranormal. They live near Raleigh, North Carolina.

Read on for a preview of Lydia Dare's

Never Been Bit

Coming September 2011
From Sourcebooks Casablanca

—

Castle Hythe, Kent—August 1817

Ever since Sorcha Ferguson had met her first Lycan, she'd been determined to have one for her very own. And her coven sister had *promised* there would be Lycans at the Duchess of Hythe's house party. Since the day that glorious news had reached Sorcha's ears, she'd planned her entire visit south around the idea of falling in love with a beast just like two of her very best friends had done. Yet she'd seen *not even one* Lycan, and she'd already been at Castle Hythe for a sennight.

There was only one thing left to do. If they wouldn't come to her, she would go to them. But first, she had to fix the shambles that was the Duchess of Hythe's orangery. Sorcha had been nearly overcome with sadness when she'd seen all the plants in such a state of neglect.

She scoffed. She was feeling very much like the plants these days. Every one of her friends had married within the last year or so, and she was the only witch in her coven left to find a husband. She snorted. She hadn't even come close to finding one, and all because those promised Lycans had yet to make an appearance.

Sorcha walked from row to row in the orangery, laying her hands on the forsaken plants. The lilies could use a kind word to boost their spirits. Their stems sagged, and there was not a single bloom to be found. She blew a lock of hair from her eyes in distraction.

A piece of Irish ivy reached out to touch her ankle. The poor thing was yellowed and aching for attention. She smiled and touched her hands to the vine, watching it strengthen and fortify itself right before her eyes. "You're welcome," she murmured when the vine stroked across the toe of her shoe. She wiped her hands together. The duchess would be appalled if she saw the dirt beneath Sorcha's fingernails.

"There you are," Lady Madeline Hayburn called from the other side of the orangery. "I've been looking everywhere for you!"

Sorcha bit her lip. She shouldn't have stopped to tend the plants. But she couldn't just allow them to suffer, could she? "I was just thinking of going out for a bit," she said evasively, avoiding the girl's gaze as she lifted herself up to sit on a low table.

Maddie's face fell. "Oh," she said with an understanding nod. But Sorcha could tell her friend was disappointed. And she'd be the worst sort of friend if she abandoned the young lady to go in search of a man. Or men. Or Lycans. *Or her destiny.*

Maddie wouldn't have any idea how to go along without her. Sorcha patted a place beside herself. "I just thought I'd pay a visit ta Eynsford Park. The ride isna too far, from what yer grandmother said."

Maddie smiled as she settled beside Sorcha, her blond curls bouncing about her shoulders. "I can't believe how wonderful Grandmamma's plants look. Just a fortnight ago, this place looked like it had died a less than peaceful death. You are a miracle worker."

Sorcha remembered. It had hurt her very heart to see the plants in such shape. "Oh, I just have a bit of a green thumb."

"Something I clearly lack." Maddie smoothed her skirts out in front of her. "What is so important at Eynsford Park?"

Only Sorcha's future. "I just want ta visit my old friend."

Maddie leaned in conspiratorially. "For years," she whispered, "the villagers swore a monster resided at Eynsford Park. Did you know?"

Sorcha knew all about that particular monster. And she could hardly wait to lay eyes on his half brothers, especially as the monster, or Lycan, in question was married to her coven sister and dear friend.

"Monster?" she giggled, determined never to give the secret away. "Cait, I mean, Lady Eynsford, would no' put up with a monster on her grounds."

Maddie giggled then too. "I can't imagine the marchioness scaring a monster away. She seems of the sweetest disposition."

"Ye've never seen Cait in a temper." Sorcha nudged her new friend's shoulder with her own. "Ye can take my word for it, Maddie. A monster would no' wish ta make her angry." Cait in a temper was a force to be reckoned with. Any self-respecting monster would steer clear of her wrath. That was what her husband did, after all.

"She sounds like Grandmamma."

The two were a bit alike with their commanding presence, now that Sorcha thought about it. "And would a monster *dare* enter Castle Hythe?"

Maddie laughed again. "Not if he had any idea of the dressing down he'd receive. 'How dare you trod upon my roses!'" She mocked her grandmother's imperious tone. "'Did you just eat my footman? Out with you, and don't come back until you learn some manners.'"

Sorcha could well imagine her coven sister barking in just that same manner at her wolfish husband. "Well, there ye have it. If a monster couldna dwell here at the castle, it couldna dwell at Eynsford Park either, if it ever did. Would ye like ta ride over there with me?"

She wouldn't be able to speak freely with Maddie about, but she hated to leave her behind. The English girl was terribly timid when left alone.

Her friend sighed. "I would love to, but Grandmamma would have a fit of apoplexy if I did. She's expecting more of *those* gentlemen to arrive, and she'll expect me to be there to greet them."

Ah, *those* gentlemen. Men of privilege the Duchess of Hythe had handpicked as acceptable matches for Maddie, men she might want to choose for a husband during her first season. This house party was an opportunity for her friend to see which men she might fancy ahead of time. It also would allow the duchess to investigate their character more closely and determine if a match might be made.

Sorcha had a reasonably sized dowry, one that would be considered large at home in Edinburgh, but it didn't compare to the fortune attached to Lady Madeline Hayburn. Hopefully, the gentlemen present would see more than pound signs when they looked at Maddie. She was the sweetest girl and deserved a gentleman who appreciated all her good qualities.

If more of *those* gentlemen were arriving today, Sorcha's excursion to Eynsford Park would have to be put off. She wouldn't throw Maddie to the wolves. That made her giggle. *She* was the one looking for a Lycan, after all.

"We doona have ta go as far as the Park. We could just ride around the castle grounds. I'll send Lady Eynsford a note askin' her ta come visit me instead."

If only there was a way to beg Cait to bring some of Eynsford's Lycan relations with her, but her coven sister was adamant that a beast was *not* in Sorcha's future, so the odds of that happening were slim, to say the least.

Maddie's green eyes twinkled almost as brightly as her smile. "Let me go get my habit, and I'll meet you in the east drawing room."

After changing into her riding habit, Sorcha penned a note to Caitrin Eynsford. That took a little longer than she had expected as she tried to find the right words to entice her coven sister to bring along her pack. Finally, note in hand, Sorcha left her chambers and made her way through the twisting and turning corridors that made up Castle Hythe. Once on the main level, she handed her note to the Hythes' stoic butler with directions that it be delivered to the Park at once.

She smoothed her sapphire riding habit into place and frowned. It was a bit long. She'd have to fix that later when no one was watching. Magic spells tended to make most people a little squeamish. Looking at her feet to make sure the hem didn't touch the ground, Sorcha started toward the east drawing room without even glancing up and promptly ran headfirst into an immovable object that blocked her path.

"Ouch!" Her head shot up. As she reached for the injury, she looked right into the black-as-night eyes of an old friend. Tall and handsome as ever, he was a friendly face in this English world, and she'd never been so happy to see him.

"Alec!" she gushed. "I had no idea ye would be here."

It Happened ONE BITE

By Lydia Dare

He's lost, trapped, doomed for all eternity...

Rich, titled, and undead, gentleman vampyre James Maitland, Lord Kettering, fears himself doomed to a cold and lonely existence—trapped for decades in an abandoned castle. Then, beautiful Scottish witch Blaire Lindsay arrives, and things begin to heat up considerably...

Unless he can persuade her to set him free...

Feisty Blaire Lindsay laughs off the local gossip surrounding her mother's ancestral home—stories of haunting cannot scare off this battle-born witch. But when she discovers the handsome prisoner in the bowels of the castle, Blaire has no idea that she has unleashed anything more than a man who sets her heart on fire...

Praise for *Tall, Dark and Wolfish*:

"A deliciously delightful read...witty repartee, scorching sensuality, wonderfully complex characters, and an intriguing plot combine to make an unforgettable story."
—Romance Junkies

978-1-4022-4510-7 • $7.99 U.S./£4.99 UK

A Certain
Wolfish
Charm

by Lydia Dare

Regency England has
gone to the wolves!

The rules of Society can be beastly...

...especially when you're a werewolf and it's that irritating time of the month. Simon Westfield, the Duke of Blackmoor, is rich, powerful, and sinfully handsome, and has spent his entire life creating scandal and mayhem. It doesn't help his wolfish temper at all that Miss Lily Rutledge seems to be as untamable as he is. When Lily's beloved nephew's behavior becomes inexplicably wild, she turns to Simon for help. But they both may have bitten off more than they can chew when each begins to discover the other's darkest secrets...

"*A Certain Wolfish Charm* has bite!"

—Sabrina Jeffries, *New York Times* bestselling
author of *Wed Him Before You Bed Him*

978-1-4022-3694-5 • $6.99 U.S./$8.99 CAN/£3.99 UK

TALL, DARK AND WOLFISH

BY LYDIA DARE

REGENCY ENGLAND HAS GONE TO THE WOLVES!

He's lost unless she can heal him

Lord Benjamin Westfield is a powerful werewolf—until one full moon when he doesn't change. His life now shattered, he rushes to Scotland in search of the healer who can restore his inner beast: young, beautiful witch Elspeth Campbell, who will help anyone who calls upon her healing arts. But when Lord Benjamin shows up, everything she thought she knew is put to the test...

Praise for *A Certain Wolfish Charm:*

"Tough, resourceful, charming women battle roguish, secretive, aristocratic men under the watchful eye of society in Dare's delightful Victorian paranormal romance debut."

—*PUBLISHERS WEEKLY* (STARRED REVIEW)

978-1-4022-3695-2 • $6.99 U.S./$8.99 CAN/£3.99 UK

THE WOLF NEXT DOOR

BY LYDIA DARE

REGENCY ENGLAND HAS GONE TO THE WOLVES!

Can she forgive the unforgivable?

Ever since her planned elopement with Lord William Westfield turned to disaster, Prisca Hawthorne has done everything she can to push him away. If only her heart didn't break every time he leaves her. Lord William throws himself into drinking, gambling, and debauchery and pretends not to care about Prisca at all. But when he returns to find a rival werewolf vying for her hand, he'll stop at nothing to claim the woman who should have been his all along, and the moon-crossed lovers are forced into a battle of wills that could be fatal.

"With its sexy hero, engaging heroine, and sizzling sexual tension, you won't want to put it down even when the moon is full."

—SABRINA JEFFRIES, *NEW YORK TIMES* BESTSELLING AUTHOR OF *WED HIM BEFORE YOU BED HIM*

978-1-4022-3696-9 • $6.99 U.S./$8.99 CAN/£3.99 UK

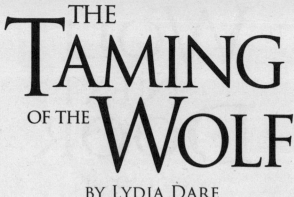

THE TAMING OF THE WOLF

BY LYDIA DARE

REGENCY ENGLAND HAS GONE TO THE WOLVES!

Lord Dashiel Thorpe has fought the wolf within him his entire life. But when the moonlight proves too powerful, Dash is helpless, and a chance encounter with Caitrin Macleod binds the two together irrevocably. Though Caitrin is a witch with remarkable abilities, she is overwhelmed and runs back to the safety of her native Scotland. But Dashiel is determined to follow her—she's the only woman who can free him from a fate worse than death. Caitrin will ultimately have to decide whether she's running from danger, or true love...

Praise for Lydia Dare

"The authors flawlessly blend the historical and paranormal genres, providing a hint of the Lycan lifestyle with a touching romance... lots of feral fun." —ROMANCE NOVEL NEWS

978-1-4022-4437-7 • $6.99 U.S./$8.99 CAN/£4.99 UK